We Come In Peace

MARK TURNBULL

Copyright © 2020 Mark Turnbull

All rights reserved.

ISBN 9798632680868

Cover design by: dkmrgn design

To everyone who loves me. I love you more.

"Life is full of meaning. It is what feeds or devours the soul."

Heinrich Galli

ONE

At an early age, I realised that there was something wrong with the world. My first best friend was nine when he fell victim to measles, the last recorded case to result in death. Perched beside his hospital bed, he told me of his fears for what was waiting for him. He asked why we live, and why we die. But the question that troubled him most wasn't what was waiting for him, or whether he would be missed, it was whether he had done in his short life, what he was meant to do. At nine years old, I couldn't answer him. And no one else possessed the kindness to even know the questions that he needed answers to, too tangled in the cruelty that would take a child from the world.

Whenever I spoke of my feelings, of the strangeness that existed, that there was more than the world we saw, the people I told were not forgiving. I was ridiculed by friends, earned concerned eyes from parents and asked not to speak of it by my teachers.

When I was eleven, I discovered another who shared my questioning of the life before us, who sought to dismantle the perceptions that my eyes and ears would have me believe, who showed me that reality was the lie I didn't know I was telling myself. His name was Heinrich Galli. The book was *A Guide to Life: The Misdirection of the Human Psyche*. Composed of fifty-six gigantic chapters, it described everything that I had felt, especially my growing belief that my life would not be merely another imitation of those that surrounded me. Despite being a fellow resident of Virginia, we had never met, but I felt connected to him. Someone who understands this life we live. This existence.

I read that book every night for four years, tucked under the covers, dreaming of the life ahead of me. He gave me a reason to question what others accepted, to believe I might find what I was looking for. But I couldn't hold on to it forever. Abruptly, the public writings of Heinrich Galli ended, and so finally, aged sixteen, I ventured to his home where his wife told me that he had taken his own life. I was so scared, so devastated by the barbaric loss of a beautiful mind that I began to conceal my views, fearing the path that I had started on. And yet the connection I felt with Heinrich Galli was only strengthened.

Time is different as you get older. Hopes unrealised. Promises broken. You look back at something from ten or twenty years ago and you can't believe it. Can't believe it happened that long ago. Can't believe that moment is over. That you will never exist in that time again. Never feel how you felt, never be who you were. Things can bring you closer to it, a song, a smell, a photograph. But it's over. You can never go back. That moment is lost to you forever.

Nothing hurts more.

* * *

I opened my eyes wide to force myself awake. The shift from sleep to consciousness was like being pulled from drowning in the ocean deep. I hung over the edge of the bed, retching, desperately straining to hack up whatever was slowly suffocating me. I heaved for breath, oxygen gradually filling my lungs. Another breath. Until I was panting, my heart racing.

Dread filled my gut as my nightmare came flooding back to me. I tried desperately to shake off the rotting nausea and come to my senses. The hairs on my arms stood on end and my legs trembled furiously. I prayed for her face to stop haunting me.

Jeri.

I pulled back the sweat-soaked duvet and jolted upright. Next to me, Jeri lay soundly sleeping. As I took a long, deep breath in and out, a little unease lifted with it. But when I closed my eyes, I still saw her terror as she was dragged across the concrete floor away from me. Felt the burning of her fingertips as they were ripped from mine. Heard Jeri's scream as she left without a chance to say goodbye.

Fighting the urge to burrow under the covers where it was safe, I clamoured out of my warm bed with clumsy footing, stumbling across the thick pile carpet and out of our bedroom. I threw Jeri a final glance as I left, face covered by blonde hair, but it was enough to reaffirm she was safe, and I pressed on towards Emily's room. Scraps sat up, jumped off the bed and followed me, as always by my side. After a few steps, I saw Emily's tiny arms clutching the teddy that I brought her back from New York last spring. It was nearly bigger than her, but she hadn't let go of it all week. Scraps gave two barks to check on Emily, but she didn't wake.

I pressed forward, and then lingered outside Kyle's room. My head told me to be rational, that everything was fine. I tried my best to stay calm, visualised Jeri waking up and telling me to stop acting stupid and go to sleep. But they couldn't all be ok.

I prowled into Kyle's room, fists clenched and ready for the worst. I dodged a different action figure or playset with each footstep, Kyle's bed almost in sight from behind the alcove. Scraps let out a bark. I waved my hand to quieten him, but he did it again. He wouldn't stop. I stepped closer, my eyes fixed on that alcove, and my foot landed firmly on something sharp. I clenched my teeth to stop from yelling out and forged ahead, getting closer, my heart beating faster with every step.

The temptation to crawl back in bed was overwhelming. If something had happened to him, until I saw it, it wasn't real.

I took one last step forward and stopped. Kyle was safely huddled up with an action figure his dad had bought him. I took a much-needed breath, gently prised his fingers apart and laid the figure on the desk. Outside the room I shuddered hard, filled with relief that they were all ok. I didn't know what was more unbearable, the nightmares or the warped sense of logic I was left with, stalking the house, terrified of what I might find.

Scraps looked up at me, waiting to follow my next direction. I led him downstairs and left him munching a treat in the kitchen while I checked the doors and windows were locked, and then I checked again, unable to let the niggling feeling of protectiveness rest. Leafless branches tapped against the kitchen window from the wind. All was safe and well in my home. Except for Scraps. I kneeled to him to stop him barking but he wouldn't, so I stood--

--I climbed into bed, trying not to wake Jeri. I lay by her side and edged my body closer to hers. I inhaled the perfume that still clung to her skin, perfectly combined with her own natural fragrance. She was at peace, so beautiful. All I wanted was to watch her sleep. If anything happened to her, I don't know what I would become.

I peeled back the covers and took the opportunity to gently rest my hand on Jeri's shoulder, careful not to wake her. I closed my eyes. Her skin was just as silky to touch as I remembered it. I wanted to hold her, imagining my arms wrapped around her body. I let go, tucked my hands under my pillow and lay my head on top to pin them down. My eyes opened and I lay staring at the blank wall, hours passing before my body finally gave in to sleep. Without the weight of Scraps' small body on the bed, I seemed to rest well.

Early morning light poured in through a gap between the curtains, but I buried my face deeper into the pillow to hide away from the harsh intensity. I rolled over and reached out to Jeri but found only an empty bed. 7:30am. I had slept in for the third time this week. I slipped on my dressing gown and spent ten minutes alone in the attic before I went downstairs for breakfast. I heard Jeri's soft voice before I saw her. An image flashed in my head of her standing beside me, holding my hand, head tilted away from me, her skin cold. A moment later and she was gone.

Even awake, I couldn't escape it. I felt sick.

I lingered in the kitchen doorway, not wanting to interrupt Jeri as she held Kyle at one side and Emily at the other. "Listen to me." She pulled Kyle's cheek to face her. "Listen, he made you both happy. He wouldn't want us to be sad, now, would he? He's gone. So, we need to forget about it now. Ok?"

Kyle gave a reluctant nod, gazing into the distance, but Emily didn't respond, tears running off her cheeks. Jeri saw me and motioned towards the garden door with her head.

I followed a trail of blood smeared across the garden pavement to a metal trashcan that stood at the end. Blood covered the inside and the tip of Scraps' nose poked out at me. I turned my head in disgust. Some of the blood from the bin managed to get onto my dressing gown.

I heard Jeri's footsteps approaching from behind and she stopped next to me. "What happened?" I asked.

"I don't want to know. It was horrible. I… I think the shelf fell on him." She held her hand to her face trying to stay composed. I fought the urge to hold her.

"Are they ok?"

"I think so, considering. They're shook up pretty bad. Kyle found him."

"Oh no, the poor kid."

Jeri tried to smile "I've talked to him about it, tried to

make him feel better. I think they just need to forget about it now," she said and made her way back into the house before I had time to object.

I tied the trash bag, replaced the metal lid, went inside and washed myself until I was clean. I felt my own eyes welling up. I remembered buying him as a puppy, how happy Jeri was, how excited Emily and Kyle were the first time they saw him.

Despite waking late, I took my time dressing in my shirt and pants, each button a labour and a blessing – as much as my own thoughts were an anvil pressing me harder and harder into the ground, I would suffer it for the time alone. Downstairs, Emily's eyes were wide with excitement; grin indented into her cheeks, all over the bowl of cereal she shovelled into her mouth. Kyle twirled his spoon slowly through the milk without taking a bite. I perched at the oak dining table in between them and seized two pieces of toast. Jeri brought in a second plate of toast and laid it on the table. She gave me a sympathetic smile and sat down next to Kyle.

I didn't know what was worse, Kyle dwelling on it or Emily's obliviousness. I wanted to put my arm around him, to pull them both close to me, but I hesitated until it was too late and I couldn't do it.

"So, what are you doing in school today, Emily?" Jeri asked, her tone exactly the same as any day when our dog didn't die.

"Painting."

"That sounds fun," I said. Jeri smiled and I liked the way her eyes lit up when she did.

"But I'm still hungry."

"Ok, Sweetie, well what have you had to eat?"

"Toast and cereal and milk and a cookie."

"And you're still hungry? We better find something to fill that greedy belly of yours then." I tickled under her arms until her screams of laughter became ear piercing and I stopped. Kyle kept staring into space. Jeri put another piece of toast onto Emily's plate.

A mug shot of a sneering young man had appeared on the TV screen followed by the newsreader. "They let him go," Jeri said.

"The kidnapper?"

Jeri detected the irritation in my voice. "People make mistakes."

"Kidnapping a fifteen-year-old girl?"

"He was only eighteen himself. And he crossed a state line, it's not really kidnapping."

"Only legally."

"Well, he deserves a second chance."

"He took her for two weeks. Her parents must have been terrified. He should be locked up. What if it was your daughter?"

"They couldn't track her?" Jeri took out a Cherry Pop and dropped it into her mouth. She closed her eyes as she swallowed it. "Divine."

I took a breath. "Her damn parents didn't put her DNA on file." The DNA tracker was the first major project that I completed at US Tech. Each tracker could hold, remotely recognise, and locate a single DNA sequence, ignoring any interference that would contaminate traditional DNA profiling.

"You don't have yours on file."

"Children should be on file," I said, earning a look of disproval from Jeri.

I did my best to stay in the room – mentally and physically. Kyle had barely looked up from his bowl. "Do you remember when we brought Scraps home?" Kyle kept his eyes on the bowl, but I saw them widen. "He jumped right out of the box."

Emily giggled hard. "And he weed on your shoe, Uncle Ryan."

Kyle's smile wrenched at my heart.

"Ok, that's enough now. We're supposed to be forgetting about it," Jeri said as she swiped away my plate with an uneaten piece of toast. "And you're going to be

7

late."

I gave the kids a kiss goodbye and told them I hoped to see them soon. Jeri walked me to the door, the pleasantness that had filled her face this morning had already started to fade. She surrendered a quiet goodbye, reached her hand out awkwardly towards my shoulder and pulled me in for a hug or a kiss. I jerked back unconsciously, and Jeri withdrew.

A flash of hurt appeared in her eyes before she slammed the door an inch away from my face. No time for me to say goodbye. From the other side of the door, her voice boomed with excitement.

What was she thinking? I wasn't trying to hurt her; I just don't understand what she was doing.

For a second, I considered giving up on my sham of a marriage.

* * *

I sat alone in my hatchback in the middle of a sea of parked cars. My eyes still felt like the lids had been peeled back and a steady tremble travelled down my body. I struggled to control my thoughts, going back and forth over the bad times. Wondering what today had in store for me. Afraid to leave the sanctuary of my car.

When I finally bolted, Jessica was waiting to greet me in the doorway of the giant rocket shaped US Tech building with Peter hanging behind. "I left you a voicemail. Bob wants you in his office in five. He's panicking again." She smiled at me. Her hair curled under the left side of her face. I tried not to think about it.

"I need a coffee," I said passing through the security scanner to access reception. "You ok for one?"

"I'll come with," Jess said. "I could do with a coffee."

Peter held one in each hand. "I just got you a latte," he said in mild dismay.

"I don't drink lattes," Jess shouted back on her way to

the coffee tap with me, leaving Peter behind the security scanner to stare down at his rejection in the form of a caffeinated drink.

The first time I saw the inside of US Tech I had to catch my breath. The curved steel arch that hung forty feet above my head was adorned with fluorescent lights small enough to look like stars. The glossy black walls featuring touchscreens and foldout tech access points were in setback in curved recesses, water fountains and coffee taps beside each one. The buzz of enthusiasm was irresistible, an undeniable epicentre of the future in the making. But now it was just another room in just another building. Its wonder wasted on me.

"So, what's got Bob so agitated?" I still felt uncomfortable around her, but Jess never stopped acting like my best friend.

Jess leaned towards me as we walked, and her eyes glowed with excitement. "The Secret Service is here."

"Are they prepping the building or something?"

"I don't know. I've never dealt with them before. Rick said they were like an army of ants when he was on the Space Lift programme."

Rick Stenson had been my best friend since college. When it came to work and his unrelenting ambition, he could be the biggest prick when he wanted to be, but if he's your friend, then he's your friend for life. Loyal like a sheepdog, he'll watch out for you, forgive anything and have your back no matter what. At US Tech, my boss, Bob had turned down my application three times before Rick persuaded him to interview me.

Bob's glass office walls were misted up, which told everyone outside that the meeting was confidential. Jess and I walked in sipping cappuccino's as Bob tapped in a fury against his glass desk. More new photos of his family had joined the half dozen others until there was barely enough space for him to lean. Rick and Peter were perched on the only two chairs in the room. "I got a call from the CEO's office. There's been a change of plan," Bob began before giving either of us a chance to bring in more seats. "I can't believe Washington laid this on us. He's moved his visit. He's coming today."

"Today? But we're not ready." Peter was right. We were hardly prepared.

"He's the Vice-President of the United States, I couldn't exactly tell him to reschedule." Bob rolled his eyes. "If that's ok with you, Peter."

Peter slumped back in his chair. "I'll hack his diary and change the date."

A professionalism aficionado, Rick had learned not to enter a slanging match with Peter, so he opted for a tension-filled blink followed by a long stare directed at Peter, rather than the profanity of the past.

"Now," Bob continued. "Vice President Palmer has always shown a great public support for the work we're doing here at US Tech, and we owe it to him and to ourselves to put on our best show. Ryan, you have the lead on this. I hope you're all ready?"

I looked around the room at Rick, Jess, and Peter. In the moment, my mind was in too much of a furore to even remember what preparation we had done. I cleared my throat. "We're ready."

"Then get your presentations on that screen and we rehearse until we're on at 1pm."

Rick jumped to his feet, laying claim to being first up for rehearsal – even though me and Jess were supposed to be up first – and used his tablet to flash the first slide onto the screen embedded in the wall. Bob let out a sigh and slumped in his chair and whispered, "Do you think we can pull this off?"

"We're at our best when we're up against it." I had become adept at portraying false confidence – I had put off and put off my preparation hoping inspiration would strike in the final hour, and I could barely concentrate enough to hold this conversation so the only thing coming out of my mouth to Vice President Palmer would be drivel and nonsense – but if Bob descended into panic then he would spend the precious time left scrutinising, which would only sabotage the preparation I knew Rick and Jess would have done (and Peter had both winged and aced every presentation I had seen him do).

Bob cracked his neck once on either side. "You're right, you're right. We've done the hard work; this is all about flying the flag. And you... you've done something very special. You're onto bigger and better things. Now you need to help Rick get polished, and I have to make an appointment." I narrowed my eyes in confusion and Bob cowered. "I've got to take Janie to the dentist. Her mom's visiting her sister in New York. She's unhappy with the colour of her braces because little Daisy has yellow ones. I don't think she'd forgive me if I cancel it again. Kids, you'll do anything for them."

"Hard not to." I didn't bother to question why he was leaving us at such a crucial time.

"What about you and Jeri? Any rugrat plans?"

Acid rose from my stomach and so far up my throat I could taste it. "No," I stumbled over my words, the acid burnt my heart on the way down. "No, not yet."

* * *

At exactly 1pm, the boardroom door swung open and two secret service staff left another four in the corridor as they hurried inside, followed by the man himself, Vice President Robert Palmer. The mood in the room lifted the second he entered, clearly someone you couldn't help but take notice of. His slim fit navy suit was immaculate and seemingly immune to creasing. He smiled and made eye contact with each of us as he strode nearer, followed by another man in a suit that made all of ours look shabby, but was still made to look like something bought from the thrift store compared to the Vice President's.

11

Elliot Brandon, the CEO of US Tech greeted him first. Brandon patted his arm and grinned like they were old chums. Vice President Palmer didn't quite reciprocate, but he was respectful. Then Bob did the usual handshake and introduced himself before the Vice President moved onto Rick, leaving Bob dabbing sweat from his brow. He greeted Jess and Peter, each of them sharing a few words of welcome and comments about how exciting our work is, and then finally, he stood right in front of me.

Ok, keep it together, Ryan. Silent. Calm. Clarity.

Oh shit, what am I going to say?

My mind was an empty shell of nothingness. I had a faint recollection of something in there, something smart, or funny, or sincere. And the etiquette: I had planned to research the recommended way to talk to a Vice President, or conversation tips, but it was the last thing on my mind when the meeting was brought forward, and with him standing right in front of me, I had no idea what to say.

"Then this must be the wonder kid?" He broke my intense awkwardness, held out his hand and laid a smile on me that reminded me of how my father eased my worries away as a child.

"It's a pleasure to meet you, sir." He had the best handshake I had ever experienced. Firm, but not too tight, long but not overly long, and his left hand placed gently on my shoulder, welcoming me into his life.

"So, I assume you all know who I am," he smiled, and all of my colleagues laughed excessively. "This is Agent Brody. He specialises in ensuring the security of our country is not compromised." Brody looked like a typical special agent, wearing a black suit and tie and a white shirt (I half expected him to top it off with black sunglasses). He travelled the room shaking hands with a vice-like grip as Vice President Palmer continued, "I am very excited by the achievements that you have made. You few in this room are part of a large movement of people who are taking our country and the whole human race to new levels of prosperity: The new wave of pioneers."

"Well, we have a packed hour for you Mr Vice President. I hope that it meets your expectations." Bob ground his teeth awaiting a response.

"Then for the next hour, I'm all yours."

The Vice President sat at the far end of the long white table and everyone except the two secret service staff – who were positioned one behind the Vice President and one at the door – clustered around him. The boardroom was not my favourite place. The chairs too heavy, the people too distant, and the large windows let in enough sun to burn my eyes out. I wished I had been more prepared, rehearsed more, and weeks in advance. This was not the time for stumbling over words or for my mind to go blank. Caffeine in full swing, I took a breath to ease my nerves and hoped the right words would find their way into my mouth.

"Eight years ago, US Tech, the largest global government-corporate collaboration in history launched a joint initiative to develop a range of technologies for the benefit of our civilisation. Three years ago, in conjunction with NASA, US Tech provided America with the Space Lift, a phenomenal achievement that allows astronauts to be transported directly to the US Pad Space Station without a shuttle. Now, we have taken the same nanotube technology that has benefited the space programme and applied it to everyday life on Earth. I present to you, the White Giant."

The Vice President smiled and nodded his head in approval at the massive cylindrical building displayed on the screen before him. The architects had done a beautiful job of the design, white walls with hexagonal reinforced windows and a domed top, it towered over every other building in DC. I breathed a sigh of relief that my constant headache hadn't affected my game.

"In 2004, the largest nanotubes were just a millimetre wide and the tallest skyscraper in the world was the Taipei 101 at 508m high. At an astonishing 3,500m high, the aptly named White Giant now stands at more than four times the world's largest Skyscraper, peaking not far off the ozone layer." Already on my next assignment, I had barely stopped to take a breath, but talking about the White Giant like this made me proud of the work we had done and I was thankful for that.

Rick leaned forward, "Between the White Giant and the Space Lift, we have shown how Mechanical Engineering, and this team specifically can trailblaze innovation to get things done, leading the way across multiple departments."

Vice President Palmer pulled a face "The space lift is an amazing accomplishment, no one denies that. But it cost more and took longer than planned. It swallowed a lot of government funding from the architectural renovation programme. How do you propose to prevent such overspends in the future?"

I felt the room tense. Palmer didn't look at anyone specific for an answer, which avoided the question being aggressive, but it only put more pressure on the response. Rick – the only member of the Space Lift project team present – choked and his head dropped, clearly not about to stick up for himself. But he had worked his arse off every day against a host of bureaucratic and ignorant decisions and I couldn't let him go down like that.

"Not everything turns out the way you want it to." Every head in the room whipped around to look at me. Elliott Brandon eyeballed me from the other side of the desk, but I continued regardless. "The people here put their souls into their work. To do it fast and to do it right. I wasn't on the Space Lift project, but I know enough to know that the plan and the budget set were never realistic, particularly given the lack of precedent." Bob squirmed in his chair, eyes darting back and forth between me and the Vice President, panic all over his face.

Silence.

Drawn out silence. I kept waiting for it to all go horribly wrong. To be escorted out of the building and away from the Vice President or fired on the spot.

Palmer bobbed his head twice and returned his attention to the screen. A spark of exhilaration lit inside me, it hit me harder than it should, like six beers after six years sober. I fought the urge to say more and took the win, subtly reorienting myself before I continued.

"With six hundred floors, the White Giant houses a three-floor conference centre, seven independent exhibition spaces, state of the art research and innovation labs, and is accompanied by more sleeping quarters than a traditional apartment block." As I clicked for the next slide the room around me fluttered like a sheet blowing in the wind. Mist rose from the floor until it surrounded me. The US Tech office walls and ceiling were gone. The long white table and empty office chairs now sat in the middle of a concrete road, towered over by buildings that reached high above the clouds, and then the clouds let out a storm. The air sweltered around me. I looked for Jeri, expecting to see her by my side but she was nowhere to be found. Unbearable screams echoed through the empty streets. I can't lose her.

I fell to my knees.

"Ryan. Ryan Ellis." Agent Brody stood in the shadows of a tall grey building at the far end of the white desk. His eyes locked onto mine, stern and unwavering, burrowing into my soul. His mouth continued moving but this time no sound came out.

Paradox. Unveil.

"Ryan. Ryan Ellis." I brushed my fingers over the oak floor that I was curled up on, Jess crouched beside me. I didn't understand why she looked so concerned. "What happened to you?" Agent Brody said from across the desk, which now stood firmly where it belonged inside the US Tech board room. He cast a perplexed look at Vice President Palmer, it was subtle, but I noticed it, and I felt like a security risk. Bob, Rick, and Peter all stood up and made their way over to me at various states of pace, but Brody didn't move.

I could see the US Tech office in front of me, but the

remnants of the empty street still felt fresh in my mind. "I'm sorry." The words came out of my mouth with difficulty. "What happened?"

* * *

I reached into the glove compartment of my hatchback and swallowed another dose of painkillers. My head had been aching since I passed out and I didn't want my dad worrying about me. He had lived in the same five-bedroom house for fifty of the sixty-three years of his life, with fantastic gardens at the front and rear where he spent most of his time.

I handed my dad a money tree sapling I had bought him and mid-thanking he was off to collect the materials. He returned minutes later to his cosy armchair opposite me, empty plant pot in hand and a bag of soil at his feet. He asked about Jeri and I told him the usual, that we're still together and trying our best. "She was very worried about you." I had heard it all before, the worry I had put everyone through, the things people think of, not knowing whether you're going to come back or turn up in a ditch. "We all were. I didn't know if you were ever coming back. Or if I was going to find you dead in a ditch one day."

"I know, Dad. I'm past that." Saying the words never seemed to make it true.

"Three days is a long time. Do you still love her?"

"Of course, I do."

"Then nothing else matters." My dad watched me carefully, waiting for me to agree.

I endured the silence long enough and changed the subject to my meeting with Vice President Palmer, and my dad was ecstatic the whole time. He always told me how proud he was of me, and today was certainly no exception. "Guess what, Dad? I've been invited to the State Dinner."

"At the White House?" I nodded and my dad couldn't contain his glee, asking every detail about it. He stood up, shook my hand and wrapped his arms around me. It was like being draped in a golden blanket. But soon the paint started to peel, nothing but a tin fraud underneath. Happiness, as ever, fleeting. My chest felt as though it was corroding into my stomach.

"What did your brother say about it?" Dad asked, pulling me back into the room.

"He was really happy for me. He wants to drop us off in his car," I said contorting my face.

"The jalopy?" He shook his head. "How is your brother?" Dad emptied soil into the pot, moulding it around the brown stem.

"He's doing good, Dad. You should go see him."

"How are Carol and my grandkids?"

"Eddie starts school next week. He-"

"I miss him." His head tilted down and sadness filled his eyes. We had gone through this conversation many times before, but my dad wouldn't budge. I could understand – this world is full of enough pain, if someone hurts you, then I say they deserve everything they get – but I wasn't even sure exactly what either of them had done that was so bad.

"Herb misses you."

"Has he told you that?"

"He doesn't have to."

My dad took a breath, deep in thought. "Does he talk about me?"

"You're constantly on his mind." Herb never spoke about Dad, at least he never started the conversation, and he did everything he could to change the subject.

"It's a cruel world, Son."

I tried to argue but the words got stuck in my throat, belonging to a version of me from long ago, not yet free of the chrysalis of naivety.

Accustomed to my silence, Dad continued, "All I wanted to do was help him. I wish your mother was still with us, she would set him straight, get him round to my way of thinking." My chest felt tight every time he spoke of her. I was desperate for him to talk about something else. I didn't know how he could just throw her name into a conversation. I fantasised about being dragged underground and swallowed up. If only I was alone to picture her in my head. The way I wanted to see her. The way she loved me. He kept waiting for an answer, but I couldn't bring myself to speak. "You think that's my problem, don't you Ryan? My way of thinking." The pain weighed on his eyes when he sighed. "I just want to talk to my son again."

* * *

The painkillers had worn off and Herb's kids were guaranteed to make it worse. When I got to the farmhouse, I could hear them before I rang the bell. Even after pressing it I considered walking away.

I had always tried to see my brother and his family as often as I could. His eldest had grown out of staying over at their Auntie and Uncle's, and the youngest two hadn't yet had the pleasure, which meant that Emily and Kyle were our most frequent residents and Jeri would have them sleeping over every night if she could.

Carol greeted me and invited me in, but I could barely make out what she was saying through the noise of kids screaming and running from one room to the next. She looked exasperated. Herb chased after his youngest, Tim, trying to trap him in a nappy. "Hey Ry, you fancy giving us a hand?" Herb asked.

"Don't worry about that, Ryan," Carol said. "Sit down and I'll make you a coffee." Herb told her not to bother because we leaving soon. I grabbed Tim as he ran past me, and I just about managed to wrap a nappy around him before he wriggled away. Herb kneeled in front of the sofa to clean smears of chocolate off it. The only time I could remember Herb getting angry with his kids was when he found his eldest daughter smoking aged eleven, which he took as a personal affront and spent weeks giving her the silent treatment.

Carol returned with a cup of coffee in hand for the three of us that Herb discreetly rolled his eyes at, then she apologised for rushing off upstairs to diffuse the chaos that had ensued, shouts and slamming doors emerging out of nowhere. Herb sat down, stretched out across the sofa, and let out a sigh of exhaustion. "I didn't know if you would cancel our date." When I didn't answer he rolled his neck around. "Still pissed then. I know. Look, I'll butt out in future, it's none of my business." I took a sip of coffee and stayed silent, made him work for it. "You're gonna make me apologise, aren't you? For shits sake Ryan-"

"Dad!" Eddie popped his head up from the other side of the sofa, apparently hiding there since I had arrived.

Herb grimaced. "For Pete's sake Ryan..." He stood up. "I'm sorry, ok?" He said hurrying out the door. Short and sweet.

After almost three hours at the Bruiser bar, Herb had glugged away a few bottles too many at the beer-sticky bar that melded to your sleeves whenever you leant on it. Every third Tuesday of the month, we sat opposite wooden deer antlers that hung above dozens of antiseptic-tasting whiskey bottles filled to various levels, never more than a dozen people surrounding us, and the same ones every week. Herb said he liked them because they were honest folk, even though the only person he had ever spoken to was whichever person was stood at the other side of the bar. We had talked about football for most of the night, which meant Herb talked and I pretended to listen, until it had grown so thin that I didn't bother, but Herb didn't seem to notice, navigating his way through varying levels of excitement with zero attention on me. I let my mind drift, wondering if Herb would even notice if I upped and left. It was becoming increasingly difficult to concentrate on anything.

Probably the painkillers.

I realised Herb hadn't been talking for a while, and he was staring at his empty bottle of beer like it was unfathomable. "I talked to Dad today. He asked about you. He talks about you a lot, you know?"

"I can imagine. 'I'm very disappointed in your brother' 'your brother is nothing like I expected,'" Herb snapped, then took a sip of his bottle of beer, the one that was empty.

"It wasn't like that." I paused knowing I had to choose my words carefully. "He cares about you. He wants to see his grandkids again."

"Is that a joke? Can you imagine what he would say to them about me?" Herb shuddered at the thought.

"He wants to see you again."

"He said that, did he?"

"I know he does."

Herb scoffed. "You're something I could never be, Ryan. You have a great job, a beautiful wife. You're a success."

I couldn't have felt any further away from being a success. "What are you talking about? Carol's great, your kids are the best kids in the world."

"I know. I'm lucky, I know I am. But I'm just... I don't know." As much as I still felt a rumbling of anger at him despite his apology, it irritated me to see him playing himself down like that, as though he didn't deserve his life, but he was too damn stubborn to listen to reason. Mom called it being 'well moulded'.

"Someone has to put an end to it. Do yourself a favour and go see him."

Herb turned back to stare at his empty bottle of beer. "I don't need to be constantly reminded that I'm a screw-up."

"You're not a screw-up."

"I'm not? Then how did I let someone steal my sheep?"

"Someone stole your sheep?"

"Five of them went missing off the farm this month. But whoever the bastard was took Eddie's dog too." Herb clenched his fist. "If you see anyone opening a new farm or butchers with a sheep dog, you let me know." He slapped me on the back with his overgrown hands so hard he nearly sent me sliding across the bar. It was only when he spoke again that my fight or flight response subsided, and I realised it was drunken affection. "Life is here to kick you in the ass. And as soon as you open your mouth to whine about it, it kicks you in the teeth." Herb turned his slouch to a straightened back and with a posh pout, said "The sooner one can accept that pearl, the sooner one can clench one's ass-cheeks and shut one's piehole." Herb sank his next beer that had been queuing up behind the empty one and returned to his usual slouch.

I could barely muster the energy to shake my head at him. "I'm going to call Jeri." Outside the bar, I managed to speak to Jeri, but it was brief. We never had any difficulty in conversation before and it still unsettled me. I wasn't even sure why I called her, old habits, maybe. But I still liked to let her know when I was heading home. By the time I got back to Herb his next beer was near decimated. "It's ten o'clock. Let's go." As the designated driver, Herb had no choice but to leave. A sober conversation with a drunken man wasn't my ideal way to spend an evening, but Herb liked the bar, and it was too far to get a cab. Besides, he needed a bit of a break and someone to talk to, and he was grateful, usually.

Driving home, a blanket of fog filled the roads, and my lights did little to compensate. Herb had fallen asleep five minutes after getting in the car. I wondered what Jeri would be doing right now, whether she still missed me. It had been so long since I felt missed.

The lights on the car ahead blinded me. They grew brighter as it got closer. Damn it. I couldn't see the road ahead. Couldn't hear the engine running. I took my foot off the gas and slammed it down, over and over but the car didn't respond.

"Herb, we're not moving. Herb!" I prodded, poked and shook him but he wouldn't wake. I pressed the button to start the engine again, but I couldn't even hear it trying. I reached out but my hand missed the handle and smacked against the door, limp. I shunted my arm at the door but my whole body was failing me.

I have to get out of here, I have to get out.

"Herb!" My tongue was almost dead. My head lolled. It's over. Whatever hell I belong in, this is it. My eyes were the last part of my body to deteriorate as they rolled to the back of my head, and I kissed my vision goodbye.

Paradox. Unveil.

What's happening to me?

TWO

Monday and I was back at work. The morning was slow and spent alone in the confines of my office. It was one of five along the corridor, including Rick's, modest in size and decor but cosy. The personal mementoes were long gone, and I managed to keep my wooden three-foot desk presenting the appearance of being on top of my work by dumping everything into the desk drawer underneath at the end of each day. I did my best to fill the time between menial tasks daydreaming about other places, other times. The notion of the past felt like a mythical realm, where I was free from worries and sorrow, until I stumbled upon some wretched memory, like finding a snake in your bed. And memories like that are never alone, as soon as one takes hold of you, they attract others like a magnet, burrowing their way into your mind, one at a time, until all you can do is hope that tonight's sleep will let them slip away.

I survived lunch, when company policy forced me to leave the solace of my office for relaxing colleague interaction to reduce anxiety or stress and improve work-life balance, allegedly. When I saw Rick, Jess and Peter at the other end of the cafeteria, I pretended I hadn't, and it was busy enough that they didn't see me. The idea of idle conversation drained the life out of me, and I knew I didn't have a worthwhile conversation in me, so I found a table out of their eye line and unpacked my sandwich. I finished the first one ok but one bite into my second, I saw the trio stand and swarm towards me. Peter second glanced back at their table and the two empty seats next where they sat, and finally back at me sitting alone. He led the way towards me and made his apologies about not seeing me, and then he fruitlessly waited for me to do the same. Jess ignored Peter and smiled at me and Rick checked I could still make the brief at 2pm. I gathered enough will to do the social rituals and clichés but it was brief and then they were gone. I stared down into my yoghurt when the chair in front of me screeched as it was dragged from underneath the table.

"Do you mind?" He said, gesturing to the empty seat. It took me a moment to search my memory, but I didn't recognise him. He waited for a response until the silence between us made my heart race and I would do anything to interrupt his empty stare.

"Sure." I gave a few nods and stuck my spoon into my yoghurt, hoping that would be the end of our conversation. He flicked the hair off his round glasses, laid his lunch tray down with its soggy mess of burger and chips and sat facing me.

"Ryan?" I didn't answer. "Rick pointed you out to me on my way in. I've been doing some work for him. It's my last day."

"You're the contractor."

"Jeremy."

I made a start on my fruit, wished that I had brought less and contemplated explaining how inedible they were. I decided it was more customary to blame a meeting that I had forgotten about and had to leave for immediately, when he started up again.

"How long have you worked for US Tech?"

"Err... Maybe too long." I smiled but he didn't smile back. He hadn't smiled at all. "Few years."

"You're married? To Jeri?"

"Sure."

"Rick talks about you a lot. Have you known him long?"

In the mood I was in, his small talk was starting to feel like the Spanish inquisition. "Since college."

"You like him, ok? He can be a bit of an ass."

He got a laugh out of me, and I noticed that I had relaxed a little. "I worked for him for nine months, so believe me, I know. We don't choose the friends we have. They just latch onto us and never let go." Jeremy smiled and stuck his hand in his bag of chips while taking a bite out of his burger. "What do you think of US Tech?"

"Impressive, I guess. I suppose you deal with some senior people in the government."

"I met the Vice-President for helping to build a really big building. Anyway," I stood up and put my leftovers onto my tray. "It was nice to meet you, Jeremy." I nearly told him the excuse about a fake meeting, but I felt bad lying to him. "I should be getting back. A lot of prep to do for a 2pm." I strolled back to my office a little pleased and more than a little surprised that the encounter turned out quite pleasant.

* * *

I walked with Rick to my next meeting and asked him if he was as much of an ass to the people that worked for him now as he was to me. He insisted that he was not and has never been an ass. "You're such an ass."

The presentation room was the same as every other in the building, grey-beige walls containing a fifty-inch flat screen, pine table and metal chairs, a sharp breeze from an overeager air conditioner and a permanent smell of new carpet. Inside, we were eagerly awaited by the head of scientific development for the research division who I had engaged with for each of the projects I had performed a lead role on, but I was surprised to see Jessica and Peter sitting at the other side of the room to Bob. According to Bob, this was just a standard progress update, but with Bob apparently inviting Rick, and now the attendees extending to Jess and Peter – none of whom were even on the project – it felt like I had walked into something else entirely. I marched straight over to Jess and Peter to find out what they were doing there. "Beats me," Peter said, and Jess gave an unknowing look. "I got an invite from Bob." A little unsettled, I felt a presence behind me.

"Hello, Ryan. Rick." The head of scientific development said. His name was a forgotten dream. Barry? Gary?

"Good afternoon. I'm sure you all remember Harry Fuller," Bob finally said.

"Hi Harry, how are you?" I shook his bony hand.

"Fine. Thank you." Harry pushed his thin rimmed glasses back onto his nose and squinted.

"Then let us press on," Bob said as he sat and mopped his brow with his handkerchief.

Harry dimmed the lights with his remote as I eased myself into a chair and he began the presentation. "I'll get straight to the point. Progress is unacceptable. We are not where we need to be. And this department is fundamentally failing the project." As the only person in the department currently working on the project, I didn't have to guess who that was squared at. If I had any doubts, his intense stare certainly didn't muddy the waters.

"Well," Bob faltered and turned to me, "Ryan, you have done a lot of great work on this."

"Let's not play around Bob," Harry said firmly. "I'm not interested in the past; this is about the future. And we don't need great work, we need results. We need answers. Most importantly, we need a working prototype. Rick, Jess, Peter, that's where you come in." He studied each one of their faces in turn. "As usual, this project is top-secret. You must not discuss the project with any persons who are not on the *documented list* of signatories for *this project*. Level 10 confidentiality forms will be issued to you following this meeting."

Bob's eyes burned into Harry's skull. I couldn't work out whether it was because he was reacting to what Harry said, or whether he already knew they were bringing in reinforcements and Harry was to blame.

With a click of a button Harry brought up the first slide. It read 'Project: Infiltrator'. And so that was that. With only a sentence I had been deemed a failure, and inept to continue on without bringing Rick and my own team onto the project to do the job right. It wasn't that I needed the extra hands, I had a team of people working for me, no, they wanted me side-lined.

"So, you're going to turn us into spies," Peter remarked.

"On the contrary, quite the opposite," Harry said. "Stealth craft go undetected on radar by absorbing the radio waves that are emitted, by detecting radar sources and deflecting them. Our scientific development team has been able to create a proposal for reversing stealth technology. Project: Infiltrator will be able to detect the radar and infrared sensors that surround the craft, creating a silhouette effect. However, the project has not yet been able to develop a prototype to gather the sensory data to perfectly pinpoint the location of the craft in real-time."

"Isn't that a military project?" Peter said.

"It's *your* new project," Harry retorted.

"But it is a military project."

"US Tech has been involved in projects that have served the defence of our country before."

"Not publicly, they haven't." I wondered whether Peter was being awkward to stick up for me in his own way, or if he was just being his usual rebellious self. Jess threw me a pity look. I looked at the door and wished I was the other side of it.

Harry was exasperated. "If it is beyond either the morals or capability of this department, I will have to-"

Bob jumped to his feet in a fluster. "No, Harry, there's no problem. Please continue. This department is more than capable." Bob's eager smile was meant to reciprocate some level of positive response from Harry, but it only intensified his sneer of discontent.

Harry continued to brief them with details of the project team, objectives, plans, budgets and everything that came with it. Two hours' worth of embarrassment while I listened to everything aspect of the project that I had been a part of and not managed to do anything worthwhile for. I wondered why I hadn't been ripped from the project entirely, or even fired, but no doubt it was down to old merits from the White Giant project. The same merits that led everyone to expect me to pull another miracle out the bag to get the anti-radar prototype operational, but I just couldn't crack it. When Harry finished, everyone left except Jess. She shuffled down two seats to sit next to me and I questioned whether it could possibly get more uncomfortable working together. I felt guilty for being in the same room as her.

"Listen," she said in a calm, warm tone. "You're the wonder kid. Just give it time; you'll be back on top. You don't need us on this with you. You'll crack it and those assholes will give you another promotion. Bob would probably promote you tomorrow if he could." Jessica held her smile and kept looking into my eyes.

"How do you know it wasn't Bob that side-lined me?"

"Bob might be a wuss but he fucking loves you. He thinks you're both alike, which you're not by the way, because you're way better. Besides, if he didn't want you on the project, he would have just told you, you know he's straight up. With us, at least."

We walked into the corridor, and I mumbled a goodbye and shuffled off into the opposite direction as her. I couldn't cope and I knew it, I just never wanted to admit it to myself. Life used to be so much easier. Maybe having a few extra people around would ease things off for me. But I couldn't shake the feeling that I was sinking even deeper.

* * *

It may have been futile at this point, but I still felt the need to work late to get my house in order before Rick, Jess & Peter started inspecting what I had done, or not done. I tried to organise my Project: Infiltrator notes and documents into some level of order but the whole thing dragged.

"Well, you look like shit," Rick had a stack of papers in his hand, which he proceeded to dump into separate piles on my clear desk. He stepped inside my office that would barely hold six people standing. Two often felt too many. He pulled up the chair next to me and leaned closer. "Are we pushing you too hard?"

"We?"

"You know what I mean..." He still liked to act like he was my boss. He took a second to restart. "Look, things are shifting at the moment in US Tech, I'm sure you sense it. You need to get your head in the game."

"Thanks *buddy*. Thanks for letting me know."

"You know what I mean..."

I locked eyes on him like I was trying to burn them all the way through to the other side of his head until he relinquished. "Not really. What are you building to ask me?"

"Nothing. I'm just saying we can finally get the recognition we deserve. Bob might transfer people to work for me, maybe even three or four. And you can get fuckers like Harry Fuller off you're back. We could blow everyone in this place out of the water." Rick's grin grew to gigantic proportions before his big finale, "Think about it, you and me on the Executive Board."

Rick's pep fell short of inspiring me to his dizzying heights of ambition and we sat in needle driving silence until Rick's eyes had wandered around my office long enough for him to restart the conversation. "How are things with Jeri?" The look on my face must have said it all. "That bad, huh? I'm sorry. Is there anything I can do?"

I huffed, half in response to the question and half

because I was still pissed with Rick. But I had learned to tolerate his well-meaning but not so helpful advice. "I don't know if there's anything I can do. I'm just so tired."

The state my marriage was in, the balance between things about my relationship I missed and things I enjoyed was enough to break the scales. When I would stumble on her best moves in the kitchen, and she caught me watching her – she never slowed down, didn't hesitate, instead she would drag me in and make me dance for her. Her Monday to Friday tradition when she would dive out of the bed and her first step would be targeted at the bathroom, every time, where she would emerge from within fifteen minutes, only a uniform away from being ready to leave. Her resistance to weekend mornings, lifting her eyelids like they were bench pressing her body weight, crawling halfway to alert before retreating under the duvet, the land of temptation that I would walk a thousand miles to enter.

Rick picked up the gold-coloured employee of the year plaque on my desk and felt the weight in his hand. I was awarded it for the White Giant project when I managed to work out how to build nanotube structures large enough to support building structures when no one else could. It was a pretty big deal. I was trying hard on the anti-stealth tech, I really was, but working on the White Giant – even though the scale was so much bigger in every sense – I found it easier. I always knew what to do. Bob had said that watching me work was like an outer body experience.

"Listen," Rick said rubbing the back of his neck while kept his head down as though he was preparing to ask me for a loan. "Thanks for sticking up for me to Vice President Palmer. I wish I could say I'd have done the same." Rick's shoulders dropped, only for a moment, and then he wrinkled his tie until it was dead centre, and the bashful Rick was replaced by a smug grin and pole up his ass posture. "Anyway, who had your back when you were out of work? If you hadn't passed probation I wouldn't have been promoted. Do you know that?"

"My hero," I said, hearing it for the sixteenth time.

"Yeah, well, you would have done the same for me. Not as well, of course. Or with as much grandiose. Now, if it's anyone other than the Vice President, you know who's got your back."

"Oh, Rick," I shook my head unable to contain my grin at his pathetic attempt at bravado. "I miss the humble nerd I met on the first day of colleague who was so enamoured with reading he wanted nothing to do with the world outside. And don't make me talk about your anorak."

"*The* anorak."

"I thought I was going to have to forcibly remove your face from that physics book, what was it called?"

Rick laughed. "You closed it on me, you bastard. That book was over a thousand pages. It took me ages to find my place."

"It took you a month to pick it back up again after I showed you where the parties were. I guess it's my fault..."

"I never partied for a month."

"College time passes quicker than normal time, don't forget."

"Can't argue with that." A smile positioned itself firmly on Rick's face. Even when Jeri took over my life, my best non-wife/girlfriend friend was always waiting for me. "Look, Jess and Peter, they're capable, more than capable, but, well... Jess' isn't as ambitious as we are. And Peter, well... but we have an opportunity right now. I can feel it. You just need to get your head in the game."

I leaned toward Rick, grabbed the back of his neck, and pulled him to me. "You're such a dick. I love you, but you're such a dick." My arms wrapped around his back, he grunted twice before he reciprocated.

He stood and rested his hand on my shoulder. "We should go out for a few drinks. Get back on college time, maybe. It's been too long." Rick closed the door on his way out.

I riffled through the papers Rick left, mostly various

documents to read and sign. I put the stack to one side and checked my personal emails on my cell. The only unread mail I had that wasn't spam was titled Project: Ambassador. I didn't recognise the sender or the project name. It was against policy to send work related emails to a personal address, and any files sent externally to approved recipients had to be encrypted, which this document was not. I opened the email and then the attachment.

The document referred to Project: Infiltrator files that I had read during my work on the project, but when I scrolled down, I found a set of schematics that wasn't in any file I had seen for Project: Infiltrator. It took me a minute to work out what they were for, and when I did, I had to read it a second time to make sure I hadn't misinterpreted them. But they were unmistakeably clear. The designs were for a prototype Earth-to-orbit shuttle with US Tech symbols all over both the document and the shuttle itself. Whoever sent it had my full attention.

The prototype shuttle would inject antimatter into normal matter, and the resulting reaction product would be vented through a magnetic nozzle to provide thrust. The problem in the past had always been retrieving and storing this energy source, but the shuttle would be entirely constructed out of nanotube technology to enable storage, and the magnetism was able to slow down and collect the anti-protons that would provide propulsion. It was years ahead of where we were thought to be.

I scrolled back up to the front page. There was the usual US Tech opening spiel, as well as similar content from NASA, and then in red block capitals: Level 20. My security clearance was the same as Rick's: level 10. Bob was only level 12.

I connected my flash drive to my cell and saved a copy, then deleted the email permanently. I paced the room, my brain working faster than it had since the early days of the White Giant. Theories and ideas bounced around inside my head. And then I realised what I held in my hands: The shuttle designs were in a file for Project: Infiltrator. The anti-stealth technology that I was tasked with developing was to be fitted to the shuttle.

I reopened the document. My heart racing, my eyes darted back and forth across the screen, taking in as much of the file that I could in a race to finish. The shuttle would be fully manoeuvrable within one thousand miles of the Earth's surface, able to travel further than the US Pad space station.

Why would a shuttle orbiting Earth need to be able to detect stealth craft?

My personal cell buzzed on my desk. I answered it right away.

"Hello?"

"Ryan. I need you to listen to me."

"Who is this?"

"I trust you received the document." I snapped to attention.

"Who is this?"

"I need to see you. Will you meet with me?" This time the voice sounded familiar, but I couldn't place it. "That's just the beginning. There's more you need to know." I picked up the handset on my desk phone, ready to call security. I was still rational enough to know not to get involved with mysterious callers and top-secret leaks.

"Ryan-"

I cut the call off and dialled. "Hello, Intelligence Security, how may I assist you?" A stern, male voice answered.

I paused. I had already deleted the email and saved a copy. I also read – if they were genuine – highly confidential files that never should have been in my possession. But most importantly, I had been targeted. I had heard of this kind of thing happening before, external agencies piggybacking on employees to elicit information about US Tech, but it usually started with information about the person they were trying to enlist, and it always led to long, drawn out investigations into how involved the US Tech employee actually was. And it resulted in every bit of personal life and secrecy that the employee ever had being aired in public. US Tech did not take security breaches lightly. And I didn't want my life torn apart for the sake of an email I never asked for.

"Sorry," I replied. "I meant to phone technical." I disconnected the call and questioned if I had done the right thing. But no one was ever going to discover a file I received through my personal email account. I placed the flash drive in my pocket and headed home.

* * *

I gazed out of the oval attic window at Jeri chasing Kyle and Emily through the long stretch of grass and vibrant flower beds. Jeri stopped to untuck the white t-shirt from her denim shorts, the sun blazing down on her from the west, until Emily taunted her to take up the chase again. Even without the kids, Jeri spent most of her free time in the garden, where her problems seemed to melt away.

I looked up at the blue sky and wondered what it felt like, what's beyond it. The way the light gleaned through the clouds, rays beaming across the sky. It looked like heaven.

The sole window in the attic was small and south facing, leaving the room poorly lit, and the ceiling hung only a few inches above my head. Light off, I moved a stack of boxes one by one and pulled out my old electric guitar. It had gotten me through bad times before, wailing songs for no one else to hear, the instrument not even plugged into an amp. I sat down, legs crossed and rested it in my lap. I held my hand over the strings, ready to make a pluck and let my agony flow into the strings and out of me. But I couldn't touch them. Couldn't strum a single chord.

I threw the guitar back behind the boxes and crouched down onto the plywood flooring. I lifted a short cut floorboard and pulled out a beautiful small box from underneath. It rested in my hand like a familiar memory in the morning. I closed my eyes and wished this moment would last forever.

Every day I took it out and placed it in front of me, usually while Jeri slept or bathed in the sunshine. She didn't like me being up here. She never said why. The smell was dank, not fresh, and our decoration of the house hadn't quite reached the bare brick walls of the attic, so it didn't possess the colour or the design consideration of somewhere like the garden, but I could be alone and uninterrupted and spent most of my day wishing I was up here.

I sat for a few minutes, legs crossed, and the box on my lap. Three birds were carved into the lid, two sitting high in a tree, and the third, smaller bird fluttered in the sky. The brass hinges were worn, and it creaked when I opened the mango wood lid. Small enough to rest easily in both hands, it wasn't the fanciest or most expensive of boxes, but it was perfect to me.

I liked to take my time and allow myself to become captivated by the contents. I couldn't have lived without it.

I was about to remove the first item when I heard footsteps on the second floor. I was sure they wouldn't get any closer, but I paused to listen. The steps changed from a dull thud on carpet to the lighter twang of a shoe hitting wood, and at a slower pace than before, each one getting nearer. I closed the lid but there wasn't enough time to return it under the floorboards, so I tucked it in between my legs and stared at the hole in the floor. All I could do was wait.

Jeri's head popped up first and then her shoulders joined her head, the rest of her body not far behind. She surveyed the attic, keeping a half smile on her face until she finally took her last step inside. She lowered her head even though it was a good distance from the ceiling.

"I made iced coffee," she said softly. "I... thought you

might like some. I've put a few biscuits on a plate too."

My nerves started to take over, I couldn't remember ever interrupting her reading in the garden or bothering her when she was planting flowers or while she moved the sprinkler around to evenly soak the grass. And I couldn't remember the last time we drank coffee together.

Jeri slowly meandered her way across the room, squinting as her eyes adjusted to the dark. She plonked herself down next to me, smack bang in my personal space. I shuffled back and held my hand firmly on the box lid. I looked down at her body, now bearing a shimmering blue dress that rested on her knees, with thin straps and matching blue shoes that struggled to maintain their sparkle in the dimly lit space. Jeri's half smile filled her face, but her eyes didn't know.

"Will you come downstairs?" she asked politely. "If you don't want to go outside, I thought maybe we could all play a game, or just watch TV or something." I couldn't look back at her, so I lowered my head and kept my eyes to the floor. "What do you think?"

She wouldn't relent. I felt lost, short of breath; the room seemed much smaller and more confined than only a few moments ago. I wanted to become part of it, a piece of furniture to add some comfort to the space or a rug to keep the floor covered. "I..." I wanted to speak but it was so hard. I didn't know what to say to her. I murmured another attempt, but that was even more botched than the first.

"Your dad called." She was nervous. We were both nervous around each other, now. "Just to ask about you. And me. He just wanted to see how we are, I guess." We held a moment of silence. "I told him, obviously. I... said you were ok, really. Just tired, that's all. You just need to sleep better, I guess. It happens to us all."

The only thing on my mind was the wooden box. I should have chanced it, hid it under the floorboards where it belongs. I felt her eyes fixated on me, worming their way into my mind, my soul. Trying to figure me out. I wished that she would just leave, go back to her garden. Leave me alone.

"Ryan."

I just want her to leave. The only reason she's doing this is because Kyle and Emily are here.

"Ryan."

I want to be alone.

She lifted her hand slowly and sailed it towards me like an oil tanker. Her fingers brushed gently across the nape of my neck, a shiver emanating out from her touch. I gripped the box between my legs. "I love you," she whispered. She pushed her lips at me and then recoiled when I didn't reciprocate. "I love you. And I know you love me. We just need to get back to it, we have to be strong. We just need to move on."

Move on. I felt a great swell in my chest as soon as the words were spoken.

Move on. It was the first time it had been said. I could have withered to the floor. I could have exploded into a million pieces. I didn't understand how she could utter the words, how the mere thought of them didn't send her into oblivion. How could she have expected me to move on?

A pain built from my stomach like a wedge forcing its way up through my chest and into my throat. I jumped to my feet. "Get out."

"Ryan-"

"Get the fuck out." I was panting, out of control. The room blared with rage screaming through me.

Jeri stumbled towards the attic door. She swung her body around and shook her arm out at me. "I give up. What do you even do up here? In the dark, by yourself."

Something caught her eye. It was the box. I gripped it tighter. She dived towards me and snatched it away. I reached out to grab it, but I wasn't quick enough. She turned her back before I could get near it. I was too late.

Jeri faced me once again, box open, squeezing a photograph between her fingers. There was only one inside the box, a picture of Jeri and me sat on a bench by Lake Ontario at the Scarborough Bluffs. At the will of a cold wind Jeri's hair danced in front of our faces with a life of its own. But the static image froze every strand like you could snap it off piece by piece until there was nothing left. My arm outstretched to capture the grins taking over our mouths as we huddled together. Each with a hand placed on Jeri's protruding stomach.

Jeri's brow furrowed in confusion at the next piece she pulled out: our twenty-week scan. The only picture in the world of our baby daughter. It held Jeri's gaze barely. Finally, a pink rattle, plastic frills sculpted around the centre and a small brown teddy bear on each side. My eyes stung, tear ducts at the ready, preparing for a well. But nothing could get past those lifeless balls in my head, too numb to cry.

Jeri's mask of pretence crumbled as she drove two fingers into the side of her head. Her mouth agape in disgust. "What is this? Why do you still have these?"

Why doesn't she understand?

"We agreed to get rid of all of this. We agreed, Ryan, you and me. How can we possibly go on when there are... reminders like this around the house?"

Jeri reached out to touch my cheek. "Get off me." I jumped back from her spindly fingers and twisted my body away. I couldn't bear to look at that nauseating face another second.

"They're a hindrance. They don't mean anything anymore. They're holding you back."

"How can you say that?"

"What's wrong with you? You're up here every day; you never want to spend time with the kids. Our kids worship you."

I couldn't believe my ears or the delusion that she had sunk into. Every word she spoke was water rising up to my head. "They're not our kids."

Jeri scoffed at me like I was being petty agonising over

38

the details. "You know what I mean."

"Yeah, well they're not ours. And they're not a fucking substitute."

Jeri gasped like I had just told her I didn't love me own child. "We're never going to have another baby, Ryan. I'm barren. These..." The photograph, the scan, the rattle, and the box, one by one she let them drop to the floor. They bounced as if they were hitting the bottom of an empty trashcan. I felt my heart drift away a little more, off into the abyss. "This isn't our life anymore."

Jeri's voice had lost some of the callous edge, but it was too late. I fell to my knees and swept my cherished items back into the box. She didn't understand. I was all alone. I knew I was. I had grown used to it. Not comfortable, you're never comfortable feeling alone, but prepared for it, maybe. I brushed past her and hurried down the stairs and out of the house. Her disgusting words echoed after me. Move on. Those hideous words. I tried to ignore them, but it stung, not like a swarm, but like a single wasp that knew exactly where to target to cause the most pain.

I jumped in my car and turned on the engine, my box safe on the seat beside me. I drove for miles until I no longer recognised the streets around me and pulled up outside a garden fence where I couldn't be interrupted. The attic is no longer safe. This will have to be it. I'll keep the spare key on me at all times. I'll clear out my glove compartment and it will stay there, with me wherever I travel.

I lifted the lid carefully. I scrutinised every piece for damage. Her greasy fingerprints littered the scan and a crease had invaded the edge of the photograph, the crumpled white of the paper breaking through. My heart sank. It was my only copy, and I hadn't been able to save the digital copy from Jeri's life wipe. I picked up the rattle and closed my eyes. I held both pictures to my chest, but I didn't cry. I could only imagine how happy I would have been, with a person I had never met.

My baby in the sky.

I closed my eyes and watched Jeri disappear into thin air.

The deadness inside of me. That's why it's there, to keep the pain at bay. I can worry, I can hurt, I can agonise. But I cannot surrender to these thoughts and feelings, or I may never re-emerge.

THREE

At exactly 11am, I was scribbling away at my desk in work when I should have been clearing my emails. I had etched two words, over and over: Paradox unveil. They had burrowed into my head, and it was the only way to let them out. My personal cell rang out. Unknown Caller flashed on the screen, and I answered.

"Hello, Ryan." I recognised the voice right away as was the man who had sent me the Earth to orbit shuttle project files. "I need to speak to you."

"Fuck off," I said and cut him off. I was in no mood to put up with anonymous callers trying to get me fired.

I let it ring another three times. The fourth I almost pressed my finger right through the phone. "Ryan, please-"

"I told you to fuck off. Don't call me again." My voice rasped this time, almost shouting. It rang again so I switched it to silent and ignored it, lighting up my desk. Five minutes passed. Then it vibrated with a text. I picked it up to see fifteen missed calls. The text read, *Ryan, I've sent you another file please read it.*

I accessed my personal email account and there it was.

I considered getting Peter to trace it and track the bastard down, but I knew I couldn't risk getting caught up in a dirty trail. The subject read *Project: Sobek. You need to read this.*

I can't get involved. There is nothing in that file that I need to know.

I held my finger over the delete button, ready to erase it.

But why had he targeted me? All I had to do was read it and maybe I would find out. No one from US Tech would ever know.

I clicked to view the attachment and within a few seconds a document was on my screen with US Tech plastered all over it along with the required level 20 security clearance. This time it was a scan of an original document, creasing showing up as lines of grey. There were pages missing as I scrolled through, names and whole sections blacked out. The opening summary detailed the intent to create a weapon to deal with significant threats to United States security. It would involve a specific trigger to activate the weapon against a planet-wide threat level. A lot of the specifics about the weapon were scrubbed out or omitted from the document. But whatever it was, the weapon was meant as a last mode of defence against something big, maybe the threat of nuclear war.

I read on intently but quickly, working my way through two pages about something call the Cognitive Expansion Group and success rates, until I found the reason I had been sent this file, why I needed to read it. On page thirty-five, not in the personnel section, or anything to do with either project resource or staff at US Tech, but under the section header *Subjects* was a list of names, most rendered unreadable by a black marker. But right there, in black ink, one of the names was perfectly readable: Ryan Ellis.

I flicked back through the document, looking for anything I had missed, any clue why my name would show up. I had never been involved in a weapons development project at US Tech and never would be, anti-stealth detection was pretty much my limit. Bob knew I would resign first.

I paced the room, going over everything I knew about the files, my experience at US Tech. I couldn't piece it together. What could I possibly be a subject for at US Tech?

The phone rang.

I gripped it tightly; my eyes bore into it. I could ignore it. It wasn't too late. My finger hovered over the red button to end the call. And then it stopped ringing.

I kept the phone in my hand, telling myself that I had done the right thing. Willing it to ring again. The black screen lit up, the tone sounded, and I hit the button to answer it. I waited but all I could hear was breathing on the other end of the line. Finally, I spoke. "Where?"

He gave me an address. I would have to wait until 7pm to find out what I was getting myself in to.

* * *

6:55pm. I couldn't remember the last time I was early. The long corridor of the Georgetown apartment block was lined with artwork and the carpet was so thick it felt like I was walking on couch pillows. After ending the call, the first thing I did was to check who the occupier was, but there was no name listed and no record of any bills, rent or anything else being paid from anyone who lived there. I switched my phone to silent and knocked on the apartment door and waited.

My brain became overwhelmed by what a bad idea it was. If I disappeared, no one would know where to look. I counted at least five locks click and the door opened slowly. I had a last second urge to run but it was too late. The pull was too strong. I had to see what was waiting for me on the other side.

The door stopped halfway. He looked back at me with an expression on his face that I couldn't quite figure out. It could have been suspicion, curiosity, or anticipation. I landed on suspicion. Of all the people that could be the other side of that door, I never expected to see Jeremy.

"You're alone?" he asked.

"Yes." Jeremy kept the door at halfway. The corridor was empty but for how long? "Are you going to let me in?"

Jeremy eyed me for a few seconds, and I didn't quite know what to do. But I knew that this was a horrible idea. If Jeremy had access to level 20 information, then what else did he have? I didn't like the idea of getting on the wrong side of him, but I wanted out.

Jeremy opened the door far enough for me to step inside. He looked down the corridor one way, then the other way before closing it behind us. I cringed when I saw that all he was wearing was a pair of boxer shorts and a build-up of sweat that moistened his forehead. He looked down at himself, and his lack of clothing and then at the watch on his wrist. "Sorry," he said. "I lost track of time."

The apartment interior was totally at odds with the long, elegant hallways outside. Clutter filled every inch of the floor except a small pathway that led in three directions: the kitchen, the bathroom and something that looked like a study. Beneath the rubble I could make out some nice features around me, but only barely.

I looked up from the mess as Jeremy set down a baseball bat beside the door next to a security monitor displaying the empty corridor outside.

Jeremy stared at me like he had fallen into a trance. "Do you get many robberies around here?" I asked.

"No," Jeremy said.

Oh. "So why did you send me the files?" I asked.

"We'll get to that." The friendly guy that ate lunch with me in work seemed like his Dr Jekyll. The small talk was gone. His face was grubby, and his hair stuck to his head "Why didn't you send anyone the file?"

"How do you know I haven't?"

"I bugged your email account."

I was furious. I gripped the phone in my pocket. "I could have sent it from work. Put it on a flash drive."

Jeremy grimaced. "That's bugged too. And I know about

44

the flash drive, but you'll find the files are corrupted. You won't be able to open or recover them."

"I could have printed it off."

He laughed mockingly. "No one does paper. That's why I do, of course. Although it generally gets stuffed in the bottom of the closet." He gave an awkwardly long pause, and I thought I was supposed to say something until he continued, "Besides, I would know if you printed them. I wrote a program for that too."

"So, what, you have, what, my whole life bugged? And I'm supposed to trust you now?" Jeremy took a deep breath. "I'm calling the police." I turned my back on him and reached for the door.

"There are other files. Your name is in one of them."

I turned back and stepped towards him. "I work at US Tech; I'm not surprised my name is in project documentation."

"You are or you wouldn't be here. You're part of the content, Ryan. Just like the last one I sent you. It's called Project: Libera. The Roman God of fertility."

The last word snapped me to attention. "Where is it?" I asked abruptly.

"I don't have it." That's convenient. "Not on me. But I've studied it thoroughly. Part of it anyway."

"I've never even heard of that project."

"It's level 20 clearance."

"And how do you have access to level 20?"

"How I got the information isn't important."

"Then what is? I want to see the file."

"I can get it." Without evidence, I was seriously questioning his credibility. Jeremy's eyes narrowed and his voice became low and subdued. "You've been having the dreams." I took a step back, more freaked out by the second, glancing at the bat.

Jeremy went hurtling into the study, placing each foot in the tiny gaps between piles of junk for no more than a second at a time. He slumped into a swivel chair. Instead of using the laptop that was already switched on in front of him, Jeremy picked up a second laptop and unfolded it. I hesitated before following him, taking the mess free pathway. Scraps of scribble-filled paper covered the room.

"Can you pass me the book on the table?" There were at least twenty books stacked on the table. The one with the blue cover, the address book." As I passed it to Jeremy, dust blew around the room. "Sorry, my house is like the moon." I didn't have a clue what he was talking about. "It's covered in three inches of dust," he said, waiting for me to get the joke. I laughed, but it was purely the nerves rather than his joke. "I guess I don't dedicate much time to spring cleaning. I don't really let anyone else in," he turned his head away from the screen for the first time "except Jacob." Jeremy gave a cold stare with a slight grin that he held for almost a minute.

I felt the need to break the awkwardness. In the middle of the heap on Jeremy's desk was a photograph in a frame of a girl who looked in her mid-twenties. "Who's this?"

"Rebecca Jones, the love of my life." He looked depressed for a man talking about the love of his life. She must have left him, though I had no trouble seeing why.

"These two things, Ryan: my laptop and address book. They hold all the keys. All the keys." There was that look again. I was one more of those looks away from getting out.

Jeremy turned back to the laptop, typing, and clicking the mouse faster than I could comprehend, and then he turned to me. His eyes narrowed and his jaw clenched. He started firing questions at me, "Ok, how often do you have this dream?"

"Often," I said.

"Be specific."

"Every night." I can't believe that I'm doing this. I haven't even told Jeri about this. What the hell am I doing here? "It's getting more regular."

"Ever when you're awake?"

"Yes... I think so. Yes."

"What happens when you're awake?"

"I'm not sure. The room and my dream, they started to... merge. And then I blacked out."

Jeremy leaned forward, bashing away at the keys. It was exactly what he wanted to hear. "Anything else?"

"I don't know... I just… I remember driving, and a light. It was so bright. I don't know what happened."

"Was anyone else ever with you?"

"My brother, but... he was asleep. I couldn't wake him." The voice in my head told me to stop talking. "We must have been driving for so long."

"Time loss."

"I don't remember getting home...I didn't even remember it happening. I was getting carried away with myself. "But I've driven that journey so many times... Sometimes you switch off, auto-pilot. It just..."

"It felt different this time, didn't it?" I didn't answer. "Have you told anyone else about this?"

"No."

"We have no idea what else is out there." Jeremy pushed his glasses up his nose only for them to slide back down. "Beyond our planet, our discreet definition of existence, we have no idea." His head shrunk into his shoulders as he got more and more worked up. "Space, time, our whole species is a blink of eye in the history of the universe. Whatever we think we know, we step outside of our small world and every rule we deem true might not even exist. Or everything may exist, somewhere, sometime. Our perception, our knowledge, our bodies they're all so limiting, we only experience a mere fraction of the truth. But we are all connected."

"Right." I had no idea where he was going, what this had to do with me. I didn't even know why I was here.

He pushed his glasses back up and stretched his neck out at me. "Do you trust yourself?"

"Yes?" I said, waiting for him to be a bit more specific.

"What about you're past self? Do you trust him?" Jeremy

asked as he peered over his smudged glasses. "You know; the guy who got you where you are. Put you in the situation that you're in." He frowned, contemplating his question. "I guess that depends on what situation you're actually in," he muttered to himself. "What about your future self? Do you trust him?"

I always thought of them all as the same guy: me.

Jeremy mulled over the answer that I didn't give. We each waited for the other to break the silence. "What did it say about me in the file?"

"We're being tested, you know." Jeremy said as if it was blindingly obvious, and I was the last person to know. "For potential beyond what you can comprehend. Maybe you failed." That was a pleasant thought.

"Maybe you don't fit the plan," Jeremy continued to mutter, "Maybe you are the plan." He sniggered to himself with more than a little craziness. "I understand, Ryan." I watched his eyes – directed at me, but I only had half of their gaze, like he was looking off into the distance, searching for the thing to fill that emptiness inside him – and I knew, he did understand.

"They exist, Ryan. And they are visiting our planet. I don't know why, but they're abducting us. The government are more than aware, of course. There have been countless departments in the Army, FBI and the CIA that deal with the threat of extra-terrestrials. Project Blue Book, Majestic 12, Sign, Grudge."

"Wait a minute. Aliens? You're saying this is aliens? More likely you're using some tech to fuck with my head."

Jeremy politely waited for me to finish speaking and then ignored what I said completely. "The people behind this. They don't want you to know the truth."

"This is ridiculous."

"Your name isn't the only one in the file, Ryan." Jeremy removed his glasses and lolled his head. When he looked back up at me, his expression was grave, all the quirks had gone. "Your wife's name is in there too."

"That's enough." I marched out of the room and towards the apartment door. Jeremy jumped out of his seat and paced after me. I spun round and poked my finger at his scrawny face. "You stay away from my wife." The anger built inside me until it was about to come crashing down on his head.

"I know what you're going through."

"You know nothing! You're a lunatic."

"A number of my sources are dead. Heart attacks, accidents. Not only is it true, but they're snapping at our heels. You dream about the end of the world. And there is nothing that you can do to stop it. You may not believe me, Ryan, but you can't deny your own experience. I know that. I know what it's like to lose someone. I know what it's like to be scared."

"I'm telling you." I grabbed him by his sticky shoulders and stared him down, without blinking, without hesitation, birthing words that came out more like a growl than speech. "Stay away. From my wife."

I slammed the door as I left.

* * *

When I arrived home darkness had fallen, streetlights casting a dim light over my house. I opened the front door quietly and crept through the hallway. I paused outside the living room door for thirty seconds or so and leaned in to listen. All I could hear was the constant hum of the fridge freezer in the kitchen. The door creaked as I pushed it and Jeri's head shot up from her laptop to look at me. I turned and headed for the stairs.

"Ryan," Jeri called from behind me. She was on her feet. My nerves were still raw from the last time we spoke in the attic. Pangs of anger ruptured inside me every time I thought about it. When I glanced at the laptop screen resting on the sofa Jeri knocked it and the screen spun out of sight.

Jeri picked up her phone and strolled towards me. Her

perfume hit me as soon as she was near, the sweet floral, familiar smell now abrasive to my senses. I didn't take my eyes off her, focusing more intently with every step. If she was about to start something then I was ready for her, my wooden box safely tucked away in my car. She moved her thumb swiftly across the screen. The slow, gentle notes that emerged failed to sooth my ears. Jeri reached towards me with both hands. "Dance with me?"

I remembered the good times and questioned whether they ever really existed or if they were conjured by my imagination, grasping at some token of a life lived. When I would hear Jeri's car pull up after work, run to the door and watch her walk up the path. She never said a word during a shiver inducing, mesmerising kiss, still in the blue uniform, handcuffs dangling from her belt, her gun resting firmly in her holster. She is the best kisser I have ever known. Or maybe she was. It only took a single day to change everything.

Jeri fumbled her lip with her teeth. Her fingers twitched. I turned and walked upstairs and didn't pause until I reached the bedroom. Until my last gasp, I would never dance again.

* * *

Over the next five days I received twenty-three missed calls, seventeen texts and nine emails from Jeremy pleading for me to contact him, telling me there wasn't much time. That he had the Project: Libera file, and that my life could be in danger. The only time I replied was when he texted me that he was going to come to my house. I told him to fuck off and warned that I would call the police if he came anywhere near me or anyone I knew. He didn't threaten that again. I feared he would call the house – no doubt he was able to get hold of my home number – and start talking this shit to Jeri, so I took a few days off to guard the phone. Bob asked if I thought now was really an appropriate time when Project: Infiltrator was going through such a transition in bringing the rest of the team on board, which is a not-so-subtle translation of 'when I'm under scrutiny for doing such a shit job'. I was unaffected; his gentle put down like stroking a dead leg, but Bob mistook apathy for upset. He tilted his head forward and peered at me with a furrowed brow curled so high it nearly met his combed back hair but it was accompanied by a sympathetic smile. "I've seen you do things no one else can do," he said. "Sometimes life likes to play monkey and throw faeces at you. But you're going to be in my seat soon. Or one that looks just like it," he added as he rested his arms on the chair and leaned back. "Mark my words."

After leaving the force, Jeri trained as a counsellor, listening to teenagers talk about their problems and guiding them out of their trauma. Apparently, she's great with them. Her working day was based around appointments, which meant she had chunks of the day at home, most of which she spent in the garden, so we managed to stay out of each other's way, and any conversation we did have was restricted to three-word sentences.

I felt so drained I could have collapsed from exhaustion at any moment. I had been sprawled out on the sofa next to the phone for a few hours when I flicked over to the news and upped the volume.

"Three bodies were found two days ago in Montrose Park, Washington D.C. All had previously been reported as missing persons. One body was identified as a Martha Weller who was reported missing five years ago. The other two bodies have now been identified as Leigh Adams and Rebecca Jones."

Three pictures appeared on the television screen. The last was a young woman in her mid-twenties who I recognised immediately as the woman in the photograph on Jeremy's desk, the love of his life, Rebecca Jones.

"Police are treating all three cases as suspicious and are rumoured to be linked to various other similar incidents across the country. Forensics at the scene stated that the time of death for all three victims was more than a year ago. In all three cases, the victims' reproductive organs had been removed. Police have not yet revealed details regarding the cause of death."

I couldn't imagine how Jeremy was feeling. Rebecca must have been missing for over a year. I stood up and gazed out the window at Jeri, her legs tucked into her chest, a book in her hand, the wind softly blowing her hair in front of her face. So beautiful. Guilt fizzed up like acid in my chest.

I checked my cell for the first time in hours. The only message I had received was a voicemail. "I need to see you. I have the file. Please. Please. I need you. For your wife. Please."

* * *

I knocked on Jeremy's apartment door and waited, discretely looking for where his camera was hidden. There was no answer, so I knocked harder, and the door creaked ajar. "Jeremy? Are you in there?" I pushed the door wide open and stepped inside. There was no one in the living room. "Jeremy?" I turned to leave when I saw something in the study.

"Oh, Jeremy, no."

A fraying rope was tied to a vent in the ceiling at one end and wrapped around Jeremy's neck at the other. His head was bent awkwardly, and his feet dangled above a wooden chair knocked on its side. His pale face was in full view, uncannily like he was staring right at me. The life drained out of him. I staggered against the door. If I had come when he asked, if I had listened to him, could I have saved him? He had lost everything and all I did was tell him to fuck off when maybe he just needed someone to care. I had to take a step back.

The blue address book and Jeremy's black laptop with a half-moon half-sun sticker on top were sat on the desk.

'They hold all the keys.' That's what Jeremy said. I fixated on one thought: the keys to what?

Next to them was a piece of paper with Jeremy's signature at the bottom.

> 'When you went out of my life the only
> reason I woke each day was to find you. I
> never stopped looking. Now you have left
> me again, I have no reason to be. All that
> is left for me to do is to hope that we can
> now be together and have faith in Ryan
> that the truth will finally be unveiled.'

I reread the note, over and over, trying to comprehend how he must have felt to be driven to this. And why he mentioned my name, why he thought I would find the truth. I marched into the living room and closed the apartment door.

I knew how suspicious it looked, my name written on the suicide note of a dead man, making reference to me finding out the truth about his dead girlfriend. I was in deep shit. He rested everything on the hope that I would take notice of his pleas to see him and return to his apartment.

I guess he wasn't expecting anyone else to visit him.

I paced from the living room to the study, avoiding the mess that littered the floor with my head in my hands. The lock on the front door rattled and I stopped dead in the centre of the living room. I heard the next lock going, and then the next. I grabbed the note and ran into Jeremy's bedroom.

The final lock clanged, and the door creaked. I backed up against a mahogany closet, just shorter than me. I stuffed the note into my pocket, opened the door without a sound, and climbed inside. As I closed the closet doors, footsteps passed and carried on into Jeremy's bedroom. I only heard one set of footsteps. I could make a run for it; get out the door before anyone saw me.

I reached out, ready to push the wardrobe door open and run. If I left now, I might not get back inside the apartment. But this might be my only chance to get out.

Adrenaline pumped through my hunched body as the footsteps grew closer and finally stopped the other side of the wooden door. There was a quiet scrape and then a tapping noise. I took small breaths, the air gradually growing stale. I felt like I was suffocating, about to burst through the closet doors in panic.

The footsteps returned, the front door creaked, then jolted shut. I finally took a full breath and burst through the doors and collapsed onto my hands and knees. I looked straight through to the apartment door to check it was shut.

Jeremy's security camera.

I jumped up and ran to the monitor to catch the bottom of a set of black pants and black shoes walking out of view down the hallway. They looked male but I couldn't be sure. I opened the cupboard next to the screen and found two wires left free: the hard drive and all its footage gone.

I paced back into the study and closed the closet doors, wiping aware where my hands had touched with the bottom of my shirt. I searched the room to see what the visitor had come for. The only thing I noticed missing was Jeremy's laptop.

I cursed to myself that I hadn't stashed it with me in the closet. But there wasn't enough time for whoever came in to have searched the place, so the laptop must be what they came for. They would have searched the whole apartment to find it and found me in the process.

Next to where the laptop had been sat Jeremy's address book, the second of the two keys. I picked it up and flicked through the pages. It seemed empty at first, but there were a few entries dotted throughout in their rightful alphabetical place. I slid it in my inside jacket pocket.

Maybe he left more than just the laptop and address book behind. I thought back to everything he told me. The contact that died of a heart attack. The photo of Rebecca

Jones. Jacob something.

I searched the address book and found Jacob Reences entry. I gently took the back off Rebecca's photo, squirming as I glanced towards Jeremy's hanging body, hoping that he would understand. But there was nothing written on or behind the photo. I carefully returned the back onto the frame, wiped it down and paced the room.

What else?

I pulled a tissue from the box and used it to protect my prints as I fumbled my way through the bookshelves. I had no idea whether the intruder was going to return, or if the police had been called, so I had to be quick. I rifled through Jeremy's drawers, cupboards and shelves, a pang of guilt as I saw photographs, magazines, socks, trousers, everything that he owned in life. I went into his closet and checked every pocket, the inside of every shoe, but found nothing.

I'm running out of time.

Paper. I wracked my brain trying to remember what he said about paper. 'People leave it stuffed in the bottom of the closet.'

I moved his shoes aside and checked inside a rucksack but there was nothing. I tapped the closet floor, and it was hollow. I hurried into the kitchen, found a screwdriver in the drawer, and worked off the base of the closet. It came off easily, but I chipped a bit of the wood. Underneath I found a stack of printed documents. I stuffed them in the rucksack, replaced the base and checked my watch; fifteen minutes since I arrived. I took one last look at Jeremy hanging in the study and left.

I hurried to my car, drove a few streets away and stopped.

What the hell am I doing? I just removed evidence from a crime scene. Whatever Jeremy was caught up in, they knew enough to steal his laptop. And now someone has the CCTV footage from Jeremy's apartment. Someone knows I was there.

* * *

I could hear the rain dripping gently outside my window, but I couldn't hear a single thought in my head. I had driven half a mile and pulled up behind a restaurant, weighing the consequences of what I had done, and what I was about to do.

I flicked through the documents until I found Project: Libera. I scanned it until I came across the list. Right there in front of me, in black and white. Undeniable.

Jeri Ellis.

I put the papers down, unable to read on. Libera. The Roman Goddess of fertility.

The pull took hold of me, itching away inside my head. There were six other names under the header 'persons of interest,' three of which I recognised: my own, Jeremy Dawson and Rebecca Jones.

I couldn't bear it anymore. I opened the car door and stepped outside, the freshness hit me, allowing me some air to breathe. Whatever happened now, there was no turning back. I pulled the documents out, leant on the roof of the car, and turned right back to the start.

The vision of losing Jeri flashed once more in my mind, bringing with it a sickening ache that I felt to my very soul.

FOUR

I was horrified at how tragic things were for Jeremy, to not know where your love is for whole year and then to lose her like that. I thought he had lovèd Rebecca so much that losing her finally pushed him over the edge. But the more I thought about it, the more I realised Jeremy welcomed death because it meant that he could finally be with her; his search was over.

Jeri didn't ask where I had been – she was never possessive or prying - she would trust me to tell her if it was important, even now. It couldn't be more important. Her name, like mine was in the file, there was nothing I could do about that. Despite most of the file being blacked out with a marker, there was enough in it to terrify me; tests that had been carried out, success criteria and fertility research conducted. What scared me most was the answers it didn't give.

The documents were too far above my security level for me to get information from anyone at US Tech – not to mention the illegal circumstances that I came by them – and Jeremy's laptop was long gone. The only thing I had left was to tell her. The idea of it weighed down on me so heavy I knew it was best to get it over with.

Jeri had her legs tucked up underneath her on the sofa. She glanced over the laptop at me then started typing away. I paused, collecting my thoughts on the best way to tell her. As I opened my mouth to speak, Jeri turned the screen to face me. There was a contemporary brick house with stone laid pathway and a ramp down to an enclosed drive.

"It's not far. Fifteen minutes from US Tech. And it even has a soundproofed room – the owner's a musician. Brass, I think. You could use it for your guitar. Upgrade your amp." Jeri's eyes left the screen and the photo of the house for the first time, her brow rose as she breathed softly, patiently waiting for me to respond. "We could decorate it ourselves," she added when there was only silence, "Keep the big stuff or rip it out if we wanted to."

I took a breath before I spoke in an effort not to flare up. "Is this a joke?"

Jeri's eyes flickered as she tried to work out the situation – it somehow seemed to have taken her by surprise. Then how did she think I felt?

I said, "You can't be serious," expecting her to bat it off and retreat.

A sigh billowed out of her mouth. She composed herself quickly and fashioned a smile. "Changing our environment might help. It could be a fresh start."

"This was our home."

"Ryan," I felt a small weight on my thigh. I looked down to see Jeri's fingers resting gently. When I looked back up her face creased with empathy for me, but I didn't know why I should be pitied. "You said was."

I jumped out of my seat putting extra emphasis on my leg to cast away her unwanted hand. "I don't need this right now. It's ridiculous."

Jeri joined me on her feet and stepped closer, she wasn't going to let me escape this time. "What's ridiculous?"

"The whole idea. We can't move house."

"We can't carry on like this; I think we both know that." Jeri bowed her head, and I knew it was only a recent realisation. She had thought a veneer life was possible, maybe even satisfying, but it took two to create the illusion and I wouldn't play along.

"Talk to me, Ryan," Jeri said as gently as a summer breeze. "Let me in."

I edged away from her but there was nowhere to go, she had me cornered.

"We've been through too much. And I can remember our old life too well. I don't care how much you try to keep me out, I'm not giving up." Jeri raised her arm slowly, like she was showing a feral mutt not to be threatened. She turned her hand over, palm facing upwards and held it out to me. I didn't know whether it was to stroke me or to distract me while she used her other hand to shove a muzzle on me. "I can help you. Why won't you let me in?"

"I can't."

"Why not?"

The walls were closing in. Jeri swayed gently, blocking my escape. "I know… you want me to pretend like nothing happened…"

"Yes," her voice quivered, desperate to hear more.

"You want us to go back to the way we were-"

"Of course," she jumped in overeager, but quieted herself, smoothing her hands over her thighs to flatten out the enthusiasm.

"But... I can't forgive you."

"You can't forgive me? What the hell do you mean, you can't forgive me?" Jeri spat the words out, flinging her arms in outrage. "Ryan, what do you mean?"

"How can you just carry on?" When the words came out, I looked down, as though I expected to see them hanging in the air before me. I raised my hand slowly through empty space to touch them.

"After everything I've been through," Jeri said, snapping me out of it. "After everything I've lost. I was finally going to have a baby. What can I do except carry on?"

"Where did she go?"

She gave me a look of confusion, dumbfounded by what I said. "They're… They're gone, Ryan."

The anger raged inside of me, built up for so long. Why didn't she understand? I felt nothing but hatred. "She was a life, Jeri, a fucking life! Just because she isn't here anymore, it doesn't change that. She's out there somewhere, all alone."

"I don't understand. They're gone."

"Her life. Her soul. Without her mother. Without her father." It felt like the air was burning around me. "How can you carry on, knowing that?"

"You can't just stop living."

"Move on."

"I didn't say that."

"That's what you want," I sneered at her, not even the hurt on her face could make me feel for her. She had abandoned our daughter, all memory of her so she could carry on living her life like nothing had ever happened, like our own baby girl had never happened. Once a life like that is created, it can't just cease to exist, it can't. Even if there isn't a body left to inhabit.

"That isn't fair. You get over it, then you-"

"There is *no* getting over it!" Jeri jolted as my voice boomed. "No moving on. There is nothing in this life that will make it right. Nothing. Every day… every day I feel like I should end it all. Because I let it happen to her."

"It's not your fault, Ryan." Jeri poured her pity all over me. I wretched. My skin crawled.

"I know that. I *know* that." I fought the urge to throw up. "I'm her father and I lost her before she was even born."

"It's not your fault." She looked so sad for me.

"Don't." I prodded my finger at it, held it strong. My hand trembled, I couldn't keep control. But my face was grave enough to show her how serious I was. Her posture deflated and she swallowed any words of comfort she was ready to say. "But every day, you keep going. Keep going. Happy. Like it's nothing. Like nothing even happened."

"You think I'm happy? I felt like I died inside. I... had to be strong. I wanted to keep crying with you, to do nothing but cry, every day, I did. But I couldn't. We're still here. We're both still here and no amount of suffering, no amount of tears will bring them back." Spit clung to her lip. Her hollow eyes didn't move. She could have been a statue.

Jeri took a breath. It made her wheeze so bad it could have been poisoned "I'm crippled by pain. Every day. This is all we have left."

Moving on. Her brave face. It was her veneer. She's as broken as me. I wanted to gaze into her swirling blue eyes but I daren't stare too long for fear she would close up. I edged my fingers towards her and gently stroked her shoulder. She didn't resist. Her body folded up and she fell against my chest. "I'm sorry. I thought... I'm so sorry."

FIVE

If Jeri knew that her name was in that file, that her inability to birth a life could be part of some secret research experiment, I couldn't take her down that road, it would destroy her.

I sank into the sofa and turned the cover on Jeremy's address book.

There were three names. The first was Major Carl Patrick. I quickly found a report online of Major Patrick's funeral, following a heart attack six months ago, just as Jeremy said his operative contact had died. My body shivered.

The next name was Jacob Reences, but my search turned up nothing, not a single person by that name, in Washington or anywhere else. I tried calling the phone number from my cell but I all I got was that annoying tone, the one of failure.

I typed the third name, Henry Russell, which returned more promising results. I narrowed the search to Washington and found Henry Russell was the father of Lilly Russell, a thirteen-year-old girl who had returned home only days ago after being missing for three weeks. I looked up their current address and added it to the address book next to Henry's name.

I found three names in the Project: Libera file, with two accompanying addresses. The first, Antonio Perez was found dead, and his wife, Lilia had been missing since and was wanted in connection with his murder. The final name was Marjorie Brown, who lived in Cardington, Ohio. I found a few basic records online, photos of her home, social media accounts, and a local newspaper article about her husband being killed in a traffic accident.

From the address book and Project: Libera file combined, I had four dead, one missing, and two leads. The closest, and therefore my first stop were Lilly and Henry Russell.

After an hour or so, I pulled up in Wolf Trap outside a huge provincial home that was surrounded by bald cypress one hundred feet tall and had a good eighty feet of grass between it and the nearest house. I rang the doorbell and was greeted by a woman in her fifties wearing an apron and a welcoming smile.

"Hello, can I help you?" She asked.

"Actually, yes. This is Lilly Russell's residence?"

"It is, I'm her mother."

"It's a pleasure to meet you, Mrs. Russell. Do you think I would be able to speak to you and your husband?"

"Well, what is it about?"

"I'm trying to help locate missing persons more easily." Mrs Russell gave a look of scepticism. "I'm sorry, my name is Ryan Ellis, I work for US Tech." I took out my ID card and held it out for her to inspect before she peered back up at me. "I was part of the team that developed the DNA tracker, and I'm leading a project to enhance the technology." I winced inside but remained confident, the project firmly closed.

"Well, I have told many people what happened, including the newspapers." The woman stepped back as though she was about to bid me goodbye.

"I'm sorry Mrs. Russell; it really will only take a moment. It could allow us to help return thousands of missing persons to their families."

She hesitated but I stood willing her to let me inside. "Well, ok. Come on in then."

Fleece blankets were draped over most of the living room furniture, surrounded by warm yellow walls. "Is Lilly home, Mrs. Russell?"

"No, she's at school. And please call me Maude. This is Lilly's father, Henry. Henry this is Mr. …"

"Ellis. Ryan Ellis. I work at US Tech," I said pulling my ID card back out. "I'm trying to understand how we can improve the DNA tracker technology to further reduce missing persons. I would just like to ask a few questions about your daughter's disappearance. It really will only take a moment."

Henry Russell shuffled in his chair before getting up to shake my hand. A few years older than Maude, his head was devoid of hair except for a thin grey moustache. His mouth curled underneath it at the corner, accompanied by a southern drawl. "Well, ok then, Ryan. We told the police what happened to Lilly, what she did. But I guess we can tell it again." Henry sat down on the sofa next to Maude.

"Thank you. So, let me just check my information is correct." I took out my tablet, in which I had written a list of facts about Lilly's disappearance. "Lilly went missing on the 2nd and returned home on the 23rd?"

"That's right." Maude said with a smile on her face, nodding and turning to Henry.

"So where was Lilly all that time?" I tried to be as coy as possible and bury the concoction of nerves and excitement fluttering inside me.

"Lilly ran away from home after an argument with her father about a boy she wanted to date. Henry told her she is too young to date boys. Lilly was hiding in a field a mile or so away the whole time, helping herself to the crops," Maude answered again.

"And do you have her DNA on file?" I asked.

"We do," Maude said.

"Then why weren't you able to locate her?"

"We think she erased it before she left, you know how children can be at times. She took the sample with her." Maude waited for me to nod along with her response, but my head remained still, my eyes fixed on hers.

"You have the sample she took?"

Maude hesitated, "Well, no."

"And she took the backup samples too? Erased the memory?"

"She did," Maude's voice had become stern, but she shook it off with a glowing smile.

Maude's eyes flickered between me and the coffee table that separated us. It wasn't the most straightforward process to do and would take a determined 13-year-old to want to disappear that badly. "So, why didn't she come home sooner?"

"Why, I don't know." Maude said, "We haven't asked her. I guess she wasn't ready to." She smiled again and patted her hands on her lap.

Maude wasn't volunteering anything. "Why did Lilly tell you that she had been abducted? Do you think she changed her story to cover for whoever really abducted her?"

"No. No, I don't." Maude said firmly. "I don't know why she made up that story. She's just a young girl, she has a wild imagination. Now is that all of your questions, Mr Ellis?"

I wasn't anywhere near finished. "Did you see a light the night that Lilly went missing?"

"Now that is enough," Henry said, breaking his silence. Maude faced me dead on.

"A light?" She asked.

"Yes." I sat forward on my seat. Maude's face flashed into confusion before she returned to a welcoming smile. "A light, brighter than you have seen before. Did it turn red?" My heart was beating faster and faster.

Henry stood up from the sofa. "Mr Ellis, I think you

should leave."

I can't go. Not yet. "Maude, did you see something? Was Lilly having dreams before she was taken? Strange dreams that didn't make any sense to her."

Maude's eyes widened and she began to look like she was in a trance. "Nightmares. I couldn't help her. The DNA tracker couldn't find her. She was gone."

"I've spoken to a man, Jeremy Dawson. I believe he was in contact with you."

Henry leaned into me, and his voice roared, "Get out! Get out of my Goddamn house!"

Maude stood up behind him and began ushering me out the room. "You have to leave. We can't help you. I'm sorry. I'm sorry that Mr Dawson's girlfriend is missing, but I told him, we can't help him. I'm sorry. I have to keep my daughter safe."

I lowered my voice, hoping the distance to the living room was enough to prevent Henry Russell following us into the hallway. Getting Mrs Russell alone was my only chance. "Maude, they found Jeremy's girlfriend. She's dead." She pressed her trembling hand against her mouth, eyes welling up. "I need you to tell me what happened. Did someone come to you after Lilly came back? What did they say to you?"

Maude stopped in the doorway, dazed eyes gazing at me. She opened the door, urging me to leave. "They're everywhere. They're always watching." She gave me a gentle shove onto her doorstep and slammed the door behind me before I could respond.

Henry and Maude's arguing was muffled but loud from inside. A man in a black estate parked fifty feet down the road stared at Henry and Maude's house. A blonde woman jogged towards me with headphones in her ears, hair scraped back. She craned her neck and glared straight into my eyes as she passed. A couple turned their heads crossing the road, the father pushing a stroller. I felt like everyone was watching me.

I had hoped to find the truth, but all I found was fear. Something had scared Henry and Maude Russell, but I had no idea what happened to their daughter.

* * *

The first thing I did when I returned home from Lilly Russell's house was to take a DNA sample and load it into a blank tracker. I had resisted joining billions of people around the world whose every movement could be tracked by their unique DNA sequence every minute of the day, but Lilly's parents had me as scared as they were, and I had to keep track of my every move. And more importantly, Jeri's. When she left the force, she gave up her car and deactivated her DNA tracker. She never told me why. With a few strands of hair from her brush her tracker was set-up.

I woke at 6:04am to the drone of my second alarm. One more day before I was due back at work. One more lead. I drove for six and a half hours to the address from the Project: Libera file for Marjorie Brown's residence with a photo of her I found online stuck to my dash. The aftermath of my night tremor still had my limbs tingling, the anxiety that I awoke with far from subdued. I spent the whole journey thinking about the one name that still evaded me: Jacob Reences. But to no avail.

I pulled up outside a white town house in Cardington with a long porch and rang the doorbell. There was no answer. I peered in through the bay window, and tapped on it, quiet at first, and then louder, but no one emerged.

"There's no one home." The voice came from across the street, a woman in her early fifties, wearing a tan coat to her knees. I crossed the street and stood next to her.

"I'm looking for this lady, Marjorie Brown." I held out the photograph. When she looked back at me, I saw the same curly black hair, the same brown eyes as the image in my hand.

"I'd say you've found her." She turned and ambled down

the street, away from her house. I followed alongside.

"Jeremy is dead."

She kept walking, looking up into the sky, like she was on a morning stroll alone and I hadn't spoken a word. "You shouldn't have come here." Her voice remained pleasant.

"I need your help."

She strolled across a stone arch bridge that stretched over a stream, water flowing gently away. She pursed her lips, but it was more disappointment than anger. At the bottom of the bridge, she stopped and closed her eyes. I felt a sense of peace inside her.

Iron railings held three bouquets of flowers, each one wrapped by a different colour that clashed with the next. The first two had been brown for some time, wilted but still clinging to the railing they were wrapped around, the outer layers of tape flaked away. The last bouquet of white lilacs was fresh. I leaned in and the heavenly smell made them seem brighter and more alive. Despite appearances, the flowers would soon rot and decay, to be removed and replaced, or to hang there, retaining their sadness and celebration in memorial of a lost loved one, just like the others.

"Can I ask? I... I know it's personal. It might be difficult. But... Do you have any children?" She didn't answer. Adrenaline started to flow inside of me. "You couldn't, could you?" I turned away from her. Jeremy was right all along. I should have taken notice of him when he was alive, and maybe I wouldn't be here, having to play catch up. "What do you know?" I demanded. "Did you see Jeremy's files?"

Marjorie took her time answering, like she had all the time in the world. "I don't know what you want from me. You're lost here."

"I want you to tell me what the hell is going on."

"I don't know what you're talking about."

"Are you going to try telling me that there's nothing happening here?" I couldn't get control of my emotions.

"That there isn't some fucking cover-up that we're both caught up in?"

"I'm telling you that there is." Her eyes fixed on mine; the gentle tones of her voice turned grave. "One so big, it will warp your mind. It will seize your life, taking hold of you and never letting go. There is no end. No respite. There is nothing you can do to escape the pull of the truth. But beneath every layer is another layer. Behind every door, another door." I banged my hands against the railings in frustration. She pushed her face so close to mine that my eyes could barely focus. "Ask yourself, what are you willing to lose? What is this all worth to you? Chasing me down here."

"I can't give in. There's too much at stake."

"Something you can't live without?"

"My wife."

"Then I pray for you. To our God and theirs. You do not know what you are up against." She turned and walked away from me.

"Paradox unveil," I shouted after her. She stopped dead. "What does it mean?"

She turned her head to the side, showing only a fragment of her face. "He was hoping you knew." She strode away, back towards her house. I passed the bridge at the stream ahead, water flowing away from me, off to join something bigger. I turned to shout Marjorie back; I couldn't let her leave.

Out of nowhere something cracked the side of my skull and sent me hurtling to the ground. I barely managed to put my hands out in time to stop my face hitting the concrete. I craned my head to look up. A boot sole smacked into my eye before I could see anything past it. I groaned in pain. Another boot, this time in the ribs. And another. My head went fuzzy. I couldn't get up. I felt my face enlarging as it swelled, numbness spreading. Spit dangled out of my mouth, all the way down to the floor. Spit and blood.

I lifted my body off the ground, but my hands gave way.

My face crashed down onto the concrete. I let out a pathetic grunt.

I have to get up. Got to fight back. Get off the ground.

Another blow banged my head down until it hit concrete, my nose taking the blunt of it. Everything went dark.

Then, the last blow. The last one that I felt.

* * *

I put my hand to the first place that hurt and winced with the sting of my lower bulging lip. My vision was partially obstructed by the harsh swelling over my left eye. It was almost too much effort to even get to my feet.

I grabbed at the bridge wall next to me and gave some small thanks that I didn't crack my head on it on the way down. My self-preservation instinct kicked in and I looked around for my attacker, but they were long gone. I didn't know how long I had been out for.

I pulled myself up and hobbled down the road, back towards Marjorie's house. I banged on the door and heard shuffling. I banged again to let her know I wouldn't wait. Hard, so she knew I was pissed. I readied my fists in case my attacker was inside with her.

A man opened the door, late fifties at a glance and short, he didn't look the strong type, but the strong ones don't always look it. "Where is she?" I barged my way in through the hallway and into the living room, flowers everywhere, patterning the walls and sofa, red, lime green and pale blue, but all with a beige background. I charged up the stairs, through every nineteen fifties style room in the house, all freshly decorated. "I said, where is she?"

"Who? I... I don't know who you're looking for," he stammered stumbling behind.

"Marjorie. I know she's in here."

"Marjorie Brown?"

I grabbed him by his collar, and he cowered. "Don't play

dumb. Was it you? Is this your handy work or did you have help?" I snatched his hands, but they were clean, not even a graze on them and soft like they were permanently bathed in hand cream.

"I... I don't know what you're talking about. Marjorie isn't here. I just rent the property."

"What are you talking about?"

"She's missing. For a few years, now. No one's seen her. Janice was the last one. Two doors down. She'll tell you."

I pulled out the photograph and held it out in front of him. He nearly choked on his breath. "That's Marjorie. But I haven't seen her, I swear. After a year or so they rented her house out to me. She doesn't have a family."

I checked every room in the house. I spoke to Janice two doors down and to missing persons. His story checked out. Over two years ago, not long after her husband died in a car accident near her house, she didn't turn up for lunch at her friend's house for lunch. No one had seen her since. Then after all this time she came back, only to disappear again into the wind. I was no closer to the truth, but I now knew one thing: I was in way over my head.

SIX

The fog enshrouds everything. Nothing can escape it. I lift my arm to shield myself from the while light blasting through the windscreen. I can't see the road. I have to close my eyes. What happened to my engine?

Herb won't wake up. Wake up damn it, Herb. Wake up. Don't you leave me.

Paradox. Unveil. Paradox. Unveil. Paradox. Unveil. Transcend.

"Ryan!" Jeri shouted, her hands on each of my shoulders shaking me hard. "What happened?"

"I... I don't know. I must have zoned out."

"Ryan, you're trembling. Your arms are trembling. And you're legs. What's wrong? Your face, it's so pale."

Every hair on my body was standing on end. My head flopped like an apple on a straw neck. I was propped up in bed, Jeri's face a blur of worry beside me. "I'm sorry. I don't know what happened."

"I kept shaking you. You were in a trance." Jeri brushed her fingers over my forehead until I calmed down.

I told Jeri I was ok, just a nightmare and hobbled to check on Kyle and Emily as Jeri craned her neck to watch every step. I crept back into the darkness of my bedroom, lit only by what light managed to seep in through the curtains and bleed around the edges from the streetlamp outside. By the time I returned, Jeri was facing away from me, her breathing barely audible. I sat on the edge of the bed the floor damp under my feet. Jeri had a glass of water next to her bed that must have spilt in all the commotion. I felt my way over to the en suite to get some tissue. There was a bang, loud enough to make me jump and it came from inside the room. I moved across the carpet, closer to where the noise had come from, but I couldn't see anything. I looked down at the floor, squinting in the shadows. I felt my hand across the carpet, and it was even wetter than the other patch. I looked up at the ceiling, but it was perfectly dry. The floorboard creaked at the other side of the room, and I jumped again.

My house rasped and groaned through heat and cold like most, but this was different, louder, like someone was in the room with me. It happened again. I took one step at a time, slowly moving towards the dresser where the second noise had come from. I ran to the noise and waved my arms around, but I couldn't see anything and all I found was squelching under my feet.

I stood at the side of the bed; my eyes fixed on the dresser. "Jeri, wake up."

"I'm awake." She didn't move.

"Jeri."

"What?"

"I think someone is in here with us."

She bolted upright and jumped to her fleet, her eyes darting around the room for an intruder. "Where?"

"Sshh. I don't know." I kept my voice at a whisper and gestured for Jeri to do the same. She scanned the room again in confusion.

"I don't understand."

"I heard them. Someone's here." I grabbed a baseball bat from under my bed. "Turn the lamp on." Jeri's hand flashed to the lamp to switch it on, and she was out of bed and fully alert in a second. Something touched the skin on my back. I jumped so hard I dropped the bat. What the fuck was that? I plunged to my knees, gripped the bat with both hands and aimed it straight ahead of me. I twisted around to face each corner of the room, examining every inch. I patted my hand against my back and rubbed my fingers together, a slimy sensation disappearing as I did.

"Did you see it?" I asked, terrified of the answer.

"See what?"

"Anything!"

"There's no one in here."

The bedroom door was half open, but I knew I had closed it after me. I clenched my bat and stormed out of the room.

I can't let it get out. I've got to find it.

I stopped dead in the centre of the hallway, searching every corner, using my foot to feel for remnants of water.

"Ryan." Jeri stood behind me, wrapping a dressing gown around her body, handgun pointed at the floor. "You need to tell me what's going on. Did you hear someone breaking in?"

I kept my voice low and quiet, "They were in the bedroom."

Jeri ran off in front of me and into Emily's bedroom, holding her gun behind her back. She should have waited; all the noise could have scared it away or given enough cover sound to escape. I took a few steps after her but as soon as I reached the doorway, she was leaving the room with Emily in her arms and heading into Kyle's bedroom. I jumped in after her and checked every crevice but I couldn't hear anything over Jeri telling Kyle to wake up.

"I'm going downstairs," Jeri said, ushering Kyle towards me.

I held up my hand to stop her but she piled Emily into my arms, gently pushed Kyle to my side and then she was three stairs down without a sound.

"Can you see anything?" I whispered as Jeri reached the

bottom stair, but she raised her finger to silence me then disappeared out of sight.

Kyle's face was grey, his eyes so wide it looked like the lids were being propped up with matchsticks. I pulled Emily's body away from me to look at her, but she only clung tighter. I couldn't leave them. It could still be in here. Hiding somewhere.

Jeri reappeared at the bottom of the stairs, gun lowered. "The alarm hasn't been tripped. All the windows and doors are locked. There's no way someone could get inside."

"Unless it was already inside."

Emily sobbed into my neck. "Uncle Ryan, I'm scared."

"Is... Is someone going to hurt us?" Kyle dug his fingertips into my leg.

Jeri ran up the stairs and Emily jumped into her arms. Jeri lowered her to the floor and wrapped an arm around Kyle and Emily's shoulder. "No one is going to hurt you. Everything is fine, there's nothing here. Uncle Ryan thought he saw something, but he didn't."

"I heard something." Sourness crept into my voice. "Something touched me; put its hand on my back. And there was water."

"Water?" She screwed up her face in disbelief.

"I don't know. I don't know what it was." I had no idea how it got past me.

"Ryan, you're scaring the children. There's nothing here. We're going back to bed."

"I heard something," the words left my tongue as a shout loud enough to wake the neighbours, but it felt like it belonged to someone else.

Fat tears bounded down Emily's face with a wail and Kyle couldn't have pressed himself against Jeri any harder without getting inside her skin.

Jeri shepherd them away and I was left standing by myself, still gripping the baseball bat. Guilt filled my gut like a tap of acid.

What is happening to me?

I crept into an empty bed and kept the bat in my arms. I could faintly hear Jeri's reassuring voice from Bethany's room.

Paradox. Unveil. Transcend.

I couldn't get the damn words out of my head.

I pulled the covers up and stared at the ceiling, listening hard until a deep sleep swallowed me whole.

SEVEN

I opened my eyes to see a green face staring back at me. My body was stiff from the concrete step I lay awkwardly over, 'GRAND ARMY OF THE REPUBLIC' carved in front of me, a relief bust just above it. I was at the Stephenson Grand Army of the Republic memoriam, in the middle of the Indiana Plaza. I had no idea how I got there.

I raised my hand and squinted at the sky. My eyes stung as though they had been smoked. My hand trembled as I lurched to a near standing position, most of my effort spent trying to prevent myself from collapsing. The entire mass of my body felt like it was stored in my head, mere spindles for legs keeping my upright. I stumbled forward and only stopped myself from falling by clutching the foot of a bronze solder.

A couple in their mid-fifties strolled by, holding hands. The woman looked on me with the pity and judgement for a man too beaten to stay away from hard liquor and the street. The man let go of her hand and marched across the street towards me.

"Hey." His face was screwed up, bulldog cheeks swollen around his eyes. "Hey, what's the matter with you? That man did more for the people of this country than you ever will."

"I... I need my car. My tracker..." In my head the full sentences were there but I couldn't transmit them from my brain to my mouth. The man's head repelled into his bulldog neck, because I owned a car or because I was about to drive it. "You… you don't understand. Just woke..."

"I understand, you rotten drunk." He breathed in deep, taking in the stench that surrounded me. My shirt was half open, hanging out of my ripped pants and twisted around my body. "You need to get your ass up out of here and show some damned respect."

He squared up to me, forcing me back against the triangular structure that towered over me. My eyes wandered down, half closed. "Need... a minute."

"That man didn't care for the brave soldiers that were sent to fight, just so you can get drunk and… and high in front of his... How can you insult..." His temper raged. I waited for a strike; my head too hazy to stop him.

He pushed my shoulder, and I stumbled back. Images flashed in my mind, each one battling for space in my consciousness. Hazmat suits tower over me, reflecting my groggy face against their surface. Bright lights line the ceiling. I can't understand their voices.

I started choking and shoved my fingers down my throat to remove whatever was blocking the airway, but I couldn't find anything. I dropped hard to my knees and wretched. I could hear the man standing over me, shouting at me to get up. But all I could see was a thin metal right in front of my eyes, shadows circling around me. My throat cleared and I gasped for air.

Scraps barks twice as he sits in front of his empty food bowl. The shelf a few feet above him is mostly bare, a picture frame and a brown mug all that it holds up. I step forward, wrench it as hard as I can and watch it crash down to the floor, cushioned by my small friend.

I choked again, this time only briefly. I was back kneeling against the base of the Stephenson memorial. The images drifted into memory.

"What the hell are you doing?" he shouted, standing over me, knocking his boot against my stomach.

All I wanted was to get out of there and get my DNA tracker, but he kept poking his foot, over and over like he was checking a dead animal. I jumped to my feet and lashed out at him. He flew at least six feet backwards and hit the floor. His wife screamed and dropped by his side. I didn't think I pushed him that hard.

The man clamoured to his feet, batting away his wife and backed off until he was at the other side of the street, his eyes fixed on me like he was waiting for me to pull a gun on him. I slumped onto the concrete base.

The last thing I remembered was sitting in the car park at work this morning. I dug into my pocket for my car key. I locked and unlocked my car repeatedly along Pennsylvania avenue until I saw my headlights flash at the bus stop outside the National Archives building.

I collapsed into the driver's seat and my head bounced off the headrest. I checked the clock. Seven hours had passed that I couldn't account for. My legs gave the occasional tremble under the steering wheel. I used my DNA tracker to go back to 8am as I arrived at US Tech for my first day back. I spent the next five hours there, then travelled directly to the Stephenson memorial.

I had travelled over five hundred miles with no memory of it.

I took out my phone to ask Rick if he knew anything, but I had three missed calls, two from Bob, one from Rick, and a voicemail. I listened to the message:

"Hey Ryan," It was Rick's voice. "What happened to you? You know I don't like being stood up." He laughed. "Anyway pal, I covered your ass with Bob. I told him you're tucked up in bed with the flu. He's gonna call you, so just make sure you stick with the same story. Anyway, let me know what kept you away. And you owe me one."

Things were getting weirder. Why did my DNA tracker

say I was in US Tech if I never met with Rick? My mind was out of control.

I picked up the DNA tracker again and followed my day. I watched the icon on the screen drive as normal until I reached US Tech where I had stayed in the car for three minutes. I zoomed in to see exactly where in the building I was, but it didn't make any sense.

I had accessed US Tech through the rear entrance, which was only for transporting equipment and supplies in and out of the building, and I didn't even have security access. Inside the building, I didn't go to my office, or the offices of anyone I worked with on the 32nd floor, and I didn't go to the Production offices on the 2nd floor where I was supposed to be with Rick. Instead, I travelled down three floors, and moved straight ahead for around 10 feet, stopped for a minute, and then took a right for fifty feet or so until I stopped dead. I sped up the tracker, but it was five hours before I moved again. I had never been below the ground floor in US Tech before, I didn't even know what was down there.

Then I travelled to the Stephenson Memorial and didn't move for another twenty minutes or so until I woke up. I replayed the day on the DNA tracker over and over.

For the last thirty minutes before I awoke, I was travelling at a steady 50mph, without stopping for more than seconds until I reached the Stephenson memorial. My car was parked outside the National Archives building but according to my DNA tracker, I never even passed it. That meant someone else drove me here, left me lying on the floor, and then parked my car so it looked like I drove myself. Which means that someone knows exactly what happened to me.

EIGHT

I heard Jeri's voice from the hallway. I grabbed the door handle to the living room to walk in but stopped as I heard my name.

"I'm worried, Michelle," Jeri continued, and I realised she didn't know I was home. "He keeps waking up, shaking violently. He strolled home full of bruises. It was horrible. He had a massive black eye, his lip was swollen."

"What happened to him?" Michelle asked.

"I don't know, he said he was attacked."

"Well, did he report it?"

"No, he said he didn't get a look at them... I can't talk to him anymore. We're just not... I don't know. Anyway... How's Teresa doing?"

"She's good. She's obsessed with this case she's on."

Jeri and Michelle met at the academy and were even partners for a while. Michelle was the only person that stayed in touch after Jeri left the force. I'm pretty sure she told Jeri to leave me.

Michelle's voice became muffled as I quietly stepped back to the front door and closed it loud enough for Jeri to hear. When I doubled back to the living room, they were sat next to each other on the sofa. Michelle was on her feet with her bag slung over her head by the time I was two steps inside the room. "Ryan, hi. I'm just on my way out."

"Oh. Ok. Listen, I can go upstairs. You don't have to leave."

"That's fine. We ran out of wine anyway." I looked at the bottle with a third of it left, and then Michelle noticed it. She gave her best efforts to produce a genuine smile and Jeri saw her out.

I made a start clearing away their plates and the last remnants of wine, but it did little to ease my guilt for interrupting their evening. When Jeri returned, she joined the clean-up. "You didn't have to do this. It wasn't your mess." She threw me a look of gratitude. "How was work?"

"Fine..." I felt bad enough listening to her outside the room but lying to her was dreadful. The incident in the bedroom had freaked her out so badly that the next morning, she told me that she didn't know what she would do if Kyle and Emily weren't allowed to stay at our house anymore. "There's… There's one of those stupid work parties coming up for the White Giant. I have to go, make a speech and stuff." I had been waiting for the right time to tell Jeri, but there was never a right time. I knew that Jeri wouldn't be too happy about me going. At one time, she accompanied me to every US Tech party, but that was before. I had tried to make excuses to get out of it, but Bob wouldn't hear of it. He told me I needed it to celebrate our achievements, build contacts in other divisions and maintain good working relationships within the team – none of which I gave a fuck about.

"That's fine, you go. I haven't seen Carol for a while."

"Are… Are you sure?" The place was clear, and I fell into the sofa, Jeri sat close enough to reach out and touch me.

"Just go. It's fine. I'm sure you'll enjoy yourself." There was something in Jeri's tone that left me unnerved but she shuffled closer to me. I rested my head back onto the sofa, exhaustion taking its toll. Thoughts collided in my mind, everything made murky by a constant hum. I felt something on my chest and flinched. Jeri had lowered her head onto me, her feet stretched across the arm of the sofa. She fitted perfectly, just in front of my shoulder. I closed my eyes and rested my hand on her side, and she let it remain there. It had been so long since I had held her like this. I hadn't realised how much I missed it. Thoughts about US Tech and Jeremy and everything else drifted away as I enjoyed the small pleasure of the touch of my love. I didn't move, didn't even blink. I sat, breathing quietly, feeling her skin against mine, hearing her quiet hum of contentment.

Soon enough a swell of guilt crept up on my fleeting moment. My gut sank and I felt wretched again. It happened every time, over and over. How could I be happy? How could I be so heartless to live on without my baby?

I looked down at Jeri, eyes closed, the small rise and fall of her body with each breath. My arms and legs gave a tremble from my morning tremors, but Jeri didn't react. I closed my eyes, held her a little tighter, and felt the wretchedness rise once more.

* * *

Everything at US Tech looked different now. The lights in reception were too bright, the corridors too long. It was no longer a building I felt safe in. I kept my head low, not wanting to look anyone in the eye. I didn't know who I could trust. I headed straight to the security desk on the ground floor. "Hello."

"What can I help you with?" I got the distinct impression that the fifty something security guard didn't want to help me with anything. He leaned on the desk, wearing the typical white shirt with navy blue tie and blazer. Behind him I glimpsed a dozen or so screens covering different areas inside and outside the building being monitored by another three guards and there were typically dozens patrolling the corridors with a few placed at the front and back entrances.

"I don't know if you can help me out, but I wanted to know if I could look at some of the security footage from yesterday."

"The security footage?"

"Yes."

"I can't give you that."

"I'm not asking for the footage, just to view it."

"That's more than my job's worth! You're not authorised to view security footage," he looked at my level 10 security card pinned to my shirt. "You're barely authorised to be in this building," he laughed and turned to one of his buddies who gave an equally mocking snigger of superiority.

I took a breath and tried to stay calm. "Look, I need to see it. Is there anything I can do? It's important. Any help you can give... I would really appreciate it."

He looked me up and down, and then bobbed his head empathetically. "You really need to see it, huh?" I nodded. "Alright. Special requests can be made. You have to put it in writing."

"Ok." I was getting somewhere.

"To the Director of Security. Good luck with that," his face produced a smug grin. "He's more uptight than me." He strolled back inside his office with an overly exaggerated "Ha," and elbowed another buddy in the head to share the joke. I felt like smashing his face onto that desk of his.

Fucking lowlife.

I stopped by my office on the way to Bob's to email the Director of Security, but only out of desperation. I strained my brain trying to mastermind another plan to get the footage, but I had nothing. When I reached Bob's office the windows were misted up but I knocked anyway. Bob poked his face out a crack in the door and then opened it fully when he saw it was me. "Ryan, come in." Rick was sat opposite Bob's desk and nodded to me. Bob's half eaten sandwich was spread out on the desk along with two empty packets of chips. "Well, you don't look half bad." He leaned towards me for a closer look, his eyes narrow and frowning. "Bit washed out. Is that a black eye?" Bob turned to Rick, "I thought you said he had the flu?" And then back to me, "And you're back the next day?"

My mind went blank for excuses, but Bob kept on staring. "Yesterday… it was the last day. I've just shaken it off."

Bob relaxed a little and smiled for the first time. He shuffled his way to the other side of his desk and sat down. "Ah, ill while you're taking your leave, huh? Well, that's no good. Welcome back, then. What can I do you for?" He nodded towards the free seat beside Rick, and I sat.

I cut right to it. "Project: Infiltrator, have you been briefed on what it's planned to be used for?"

"Well, Peter was right; it will support future military operations."

"What military operations?"

"I don't know."

"Anything else?"

"I… I don't know."

"What about Project: Ambassador?" Despite the level 20 security clearance for the Earth-to-Orbit shuttle, Bob must at least be aware of the existence of a project by that name, particularly as it was so far along in the development lifecycle, even if he doesn't know the details.

"Never heard of it."

"What about a joint venture with NASA? Something that the anti-stealth tech will be equipped to?"

"I don't know what you're shovelling on about, Ryan? Do you know what he's getting at?"

"Haven't a clue," Rick replied.

I tried to determine whether Bob knew more than he was saying, but he looked genuinely confused. He tried to pull me into small talk, so I made my excuses and left. Rick followed to my next stop, analysing me all the way. "So, what happened to you yesterday?" he asked.

"I blacked out."

"All day?" he gave a laugh as he said it. When he saw my reaction, he stopped laughing. "Oh man, how did you black out?"

"I don't know. Look, don't tell anyone, will you?"

"Of course."

Rick stopped and pulled at my shoulder to hold me with him. "You haven't told Jeri, have you?" I didn't answer. I wanted to tell her. "I wouldn't. It sounds ridiculous. Aren't things bad enough?"

"I know, I know." We walked on until we reached the lift.

"Just look after yourself, ok?" Rick stared at me, his eyes filled with concern until I nodded and left him behind in the corridor.

One of the key functions of the DNA tracker was that it could provide the vertical location of a person as well as their horizontal position. Another feature was that, if activated, it possessed a memory bank that could store all of the locations travelled by a person for up to eighteen months, or until erased. A lot of people didn't want their every move tracked, which was why the feature had an off switch, but there were many benefits. For me, I was able to track my whereabouts a day earlier to the exact position within US Tech.

The elevator pinged as I arrived at the -3rd floor. A narrow corridor stretched out in front of me with numerous doors either side, each with a standard security scanner to grant access. My eyes darted between my DNA tracker in hand and the doors that passed as I progressed closer to my destination. Then the small bleep and the flash of a light on the handheld device, signalling that my exact whereabouts between 8:15am and 1pm the day previous was about fifty feet away on my right-hand side, the other side of a set of double doors. I swiped my card and held my breath.

LEVEL 20 AUTHORISATION REQUIRED

Shit.

Without a level 20 security pass, I wasn't getting in that room. I went back to my office and mulled over what to do next. They could be watching me right now. And without Jeremy's laptop, I had no more leads, nothing to go on.

I took Jeremy's address book out of my jacket pocket and thumbed through the pages. My mind constantly replayed the way Jeremy looked at me when he told me about Jacob Reences. He must be at the centre of all this, him, and the address book. If only I had picked up the laptop and ran.

Him. He. She.

I grabbed a pen and paper. I scribbled down the two names, Jacob Reences and Rebecca Jones and crossed off the corresponding letters one at a time.

Shit. It's a fucking anagram.

So, Jacob Reences wasn't a person and that wasn't a phone number. Then what?

I made a list of what it could be, from coordinates to some kind of code but each one proved fruitless. I stared at the twelve letters continuously until I decided that wasn't working and paced the room instead, throwing and catching a stress ball to spark my brain power.

Where would Jeremy leave a trail for me to follow? And then I realised the clue was all around me, one of two places that I knew for sure that we had both been: US Tech.

I crashed down into my swivel chair, pulled myself close to the desk and typed Jacob Reences into the user account database. Success. I double checked it against the employee database and found nothing; Jacob Reences never existed; Jeremy must have managed to set-up a dummy account.

I logged out of my ID and inputted 'Jacob Reences' into the user ID and the dummy telephone number into the password field.

PASSWORD ACCEPTED

I scanned my level 10 security card onto the screen.

LEVEL 20 AUTHORISATION REQUIRED

Shit. Not again.

I jumped out of my seat and grabbed the stress ball. The White Giant party was planned to be held at US Tech. Hundreds of people would be there, most of them drunk, and more than a few with level 20 security cards.

* * *

Waking up at the Stephenson Memorial wasn't the first incident when I had lost a chunk of time. I had tried my best to forget about it, but the similarities were not lost on me.

"Howdy," Herb said answering the phone.

"I need to ask you something." Talking to Herb about that kind of thing was always difficult but if I could get past the buffoonery and snide comments, he could actually be helpful. "You know, when I took off for a few days?"

"You mean when you went on a bender?"

"It wasn't a bender."

"It wasn't? You said it was a blur. You turned up rotten drunk."

"I'm not sure that was it."

"Then what? Was it Rick? What did that piss ant get you into?"

"It wasn't Rick."

"Oh no, tell me you weren't with that bitch."

"Will you just listen to me?" It's a waste of time. I don't know why I called him. "I... I think something happened then. Maybe I blacked out."

"For three days? Are you serious?"

"I don't know. I never made it to work yesterday. I don't remember what happened... The entire day is just gone to me. I don't know if it's connected. Last time, you were there when I got home. Are you sure I was drunk?"

"You were out of it. Rambling about nonsense, said you were lost."

"But are you sure I was drunk? Did you smell booze on me? Was I just out of it?"

"I don't know, man. I don't remember how you smelt.

Geez, I thought I was the problem child." The phone went deathly quiet. I thought about hanging up. I had said too much. "Do you think you need to see a doctor?"

"I don't know."

* * *

Jeri popped her head through the kitchen door to peer into the garden. She saw me at the table surrounded by place settings, cutlery and two glasses of red wine. Jeri approached cautiously. "What's this?"

"It's warm, I thought... why not."

Jeri beamed but brushed it off quickly like I might change my mind if she was too happy about it. She slipped into the chair opposite me and took a sip of wine. We sat in silence at first, reacclimatising ourselves to the situation. "How was your day?" she asked.

"Fine. And yours?"

"Good, thank you."

"Great."

We were like awkward strangers, so unaccustomed to such a mundane activity between married couples that it seemed foreign to us. All that time spent living together but living apart, I genuinely didn't know what to say to her.

I gestured to the house and dashed inside. I brought out Thai chicken curry with rice, seared eggplant, mushrooms and bok choy – one of Jeri's favourites. For the first few minutes, we alternated between food and wine without saying a word. Jeri looked out across the garden at the lawn and the flowers bedded on either side. Her hair fluttered in the cool breeze.

"It's been a while," she said. "Since we ate out here together." She casually tossed a spoonful of rice into her mouth, but I knew she was waiting for an answer to the question she didn't ask. "It's lovely. There's really no reason?" Apparently, I still knew her well.

"Not that I'm complaining." She smiled at me and rested

her hand on top of mine. "This is good, Ryan." Her smile held and her hand remained like a soft blanket covering my own. "I saw Herb. He reminded me that he's driving us to the state dinner."

"I'm sorry."

Jeri laughed. "I think it's brilliant. Do you think we'll be the only ones not in a limo?"

"I think they might refuse us at the door. Chase away the hobos."

"It's been a while since you saw Herb?"

"Yeah, a while."

"You didn't go to the bar this week? Or last week. You should definitely go this week. Relax a little. Maybe give him a call?"

"Sure." I didn't have time to go out with Herb. I had too much to plan for the White Giant party. Too much at stake.

"Bob was ok with you being off yesterday?" I hadn't told Jeri I had stayed off work. She fixed her eyes on mine. "You didn't go into work, right?"

"I... that's right."

"You feeling, ok?"

"I just had some things to take care of."

"Oh, I see." There was another silence, but this one was awkward. She expected more. "Your eye is healing well." I nodded. "Did you report it to the police?"

"No. I didn't have much to report."

"Why would someone want to attack you?" She said empathetically. "For no reason?"

"It happens, I guess. I'm sure you've seen plenty of cases like that."

Jeri set her fork down. "Still, it would be good to know the truth of it. Why they attacked you, that is. I could ask at the station... If they've had other reports."

I shook my head.

"Just so much going on these days. Like that intruder the other night? The one who didn't break any windows or doors to get in? Didn't take anything."

"It must have been nothing."

"You imagined it?" Her tone had become accusing. With every word I liked where this was going less and less.

"I thought I saw something."

"But you didn't. Kyle and Emily were terrified; hell, I pulled my gun out in front of them. And now Herb doesn't want them staying here for a while. Did he tell you that?" She locked eyes with me. I was breathing fast and shallow. "I was scared. I don't even know what I'm afraid of, Ryan. Do you know?"

"I... I thought I saw something."

"And yesterday? You don't know what happened, then? "And two years ago?" Herb, the treacherous bastard. "You're trying to change the story on that one?"

"What did he tell you?"

"More than you did. What are you hiding from me?"

"You don't know what you're talking about."

"How could I? You don't talk to me. You can talk to your brother, but you can't talk to me?"

"I'm talking to you right now."

"No, you're not. You're speaking, there are words coming out, but they don't mean a thing. Lying isn't just speaking an untruth, it's when you omit the truth. Hiding the truth. You do all this, give me hope... I think I preferred it when you just told me to fuck off and ran away."

I dropped my fork and jumped to my feet. Jeri dived out of her seat and blocked my path to the house.

"Where are you going? Face me. For once, Ryan, tell me what is going on with you?"

I don't know why I did this. Why I thought I deserved to be happy. I felt so bad thinking she had just pushed aside what we had lost, when all she's doing is plastering over it.

"I'm your wife. Your partner. Your companion. This isn't how you're supposed to treat me."

"I don't know what you want from me." I just want to leave.

"I want my husband back. I want to know why you're

waking up every night terrified, shaking uncontrollably. I want you to tell me what happened to you yesterday, and why you can't remember it. I want you to open up to me. I want things to go back to the way they were."

The food had already started to congeal. "I tried… to have time together. Where we could just eat. And talk. I tried."

"It doesn't matter. What's the point, when you're lying to my face? You make the right noises, make the right moves. Behind my back it's the same nonsense."

I picked up my plate, rice spilling over and slammed it onto the pavement. Curry splattered everywhere; jagged ceramic shrapnel's shattering beneath us. I darted past her. She grabbed my arm and stopped me dead.

"Look at you. You're like a teenager, raging hormones and emotion. Obsessed with spending your life suffering alone. That's not even a life. It's pathetic."

I pulled free from her grip and escaped through the house and to my car as quickly as I could. I could feel the air start to poison me, the ring on my finger burning, a stinging mockery. I took out my wooden box, wrapped my arms around it and buried it into my chest.

NINE

Jeri and I had barely spoken since my attempt at dinner. I took some solace in that it was the night of the White Giant opening party, where thanks to US Tech protocol, I would finally get close to more than one distracted or drunk employee with a level 20 security card. The plan was clear: get a security card, use it to access Jeremy's fake account and then the basement, then get the security card back to the owner before it was discovered missing.

I jogged upstairs to get ready. Jeri was already in the bedroom sitting at the dressing table. One sparkling gold earring dangled from her ear while the second hid behind her hair that swept across one shoulder.

"You're going out?" I asked.

"Uh-huh."

I breathed a sigh of relief. Jeri being there would make it tricky to do what I needed, but her being at the same party as Jess made me want to take the White Giant and pull it down on top of me. "With Carol?"

Jeri stood; her dress was a good distance above her knees and shined brightly with the reflection from the light. "What time are you leaving?"

"Around eight."

"I'll be ready," she announced fastening the straps from her shoes that wrapped around her ankles, heels six inches high. My heart throbbed in my chest.

I didn't want to outright say that Jess was going to be there. "Are you sure?"

"Maybe I'll see what you're up to." She widened her eyes, encouraging submission. I wanted to check again if she really thought it was a good idea to go but I stopped before I opened my mouth. The drive to the party was without words but filled with me envisioning Jeri tasering Jess and dragging her away cuffed in a cop car.

We passed through the security gates and pulled up outside US Tech. A valet took my keys and Jeri dashed out of the car and into the party as I trailed behind. The event was held in one of the larger suites of the main US Tech building and the open plan room was decorated in balloons, banners and a twelve-foot replica cake of the White Giant in the centre of the room that was big enough to feed the entire company. The place was bursting with people from every department and every level of the business as well as a small media crew who did their rounds with strict orders that all material would be audited before any release. It was a fun time for everyone, apparently. I understood how flies felt when they found their way into a spider web. I looked but couldn't see Jessica and fought the urge to ask anyone if she was there. I hoped desperately there would be enough people in attendance for Jeri and Jessica to never cross paths.

We found Rick and Peter stood side by side at the edge of the dance floor, each with a drink in hand. Rick gave a friendly hello to Jeri. Before she could reply, Peter jumped with excitement and grabbed her by the hands. "Come dance with me." Jeri pulled a face. "Come on, I can't take much more of these stiffs." Rick looked around, the only one there, and retreated to his drink.

Jeri leaned across to me and placed her hand firmly on my shoulder. "Wait here for me?"

"Ok. Sure," I replied, but it felt more like an instruction than a question. Jeri made her way to the dance floor, Peter in hand, and left me standing sheepishly near the entrance with Rick. I studied the room for the faces of US Tech executives, but none had emerged yet. They were probably in an office somewhere having a private bottle of something that cost more than my first car. After an hour or so, Bob stumbled towards me with a four-pint pitcher in hand all to himself. "Ryan, my prodigal son, how are you?"

"I'm fine, Bob."

"You're having a good time?"

"I am." I didn't bother to act like it was true. Bob always stayed surprisingly sober for what he poured down his throat, but even sober he didn't seem to notice.

"You're the man of the moment," he said. "The press wants to do a segment on you and your wife."

Rick pulled a face.

"I don't think so," I said to Bob. "Jeri wouldn't go for that. Not tonight."

"I'm sure you can talk her round. You can be quite the charmer."

"I'm sure Jess can vouch for that," Rick said with a smirk.

I looked around the room to see if Jeri had heard Rick's shitty comment, but she was far away at the bar chatting to Peter. Bob acted oblivious, unaware of my history with Jessica. "What do you think?" he asked.

"I'll do whatever press I need to, but I won't put Jeri through it." I waited for another snide comment from Rick, but he stayed quiet. He had done so much for me over the years but sometimes he was a real prick. Bob smacked me on the back and joined a three-person conga burrowing through the crowd. How many people want to know you when they think you're on your way up? I wondered how their interests might change if they were watching me fall.

"Are we losing you buddy?" Rick held a drink out to me that had been sitting on the table in reserve.

"It's just a little overwhelming."

"I know, I feel it too." The drink felt cold as it went down. "Jeri looks like she's doing ok."

"What do you mean by that?"

He took pause to choose his words – a rare sight for Rick. "Just with Jess being here, and everything that's happened. It can't be easy for her. She looks like she's having fun with Peter, though." They were taking turns to swirl each other around in front of the bar. "You know, a lot of people don't even count kissing as cheating."

"Well, I do," I insisted vehemently.

"Alright, I'm just trying to be supportive."

"Touchy subject." I lost myself watching Jeri dance, time drifting by. It had been so long since I had seen her let go like that. Once upon a time we went out dancing every week.

Jeri strode across the dance floor towards me. She stumbled a little on her way with an empty shot glass in her hand. "Are you ok?" I asked.

"I'm having a great time. Peter's a hoot! What's wrong with your face?"

"Nothing. You're just a little drunk."

"I think it's about time I let my hair down, don't you? Or does she wear it up for you?"

"Hey partner." Peter danced over to Jeri with two more shot glasses and handed one to her. She drank it in one gulp, and they clanged empty glasses before resuming their dance next to us. Peter twirled her around and her dress went out like a spinning top. When I closed my eyes, it wasn't Peter that took her hand, it was me. Even Rick couldn't take his eyes off her. Mostly, I was wishing for the night to be over. But I still had work to do.

Jeri caught me watching her and signalled to Peter to follow her back to the dance floor. As Peter turned to comply, Rick grabbed his forearm. "What the hell are you playing at?"

"What?" Peter tried to pull away, but Rick only dug his fingers in harder.

"That's your boss's wife."

The realisation of Rick's attack dawned on Peter's face. I put my hand on Rick's to bat it away, but his fingers were buried too deep into Peter's skin. "Rick, it's fine. Let go."

Peter looked between me and Rick's cold stare. "Ryan, I would never... we were just dancing."

"Let go," I said again as I banged Rick on the hand until his fingers released like a bear trap being reset.

"Geez." Peter shook his head as he shuffled away. Rick's lip curled up in disgust.

"What was that?" I asked expecting Rick to shake it off and admit to overreacting.

Rick didn't even offer me a glance. "He knows what happened, what's he trying to do to you?"

Rick had my best interests at heart – at least he had that over Herb – but at this rate his interference was just as unwelcome. Peter gradually resumed dancing with Jeri at half the speed and enthusiasm as before, but Jeri moved at full pelt, thankfully unaware.

Behind Jeri, wearing full suit and matching tie, one black, one navy blue, I spotted two targets leaning against the bar yakking like old friends. In truth, Alex Little and Timothy Calderbank hated each other. They would steal the shirts off each other's backs if it would further their respective divisions – not that they cared about anyone else in the division, it was all for personal glory. I darted towards them, leaving Rick grumbling and alone. I slowed on approach and rested a hand on each of their shoulders. Time to go to work. "Excuse me, gentlemen. How's your evening?"

Timothy screwed his eyes, my face obviously not one he thought to remember. "Ellis!" Alex exclaimed resting his own hand on my shoulder, allowing me to slip mine lower to discreetly feel around his jacket pocket from the outside.

"Oh... yes, Ellis," Timothy stammered. "Some good work, some very good work from you here. We're always on the lookout for new talent in Production, you know."

"Ellis is very happy in R&D," Alex retorted. "Tell him

Ellis."

"Of course." I found no trace of Alex's security card. Pants pockets were a little too risky. As Timothy sat back in reproach, a lanyard peered out from behind his jacket holding exactly what I needed. I leaned in close to Timothy and he leaned towards me eagerly. "But I'm always interested in a good offer," I whispered in his ear. Timothy rested back against the bar with a knowing grin and a nod of the head as I stepped away, his level 20 security card tucked securely in my hand.

* * *

I squeezed past crowds of dance circles and riotous huddles and dodged five colleagues who tried to call me over to their conversation. I made it through double doors, down the corridor and straight to the nearest office on the ground floor. The motion sensor flashed and automatically lit up the room. I used a random computer terminal so nothing could be traced to me and was glad I let Peter show me a few of his tricks when no one else would. When I logged on I rerouted the location to the fifteenth floor so if anyone checked CCTV footage, they wouldn't look in a ground floor office. I typed the user ID and password into the terminal and scanned Calderbank's level 20 ID card.

AUTHORISATION ACCEPTED

I searched the memory and found a handful of files. I stuck my flash drive into the unit and copied them over: 3 minutes to complete. I heard something in the distance. Footsteps and they were getting closer. I reached, ready to pull the flash drive out, still 3 minutes to go. The footsteps were louder, heels clacking on the linoleum floor. I pushed the chair back, got down on all fours and crawled under the desk. I hoped whoever it was were down here for a reason and just passing through, because I was in the only office that wasn't in darkness.

They kept coming until I could hear them in the room

with me.

"What are you doing? You don't even work in this office." I shuffled my knees backwards across the floor and popped my head out from under the desk. "The party's that way," Jess said standing over me, a thin fabric draped from her shoulders, fitted to every curve and resting halfway up her slender thigh. Sandal straps wrapped their way up each leg like a snake to almost meet the dress. She always managed to look effortless. It really didn't help that Jessica was honestly beautiful. I wanted to cry for thinking that. "You're hiding from me, aren't you?"

I fumbled for a response that didn't give her the impression it was specifically her I was hiding from and didn't give away what I was really doing down here. Realisation flashed across Jess' face. "Is Jeri here?" She concluded the answer before I could say it. "Shit. Shit, this looks really bad. I just came down to see if you were ok... I wasn't going to. Shit."

Jess backed away towards the door, "You need to get back upstairs."

2 minutes remaining. "No-"

"Yes, its fine, I'll stay down here until it's clear."

"Jess, listen, you go up-"

"No one's expecting me up there. What happens if Jeri comes looking for you and finds me on the way?"

Total disaster.

1 minute 30 seconds remaining.

She's right. I have to keep her distracted, get the flash drive out and log off without her seeing.

1 minute 15 seconds remaining.

"What do you keep looking at?" Jess craned her neck to see the screen.

I grabbed her shoulder to turn her to face me. "Listen... I..."

Jess' eyes narrowed, she pulled away from me and yanked the screen to face it full on. "What are you downloading? Is this above board?" She looked down at

Timothy Calderbank's security pass that I left on the desk in my panic. "Holy shit, what are you doing?"

"I... I've got an idea... about the anti-stealth prototype. Calderbank got a hold of my designs."

"How?"

"I have no idea. But I can't let him take credit for it."

"Shit." Jess stared down at the ground, her eyes darting around deep in thought. "How can I help?"

"Just get out of here."

"I can't just leave you here, let me help."

"I don't want you getting caught up in it. And Jeri could come looking for me any minute." Jess took a step to leave and then stepped back. "I'm almost done. Thank you, but please, get out of here."

Jess gave a reluctant nod. "Just be safe. Come and find me later?"

"Sure," I said knowing there was no way I could be near her.

* * *

The elevator pinged at the -3rd floor. I could imagine people scurrying, in and out of rooms scanning their security cards along the way, but today, the corridor was empty. I followed the same route to reach the secured room that according to my DNA tracker I had been inside. I reached into my pocket for Calderbank's security card. The lift doors clattered open behind me.

Rick stepped out of the lift, looking each way down the corridor until he found me. "What are you doing down here?" He walked briskly towards me, but I froze, still fumbling around in my head for something worthy.

"How did you find me?"

"We couldn't find you upstairs, so I got Jimmy to check CCTV for you."

The security scanner was so close I could have reached out and touched it. I wouldn't get another chance. "Why did you come looking for me?"

"Jeri asked me to." Rick grimaced. "I think you'd better come up."

I pulled Calderbank's security card out of my pocket and held it by the scanner.

"Don't do it." Rick held his hand out to reaffirm the warning. "Whatever you're doing down here, Ryan... don't do it."

"I need to-"

"I don't want to know. Just put that thing in your pocket and let's get back up to the party." Rick faced me legs parted, hands by his side and eyes fixed like he would draw on me if I made the wrong move. Beneath the look to urge me not to do it, I saw worry.

I bent my wrist and pressed the card against the security scanner. Rick's shoulders collapsed in a heap.

AUTHORISATION ACCEPTED

PASSWORD REQUIRED

Level 20 was the highest clearance I was aware of in the organisation. If Timothy Calderbank doesn't have clearance, then who the hell does?

* * *

Jeri was waiting for me at the other side of the double doors. I raised a slight smile to greet her but there was no reciprocation, a sombre expression the only thing that her face had for me at that moment. "Where have you been?"

"I... I was just-"

"She's here." Jeri didn't let me finish. "Was she with you?"

"Is that why you sent him after me?" Rick looked at me sheepishly. It wasn't the first time he was stuck in the middle of us.

"I don't know what you're talking about."

"Whatever."

While we were locked in a silent gaze, one of the double

doors opened behind me. I didn't need to turn around to know who it was, Jeri's face told me everything. "I see." Jeri's voice quietened.

"Hello, Jeri," Jessica said timidly. She waited, eyes wide for a response. She would have to wait a lot longer.

Jeri took hold of Rick's arm, "Would you like to take me home? I think I need to leave." Rick's eyes darted back and forth between me and Jeri.

"You don't need to leave." Jessica's voice seemed to softly emerge through the noise of the party. "I'll go if you want. But neither of us has to, really." The music quieted, dropping into the background as my colleagues and their guests gradually hushed around the room. I wanted to jump in the middle of them and stop either one saying another word, but I resisted, painfully aware that any wrong move could hurt Jeri even more. "I'm sorry Jeri."

"I married him. He's my husband and I kiss him, not you. He doesn't love you." I could see the hurt on Jessica's face as her eyes welled up, like a starved kitten being poked. I think that was the first time Jeri realised that it wasn't just some office fling for Jessica, that her feelings were more serious. Jeri's scowl lessened but didn't disappear completely. "He's, my husband. I want you to stay away from him." Jess's pleading eyes found me before she closed them tightly and ran into the toilets, mascara dripping slowly down her cheek.

Jeri followed Jessica with her eyes until she was out of sight and gave me one final glare of hostility before she walked away from us all. From across the room, Bob looked upon me with pity, which only made me cringe even more. I caught up to Jeri and took hold of her arm. "Where are you going?"

She broke free from me. "Away from the two of you. Sneaking off together, doing who knows what. I bet you do it over your office desk with that little slut."

"Please don't say that. Nothing happened. I'm sorry, but you knew she was going to be here. You wanted to come."

"Fuck you, Ryan."

"Can we talk outside please? I'll explain, I promise." She marched through the entrance hallway and out of the building. On my way out, I handed Timothy Calderbank's card into reception and said I found it at the bar. When I caught up to Jeri, she was sat on the edge of the pavement near the exit with her back to me. The cold air made her shiver. She let her shoulders round and lost the bold poise of moments earlier. She dipped her chin and pushed her hair to the side to reveal the nape of her neck, soft and delicate with a slight paleness from an avoidance of too much sun, her head resting in her hands. In that moment an intense feeling returned to me, of something I had known since the moment I met her, that no other woman would ever be as beautiful to me as my Jeri.

"I'll keep apologising as much as you want. I'm sorry, I truly am. But I wasn't with Jessica tonight. I saw her, we spoke, but nothing happened." Any words I could use seemed feeble. None of them could fix what was broken. "You don't know how much I wish I could change the past."

"You stupid, stupid man. You think that this is because you two kissed? Just shut up." The distance between us seemed to grow with every word. "When you came home and told me that you kissed another woman, I thought that you were going to leave me."

"I would never leave you."

"You abandoned me. I lost our baby, and you disappeared for three days. I thought that you were never coming back." Jeri tucked her knees into her chest.

"I'm sorry."

"All I've been doing is waiting for you to disappear without a trace. I started to wish that you would just leave. Get it over with. And now I feel like it's all happening all over again." Her words hit me like a freight train. "I don't know what you're caught up in, but what if you don't get up next time? What if they leave you for dead? I wish I was strong enough to walk away."

A storm could break me in two and Jeri would still be standing like an oak she was so strong. So, what's stopping her from walking away? "I don't know what I'm caught up in. I blacked out." Jeri's eyes widened. She was hanging on my every word. "When I missed work… And maybe when I… When I disappeared. I don't think I was drunk."

"Then what were you? What would make you leave your grieving wife for three days?"

I tried to tell her. I wanted her to know. But I couldn't do it. I was in too deep to drag her down with me. Jeri looked so disappointed.

I understood what Jeremy wanted from me; we can't judge people in grief. But it could still all be a suicidal man's desperate attempt to rationalise the death of his love. Even if it was true, some truths are better left unknown. "I'll drop it. I'll drop the whole thing."

I lowered myself next to Jeri and she let me get close enough to place my arms around her shoulders. I wanted to hold her tighter, but I didn't squeeze too hard in case it made her recoil. I let go and held her hair behind her head as she vomited in the street.

TEN

My unconscious mind obviously didn't care about my pledge to Jeri because nightmares plagued my every night for a week, each night worse than the last. Every morning, I woke up trembling in an oily sweat. I fell into a trance twice; the second time, Jeri had the phone in her hand to dial 911 before I came to. She insisted I see a doctor, but he declared it symptoms of chronic insomnia. Each one felt more traumatic and real than the last.

Jeri hadn't mentioned the White Giant party and acted like it had never happened. She tried to talk to me like we were a normal married couple, even when we were alone, with no sign of the resentment between us that had always seemed to bubble beneath the surface. I think she appreciated the fact that despite my agony, I had let it go.

I lay awake trying to remember past birthdays and celebrations, nights cuddling on the sofa. I pictured our old life together, hoping it would find us once more, to return me to a world of promise, when we took hold of each other's hands and didn't let go. The first time I laid eyes on her, Rick and I were only out to relax, sat in a grimy corner of Taylor's bar, final's stress gradually dissipating as the empty bottles steadily stacked up. The music, quiet at first and then rising gradually to chorus. As it does, Jeri moving slowly across the dance floor, her feet taking each step like it was expertly choreographed to be purposely casual, harmoniously attuned to the beat. A smoky haze of fog lingering in the air between us. But I can see clearly. She motions to someone I can't bear to look at and slides her hands slowly up and down her body, inviting me into her life. With one hand and a flick of her head, she lets her hair fall out of the ponytail to caress her shoulders, barely touching them. Moving with the beat, grinding her body, her legs, unbelievable and captivating, steadily moving faster and faster until the guitar screams out and she shakes her whole body from side to side, the only person in the room, thinking only of herself and the music. Her head swaying side to side, reflecting light with the glitter that adorns her face, a soul far removed from the complicated existence that plagues the lives of every other unfortunate soul.

I can't look away. I'm captivated by this woman who doesn't care about anything but now. Moving with too much precision and brilliance to be under the influence of more than a glass or two of alcohol, she pays no attention to any man in the room; this dance is only for her. She holds her position perfectly, a mere few feet away, gazing straight ahead, looking only at me. I'm mesmerised. We catch each other's eyes like I've just entered her room and I'm paralysed, intoxicated by this woman who I know I can't live without. I could walk right over to her, play it cool, try to impress her, offer a drink, ask her to dance, complement her or try to kiss her, but oh no, nothing will jeopardise this perfect moment. And just like that, she moves to a gradual stop, picks up a pleather jacket from a barstool and leaves. Rick's voice faintly nagging at me in the background, there was nothing in my head except her face, her body, her soul.

All alone, I lay on the attic floor, no more likely to sleep here than in my bed. Thinking about my fairy-tale life and how it had slipped through my fingers when I had held onto it so tightly. Maybe it was never really mine.

I took the flash drive out of my pocket and held it up in front of me. It had become more than just an object; a Pandora's Box that represented a path that lay ahead, and every action I had taken so far. Jeremy's breadcrumbs that he had left for me in a fake name and a fake US Tech account. Whatever was on it would forever remain a mystery.

I wanted to be myself again, to live the life I missed so dearly. Yet I was trapped by the object before me and its magnetic pull, unaware of its own significance, urging me to plug it in, to power up my laptop and devour the secrets it contained. Otherwise, it was without purpose, and without a purpose I didn't even know what it was doing in my hand. Was it a flash drive or an anchor pulling me under?

I couldn't bear to see the devastation on Jeri's face if I let her down. I made a promise to her. Hearing her screams as she is ripped away from me, feeling the burning of her fingertips as they tear away from mine, seeing her face as she leaves without a chance to say goodbye. It is just what I must endure for her. My pain to bear.

But Jeri's screaming face was all I saw. The burn of her fingertips. Gnawing at me. The answers were in my hand. The truth. Or a path to it.

Tormenting me. This could be how I lose her, how I let her die, because I did nothing. When I could have saved her.

What if I'm supposed to open it? All I need to do is read what's inside. The first file could have every answer I need. Or it could tell me that I'm crazy. That there is no conspiracy, and I can get back to this life exactly as if I'd never even plugged the thing in.

Or it could be the only way to protect her.

It screamed out to me. Plug it in. I only need to read it once. Just open it. Then I can stop. I can give it up at any point. *Paradox. Unveil. Transcend.* I've heard those words every night while I sleep.

My pain to bear.

The light flickered and the shadows climbed the walls

around me. It wanted to drag me under, that small piece of plastic; to consume me. To pull me back in and never let me free again.

So, this time I let it.

* * *

The flash drive contained every file that Jeremy had sent me, everything I found printed underneath his wardrobe and more. 'Project: Ambassador' detailed how the Earth-to-orbit shuttle was about to enter full production, with an initial run of one hundred due from US Tech on behalf of NASA only a week from now. Most projects in development at US Tech started with extremely tight security to prevent leaks to competitors and to limit customer awareness before official customer engagement programmes had kicked off, but I had always been briefed before they reached production. I read on, to the project team, where I found both Timothy Calderbank and Alex Little named, to no surprise. Especially compared to the next name I read: my own best friend, Rick Stenson.

He was there when I questioned Bob and he said nothing. Even when on the Space Lift project, and Rick had been under a non-disclosure agreement, he still told me in strict confidence what he was working on. I had no idea that he had even been working on another project. He saw how much it meant to me and still he said nothing.

Adrenaline fired through me as I moved on to the next file, a mash-up of dozens of cases that had been collected together. There were reports of abductions, all of them sharing the same symptoms as me: fractured dreams, frequent trances and missing time. One of the files detailed the abduction of the young Lilly Russell. There was a full report by Major Carl Patrick, the man named in Jeremy's address book who died of a heart attack, and his experience of UFO investigations, including the retrieval of an alien lifeform.

Photographs of craft were scattered all over one of the reports, an oval shape on its side, all of them identical. The same report detailed how they move silently at speeds estimated to be above 100,000 km/h and could not be detected by radar. My eyes danced across the screen. It was everything Jeremy had led me to.

The last document was different. I figured it had been put together by Jeremy, as a collection of articles from various sources, notes annotated underneath each one. It was titled 'Apex Guard'. There were news reports of dozens of missing persons, many of them later found with reproductive organs missing. There were even financial reports that linked US Tech funding back to Apex Guard. In each set of notes, Jeremy referred to Apex Guard as an entity or person.

There was no turning back.

I copied the files onto another flash drive and made a set of printed copies – as Jeremy said himself, nobody does paper. I put the second flash drive at the back of my desk drawer in my study and hid the printed copies of the files in a compartment under the closet.

But the question still remained, what to do next. Jeremy had led me this far, but from death, his reach had to come to an end. I was most unnerved by why he had placed so much faith in me.

ELEVEN

My eyes were tired after hours of research that had continued from the weekend at home into Monday afternoon at work – re-reading Jeremy's file, scouring the internet for reports of abductions, sightings, half looking for a lead and half trying to process it all. I had told Jeri I was catching up on work and she believed me. I washed my face trying to regenerate some life back into it. Water splashed on my shoes, but I didn't mind. I looked up into the mirror and locked eyes with the person staring back at me. I wasn't proud of what I saw. Bob only said one thing about the events of the party, "Things like that, they happen," but he could barely look at me.

I didn't take my eyes off Rick as he entered Bob's office for the scheduled progress update for Project: Infiltrator. He eased himself into the chair, not a care in the world.

Play it smart. Wait until he's alone.

Jess was sat at the opposite end of the white veneer desk at an angle away from me, yet to make eye contact. Peter leaned back on his chair next to me, gazing around the room in a daze.

Bob made even more effort than usual to be welcoming and upbeat, and even pushed a cup of coffee across the desk

110

to me that I hadn't asked for.

"Hey, where's mine?" Bob finally had Peter's attention.

"You'll get yours when you have one of his breakthroughs. Isn't that right, Ryan?"

I smiled, wishing I was anywhere else, far away from the woman my wife didn't want me near, and my best friend, the liar.

"Ok, let's get going," Bob said glancing at his watch, the usual agenda on the screen. We drifted from what had gone well to talking about a new development, which was how the technology would be utilised through mobile devices, likely masts that would be positioned at key locations. Then Bob called time and we moved on to what we could do better. Every second was stretched beyond capacity, every word Bob said a drone in my ears. The only thing to spike my interest was Rick's occasional interruptions to garner credit or attention, each one forcing me to push my self-control to the limit to silence my tongue.

"We should have been fully dedicated to the project from the start," Rick said. His personal attack caught me by surprise. A red flag waving in front of my face.

"Rather than secret projects on the side?" Rick's poker face gave nothing away. My moment had arrived. "Like your shuttle project?" My venomous tone instantly created an air of tension in the room. "Rick here hasn't been working on enhancing existing tech like he claims. He's had a full-blown project underway."

"What are you talking about?" Bob said, already exasperated by the situation. "What project?"

"To create an Earth-to-Orbit shuttle, fully manoeuvrable within a thousand miles of the Earth's surface. They're already in production, aren't they?" I glared at Rick, but he kept staring straight ahead at the TV screen.

"That's absurd," Bob weighed in.

"What else do you know, Rick?" I demanded. "Do you know about Project: Libera?"

"Ryan, calm down," Bob insisted.

"Calm down?" I stood up and loomed over the desk at Bob. He craned back in his chair to stare up at me. "Ask him." Rick shook his head at me. My fists trembled. "Why is my wife's name on that list?"

Bob put his hands out, palms faced up in a 'non-threatening' way that only patronised me. "I think you should get some air."

"Do you know about this?"

"There is nothing happening in my division that I don't know about," Bob replied.

"Is that an admission of guilt or stupidity? I've read the files, Bob."

"Ok, Ryan, that's enough. Leave my office now please, this appointment is finished."

I turned to Peter and Jess who were sat rigid, their eyes darting back and forth until Peter's landed on me, and he winced, knowing he was no longer going to be part of an invisible crowd. "He lied to us. You don't know what's going on here. Right under your noses."

"Get him the hell out of here," Bob's roared. Jess jumped up and ushered me towards the doorway. I stormed out, slamming the door behind me. I panted for breath, my anger gradually fading. I had no leads, no one to turn to. I was scrambling around in the dark.

"What was that?" Jess searched my face like she was trying to find the answer.

"I don't know."

"I've never seen you like that before."

"I saw the files. I need to find out how much Rick knows."

"About what? A classified project he's working on? What are you trying to do to your career?"

"Fuck my career. I need to get back in there." I charged back towards Bob's office. Jess jumped in the way and pushed me back.

"Are you serious? You go back in there and I can't help you." Jess stood tall. I would have had to forcibly remove her to get back into the meeting room.

I was supposed to play it smart. But it was one cock-up after another. "Bob's probably going to make me take some leave, isn't he?"

"Might not be a bad idea. How many hours are you putting in?" It wasn't the hours spent working that was the problem, it was the sleepless nights. The fear. I shrugged it off.

"Look, I know we probably shouldn't be alone right now... I'm sure Jeri doesn't even want you speaking to me... but do you want to get some air? Grab a coffee? I understand if you say no. It's probably not a good idea." Many people connect over many different rituals. Sometimes Jess and I connected over alcohol, sometimes tea, but more often than not, it was over coffee.

"Jeri still hates you."

"She should. But you look like you need a friend."

"I... I really shouldn't."

"You say no one more time and I'll accept it. But we both know nothing is going to happen between us. We're friends, just like before. And as a friend I'm worried as fuck about you."

I agreed and Jessica went back in to excuse herself, but Bob had already left. At Fringe cafe, she made sure to talk about anything other than work and Jeri. Anytime I started showed signs of stress, she had another conversation ready to change the subject. "Good to see you've still got your sense of humour," she said sipping at her mocha.

"Looks like it was still in there somewhere." Under soft lighting and nestled in a cosy armchair with the warmth from the coffee, I began to relax. It had been Jess' favourite place to meet since I had known her, and we had spent many lunch hours together, just the two of us, or with Rick and Peter, laughing, passionately debating, watching Peter storm out of the place because he was pissed at Rick. Even during peak times, it was quiet and the grey painted brick walls with lowbrow artwork, soft cream carpets and various exotic plants dotted around provided character. It felt strange being back here with Jess. It had been so long since she last told me tales of her boyfriends over a flat white and asked for my judgement on whether they should end up on the scrap heap as we toppled pastry after pastry. It always seemed ludicrous to me how a girl so fascinating always ended up with some self-proclaimed 'real man' who lacked a shred of independence or an iota of kindness, never appreciating what they had until she had moved on.

Jessica gave me her full attention, and after half an hour of comfort conversation, it felt like she was waiting for me to spill open my head and heart. Before I knew it, I started to oblige. "I just feel different."

"Different how?"

"I find it hard to concentrate, to stay focused on anything. I'm bad tempered – which you witnessed first-hand with my Bob-tage. I see the face of Heinrich Galli, staring at me".

"The physicist?" She peered over her shoulder, expecting to see some long-haired bearded scientist leaning over her shoulder.

"He looks so disappointed in me. Every night when I sleep. And Jeri. I'm terrified I'm going to lose her."

"Because of me." Jess put her mug down and sat forward, ready to leave.

"Not like that. It's... I can't help feeling like something terrible is going to happen to her. I mean... you know what I mean. My nerves are destroyed."

"Guilt can eat away at your subconscious."

"There's guilt. Plenty of it. But it's more than that."

"What does Jeri think?"

"She wants me to forget about it. Pretend it's not happening. I don't know. I can't really talk to her about it."

"How is she?" Jessica cringed, a double-edged question that she probably didn't want to ask but had to ask.

"Shit." My life's shit. My marriage is shit. And I know it's my fault but I'm also pretty sure there's nothing I can do about it."

We sat in silence, but it wasn't uncomfortable. She leaned back in her chair and broke the quiet. "This project Rick's on. What's the big deal?"

"I..." I wanted to tell her more, but I couldn't get her involved. Have to play it smart this time. "I don't know. I just thought he should have told me, I guess."

Jess eyed me, unconvinced. "Bob doesn't seem to know anything about it. Rick denied it when you left. Then he said something about me not being ambitious enough. I love the guy but when it comes to work, he's such a dick."

"Tell me about it."

"It was after I shouted at him though." Jess' eyes drifted. I took another sip and laid my cup down. When I looked back up Jess was staring at me. "If we had met first, maybe... maybe things would be different?"

"Jess-"

"No, please. I don't want to know. Either way it'll do me no good. Because I was second. So, go home." After a gentle sigh, her sad eyes were replaced by a smile of contentment. "Sit down with your wife and tell her how you feel and ask her to understand, or to at least listen. Tell her whatever it is you're not telling me."

"I can't"

"You fucking better. Or you will lose her. This shit that life throws at you, and just expects you to deal with, that's exactly the kind of shit that people who love each other are supposed to deal with together."

I lifted my hand up to Jess in some pitiful attempt to reject her advice. "Too much has happened. I've tried."

"Have you?"

"It's hard. It's so fucking hard."

"I know. I know. But I'm pretty sure it's worth it."

* * *

I spent the rest of the day driving aimlessly around DC, Jess' words running through my mind on a loop. I arrived about an hour after dark, the same time I would have if I had finished work at the usual time. As soon as I pulled into the driveway, I saw my front door wide open, but there was no one in sight and I couldn't see any lights on. I ran inside. Everything in the hallway had been tossed around and the living room was the same.

"Ryan?" Jeri shouted. "Is that you?"

I darted upstairs where Jeri was hunched over at the end of the bed smearing tears across her cheek. "What happened? Are you ok?" I examined her but I couldn't see any sign of injury. "Are you hurt?"

"I couldn't stop them."

"Who?"

"They searched everywhere, they wouldn't tell me what they were looking for."

"Who did?" My patience was gone, and I was ready to give it to whichever bastard had broken into my home. I picked up a brass candlestick off the dresser, brandishing it in case they hadn't yet escaped.

"They were from the government. What's happening?" Jeri's voice was almost pitiful. "Why are the government searching our house?"

My heart sank. There was no good reason for the government to search your home. "You're not hurt?" Jeri shook her head.

I paced around the room, trying to keep a clear head, but I knew this was it, Jeri wouldn't let this go without answers. "I was contacted by someone. His girlfriend went missing, and… she was found dead."

"What are you talking about? Who's dead?"

"Rebecca… But I… I got security files from US Tech, they were restricted to level 20, and her name was on a list of persons of interest-"

"You're level 10," Jeri interrupted. "They moved you up to level 20?"

"I got it from Timothy Calderbank."

"You stole it?"

"You haven't seen what's in those files. It all ties together."

Jeri put her hand to her mouth and recoiled. I knew it was hard for her, but it had gone too far. She had to know the truth. "I don't want to hear it," she groaned through the gaps between her fingers.

"Jeri, we're both on that list."

The expression on Jeri's face had unmistakably turned to one of horror. I was expecting her to get her head around a mire of questions and unknowns but there was no time for anything else.

"I know it's a lot to take, but I can prove it to you." I dashed into the study and scurried through the drawer, but the flash drive was gone. I lay on the carpet and reached into the compartment under the closet and stretched my fingers out, but the printed copies were gone. They knew exactly what they were looking for.

I grabbed my laptop and took it into the bedroom. Jeri hadn't moved. I took my original flash drive out of my pocket, plugged it into my laptop and switched it on. "They took my backups, but I've got the original." Jeri stared into dead air ahead of her. I had never seen such worry in her eyes. Part of the reason that I fell in love with her was her inner strength and resilience, but she looked like a broken woman. "I don't know how they found out I have them," I muttered to myself.

Jeri broke her silence, and when she did her voice boomed. "Look at what you're doing to us. Is it worth it? Ask yourself, is it worth it?"

I wrapped my hands around hers and held them close to me. "I'm sorry. But it has to be."

Jeri pulled at my arm, squirming in front me. "I'm asking you, please, just let it go."

"I'm trying to protect you."

"You're tearing us apart."

"Jeremy… he thought there was some kind of cover-up." Jeri escaped to the corner of the room and dug her fingers into her temple. "You need to listen to me. The government came looking for these files. That proves that Jeremy wasn't some UFO nut searching the Internet. He knew something real and it's right here."

"Aliens?"

"I know how it sounds. But the files... You need to see them."

Jeri was horrified. Her voice became quiet. "How did I let this happen? How could I let it go this far?"

"It all makes sense. The dreams. The trances, the-"

Jeri cut me off before I could finish. "The time loss? You told me you would drop it. You promised me." She spoke slowly and quietly so I could barely hear her, "I... I can't believe this. I thought we were getting over it."

"I'm finally trying to tell you everything. I know how it sounds." My heart beat faster, I was losing control. My arms and legs shook as I paced up and down the room. I took a deep breath. Hate and rage and anxiety boiled over; images churned through my mind, taking away my control. "I'm trying to protect you."

"You don't need to protect me."

"I know how strong you are, stronger than me. But you don't understand. These dreams are happening to me for a reason. I can save you."

"I can't handle this right now. I can't be here." Jeri didn't say another word. She turned her back to me, picked up her overnight bag and stuffed it with clothes.

I took hold of her hand and gently turned her around. Black mascara stained her face once more, spreading across the collar of her shirt. My voice became a whisper. "I'm doing this for you."

Jeri turned her head away from me, stretching her neck out as though I was a disgusting creature that she must avert her eyes from. Her hand slipped out of mine and she walked out. I heard my car engine start and then she was gone.

Only one thought was in my mind: I love her so much.

After everything that happened, I expected that we would never be happy again, not true happiness, not contentment. We might get through the day together, we might find a rare moment to take some small pleasure from, but life could never again be what it once was. Despite this, despite the pain that came from being around each other, the constant reminder of what we had lost, what we could have had, I couldn't let her go. Without Jeri there is nothing left of me.

I sat in front of the laptop, ready to immerse myself once more, to let the rest of the world drift away. But I was anchored down by the sound of Jeri's voice, telling me that I am tearing us apart. She's so much stronger than me, able to step away, to do what needs to be done.

A box popped up on the screen 'Deleting files'. I hadn't asked to delete anything. I hit escape, enter, every button I could press. But it was too late. The box ran its course and disappeared. I refreshed the drive, but it was empty. All trace of Jeremy's files was gone.

TWELVE

Morning approached and I had slept like a caffeine-addicted insomniac. The one time I nodded off, I woke minutes later clutching my head in pain. The nightmare was the same, but I felt only cold, sweat soaked sheets where Jeri once lay. I stretched out for the DNA tracker. Jeri was still at the Regent Falls hotel. It was never meant as a way to keep tabs on her, but without any contact, it was my only indication she was safe. Though it did little to ease my fears.

I had been suspended from work for three days without pay for accessing confidential and secure files without required security clearance. Bob apologised profusely for reporting me. He said it was his job, that he didn't know they were going to search my house. Bob had never done a thing in his life that wasn't by the book, protocol, following the rules.

"What did you expect?" I had asked him.

Still, I was lucky to keep my job, and only did so because I lied, telling the internal security intelligence team that I had accessed them from a non-secure drive, that someone else must have put them there, with no mention of the Jacob Reences account. And I accepted responsibility for not reporting it. Still, someone must have pulled some serious strings for me to get away with it. Because they believed I hadn't proactively retrieved the files I wasn't considered a security threat, so I was allowed to attend the State dinner at the White House, though Bob told me it was a definite no, until a last-minute swing decision from on high to let me go. Probably to mitigate any negative impact to public perception – particularly as I had been so closely linked to the White Giant and one thing our CEO Elliot Brandon hated was a scandal – but it only served to ramp up my paranoia.

In that time, a press statement was released about an Earth-to-Orbit shuttle that had been prototyped through a joint venture between US Tech and NASA, but there was no mention that the shuttle had already commenced production. Rick had been lying to me the whole time.

Without Jeri or work, there was nothing to occupy my attention, so it was early afternoon before I left my bed. Jeremy's trail had run out, and what I did have had evaporated from my possession. I was adrift in the water with barely a fucking doggy paddle to keep me afloat. I took the State Dinner invitation out of my drawer. Only a few hours to go. The timing was bittersweet; a good opportunity to corner Rick, now my only lead, but I dreaded the possibility of attending without Jeri. I wanted to call her, but I was too scared to do anything except give her space. I spent an hour watching the door and when the phone rang, I jumped up to answer it. When I heard Herb's voice my whole body slumped. He was checking what time I wanted him to pick us up. I couldn't bring myself to tell him that I had no idea if Jeri would even be going with me.

I took out my tux and hung it on the front of the closet. I can't go. Not alone. I finally plucked up the courage to pick up my cell phone and called her, but it went straight to voicemail. I closed my eyes and listened to her soft voice, and for the briefest of moments, I felt content. As the inevitable beep came and Jeri's message ended, the recording of the words she once spoke stung like they were taunting me, their friendly tone not meant for me.

I picked up my tux and started to undress. If there was even a chance that Jeri was going to show up there, I couldn't risk leaving her alone.

$$* * *$$

A beat-up orange pickup truck, still possessing a lingering odour of animal faeces was definitely not how I had dreamed of arriving at the White House. But Herb insisted on driving us so he could get as close to the event and the White House as possible, and he refused to drive any car but his own. I hadn't possessed the will to object more than twice. The oncoming headlights reflected off the front of Herb's balding head.

"Talk about cheese."

"What?" I asked, trying to work out how ten minutes of silence had led to a conversation about cheese.

"President Walker likes cheese."

"Thanks for the tip," I said with sarcasm, but Herb gave a 'you're welcome' nod for his wisdom.

"I just want to get close to it, you know? Not inside, just in the vicinity." Herb looked at me expectantly to show an interest. I hoped he would return to quiet – my desire for small talk reaching an all-time low – but it was rare, so I didn't hold out much hope. "So, how are things with you two?"

"Good. Things are good." I answered without conviction and my mind still partially on cheese.

"It's not at all odd that she's meeting you there." A raised eyebrow accompanied Herb's childish grin. I didn't respond so he waited a few seconds and then pressed, "You sure you're, ok?"

"I'm fine," I said, painfully aware that my private conversations with Herb were never private when Jeri was involved, a lesson I should have learned a long time ago.

"How's the job?" Herb gave me a couple of glances

while trying to keep his eye on the road.

"Fine."

"How are you sleeping?"

"Fine. I'm just under a lot of pressure recently." Shit. As soon as I said it, I knew I was in for pain.

"I thought you said there was nothing wrong."

"You know, work stuff, I guess." Over the years Herb's hair had created indents in each corner of his forehead in a bid to retreat from his face. The indents began to annoy me.

Herb took a long pause. He tried to act coy; unwillingly making it obvious in the process that he was building up to something. "You still see her at work, don't you?" he blurted out followed by a grimace that turned his double chin into a triple. "Even after the party?"

"Stay out of it, Herb."

"Just looking out for you, little brother."

"Looking out for me? Are you serious? You told Jeri I blacked out. That I didn't believe I was just off getting drunk somewhere for three days."

"She's your wife. You're supposed to tell her yourself."

"That's none of your fucking business."

"Cool it. I'm doing you a favour here." I gritted my teeth and let out a deep growl of infuriation. "You're going to lose that woman one day, I swear. And Dad says I'm the screw up."

If I had bitten my tongue, I would have bitten it clean off. I had to fight every urge in my body to jump out of my seat and choke his bloated neck. One thing my marriage didn't need was Herb's festering interference. The rest of the journey was in stone cold silence. I'd press my fist through his face rather than say another word to him.

"Have fun," he said as he got his vicinity and drove off. Asshole.

I walked to the Entrance Hall door at the rear of the White House as instructed, passing through tight, but efficient security to reach a sea of photographers snapping away at the guests. Everyone I saw was holding hands, wrapped arms around each other, or at least gave the occasional peck, and here I was, all alone. Herb still had me seething. I wasn't sure if it was because he was so irritating, or because I knew he was right. I never had a problem talking to Jeri about anything before. Bastard.

Inside the massive marble-walled hallway, imposing portraits of the most recent Presidents were hung every few metres. A few guests ahead of me were mingling, leaving the lone stray trailing slightly behind and excluded from any conversation. I hoped that Jeri wouldn't let me down, that she would be waiting for me. She left her blue ball gown that she looked so elegant still hanging in her wardrobe, but maybe she had bought something new.

The massive East Room and its immaculate white walls were already filled with people. Only a few steps in, I caught a glimpse of Bob and his wife across the hall. I ducked my head, not wanting him to see me there without Jeri. I knew the team at US Tech would be sat separately amongst the one hundred and forty guests, so I had the sound plan to avoid them completely, at least until Jeri arrived. Air Force Honour guards in full dress uniform lined the immaculately white walls and I was guided to my table, but the only thing waiting for me was an empty silver seat and curious glances from the guests sat on either side of me. I looked up and saw cupids and flowers engraved into the ceiling. And I cursed myself for everything that had led to this.

Once the guests were all seated, Jean-Luc Franco, the phenomenal concert pianist accompanied the entrance of President William Walker and his wife Betty into an otherwise silent room. They stopped behind a long, rectangular table in the centre of the guests, warm smiles beaming from both of their faces. Jean-Luc's piece ended, and President Walker said a few words on behalf of himself and his wife Betty, about how there was no shortage of astonishing people to celebrate and that we were all astonishing people. I kept getting lost in my own thoughts, so I missed chunks. I thought about how the moment should have felt to me. I knew that I should be proud, but my lack of pride or pleasure only made me feel that I deserved to be there even less.

President Walker finished with a quote from George Washington: "Let there be no sectionalism, no North, South, East or West. You are all dependent on one another and should be one in union. In one word, be a nation." President Walker gave a subtle nod of respect to a full-length portrait of George Washington behind him, holding out one hand and holding a blade in the other. After resounding applause, President Walker left the stage.

Seated to my right was the wife of Remy Johnson, Point Guard for the Chicago Bulls, who spent most of dinner picking up her husband's finger to flash his newly won championship ring around the room. On the left, an empty seat away, a state official, Olivia Greene introduced herself and did her best to lean towards me for an exchange or two with me, but I struggled to muster anything that resembled an interesting conversation. If only Jeri had been here. Tonight, would have been so different.

Or would it? With the current state of our relationship, maybe it would have been a disaster. I pictured Jeri storming out like she did at the White Giant party at the first sight of Jessica. Despite the loving relationship she portrayed while we were in company, Jess was the potential spark that could set her off at any moment.

When all of this is over, I need to find a new job.

* * *

After four courses, we were ushered into the massive state dining room, where dinner had usually been served since 1874, but President Walker liked to do things differently, using the room as the after-dinner venue. I was eyeing the room, from the intricate carvings of the crisp white walls to the delicate twelve foot gold mirror when I felt someone approach from behind. I turned and saw two instantly recognisable faces. "Good evening, Mr Ellis. It's a pleasure to see you again." Vice President Robert Palmer's hand was held out towards me, paired with a warm smile. As I shook it, he continued, "Mr President, allow me to introduce you to Ryan Ellis."

"Mr President." Charisma exuded from him, his presence filing the room as he shook my hand as at least half of the guests looked on. "It's such an honour to meet you, Sir."

"And you, Ryan. I hope you're enjoying the evening?" Words poured out of his mouth, slow and easy.

I marvelled around the room at the fine wool rug that matched the moulding of the ceiling and the dozens of lights mounted on the walls and were hung from the elegant gold chandelier. Despite how impressive I knew it was in my rational brain to be standing here in this company, I was emotionally unaffected. But I had become far too proficient at feigning enthusiasm. "This whole estate is fascinating. It must be incredible to live here."

"It is. I know how fortunate I am."

I desperately tried to pull myself together and make a good impression on them both and realised I had lost track of President Walker's words. His gentle gaze was upon me, pressing for a response. I waited for him to say more and gave a feint panic laugh, but neither laughed along.

"Come on, William," Vice President Palmer said, and I let out a breath. "You can't ask a young man that."

President Walker laughed, and I laughed along, the tension seeping away. As I focussed my mind, I gestured to my side to introduce Jeri. The empty space at my side sucked every spec of happiness I should have had. I could do nothing but leave my hand jutting out awkwardly.

VP Palmer rested his hand on my shoulder, sweeping my unease away. "Ryan delivered an excellent presentation to me about the White Giant, he's the mechanical engineer that deduced how to build nanotube structures large enough to support building structures. He's quite the genius." Apart from collapsing in the middle of the speech.

President Walker nodded with a smile. "Yes, very impressive. Based on Galli's theory?"

"That's right."

"And you weren't too well, I recall." VP Palmer said. "How are you now?"

"Much better, thank you."

"Are you here alone?" William glanced at the ring on my finger. I struggled to conjure a convincing answer that didn't peg me as pathetic and pulled out the first thing that came to mind.

"My wife... she's sick. Really bad cold." William gave an understanding nod, and he reminded me of my father. It was the kindness in his eyes, like a Labradors.

"That's a shame," VP Palmer said. "I would have liked to have met your wife."

"She's devastated not to be here. She's been looking forward to meeting all of the guests, especially both of you, of course."

The Vice President laughed. "We're probably the most boring two at the party, eh William?" President Walker laughed along, seemingly in genuine agreement. "Anyway, I'm sure this won't be the last opportunity she gets."

President Walker shook his head, "I'm sure it won't."

"Ryan also created the first DNA tracker prototype." VP Palmer clearly had his staff prep him about me before our meeting.

"Such a marvellous invention," President Walker replied. "Though, you may know, I wasn't entirely supportive of the technology. The potential for misuse is staggering, of course."

"Of course. As it is with most technical advancements, it's what you do with it that counts."

"Precisely," President Walker nodded. His demeanour was gentle but firm. I easily imagined him calmly picking up his son or daughter after they had fallen and dusting them off. Carrying grandchildren to a rowboat to sail across the lake at the crack of dawn.

"While I was developing it, I imagined people holed up in a dark room tracking the whereabouts of every person on Earth."

"There were a few people that wanted it that way, you can believe that. But we must have faith in people, if they are to have any chance of doing the right thing." President Walker had secured a National Rights Act, which had, among other things prohibited the collection of DNA to be used in a tracker without a person's consent, especially prohibiting any type of central or government held information. There was much opposition across various security agencies due to the potential opportunities against crime and terrorism, but liberty had won the day. A liberty I had both supported and then betrayed, to ease my own fears.

"I do wonder," I said noticing that I was in the swing of conversation, "whether it should be used for criminals. Can you imagine how much it could reduce burglaries, or murder? The difference it could make to innocent people's lives?"

"It's a dangerous road, segregation always is," President Walker replied, the friendliness in his voice reminding me of the growl that dogs give off to warn other dogs away.

"But the likelihood of re-offence-"

"May be high but may not be helped by keeping tabs on people."

"Criminals deserve to be punished."

"Perhaps, but it doesn't stop them doing it again."

"So, you're saying we should let criminals off the hook? Let them destroy some other innocent person's life?"

"I'm saying that when a person makes a mistake, they are often greeted by a hostile hand, when often all they really need is help." President Walker's face became sombre. I regretted not taking the conversation down a lighter tone, but that was difficult in the frame of mind I was in. "I'm afraid I have to mingle. Before my wife comes to collect me." He smiled at me, and I gave a brief smile back. "Enjoy the rest of the evening. I look forward to our next meeting; hopefully, we will have more time for you to tell me about your next great achievement."

Vice President Palmer nodded to me as he and William moved to a group of guests that I didn't recognise. I blew it. Why couldn't I have talked about cheese?

I felt a heavy hand weigh on my shoulder. Vice President Palmer's face leaned in towards mine. "Most people wouldn't dream of holding their ground against the President like that, even one as reasonable as William. You're almost as stubborn as he is. I'm impressed." He grabbed a glass of champagne from a passing waiter and smacked me on the back twice before he walked through a parting of the guests.

I was left loitering at a beautiful white mantel, two bison heads among the intricate carvings and adorned by two ornate candlestick holders. Thanks to Vice President Palmer, I congratulated myself on not completely ruining my first meeting with the President and looked up at the large portrait of President Lincoln sat, leaning forward expectedly. Below it was an inscription:

> *I pray Heaven to Bestow the Best of Blessings on THIS HOUSE and on All that shall hereafter Inhabit it. May none but honest and Wise Men ever rule under this roof.*

* * *

The first trans-shuttle set off to a tent the size of a football field where the evening event was being held. I boarded the second with another two-dozen guests, heading for the party in search of Rick and the truth.

The giant tent housed all of the guests, three bars, a dancefloor, stage and plenty of amenities and bared no resemblance to a tent at all. When I entered, I was surrounded by guests that should have had me bouncing off the walls with excitement: the governor of California, Nobel prize winner and physicist Pieter Baddiel, and the lead singer of the Dead Scarecrows. With a Futurist theme, the place was littered with silver and black decor, wavy glowing tables, and thick, domed chairs clustered around the room. I found Rick at the outskirts of the party, close to a ten foot, abstract-style, metal weeping willow. He introduced me to his date who stood underneath the tree, its branches wilting just above her head. Rick told me that she was there in honour of her father, Heinrich Galli. After the briefest of introductions, Rick said he was going to get us all a drink. I tried to follow but he stopped and insisted I stay with Vera before he voyaged off. I resisted causing a scene, doing my best to learn from at least one of my mistakes.

Vera only occasionally looked up from her last drop of wine, and when she did, it was to observe guests talking in small circles around the room, or the few that had started to dance at a little before 8pm. I couldn't take my eyes off her. I couldn't believe that the daughter of the man I so revered and devastatingly never got to meet was standing right in front of me. Even without Jeri with me, I thought I might be able to salvage some enjoyment from the night. "Are you having a good evening?"

"It's overwhelming." Vera said nervously. "There are so many expectations of you at an event such as this." A native of Switzerland, her German accent was still lurking beneath the more generic accent that most DC residents carry.

"I read your fathers books many times. You must be honoured." The image was burnt into my mind of Heinrich Galli's face, staring back at me with disappointment. "Your father, he…" I finished the sentence in my head. That I had been seeing his face every night whilst I slept, to ask her what it meant, why her father was haunting me, but I stopped long enough for Vera to interject.

"I was very reluctant to attend," she said, her face stern. I waited for her to continue but she didn't. If I hadn't spoken, she may have stood in silence until Rick returned.

"How do you know Rick?"

"Through a friend. We met once... briefly."

I knew her reaction was warning me to stay away from the subject, but I couldn't let the opportunity to give thanks in some way to the man who had such an influence on my early life pass me by. "Your fathers work helped me through difficult times-"

"My father caused me difficult times." She saw I was taken aback, and her face softened. "We are many things to many people, not all of them good." The awkward silence returned, and I spent every second regretting not going with Rick and leaving Vera where she stood. When Rick finally returned, we kept the conversation light and mostly about the event until Vera left us to use the ladies. Rick poured the remains of his whiskey down his throat, then stared ahead, clenching his teeth so hard I could see he cheeks tense.

"You don't look yourself," I said.

"I could say the same about you." Rick's grip on his glass was tightening. He let his gaze fall to the floor.

"Talk to me." My voice was severe. I had little patience for idle chatter or lies.

"I've got nothing to say."

I grabbed him by the collar of his suit, my face close enough that he could feel my breath against his cheek. "Tell me everything you know."

"About what?"

I clenched my fist, to sate the urge to throw him against the wall. "About the shuttles."

Rick knocked my hands off and backed away. "Don't start this again."

"They raided my fucking house!" Surprise filled Rick's face and I got more than a few looks of disapproval from the guests that heard me over the music. I managed a few deep breaths to calm myself. "They tore the place apart."

Rick grabbed my arm and pulled me away from the crowd. "Who did? What the hell is going on with you?"

131

"The government. They took everything I had. Bob reported me."

"You can't spout off about classified information and not expect ramifications. What did they take? What did you have?" Rick leaned in for an answer. My eyes roamed around the room, anywhere but on Rick. He gave an exaggerated sigh like I was another disappointment.

"Why didn't you just come to me?" he asked.

"I did."

"In private."

"So, you would have come clean?" I felt the anger remerge.

Rick shoved his hand in his pockets. "It was a classified project, you know protocol, I could lose my job."

I shook my head at him.

"Come on, it's NASA we're dealing with," he said, his expression sympathetic. "I couldn't even tell Bob. It's a shuttle project, for fuck's sake. It's a big deal, but there's nothing more to it than that." I stared into Rick's eyes, waiting for him to flinch but he didn't. I knew when Rick was lying and when he was telling the truth, and there was nothing in his face that told me it was a lie. My own fears had gotten the better of me. If I couldn't trust Rick, then I couldn't trust anyone. And that was a notion that could ramp up my paranoia passed ten. He stepped closer to me, and his voice quietened to a level that I could barely hear over the music. "What's got you so worked up about it anyway?"

I had been burned by trying to tell Jeri the truth and I had no idea if Rick would react any better. I couldn't risk him telling Bob, not even for the right reasons, who would force me to take leave, or get me sacked, and I couldn't lose access to US Tech. Even worse, I could take Rick down with me. I watched the guests moving around the dance floor, all of them in pairs. "Jeri left me."

"Shit, Ryan, I'm sorry. For good?"

"I don't know. I thought she would be here." I rested

my arm on his shoulder. "I think I'm going to head home."

"No, stay." I pulled a face, but Rick wasn't about to give up. "When will you have the chance to party at the White House again? Come on. I think Vera likes you." I laughed and thanked him in my head for getting that out of me. "Well, at least she likes you more than she likes me." As much as every part of me wanted to curl up in a ball at home and wallow in self-pity, Rick had a knack for pulling me out of a hard time, so I gave in and spent the rest of the evening with my best friend.

* * *

I took a cab home, earning me an angry voicemail from Herb to say he would wait another ten minutes before he would leave me there alone, which I ignored.

When I arrived home, I felt exhausted but I couldn't bear another night in bed alone, so I stopped at the sofa and lay down; pulling a thin blanket over my body like it was an afternoon nap. Taking care to make sure it covered me completely, I held it tightly under my chin. The shoulder pads of my tuxedo trapped my shoulders, but I was so tired that I didn't notice it after a while. A few creaks in the room caught my attention but not enough to stop my heavy eyes from closing, finally giving in to sleep.

I leapt from the sofa, completely alert. The blanket fell to the floor. I didn't know how much time had passed but it was still dark outside. I felt someone in the room with me.

I stepped towards the hallway, about to shout Jeri's name and the carpet squelched between my toes. Something touched my neck. I spun around but there was no one there. I reached under my shirt collar. My fingers were drenched in oil.

A blinding light bleached the whole room white. I cowered behind my forearm, able to see less than if it was pitch black. Something slimy stroked my cheek. I pressed my hand against it and found oil dripping off my face. A caress on the back of my neck.

I spun round and shouted out, but the words disappeared into a vacuum. A silhouette darted past me and stopped a few feet away. I squinted, barely able to make out the figure in front of me. My legs became shaky, scarcely able to support my body. I couldn't feel my toes. Gradually, the loss of sensation travelled up my body, until I hit the ground, struggling to breathe. A cold breeze blew against my neck making me shiver. I shouted only half of her name before my voice no longer worked. My eyes rolled to the back of my head and the world around me seemed to merge as I became lost in a sea of red light.

THIRTEEN

Sirens roared around me, urging me inside. I stalled as long as I could, knuckles white, until the ache in my stomach that had kept me at a standstill made it impossible to stay outside any longer. I felt every second. The anguish. The anxiety. The pain. I couldn't bare the pain.

I watched through the glass at distorted shadows moving inside the hospital room until one approached the door. It's my turn. I don't want a turn, why does anybody have to have a turn?

The door shut behind me and I realised I was now the one peering out through the glass at figures in the corridor outside, wishing I was on the other side. There was no escaping it. Everything was silent – not only the absence of voice or any other sound made inside the room, but everything outside of it seemed to have stopped. Jeri's head was buried in my father's shoulder, and she only looked up for the tears to run off her face. But I still couldn't hear a sound.

A calm voice emerged from behind Jeri, so soft, so gentle. "It doesn't hurt." How can she say that? How can she lie to me? "I lived a happy life. With my two beautiful boys, two wonderful men. And my lovely husband." She looked up at my dad and they shared an identical smile. She looked back at me, smiling as much as she could. "They need you. To keep our family together. They're too much alike." My dad grumbled behind me, shuffling from foot to foot. "They love each other, but they're too much alike." She stroked my arm, but I could barely feel it. "I love you, my boy. My beautiful boy." The silence was bearing down on me. I couldn't bear to speak. I hoped the words didn't need to be said, that everything in my heart was already felt. I didn't let a single tear out; they could wait. I held her hand, leaned down and rested my head.

Her life meant something. Her passing did not.

It was just another loss, another death blow, a hint of things to come: the misery, the pain. It all has to start somewhere, converting a happy life into an unbearable existence. Gradual at first, always gradual and then, bang. Something hits you. Maybe someone's dead. Maybe you lost someone into the abyss.

Bang! Your life is changed.

Bang! Your life is over.

Bang! You're dead. And now it's everyone else's turn. You just fucked up the lives of all of those around you, taking away one of the masquerades of joy that you were in their fabricated lives. If only you had known what you would eventually become to them, maybe you would have disappeared long ago, before any attachments could be made. Or let the whole thing turn sour until they resented you and you became just another regret. 'I couldn't stand that kid,' they would say when it happened. 'That Ryan kid. What a shame. I couldn't stand him though.' It would be better that way.

I felt her slipping away from me, leaving gradually and taking a part of me with her. I wasn't selfish when it happened. I wasn't thinking of my pain, or my suffering. Any consideration of me never entered my head. Not with everything she was going through, everyone she was leaving behind. I could have wailed right there if I thought she couldn't hear me. I could have splattered my head against the wall just to escape the unbearableness, could have drunk all the morphine on the ward if she didn't need me. But all she wanted was to have her family around her as she said goodbye. To give her that, my torment could wait.

* * *

Lake Ontario glistens in front of me, a mirror of the perfect blue sky. The sun beams down on us, white rocks peeking out from lush greenery, trees hanging over the edges. The air is crisp but all three of us are wrapped in thick jackets. Jeri grabs my shoulder from across the bench and pulls me closer to her. Her eyes are wide and seem bigger than they had been, more optimistic. Jeri's hair flows; golden, like it's breathing and feeling all by itself. She stretches her arm out and prepares to take the photo when another head pops up between us.

She fits perfectly, pressing her cheeks against the two of ours. We all smile and watch the red light of the camera blink. Jeri pushes her face towards me, lips protruding out, and eyes closed. I hear giggling, and Jeri and I open an eye each, our lips still pressed together. The beautiful little girl stands grinning in front of us, blue jeans tucked into her welly's, her hands held out to us, such kindness in her eyes. Jeri rests her hands on her stomach, where the little girl used to be. I hold out my hands to her, but I can't reach, she seems so far away.

The lake before us, the sun behind, I lean closer to Jeri's stomach until my cheek touches her skin. "I'll never forget you. I promise."

I tried again to reach out, but I could barely move my arm. Jeri was still by my side, but my little girl was almost out of sight. The sky turned grey, pulsating with light. It felt like the oxygen was being sucked out of the air. I heaved to inhale until my chest hurt. My tongue felt so dry it was like leather cracking, my teeth piercing the skin. I became so lightheaded that everything turned into a blur. I wanted to grip my throat with both hands to force air down it, but I couldn't move my arms. A feeling started at my shoulder, only slight at first but becoming increasingly painful, like air was being pushed into my pores and through my skin. My body seared with pain as I drifted in and out of consciousness until air was shoved into my lungs like it didn't fit. My body jolted and spasmed, but something held me down. I tried desperately to see more than the translucent grey ceiling above, but I couldn't lift my head high enough to see anything. Metal lay underneath my body, cold as steel, a thick glob that moved with every part of my body during the tiny adjustments I made. It covered my face and pinned me down like I was clinically insane. It flexed as I wrestled with it and tried to break free of my constraints.

I attempted to sit up, but my arms were numb as hell and couldn't support the weight. I tried again, arching my back to get high enough to see my legs but my neck snapped back down under the force of the thin metal that covered my face.

Jeri. My mind entered a whirl of panic. I clambered as high as I could, fighting against the blanket that covered me. I have to find her. I have to keep her safe. I have to get out and I'll… I'll…

I sank back down under the force of my freezing cold restraint. Utterly helpless.

Why did I welcome this? What good is the truth when I'm dead and can't do anything about it?

I kept as still as possible. The metal-like blanket steamed up with every heavy breath I took. Shadows appeared as the light pulsated from the ceiling, then disappeared into darkness. My body froze. Wheezing. Scared. Alone. Terrified of what might be happening to Jeri.

The walls around me were different, only barely but enough to realise I was drifting slowly around the room, rising from the ground. I held my breath long enough to see a large liquid filled container. There was something floating inside but I couldn't make it out. I strained harder and held my breath for longer until I made out a dog's head bobbing up and down, completely detached of its body. More containers were spread around the edge of the domed room with lambs and calves, their limbs and faces mutilated and deformed. Then the last. I squeezed my eyes shut to keep from welcoming my own death. Unlike the others, its human limbs were perfectly formed; two legs almost touching the bottom and two arms floating by its side. It stood two feet tall with soft pink skin and black glassy eyes dominating its mouthless head.

I was too afraid to open my eyes again. They won't leave me here forever. They'll be back. Or are they still here? Are they here right now, surrounding me? If I open my eyes, will I see them?

My breathing became more rapid. I squirmed to break free, but with every pitiful attempt I was tighter in its grip. I prayed for release.

The only sound was a steady hum and the faintness of my breathing. I gathered any courage I had left, held my breath, and forced my eyes wide open.

I jolted back. My own petrified face stared back at me in the harsh black reflection, a glassy eye protruding out at me. The metal sheet that covered me was stripped away, leaving my head exposed except for a small piece that remained over my mouth. Its grey face leaned closer, moist skin dripped onto my skin. My stomach wrenched and the metal blanket sank further down my throat until I choked.

I was desperate to scream but it wouldn't have mattered if could; the thing had no ears or mouth. It floated above me, almost translucent, arms bent and angled into a complete circle. The creature extended its arm quickly as more surrounded me, drifting closer. Their limbs retracted and extended in turn like a ritual, clicking in my ears with every movement.

Its spindly fingers stretched out at me, nearly touching. I jerked back as far as I could. Its arms retracted suddenly.

And then it started all over again, pointing at my face, an inch away from my skin. There was nothing I could do to stop it. I closed my eyes and thought about how worthless I had become, wanting to know the truth, trying desperately to understand my nightmares. And now this is where it ends. I whispered a silent sorry to Jeri, wherever she was, and awaited my fate, praying for release.

Four slimy fingers stroked my temple. One slid down my face, leaving a wet trail behind. I could almost see myself lying there covered, starved of oxygen. My insides felt cold and empty. My eyes were closing but there was no bright light and no one to welcome me. I felt trapped by more than the restraints that pinned me down. With a gasp I managed a breath, enough to keep me conscious. And then it started again, like I was being pulled out of my own skin. My breathing slowed until it stopped completely. The quiet of the room was lost to a barrage of high-pitched wails and screeches. The world around me turned whiter, until the pieces broke apart, floating freely, unbound by the ties of reality. And then the deafening noise became clear.

I no longer felt afraid. I felt nothing at all.

FOURTEEN

The air swelters around me with an impossible intensity. Of all the disconnected moments in time, this one leaves me ill at ease with my surroundings. Winds rage, tossing the dust that has fallen to the street, causing me to hide my face. Jeri stands at my side with her head tilted away from me, a warmth radiating from her that makes my skin tingle. I shroud her hand in mine; embraced. This is what it has all been leading to. This is where it ends.

The sky above lets out a trickle that lands on my shoulder before it runs off and falls to the ground. It won't be long until the fury, and the clouds let out a storm.

A man stares at me, a long flowing mane and wild hair across his face. All I can see of him is his head and shoulders – that is all I have ever seen of him, of dear Mr Galli. His brow furrows. I look to him for answers but it's too late.

They line up in the thousands, each one terrifies me. They can do what they want to me, but they can't take her. Please, not this time; please don't let them take her. I'll do anything. Her head hits the ground without the gentleness that I would hope for. Her fingertips burn as they're torn from mine. She looks so scared.

She is gone and I'm too weak, always too weak.

The thin fabric of time rips apart in my fingers. The light it spat out hurts my eyes, tastes of aluminum. The space where Jeri once stood by my side is empty. She's so far away. I reach out in desperation but there is nothing left.

My fury builds, amassing into a blinding rage. Bodies cover the pavement, ready to be blown away in the wind. Blood and devastation, from bombs and bullets and so much worse. There is nothing left.

It is the end of the world.

And I am all alone.

FIFTEEN

The rear wall of my house phased in and out of focus, awaiting my return. It seemed only minutes had passed, but my grasp on time was wavering. Every hair on my body felt like it was standing on end. My head ached. The sun that had risen that morning hurt my eyes. I didn't squint; I felt the uneasiness.

Four words. I couldn't get them out of my head.

Paradoxical end. Unveil. Transcend.

I stumbled towards the house and stopped, absorbing my surroundings. They were different than before. The flowers were brighter, their smell reaching me from a few feet away. Their soft, delicate touch reached out to me through the dirt and grass beneath my bare feet. The veil that draped over the world flickered in front of me ever so slightly, revealing something beyond it, like the word that you know in your deep consciousness, but can't quite summon to leave your lips.

I wandered further, the air buzzing around me, the breeze keeping me upright, until I found the door into the house. I stretched my fingers out and touched it to see if it was real, felt the smoothness and the occasional jaggedness of the wood grain, the skin wrapped around my fingertips smeared its way down, but I still wasn't convinced. I lost my footing and tripped on a plant pot, spilling it onto its side with a clatter. I steadied myself as the door swung open. As soon as she saw me, Jeri's eyes flared wide open. Her face filled with fear and desperation. She hesitated before she spoke.

"Where have you been?" I couldn't answer. "I called the police; I told them you were missing." Jeri continued talking and the words drifted on by like music that was satisfied to float in the background not demanding to be heard. The breakfast table behind her drew my attention, dangling between the ceiling and the floor, struggling to understand its place, its purpose.

"Worried... Help... Gone..."

I had seen that table so many times before – even used it – but only then did I truly understand it. I took a plate out of the cupboard and placed it on top. I stood back and admired what I had done. Jeri's panic was only interrupted by herself. "Ryan? What are you doing, you're trembling." She was shaking herself. "Ryan, your face. Your face is so pale. What happened to you? Please, speak to me."

Jeri rested her hand on my cheek but removed it quickly. She rubbed her fingers together trying to be subtle, but I noticed; my skin was drenched in oil. She was desperate for answers. Even more desperate for me to speak. As if that would let her know that I was ok. I opened my mouth to talk but no sound emerged. Blood dripped from my nose and off my chin. Jeri pulled a tissue from the box on the worktop, dabbed the red stain on my face and stopped the next droplet before it could form. She looked at me in a different way entirely.

"Tell me what happened to you. Where have you been?"

I no longer possessed the energy or will to speak. The daytime light had almost turned to shade in front of me, like a summer's day when the darkness creeps up on you from nowhere. I shook like a junkie, pumped up to the eyeballs and then going cold turkey the same day. I don't belong here.

Jeri pressed her palm so hard against her cheek that she became a waxwork that was slowly melting. She took an uneasy breath and pulled me by the hand into the living room and guided my body down to the sofa. "Ryan..." She stopped to compose herself, taking care to fully consider her words before she let them leave her mouth. "I came back here because... I've been waiting here for you to come home. To make sure you were safe. You see... you've been gone three days. And..." She stared at me, waiting for a response. In part, because she wanted an explanation from me, but mostly, because there was more, she had to say, and she didn't know how to say it. My eyes darted around the room, my body perfectly still. I assessed each corner, each item. I saw it all through new eyes. "I need to show you something." Jeri turned away from me sheepishly, cowering almost. She pressed a few buttons and the screen lit up. President Walker stood at the stage in the Brady Press Briefing Room at the White House.

After a long pause, he began to speak:

"Members of the press, I have invited you to this emergency announcement, because a day that we have so often imagined has finally arrived. I can now confirm that our ongoing search for extra-terrestrial life has reached a monumental point. Intelligent extra-terrestrial life has in fact visited our planet.

"We do not yet know their origin, but we believe that contact between humanity and the extra-terrestrial visitors has already occurred." The TV screen flickered with distortion.

There it was. I had all the proof and explanations I needed. Without any of the relief or satisfaction I had longed for.

I am as helpless now as I was in their captivity. They can take me away and there is nothing I can do about it. Whatever happens to Jeri, I've brought it upon her. I've led them to her. And I can do nothing to protect her. We're condemned, and there is no hope left.

I wouldn't let myself fall asleep. I hoped for Jeri to hold me in the night, but she didn't. I lay perfectly still, listening, waiting for them to come for me while the darkness hid their dripping wet faces. Holding out their shiny limbs, watching me with the void that is their black, glassy eyes. No sound to be heard from their mouthless faces.

I forced my eyes apart, willing the night to end, even though I knew the day would bring no more safety.

Tomorrow will be so strange.

SIXTEEN

Rain banged against the roof of my car like it was trying to get inside my head, but there was no space left to occupy. The roads were deserted. I could only assume that families had stayed at home for their own protection, but I knew that no house existed that would make you safe. The day resembled the morning of a funeral. I expected the moment to come when I would break down in tears because things were so dire, because everything had gone so wrong. But it never did. I couldn't bear a moment of happiness or hold a shred of hope after what I had seen. If only I had been crazy, at least everyone else would have been spared.

There would be others who had been taken and returned, and US Tech had already established strong ties to the government, so Jeri insisted that I go back to work because US Tech was my best chance of getting help.

The extreme desertedness of the streets was matched equally with the extreme of the populated and manic US Tech. I went straight to Bob's office to ask for help. He was rambling on the phone, moving papers around his desk in frenzy. I stepped inside and he waved his hand at me to sit down. Bob paced behind me to shut the door and then back around to the other side of his desk. "It's the big one. On

147

the seventh floor. Yes, he's here now. Ok." He hung up and took a massive breath.

"I need to talk to you." I had no idea how he would react to me being abducted. From one of the people who had 'made contact' it was not the momentous occasion that our President was describing it as.

"About what? And where were you yesterday?"

"I- "

"Never mind, we can talk later. Right now, I need you with me. The Vice-President is here. He asked for you personally, or so I'm told." Bob grabbed his tablet, hurried to the door and held it open for me.

"It can't wait."

"Didn't you hear me? The Vice President is here." He raced down the hall and into the elevator as I trailed behind. I tried twice more on the way down to floor seven, only to be told that now wasn't the time, before Bob dived inside the Executive meeting room on the left, where a dozen or so people filled seats at an oblong table. Bob stopped at the back of the room, so I stood next to him. I propped myself up against the wall and wished I had taken a seat. I only recognised a few faces around the room. Alex Little and Timothy Calderbank were sat on the right-hand side of me, engaged in a debate that I couldn't make out. Elliot Brandon, CEO of US Tech and Agent Brody sat at the far end of the table, either side of the only empty chair. The door opened and everyone in the room stood. Vice President Palmer entered and took the empty seat. I questioned exactly what I was in the middle of, and why Vice President Palmer would want me there. If they already knew about my abduction, surely, they wouldn't address it here, like this.

Good morning." The Vice President's voice instantly silenced all chatter around the table. "Now we're public, I'm sure all of you can appreciate how critical the next few days are. Cells across Washington have been tasked with various objectives during this crisis. With its advanced facilities, personnel and experience with untested circumstances, US Tech is now HQ, our base of operations for dealing with the extra-terrestrial situation. General Day will be posted here to lead Defence Operations." Vice President Palmer motioned to a woman in her early fifties, wearing full military uniform, the other side of Brody. Palmer leaned forward, his voice even more commanding than usual, "I cannot emphasise enough, the importance of this operation. Agent Brody will be my representative based here at US Tech. He will co-ordinate all areas from this building and will liaise with me directly."

Brody firmly placed one hand on the desk. "Thank you, Mr Vice President. There will be five operations," he said. "Identification, Recovery, Response, Communications, and Production. The first four are strictly R&D, under the supervision of Alex Little." Alex did his best to contain a smug grin, but it crept up at the sides of his mouth regardless. "Timothy Calderbank will then be responsible for moving the output into Production. Leads for R&D are Identification, Bob Blunt, Recovery, Karen Holmes, Response, Cedric Johnson, and Comms, Ryan Ellis."

I looked up at Brody, unsure if I heard him right. Apparently, Alex Little felt the same, "I need to review the new appointment for comms, Agent Brody. Ellis is not qualified-"

"The list is final," Brody stated calmly. Little's grin became a sneer. Bob gave me a nod with a half-smile of pride.

"How many abductees do we have in custody?" Karen Holmes asked. She was in her early forties with light blonde hair trailing down her back, her face permanently devoid of expression when she spoke.

Brody glared at her, but I wasn't sure whether it was because Holmes brought up the subject, or because she was taking Brody's brief on a tangent. "Ten additional. They're being prepped for assessment and interrogation before transfer to quarantine with the others. We're ramping up this operation significantly."

Assessment and interrogation. Quarantine. The sweat dripped from my forehead onto my shirt. Bob threw me a look and I did my best to slow my breathing, but I was only moderately successful; the panic had set in. I could faint at any moment.

The brief continued and we were assigned locations within the building to work from, each lead had a strict schedule of deliverables, with daily status updates to be provided to our department head and Brody, as well as periodic reviews with Vice President Palmer. The leads around the room gave updates on various technologies that were in progress, including the Earth-to-orbit shuttles, and Bob stumbled over the fact that the anti-stealth tech wasn't ready. Brody gave Bob an ice-cold stare and told Bob he had three days to complete R&D and move it into production. As the meeting closed, Vice President Palmer gave a final address. "We have to tell them we are serious. And I would rather do it with words than with actions. We must exhaust all options to ensure a peaceful union between our two civilisations. You few here today are essential to that mission. Thank you and good luck."

As the attendees marched out of the room, a silver-haired man approached me and told me he would send me over the details of the progress he had made on the communications device, "I guess it's time for a new set of eyes," he said keeping his head bowed. "I'll make sure you're fully briefed today."

When he left the room, the only people left were Brody and me. He hadn't moved from behind the desk, his eyes burning into me as I headed for the door. "He's putting a lot of faith in you." I stopped dead. "He says you're full of potential. You know how important this is. Don't let him down." His words reverberated in my ear, refusing to leave.

Bob was waiting for me outside. "I'm going to end up working for you soon, aren't I?"

"I doubt that."

He shrugged. "So, what did you want to talk to me about?"

I had rehearsed how to tell Bob that I had been abducted, imagining how he would react; in horror, pity, or maybe he would be scared of me, afraid that he would be there when they returned for me. I handed him a flash drive with the standard encryption.

"What's this?"

"The anti-stealth tech. You'll hit your deadline." He looked at me in shock. "I cracked it and did a full design spec this morning. It's all in there."

"Are you serious? This morning?" Bob tucked it into the palm of his hand. He scuffed his hair until it puffed up like brown candyfloss. "Are you sure it will work?"

I smiled at Bob, absolutely certain it would.

* * *

When I opened the front door, Jeri was stood in the hallway, eyes wide. "What... What did they say?"

"I didn't tell them."

She sighed in frustration like I had failed her again. "But they can protect you, we don't have anyone else to turn to."

"They have other abductees. They're holding them in custody, like criminals."

Jeri rubbed her hand across her forehead, lost in thought. "Can you talk to them, the abductees?"

"I don't know. I don't want anyone at US Tech to find out about me. They've been preparing for this for a while, Jeri. The Vice President was there. He's in charge of the whole thing."

Jeri was having a tough time taking it all in. I knew how she felt. I traipsed into the living room, sat on the sofa and she perched herself next to me. She moved closer, took hold of my hands, and locked her eyes dead on with mine. "You need to tell me everything."

I told her about Jeremy's research, about how he took

his own life and the note he left, handing the baton to me. I recounted every detail I could recall from the files that were taken from our home, about the Earth-to-orbit shuttle, Project: Sobek to build some kind of weapon, Project: Libera and the mention of our names, along with Jeremy, Rebecca Jones, Marjorie, and Lilly Russell. How, after waking up in the street with no memory of the day, I followed my whereabouts on the DNA tracker to the basement of US Tech, where the highest security clearance wasn't enough. And then I told her, in horrific detail the nightmare that tortured me. And how I would do anything not to lose her. Yet I had watched it over and over, every time I closed my eyes.

Jeri didn't utter a word. Her eyes never left mine. "I don't think it's the first time," I said. "I don't know whether they're coming back for me. Whether they'll bring me back next time."

Once again inside her own thoughts, Jeri spent minutes staring into nothingness. I waited quietly until she snapped out of it.

"What's Project: Libera? And what has it got to do with us?"

I hesitated. Swallowed hard. "I don't know." I couldn't look her in the eye. "But Rebecca Jones was abducted, and Lilly Russell. Maybe other people on the list, I don't know."

"Does that mean US Tech already know you were abducted?"

"It's possible. Or maybe they just suspect. Otherwise, wouldn't they have me in custody too?"

"You need to ask them."

"I can't. I don't know who I can trust."

"What about Rick? Can he help us?"

I shook my head. "He's just working on the shuttle project. He's as in the dark as I was, otherwise, he would have been in the room today."

Jeri took her time to process the situation. The only option I could see was to help Vice President Palmer do what he needed to do to stop the bastards. I hoped that he could do it before they came for me again. Before it was too late.

"What are they doing here? What do they want?"

"No one will say. They've asked me to lead R&D for comms, but I only have access to anything that strictly relates to my department. Even then, they refused access to most of the information I requested. I'm not sure if anyone knows."

Jeri squeezed my hand and leaned closer to me. Her sympathetic smile forewarned that she was about to tread into sensitive territory. "What happened, Ryan? When they took you?" I pulled away but that only caused Jeri to move closer. "You have to talk about it." Her voice remained calm and soothing, only causing it to grate against my nerves. The false veneer of politeness concealed a barbed question that could tear apart my very being. I leapt out of my seat.

"That... No. No!" Jeri stood alongside me and tried to wrap her hands around my arm, but I kept thrashing until it was free.

"You don't understand. You don't understand!" My hand flew up against my head, stabbing it with my forefinger. "They were in here. They were in here."

"I know." She curled my hand into a ball inside her own and lowered it back down to my side, still enveloped inside hers. "I know."

"You don't know. No one knows. They got inside my head. What if they never left?"

Jeri sat, easing me down with her. Her presence no longer felt unnerving. It felt warm to me, reassuring. My calm was only possible because I knew Jeri had finished trying to eek out of me the wretchedness. Their long, slimy fingers. Their horrible, huge glassy eyes. The vile contents of their large-

"We can do this, Ryan. We can do this," she hesitated before she said the last word, but when she finally spoke it, it was with conviction. "Together."

Together.

The word was different than before. So much more than eight letters. More than something you say in passing or as part of a sentence. With a mere mention of it, I felt the urge to look around the room for another person or two that I might have missed on my way in, usually Kyle or Emily, who would cause Jeri to add the social veneer. But we were alone, just the two of us.

Together.

SEVENTEEN

I had assistants everywhere, a team of scientists, more project managers than a project management convention and my own mechanical engineers transferred from the anti-stealth project. And I had their full support – every one of them committed long hours with few breaks. They had put their faith in me to lead them to success, but after an early flurry of progress, we had suffered weeks of nothing. Without a live being to communicate with, we were padding around in the dark.

"We've tried increasing the focus on the auditory cortex, but there's still no response," Peter said cross-legged on the table.

Jess supped her cappuccino. "They could be ignoring it."

"We would know." I ambled from one side of my office to the other. "We would at least be able to register a response."

"Ryan," Alex Little shouted before barging into my office. As my interim manager, he had spent most of his time with my research team, and the rest emailing or calling me to demand updates by the minute. In our first conversation, he told me outright that my recent failure on Project: Infiltrator was not tolerable and could not be repeated, completely ignoring the fact that I was the one who created the design to finally build a working prototype.

Little stepped towards me but his eyes went straight to the whiteboard filled with our scribbles and diagrams. He looked between the three of us as though he has had stumbled on us plotting his death. "What the hell is this?"

Jess and Peter's eyes darted to me to answer. "We're just throwing some last-minute ideas around."

"Last minute," Little said as though the words themselves were ridiculous. "This is going to be another failure to add to add to the list." He narrowed his eyes, gathering the worst he could muster from the depths of his dirty soul. "Because you're a failure."

"What?" Jess piped up. "Ryan's had us working every minute of every day. And he's putting in twice the hours himself. Trust me, he's doing everything he can to get it up and running."

Little's eyes narrowed. He sneered as his penchant for uber-professionalism over actual value took a hit at the sight of Peter still perched on the desk. "I'm not buying it." His eyes returned to me with a glare, probably waiting for me to say the wrong thing and hang myself. "I had to stand in front of the Vice President of the United States and tell him that you are failing. And that means I'm failing. Do you understand why that is not an option? Do you understand what will happen to you?" I wanted to ask him if he understood how go fuck himself. He had no idea what we were even up against. "You make this work. Today."

I found ridiculous deadlines and heinous threats so motivating.

On the way back to the test lab, Jess brushed her shoulder against mine and gave me a sympathetic smile. "You're testing his patience," Peter warned earning an elbow in the ribs from Jess in response.

The rest of the team were loitering around the lab. It was triple the size of the research department for the White Giant, and this time the project and every person assigned to it were under my leadership. A few hushed words passed as they waited for me to tell them what to do. I couldn't assemble a clear thought in my head.

"Alright people," Jess shouted. "Let's get started. We need to be ready in five."

Dr Curtis, one of the lead science officers edged towards me. "Ryan, I could do with your help. Before we get started." He gave me a meek smile.

"It'll have to wait."

"It will only take a moment. I just want to make sure-"

"I said it can wait. I don't have time, not today." It came across more severe than I intended.

Dr Curtis crept away, mumbling sorry to me. He was one of the best people I had on the team. I cursed myself for letting Little get to me and made a promise to square it with him later.

The doors swung open. Brody marched in with two women in full suit and tie, six military officers cradling light machine guns and the three scientists in clinical white hazmat suits pushing a large metallic dome on a stainless-steel gurney. Brody stopped next to me.

The three scientists pushed the dome past and into a twelve-foot square air-tight plastic containment unit. Seconds later, they re-emerged outside the unit into the sealed control area and punched away at the panels. All I could hear was the steady hum of machinery and the rhythmic inhale and exhale passing through my mouth. I gazed ahead at water rising inside the containment unit, hazy thoughts failing to evolve into coherence. Brody turned to me and paused before he spoke. "Are you ready?"

They expect a miracle from me. "We're ready."

I walked slowly towards the plastic screen. My reflection moved closer to me with every step. As I trembled like I had been left out in the cold, it was right in front of me, perfectly at ease. I sank into the emptiness of its huge black eyes staring back at me. Bobbing up and down, electrodes stuck to its skin, dry and flaky in the harsh light. Its arms darted out at me and curled back in, over and over. My throat swelled. When I closed my eyes, I could feel its oily fingers touching me.

"It's still disconnected from the central consciousness?" I hoped no one else detected the quiver of fear in my voice.

"Confirmed," Peter replied.

We knew so little about them and what they were capable of. If we could only lock them all away.

"Ellis." Brody called out from behind me, "We need to get moving."

I nodded. Pull it together. It's all alone here. It can't hurt anyone now. "Run program seventeen. We're going to incrementally alter the frequency a degree until we hear anything that sounds like a language."

The first attempt tried and failed. So did the second, third and fourth. Its eyes followed me around the room.

"Looking good," Jess said. "Test subject's brain activity is increasing." I waited, desperately fighting the urge to hope. Jess shook her head.

"Can you enhance the signal?" I asked. Jess did and the test subject's brain activity doubled." It barely moved, no eyelids to blink.

"What about giving it an incentive?" Peter asked. "Deliver the electric shock treatment."

"No." I couldn't believe Peter was even suggesting it. "Up the frequency point one degree."

A quiet crackling hummed in my ear. "Did you hear that?" I listened intently; sure that I heard something. We looked around the room at each other's faces, willing this to be the moment.

"I don't hear it," Jess replied. I was so sure when it happened, but no one else spoke up.

"The test subject's brain activity is reducing. It's falling below normal." Jess gave me a sympathetic smile. It seemed impossible.

It doesn't want to communicate any more than it wants to be locked inside that vat. When they spoke to me, it was

158

in their craft, and I was at their mercy. Only they didn't speak, I never heard a single word uttered in my head. It was visual, like a memory being replayed. "We're trying to communicate like humans. Change the target area to the hippocampus, frontal cortex and the visual cortex."

Jess stared at her control screen in confusion. "Brain waves increasing. They're off the chart."

This is it.

It hit me like ten thousand volts electrifying my brain. I grabbed for the desk to stop me falling, but it was no use. I saw myself stumbling forward as the desk disappeared before me. A flash of bright light and they were lined up in a row beside me, black eyed, not a movement to be seen, each of them facing a shiny metal surface, a domed ceiling a foot above our heads. Two circles glowed like the eyes of the sun. The metal shifted, from a flat panel to a tall dome. The glowing circles split into four and it felt like I was moving with them. Half a dozen humans and three times as many animals were stretched out and unconscious, except for one woman who was as terrified as ever I've seen a person. I looked through the eyes of every one of them, from the sea to the stars.

Moisture drifted in the air around us, seeping in through their skin. So calm, devoid of emotion. It rushed over me like a wave, washing away all of my hatred and bitterness. It didn't stop. It reached further, tugging at the warmth inside me. My mind's image of Jeri was drained of its luminance, becoming bereft of any glimmer of hope. I no longer loved her. I didn't love anything. I felt nothing. And I had no desire to resist.

"It's breaking through." Peter's voice seeped in and with it, the lab returned to me like a thin veil draped over the eyes of every alien being that I looked through. Another flash of light and I was back in the room to see a crack slowly run down the plastic screen of the containment unit, water seeping out onto the floor.

"Shut it down," Brody shouted. He pulled a gun from

under his jacket and flicked off the safety. The gun flew out of Brody's hand and spun across the room.

"Electric," Brody shouted, but it was too late. The electrodes were repelled from its body and with the sealed environment compromised, gas was no longer an option.

The thick plastic ripped in two and flew across the room. Water gushed out and fried the controls in front of the containment unit. It leapt out, landing a few feet away, stretching its arms out towards me.

The cage was open. The animal loose.

Its face didn't flicker, water trickling at its curled feet. Peter looked back and forth between the alien and Brody. Soldiers around the room trained their guns on it. Brody glared at it, ready for an attack. "Keep it alive. No kill shots."

Its horrific screech sent everyone reeling to the floor. Guns blazed from behind me, then flew overhead. Before her gun could be snatched away, one of the soldiers managed to unleash a few rounds on the alien's stomach. She flew across the room, still gripping her gun until her body splattered against the wall.

"Stop!" Brody screamed, "We need it alive."

Two more soldiers launched into the air and crashed into a glass cabinet. Its black eyes didn't need to look where it was throwing them. Dr Curtis shook violently, his head fixed in place. As he peered at me from the corner of his eyes, his body burst apart, splattering chunks of flesh across the lab, showering Peter in blood and fluid. There was nothing left of him bigger than a plum.

It lifted Peter and three other scientists into the air, shaking violently.

Brody planted his feet in the ground and pulled out a second gun. He sprayed bullets into its arms and legs. No kill shots. "I need tasers in here, now."

My foot hit something. Brody's gun. I grabbed it and pointed it at the alien being while trying to stay upright. I fired every bullet at its head until it collapsed to the floor in a bloody mess.

Brody squared up to me. "What the hell was that? I said I wanted it alive."

"I… I had to."

"We needed that thing to get the comms device working."

"Innocent people were being slaughtered. Their blood is on your hands." It would have killed us all. "Besides, we got what we needed. Your comms device finally worked."

"You disobey a direct order again and I'll have your head."

"Ryan," Peter's voice came, quietly from behind me. He was hunched over the desk shaking hard. "It's brain waves dropped off again. It didn't work."

* * *

Since President Walker's announcement, the Press were not calm or quiet and had been buzzing with anticipation. Shopping centres closed and whole cities ground to a halt; people didn't want to spend their last days at work. Some camped outside the White House in hope of seeing an alien visitor and maybe even having the honour of being taken. They were regarded by many as some form of saviour, here to rescue us from the malevolent corporations that we had become subjected to; so fundamentally flawed.

Alex Little gathered my whole team together and proceeded to tell us what a disaster it was, what a disaster we were. I tried to interrupt to tell him that no one here was responsible for security, that I had no choice to kill it, but he bulldozed over me. After ten minutes of raging abuse, he stormed out. Peter broke down in tears and I wondered why I let Little trample over me like that. Trample over my team like that. I still felt the weight of the gun in my hand.

I had been preparing to give a formal progress update on communications in person to Vice President Palmer. I submitted a report in advance, which was nothing more than analysis of all the tests completed so far and further research and hypothesis about how to get the thing working, with no mention that it had worked for me and me alone.

I waited in the seating area that had recently been created outside the Vice President's office at US Tech. Five secret service agents with curly wires in their ear stared straight ahead, one positioned by the water cooler, two near Palmer's office door, and one in the corridor at each end of the seating area. A sixth stood against the wall directly opposite, glancing down at me every thirty seconds or so.

After a few minutes, Palmer's assistant flashed a smile, in between stern expressions and led me into his office. "Ryan, it's a pleasure to see you again," Vice President Palmer said as he appeared from the private rest room in the far corner of the office. He reached across the desk and shook my hand. I tried to conceal the muscle in my right arm that twitched indignantly every few seconds.

"Thank you, Sir. It's a pleasure to be here."

"This afternoon is incredibly important." Vice President Palmer gestured to the chair and we both sat. His large office was empty except for the large traditional oak table that sat between us, a tall bookshelf behind him and photographs changing from the Vice President with one important social figure to the next. I felt uncomfortable in the open space, vulnerable. I tried to keep focus. "President Walker has declared that he will be joining us, this afternoon." He was clearly not happy about it. Palmer picked up his tablet. "I've read your briefing notes. Tell me, how you are going to produce a working prototype."

With no mention of what happened in the lab, it was entirely possible that Brody or Little, or both of them had concealed the breakout and all of its devastation from him. "We had a greater response targeting the hippocampus, frontal cortex and the visual cortex, or at least what we believe to be their equivalent. We have a test procedure mapped out that will take seven days. It is estimated-"

Vice President Palmer waved a hand in front of me. "I don't need to hear that. Tell me how we can get this thing to work. Our one hope to start on the right foot with a new civilisation is by overcoming communication barriers. President Walker is putting the pressure on to be ready for an imminent engagement. We get that wrong and we could start a war. Right now, your operation is my number one priority. So, what's blocking you?"

I wanted to tell him the truth, but if the government knew I was the only one who it communicated with, then I would be held in quarantine and helpless. I couldn't let that happen.

"There must be a way," he added.

"We're in uncharted territory here, an alien physiology, so many unknowns."

VP Palmer smiled at me. "I got a lot of raised eyebrows when I put you in charge of comms. Only one spoke up – I'm afraid not many people do when you're the Vice-President – but I hear things. I saw the reactions on people's faces." The smile vanished and Palmer leaned into me and lowered his voice to an impassioned whisper. "But I did it for one reason. Do you know what that is, Ryan?"

"I... I have no idea."

"I know you can do it."

I sat back, rattled by guilt. I knew how important this was. Maybe more than anyone. "We can't find a frequency that both humans and the alien race can operate on. But what about abductees? There are reports from Response that show more higher neural activity in abductees. Their brains have already been accessed through communication with the alien species, so they may be more predisposed to telepathic communication."

"Will it work?"

"It's a theory," I was cautious that this theory had not been included in the report, which had been carefully vetted by both Little and Brody. "It follows the principles of Galli's theory of absolute consciousness. I think it might."

VP Palmer considered my response, and then nodded. "You were right not to include it in here. Progress that line of research immediately." Palmer smiled and put his hand out as he stood, which I took as my queue that we were done.

* * *

Before I tested the comms device using an abductee, Vice President Palmer gave a statement, announcing that an official meeting had taken place with the visitors to our planet, revealing nothing about the engagement. President Walker was strangely absent.

At 10am, Vice President Palmer stood alone in his office at US Tech, immaculate as ever. His suit gave a radiant sheen, and his royal blue tie was positioned perfectly between each corner of his shirt collar. No matter how much pressure he was under he always maintained complete control. "Hello, Ryan. My apologies if I have kept you waiting."

I mumbled something intended to dismiss the need for an apology.

"I wanted to congratulate you. You did a fantastic job. Even faster than I hoped for."

"Not fast enough." Press stories were rampant about the President being an alien or being taken back to an alien planet and held hostage. And they were among the more rational explanations for his absence.

VP Palmer gave a grave frown of frustration. "I'm afraid he wouldn't wait any longer. Despite the risk. Thanks to you we now have the technology that will allow us to communicate with them."

Palmer strolled around me until he reached his chair, and then sat so I took his lead. "These are dangerous times, Ryan. And I do not feel that we are prepared for what lies ahead. This is not the time for the bureaucrats, career builders or the self-serving. if we're going to make it through this, I need talented people like you who are willing to serve the greater good. Although we have tried to ready ourselves should a situation like this arise, I don't have confidence in our current capabilities to protect our planet from these beings." He leaned forward towards me, as though he was about to whisper. In eagerness I leaned forward too. "I know what kind of person you are. Frequently late, easily distracted, possibly prone to depression." It was feeling a little too personal. "You're not made for the nine to five. But you are also passionate, obsessed by a problem until you have reached a resolution. You see things differently to other people. And you care about people, perhaps to your own deficit. Those are attributes I need in spades. If we are to be ready for what is to come."

"What's to come?"

Vice President Palmer sat back and considered the question. A blue light flashed repeatedly behind me. I turned and saw it placed on the wall, buzzing quietly. The office door swung open, and Agent Brody stepped inside. "Sir, we have a situation."

I looked to the Vice President, but he was still seated. "Ryan," his eyes focused, and his hands clenched tightly together. "I want you to come with me."

* * *

I strode alongside the Vice President through a claustrophobic passage within the underground depths of US Tech, flanked by three members of his security force and three following behind, while Agent Brody led the way. Vice President Palmer remained silent as the steel walled passageway narrowed, until two people could barely fit side by side. As I looked up at the steel ceiling that hung just above my head, Palmer finally spoke. "You are one of only forty people who are aware of this location."

"What location is it?" I asked but Vice President Palmer didn't answer. He was considerably strong in such a 'situation', and I was very eager to see what he had up his sleeve to give him such strength. Brody held up his hand to bring us to a standstill. One member of Palmer's security force marched ahead to a door at the end of the dimly lit corridor before waving us on. When we reached the door a number of beeps sounded from both sides. A small keypad emerge from behind a steel plate beside the door and Brody inputted his fingerprint, a retinal scan and a DNA sample via his saliva. The security officer repeated the process and the door opened.

I followed the Vice President and three of the officers inside. A wave of heat poured over me along with the layers of sweat in the room. I heard the door close behind me, my attention on the tech that had spread through the room like vines in an abandoned garden. A bright light flashed repeatedly, turning the concrete walls and floor crimson. Ten people were already inside the room that was half the size of a basketball court, two communications officers wearing headsets, four sat at computer terminals and four wearing military uniforms. I was in the President's war room.

* * *

Vice President Palmer occupied the centre of the room as General Day stepped aside. "Status report, General."

The General replied immediately, "We have identified two Class 3 alien craft within Earth's atmosphere, Sir. We have six Tactical Interceptor planes ninety seconds away from them." She lifted each hand to the side of her grey hair pulled back into a ponytail and moved her fingers around her head in unison until they met at the back.

A prototype anti-stealth detection screen stood tall in front of Vice President Palmer, with two alien craft dead centre of the display. I felt a cold shiver run through my body.

"We are approaching targets," A voice came over the digital audio transmitter.

"Do you have capable detection?" The general said.

There was a short pause before the reply, "Affirmative, anti-stealth detection system is operational. They are showing on our radar."

"They're not responding," The communications officer said. I instantly recognised the all too familiar comms programme displayed on the screen. The officer operating it must have been an abductee – at least some were allowed to roam free.

VP Palmer didn't take his eyes off the anti-stealth screen. "They are in United States airspace without authorisation and are not responding. Fire at will." I couldn't believe what I was hearing. Surely, he can't do that. But the Vice President was more than ready to defend our country. One of the communications officers repeated the last of Vice President Palmer's words into his headset. After that, the only sound in the room was the exchange between pilots.

"On my command. Ready US 2. Fire!"

"My missile won't launch."

"I've lost power! I'm going into a nosedive!"

"Affirmative. I've lost control."

"My God… It's so bright."

"One disappeared from radar. Where did it go?"

"They merged together, two of them merged into one!"

"It's too bright, it's coming right at me."

"Fire, US 4"

"I can't!"

"Take evasive manoeuvres."

"I can't!"

Everyone in the room had held their breath since the words 'it's coming towards me.' We watched helplessly as every Tactical Interceptor plane was forced away from the craft into different directions, all except US5 that seemed to be out of range. US5 shot a missile through the sky as the door swung open behind us.

President Walker burst in the room, a cluster of secret service slipping in behind. "What the hell is going on here? Abort this mission! I did not authorise this."

The communications officer looked to the Vice President, but he gave no response. He didn't even acknowledge that William was in the room; he remained focused on the anti-stealth detection screen, ignorant of everything else.

The long, rounded missile grew closer and closer to the alien ship. Everyone including William was now fixated on its image. Until it disappeared from the screen completely. The pilot of US5 started to shout, "The missile disintegrated! A light originating from the ship disintegrated the missile!"

"Damn it, Robert, stop this now!" William's voice boomed as he strode towards VP Palmer.

"They're retreating." General Day said.

A deafening screech rained down on me. The communications officer threw down his headset and grabbed the desk to stop him from falling as he toppled off his chair. The horrific noise ended, and my head flopped down in relief.

Vice President Palmer looked towards the General, unsure of what had just happened. William cried out in pain and dropped to the floor right in front of me. One of the secret service officers dived for him but couldn't reach him before he hit the ground. "He's still breathing," the officer said, kneeling over him.

The Vice President's attention darted to President Walker, as though his collapse had only just gained hit him. "Get him to medical." He turned to the General, doing nothing to conceal his concern. "Why didn't it kill them?"

"It didn't have to," I said with regret. "We don't threaten them."

EIGHTEEN

Reports of the incident were plastered over traditional and social media, sending the world into panic. Anti-alien groups formed, and civilian watch parties stood armed on street corners. I could feel the chaos about to ensue.

Vice President Palmer requested that I accompany him to the medical facility at US Tech where heavily armed guards were dotted every few feet. There were no other visitors in the ward and only one quarantined room was occupied. Palmer looked through the window at President Walker lying still.

"How is he?" I asked, resisting the urge to jump straight to why I was there.

"He has the best medical care in the world. But it's unlike any coma his doctors have ever seen. They don't think he'll wake up."

"Do they know what caused it?"

"When he came back from meeting that... that thing. He was shaking. He told me that he was ok, but he wasn't. I knew that. But I let him continue, I obeyed his request to remain in office. He went in raw. I tried to get him to wait." The Vice President stood in silence. His jaw clenched, neck hunched, he wore the pressure he had been under since

William entered a coma all over his face, but his eyes hadn't lost any of their intensity. A smile found its way through the strain, but it was gone in a moment. "I knew you would come through. But he just let them poke around in his mind and God knows what else."

I squirmed inside. If I had told the Vice President that the comms device worked for me, he wouldn't be there.

"They agreed to stay out of our airspace," the Vice President continued, "unless we gave permission to enter. They're already breaking our agreements. He called them magnificent."

Taking people against their will was anything but magnificent. Rebecca Jones didn't ask to be taken. No one asks to be taken. VP Palmer paced to the other side of the room. For a few minutes we both remained silent, as I contemplated President Walker's reliability and his intentions. "I wish I knew what happened," VP Palmer said. His gaze was fixed on a painting hanging on the corridor wall, a single warrior standing tall in a field, surrounded by men in the same navy-blue uniform, all injured or dead.

"You weren't there?"

"I was. But all I saw was that..." He clenched his teeth in distaste "thing touch the Presidents head. They surrounded him; we looked weak. They were testing us, examining our defences. And we had nothing but firearms. Can you believe it? The strongest damn nation in the world. The only thing he cared about was trying to make peace, we all want peace. Now the safety of our entire planet may be at stake." VP Palmer's words were making more sense to me than the President's actions. "There are no unauthorised alien craft allowed in our atmosphere. We have to stand firm."

"What happens when they come?"

"Answer me this, Ryan. Do they read our minds? Or do they control them? I have a list of one hundred names, where there is compelling evidence of abduction, people who were found dead. Their bodies mutilated. And they're the ones we know about. They can take you for days or grab you while you sleep and have you back in bed within hours. You would never even know you were gone." He raised his voice, almost shouting. "How can we sit back and let this continue? How can we let them murder our country?" The Vice President's words held bite and I'm sure there was resentment, possibly for those like the President who placed our world in jeopardy.

My heart sped so fast it was almost tripping over itself. My anger matched the Vice President's pound for pound. I nearly told him everything there and then. "If someone hurts you or someone you care about… you have to make them pay. Or they'll only come back and do worse."

He became calm again, his eyes fixed on President Walker, lying helpless. "I couldn't agree more. We should have taken steps to prevent this situation before it began. The best defence is a good offence. Well, I don't think the wrongs they have committed against us are at an end. So, it's time we worked on our offence."

"What do you need from me?"

"I have to make the difficult decisions. Some are almost impossible. Our society rests on the countless civilisations that we have built upon. The Parthenon of ancient Greece, the creation of writing to pass down masses of information and perspectives through generations. Mozart's serenade number thirteen. The African Stonehenge. The Native American calendars. We have achieved so much. How many of our societies have reached such astonishing levels of achievement, only to be destroyed or oppressed by strangers from another land?"

Vice President Palmer, letting his passion settle his stare pinpointed directly at me. "I see the desire in your eyes. There is a sadness casting over it, but it burns on. The need to do whatever you can. And most importantly, I think you want to have seen the last of this damned alien race as much as I do."

"So, what do you want from me?"

Having reached the moment he had been building up to,

the Vice President locked his gaze onto mine. "Your security clearance is about to jump up a few levels." He studied me, until a gracious smile appeared momentarily, and then it was gone again. "Before you took over, a team had been working on the comms device for months. You cracked it in weeks. You created the anti-stealth designs, a prototype DNA tracker and you worked out how to build nanotube structures large enough to support a space-scraper. You have a unique talent, Ryan, which you are not aware of. The technology that you have been using for the comms device-"

"You have their tech."

"We found a ship. It was enough to start reverse engineering it to launch a number of initiatives to adopt that technology for the advancement of our society."

"Galli's theory."

The Vice President nodded. "Most of them struggled to get out the gate."

"The Earth-to-Orbit shuttle?"

"Yes, one of the few successful projects that you haven't been involved in. No one else has been anywhere near as proficient in developing their technology as you have. But there is information that you have not yet had access to. I want to make this information available to you."

"You know why they're here."

"You like to be a step ahead, don't you? So, do I. Each being has lived for almost a thousand years. They constantly evolve. But their advances in genetic manipulation only stalled the process of death, and now their lifespan is coming to an end, one by one. We are the only other intelligent species they claim to have found. They tried to use other species to help them to reproduce but without any real success." The image of large vats containing a variety of monstrosities had buried itself in my mind. "William only saw the possibilities of what we could achieve together."

"They want to use us."

"If they have the technology to travel across or through

space to reach our planet, along with many others, what else can they do?"

"If they wanted to attack us-"

"Then they would have. They're not mindless conquerors. They want us alive, it's in their best interests. Until they solve their problem, that is. And then what?"

Then we don't stand a chance.

The sternness on the Vice President's face broke. "Should the situation arise that we need to defend ourselves, then we have to be ready."

"So that's what this is?"

"That's what this is. The communications device. I need you to weaponise it."

"I thought you wanted peace."

"I do. More than anything. But I'm not naive, Ryan. You saw what they did to our fighter jets."

"Is this personal?"

"It's my country. My planet. My people. Of course, it's personal."

I took a deep breath before even considering what the Vice President had asked of me. I couldn't look at President Walker's lifeless body any longer. "I don't kill. And I don't put weapons in other people's hands."

"I know what happened in the lab. You did what needed to be done."

"That was self-defence. It would have killed everyone there."

"And it would only be used under the same circumstances. A last resort." VP Palmer's imposing stature faced me full on. "They got to our President. Our President. I am as reluctant as you are to up the stakes in the development of weapons, but we just got bumped up a few leagues in the galactic arena and now we need to shift the balance decidedly in our favour or we are lambs to the slaughter. We know that they possess a single consciousness, functioning as one. If the situation becomes so dire, we'll be able to end their consciousness simultaneously. We have to be ready."

"All of them?"

"Instantaneously. I'm told it would be almost painless. It may be an impossible decision. But we have to be ready to defend ourselves."

"I'm not ready to become the next Oppenheimer."

Vice President Palmer paced slowly about the room. I thought he had given up until he bobbed his head again, this time like he was gearing up. And then his posture relaxed, his arms lolling by his side, his shoulders rounding. And his face showed tiredness I hadn't seen before. "I was very close to William," he said softly, the assertive tones that were usually expelled from his mouth were nowhere to be heard. "He was a very close friend, indeed. A marvellous man long before he was a President. I believe in him. But he may be gone. And as much as I loved his idealism, his caring for others without refrain, I believe we have to put the safety of those here, in our home, on our planet before everything else. William told me that these aliens could control short-term memory. Think about how many people could be being taken without us even knowing. If they take whole families, when will they decide that they no longer need to bring them home?"

The Vice President's body straightened up, returning to his impeccable posture, his eyes wide, which delivered a renewed freshness to his face. He clenched his fist and released it, over and over, the only sign that the situation was wearing on him. A crack in his armour. "I am asking you to do this," he continued. "Your President is asking you to do this. To protect your country and its families."

Vice President Palmer had dissected world politics and discarded petty spin and the marketing extravaganza that always came with it. Years of build-up had come to a head when he released his 'I vote for my country' campaign that had centred around the ideal that the person in presidency is less important than their vision and how they put the people first. This man stood in front of me asking for my help to ensure the survival of the human race. I took a deep breath to steady my resolve. "I will do whatever you need to improve our defences. But I'm sorry, I can't build a weapon for you."

"Don't give me your answer now," the Vice President insisted. "Please, just consider it for me. That's all I ask."

* * *

Sat in the packed Brady Press Briefing Room at the White House, there were a handful of people I recognised: Agent Brody, General Day, Alex Little, Timothy Calderbank and CEO of US Tech, Elliott Brandon. Vice President Robert Palmer walked on stage and gave his welcome address to the buzzing press. No person alive had such a variation of blue in their wardrobe, immaculate in a crisis.

Palmer stood firm, about to give the most important speech of his life. "I can officially confirm that William Walker is still in a coma and is not expected to recover." A rumbling of upset and devastation spread through the room like a minor earthquake; William was beloved by the people and for good reason. "He was the greatest President that this country has ever known, but he also is the greatest man that I will ever know." It wasn't just kind words that Palmer was saying about a respected and revered President, there was compassion and concern in his voice that spoke of true friendship.

Vice President Palmer took a breath to compose himself, "Our country has suffered a great loss. We are in the middle of an unprecedented situation, not only in the history of America, but of humankind. I emphasise that we are in the middle, because we are now at a crossroads. And for our society, our civilisation, to be able to survive through this, I need to share with you some events that will alarm you. When President Walker met with the alien race that has visited our planet, he reached an agreement that no craft was to enter United States airspace without prior authorisation.

That agreement was violated, and United States forces engaged with an alien craft. I can also report that following an in-depth investigation, we have confirmed a number of genuine abductions, many resulting in physical harm to the abductees."

"But we have a choice." Palmer thrust his hand into the air. "Our people are being taken, abducted from their homes. And we have reason to believe that not all of them are being returned alive. But we have a choice. We can run and hide and hope that it is not ourselves or our family members that are taken. Or we can choose to do what our great nation has done so many times before, and we can rise to the occasion. I ask you to have faith in what is right... And there is no greater right, than the safety and wellbeing of the people of our great world. We must defend our freedom and our lives. But we must do it together. I need your help, the help of everyone in this room. The help of everyone watching at home, at work, or with friends. To support me, in undoing the wrongs that have been done. To protect this country, our society, and the entire human civilisation."

The crowd gave an uproar of support. VP Palmer stood back. A man leaned toward the microphone, "President Palmer will now take questions from the Press."

Hands flew into the air. Palmer's assistant gestured to the first, "Mr President, do you think that President Walker's condition is related to his meeting with the aliens?"

Palmer leaned towards the microphone, "I do." I reeled in shock with the rest of the crowd. His openness was certainly unconventional but undeniably admirable.

The next reporter lowered her hand, "What do you advise the public to do, Mr President if they believe that they are being abducted?"

Another shouted over the last, "Mr President, do you know what happens during the alien abductions? What do the aliens do to their victims?"

"We are currently investigating the events that transpire during an abduction incident. In almost all cases they have little or no memory of ever being abducted, and only become aware through some form of intervention, most commonly hypnotic regression."

"If you believe that you are being abducted by extraterrestrial beings, I urge you to come forward, so that you can get the proper help and support. We will investigate all genuine reports, and an encounter web address and hotline will be provided at the end."

The questions continued but my attention waned; my mind plagued by what President Palmer had asked of me. I felt indebted to him for placing so much trust in me, and to have the courage to face off against the threat and protect our country. But the idea of creating a weapon of mass destruction against any enemy terrified me, and there was no way to know if it could be turned against us.

I broke out of my trance to hear the Vice President's closing statement, "We will stand united to preserve what humankind has built."

NINETEEN

I fastened the buttons on a casual shirt as Jeri watched me from the doorway. "You won't be out long?" She asked, leaning into our bedroom.

"No. I don't think so." Every time I looked at her, I saw their dripping wet faces. The idea of being back in their clutches left me reeling, but the dread of when they finally came for Jeri left me almost unable to function.

Jeri nodded. She pulled at her lips with her fingers. "Will you be back by eleven?"

Rick had suggested a late night, that we were all in desperate need of it and had plenty to discuss, but seeing the worry on Jeri's face, her not knowing whether I was relaxing in a bar or held captive, I decided then that I would be home early. "Ten at the latest." I regretted agreeing to go out entirely.

I sat down on the bed to tie my boot laces. Jeri nestled up next to me. "I know she'll be there. You made it obvious without outright saying it. Which I appreciate… and I trust you." I put my arm around her, pulled her towards me and kissed the soft hair on top of her head.

* * *

They were waiting for me by the time I arrived at Urbane2, which was pretty much Urbane one, but with a new carpet and black waistcoats over the staff's white shirts. Its octagon tables in the middle of garden-style benches remained and Rick, Jess and Peter occupied the one in the furthest corner. "Greetings, fair leader," Peter shouted as he saw me enter. "Our night begins."

I sat beside Rick and put on my best false smile. Peter launched out of his seat and headed off, returning a few minutes later with a round of beers.

Rick had recently been working on the shuttle project full-time as part of the response team, so I had barely seen him since the State Dinner. I asked if he had seen Vera again, but she had politely told him that she most desperately wished she had attended the state dinner alone. Rick seemed doomed to a never ending cycle of picking the wrong woman. It was nice being with friends and I quickly lost myself in conversation.

"Shots!" Peter cried out, coming back from the bar with a tray full.

"I'm fine. I'm not staying late." But Peter still laid a shot down in front of me and urged me to drink it. I began to question what harm it could do. Maybe I should relax. Forget about the world outside the bar. Drown my sorrows and my secrets. Mine was the only glass still full. Peter was tempting me, taunting me to drink it. I wanted to so bad.

I shuffled my hands under the table, ready to make a grab for it. Before I could get near, Rick had emptied mine down his throat and slammed the empty glass back on the table. As Peter cheered, Rick gave me a nod and smiled.

* * *

When I got home, lights were on all over the house. I searched every room downstairs, nerves frayed, but there was no sign of Jeri. I was about to head upstairs when I noticed a set of keys in the door to the garden. Jeri was under a cherry blossom tree sat at the picnic table alone in the open space. I took a step towards her, and another step, and another, until I was halfway there, on a sandstone pathway that split the long stretch of grass in half. A cold breeze blew against my face and my body craved the enclosure of being indoors.

"What are you doing out here?" I asked.

"I needed some fresh air. The stars. They're so bright. What time is it?"

"Eight thirty." I walked to the other side of the table. Jeri took her eyes off the sky for the first time and turned to face me.

"I was so worried."

"I'm home now."

"That's not me. I'm not a worrier. I don't even recognise myself anymore."

I sat by her side and took a deep breath as if I was about to say something meaningful or important, but I couldn't think of any advice or opinion that would be of value. We stared ahead at the grass and the vibrancy of bright red and deep orange roses at the edges, accentuated by the moonlight. The cool breeze and Jeri's breath became the only sounds I could hear. It felt like ten minutes before Jeri broke the silence.

"Nothing is the same, is it? We don't even know when it changed."

I looked up at the sky and wondered how it would feel to be up there, what's beyond it. The way the moonlight gleamed through the clouds, it looked like heaven. I held out a white rose that I picked up from a street seller outside the bar. Jeri smiled and brought it close to her chest. "Hold me," she said.

I put my arm around her, and she turned quickly, her face so close, her lips parted and moving steadily towards me. My eyes were still open when her mouth met mine and her tongue began massaging my own. I lowered my hand

and took hold of her waist, but she pushed it away. I peered out of one eye as her arms moved towards me, my shirt gradually unbuttoned. She got about half way down and then pulled her vest-top up, over her head, leaving me to finish the job. She let it fall to the floor and I did the same. The small pile of clothes grew bigger, until only boxer shorts and a briefs remained. She shifted across the bench to get closer to me, close enough for our skin to touch. She leaned down to slip her last garment over her legs and I fumbled mine off. Bearing all, her crystal blue eyes gazed at mine.

A warmth started in my chest and spread like fire across my body. We moved from the bench to the cold, slightly jagged paving. She touched my cheek and it no longer felt like the paving beneath me was trying to pierce my skin. The breeze that moments earlier caused an occasional shiver had become silk draping over me. Jeri lay the white flower down next to her. She buried her nose between its soft petals, closed her eyes, and inhaled its sweet scent.

Entwined, enveloped in the far reaches of each other's being, Jeri was now a part of me, as I was a part of her. Under the stars, with the White Giant spacescraper looming over us, we made love.

* * *

The duvet cover leaves only one eye, a nose, and half of Ryan's mouth visible as he sleeps soundly. I scan the bedroom for what caused the noise that woke me, but we're the only ones in the room. I pull the covers off me, long, slender legs half covered by my nightdress.

I step onto the floor and the soles of my feet feel wet. The floorboard creaks at the other side of the room. I turn quickly but no one is there except for Ryan, still sleeping. I reach down and run my fingertips through the thick pile and feel the wetness expand across the carpet. Padding the floor with my feet, I find a trail leading all the way to my bedroom doorway.

I whip my head around at the sound of a bang. It came from downstairs. There's someone in our house. My heart is racing. I rush to wake Ryan. The trivialness of last night's argument flashes through my mind. Before I can get to him, I'm stopped dead. I can't move. I've never felt a sensation like it, not on this Earth. I grunt because even though they're in my head, the words won't form. No matter how loud I groan Ryan doesn't wake.

Please wake up.

My feet have grown so cold. It creeps slowly up my legs, all the way to my neck like I'm lying naked on a steel mortuary trolley. As it reaches my mouth, there's a metallic taste. I close my jaw quickly and try to lift my arms to stop it, but they're trapped at my sides. The metal creeps down my throat and the last thing I see is my bedroom through the semi-transparent material that now covers my face. I scream out but no one hears me. Ryan sleeps soundly as they take me away.

Paradoxical end. Unveil. Transcend.

A scream brought me back to the garden, cold concrete under my skin, Jeri's breasts clearly visible to me now that my eyes had fully adjusted to the dark. Flashes of my latest nightmare tortured my mind. But it wasn't my nightmare. It was Jeri's.

Jeri lay next to me and placed her hand on my cheek. Her expression was no longer that of someone losing themselves in the moment, it was overcome with concern.

"Oh, Ryan. Their eyes. Their horrible, big, black eyes. What did they do to you? I can't imagine how... terrifying...Their skin, so slimy and wet. And the creatures, those dead creatures floating beside you. Oh, Ryan." She brushed her thumb against my cheek repeatedly, each time softer than the last. I kept my eyes down, ashamed of the dark corner of my mind that she had crept into.

"You saw it?"

"Like it was happening to me." It wasn't a nightmare at all. It was a memory.

I had dreaded the day that they came for Jeri. It was a black shadow on every moment of my life. Waiting for it. On my knees in the dark. I always thought that was worse, the dread, worse than the harshest reality, when the light shone, and the bad thing finally happened. But now I know that's not true. The dread isn't worse at all.

Despite the pain from the cold, solid floor, and the numbness that crept up on us, we didn't move for some time.

* * *

For an hour or so we had been content with each other. Groping around, sensations mounting. Infatuated. It was no more than a fleeting memory, now. Jeri stared into space as the kettle boiled and I waited at the kitchen table. She had barely spoken a word. She rested the steaming mugs down, but she didn't sit. A dim floor lamp cast a shadow across her face. She took a deep breath, mentally preparing herself. It should have been a time of happiness, to take pleasure. But I felt nothing but dread for our impending conversation.

"What happened…" The words crept out of her mouth quietly. Seeing her that hesitant, I felt pity for her.

"It's ok," I said taking hold of her hand gently. "I know how it feels."

Jeri pulled her hand away quickly. "That's not what I meant. What happened between us… It was special."

"I saw what happened to you. And you saw me. Do you remember anything? Bright lights? Have you blacked out or lost time?"

Jeri placed her hand on mine and gave a pitiful smile. "It doesn't take anything away. From what happened between us."

"What I saw-"

"I don't want to know what you saw."

"We can't just hide away from this."

Jeri snatched her mug and tipped it into her mouth. I

reached to take a drink, but my mug was too hot to touch. "And we can't just sit around, moping about it. There's nothing more to say," Jeri said forcefully. She banged her cup down and sidled up next to me. She brushed her soft fingers against my cheek and stood between my knees. "Just kiss me."

"Don't." I jumped up from the chair and marched away from her. My skin tingled at the thought of what she wanted from me. It was too late for that now. "We need to know when it happened. How many times they have taken you?"

"This is ridiculous."

"What do you remember?"

"I don't want to talk about it. We... We don't even know what it was."

"I can't believe this." I shook my head, desperate to escape from what I was hearing. "I saw them take you like you saw them take me." She sipped at her steaming tea, looking everywhere but at me. "You remember. You, do don't you? Why haven't you told me?"

"We're in this together. That's what's most important."

I squirmed, the hairs on my arms doing their best not to touch my skin. "How many times? How many fucking times have they taken you?"

"Stop it. That's not going to help anyone."

"Tell me what you remember." I could hear a voice inside, telling me to stop, to calm down, desperate to be heard, but the voice was so small, drowned out by scorching fear. "How can you do this to me? You've never had the nightmares, never came to me, and never told me anything about it. It can't be happening to you, it can't."

Jeri was as though all of the air had been deflated out of her, someone reeling from bad news or an accident, but apart from seeing what happened to me, she wasn't surprised. "Did you know? Jeri, did you know? Answer me."

"I don't know. Maybe... I suspected but I-"

"Fuck. Fuck you."

"You can't blame me for this. I didn't ask for any of it."

Jeri stayed calm. Always so calm, forever in control. "All we can do is put it behind us, whatever happened, and move on."

"I know why your name was in the file. I know why they're here. I know why they took you."

Jeri was about to interrupt me, but she bit her tongue.

A sickness filled my gut. The voice told me to shut my mouth. That no good could come of it. But I didn't listen. I spat out the words and waited for the fallout. "They can't reproduce. That's why they're here."

Jeri fell back against the kitchen worktop, fumbling to hold on. Her face ghastly pale. I searched for the right words but nothing materialised.

* * *

Come at her with fists or a weapon, and Jeri could defend herself better than anyone I knew. But those abilities that had served her so well in the force had been rendered almost useless and she knew it. Draining a third coffee, it was agonising to be away from her side – even with only a flight of stairs between us. I just needed to see that she was ok, that she was still upstairs and not far away, their oily skin stroking her face.

I sighed in relief at the sound of Jeri's footsteps descending the stairs. She asked me to come and sit down and I followed her into the living room where she perched on the edge of the sofa. I remained standing. Jeri spoke so quietly that I could barely hear her. "About last night... What you saw..."

"I'm sorry-"

"Just listen to me." Her voice was steady. So calm. "You hold onto things so tightly. Onto what you've lost. What you're scared to lose. About what happened last night... I need to work it out."

"I know, we can do this. We'll do it togeth-"

"By myself."

My chest tightened.

"Sit down," Jeri said.

I sat as far away as I could and then my eyes finally landed on it in the hallway, totally out of place, transforming the room. In a different context, a different setting it would have meant something else, a holiday, or a business trip, but I knew exactly what it meant. I had been expecting it for a long time. But not now. I thought things were better. I thought we could get through this.

"There's still love between us," she said. "I know that. But you need to give me space. I'll contact you... When I'm... When I'm ready."

I wasn't convinced. I fought the urge to beg her not to leave and forced the emotions back down, deep inside me.

"Ryan, talk to me."

"I don't know what I'll do if you leave."

"I can't go back… Not to how things were. You need to process things, to dwell and wallow in pain. You're obsessed. Do you hate them?"

After what they've done to her, any sane person would. "Don't you?"

She took a deep breath to control herself. "I can't be around that, right now. Sometimes, you need to take yourself out of a situation to fix it. If I don't, there'll be nothing left of us."

"I can't protect you out there."

"You can't protect me here." A punch in the gut. "This hate... you're going to kill yourself trying." I could have thrown up on her white leather heels.

Jeri craned her neck to look out the window, at the sound of a car engine revving. She rushed to the door and said I couldn't tell anyone about what I saw while I trailed behind. Herb sauntered from his truck up the path towards us. He picked up her case and carried it to the car without ever letting me look him in the eye. I didn't understand why he was here. I could have driven her. She could have taken the car.

186

She opened up that orange piece of shit and hesitated, looking back at me with sympathy. I wished that she would just get it over with and leave. I told myself it was for the best. That we needed some time apart.

I felt sure of it.

I couldn't stop my hand from shaking.

* * *

Dribs and drabs of hatred slipped out of me throughout the day. I didn't mean for it to happen, but it did anyway. Everyone who came into contact with me felt the brunt of it. I was utterly helpless. Even with Herb and his family, Jeri may as well have been alone. If anything happened, they couldn't do shit. At least I knew what she was going through, I understood better than anyone.

I requested an urgent meeting with Vice President Palmer, who had largely based himself at US Tech since the alien craft incident. He hadn't contacted me since asking me to weaponise the comms device, and I appreciated that he hadn't continued to pressure me, particularly given the urgency. I sat holding a wad of papers, alone outside Palmer's office except for the usual security force and assistant. When I closed my eyes, I saw Jeri standing in our bedroom. Felt the thin metallic blanket wrap around her, forcing its way down her throat.

Vice President Robert Palmer emerged from his office and asked me to accompany him, down into the depths of US Tech once more, but this time we stopped at a different door. 'Magenta' was written on a gold plaque with the usual security mechanisms below it. Palmer supplied his own retina, fingerprint and DNA and the five guards that accompanied us remained outside when the door closed silently. We stopped about halfway down the corridor at one of rows of labs with blacked out windows. Vice President Palmer opened the door for me. Moisture swarmed my skin like I was in a steam room, but it made me shiver, the temperature a few degrees lower than outside the room. "It died within a few hours of retrieving it," he said. As soon as I walked through the door, I was on top of it. The flaking body lay in the middle of the table, nothing else in the room. "Touch it. Go on, not many people can say they have."

I stared at Palmer, taken aback at his casualness. It looked different in clear view under the harsh fluorescent light. I reached my hand out slowly until it met the flaky skin. "It feels empty." I felt bitterness towards it. It was no longer moist.

"It's not. Not physically anyway. It has organs, not completely dissimilar to ours. It has sexual organs, but they possess no reproductive capability. We don't know why. Evidently, neither do they." VP Palmer's gentle smile reflected up at me in its glassy black eyes.

"They look so peaceful. Innocent. Almost childlike. But it would be a mistake to treat them as such. We don't truly know what they are capable of." He kept his voice low and calm, his face mostly devoid of expression, leaning into me, the conversation feeling intimate in the small room. He knew not to pressure me. "Are you ok? Did something happen?"

I handed him the papers I was holding. "Why is my name wife's name in these reports?"

Palmer flicked through the pages. He stopped on one and held them against his chest. "I'm sorry. I know about the problems that you and your wife had conceiving." He gave me his best attempt at an empathetic smile. I almost regretted asking about the files. But he didn't hesitate, didn't take any time to fabricate a response. "Working on the projects you have... with that biological history. And your capability to adapt their tech, that's three for three. You were top of the list of potential people to be brought in once we went public. We had to be sure."

"And?"

"I am very happy to say that we found no evidence of abduction or contact. In either of you."

"That's why I was brought into US Tech? When I blacked out."

"It was protocol. I hope you understand." Palmer waited for a response, eyeing me up to determine how I would react.

"What about the people who have been abducted? What happens to them?"

"As soon as this is over, they go free."

"Ok, I'll do it. I'll weaponise the comms device." A smile grew on the Vice President's face, wide and welcoming. "We have to stop them, Vice-President. No matter what."

He nodded, understanding completely. "Thank you, Ryan. You're doing a great duty for our civilisation. I hope you know how much I personally appreciate that. And please, call me Robert."

Robert shook my hand and led me back to his office. He told me that if I needed anything at all, to contact Agent Brody, that my mission was the most critical of the entire operation. He handed me a glass of scotch a few years my senior and clanked his against it – a drink to our future. With every sip, the ghastly screams of Jeri's flopping body faded into the recesses of my mind. Robert Palmer had brought me hope that a power could exist in this world that could stop them.

I vowed to do everything in my power to protect her.

TWENTY

I slid down the leather seats of the rental-fresh hatchback, so my eyes were slightly above level with the dashboard. There were a few lights on in the house, even though daylight lingered, and although Jeri's DNA tracker confirmed she was still inside, not a soul was to be seen.

It had taken me hours to trawl through every document on my tablet that Robert gave me access to. I read everything we knew about their shared consciousness, and the theory that an artificially generated EMP could be released to dissolve the intrinsic connection that existed between every member of the alien race, effectively causing mass brain damage that would shut down their biological functions.

There were dozens of validated abductee reports. The first was similar to Rebecca Jones, missing for months and then found dead, ovaries surgically removed. No initial suggestion of extra-terrestrial intervention, just a dead girl and her devastated family. During the autopsy, the coroner discovered a type of laser incisions that were impossible with current technology. I insisted that Jeri's story would be different, until it was the only thought in my head.

Carol appeared first, squirreling food from the kitchen

into the living room. Then an occasional head bobbed up intermittently at the bottom of the window that I thought was Emily. It had been so long since I had seen her. It wasn't just Jeri that I was creating this weapon for; it was every child on the planet and everyone yet to be born.

The rest poured through the house, a wave of children and Herb, all rushing to the table, overtaking one another until they claimed their chairs. Jeri ambled behind, following their path, but in no rush to get anywhere. I was parked far enough away that she couldn't see me, none of them could. A peeping Tom. An intruder to their home, gazing in at their lives.

I had texted her, despite what she asked of me. It was a weak moment and I berated myself for letting her down. I'm ok. Please don't contact me again, she replied. Even though I knew she said she was ok to get me off her back, I was elated with the possibility that it was true.

Even from outside I got a sense of warmth coming from the house, a place for family. My own home no longer appealed to me or felt like any kind of haven. Any meaning once associated with the building left with my wife. Behind the windscreen of the car, I at least felt protected from their eyes. But it was really their ignorance, their indulgence in those daily tasks that maintained their insulation, cut off from anything happening outside their world.

I took one more sip of my corner store whiskey and opened Heinrich Galli's *A Guide to Life: The Misdirection of the Human Psyche*. Ten years since I deciphered the defining word on Galli's theory, I prayed that he possessed the power to help me now. I wasn't sure what I expected from a dead man.

> There will be an awakening of humanity that will bring about the end and the beginning. The current reality we find ourselves in cannot be fully known through technology or science, only through an

191

> internal knowing of the human mind, and
> all that it is truly capable of. To fully tap into
> a consciousness that may be physical,
> beyond physical, or non-physical, we must
> first hold onto the pleasure and the pain
> that permeates our everyday lives, whilst
> perceiving beyond our own constraints and
> mental barriers to understand the true
> nature of consciousness.

A half smile surfaced and quickly furrowed as I recalled the warmth of long forgotten pleasures, and the pain that followed.

Jeri's smile beamed occasionally in reaction to one of her nieces or nephews, but I knew it as the mask it was, carefully concealing the truth. I wondered what Jeri had told Carol and Herb. How much they blamed me.

I hoped she didn't find it hard being around the children. Every day I had spent with them had been such a conflicting time of love and sorrow. I hoped they brought her happiness.

It's the smaller mistakes that often cause the most pain. The unsaid word, the ill emotion conveyed. It should be easy. I tried to tell myself that my actions betray my feelings, that it's possible for something inherently good to falter and produce something abhorrent. Perhaps there is another version of me somewhere, who isn't crippled by their mistakes and the cruel whims of the universe. Someone fulfilling the potential of a life such as this. A family strong enough to face anything that the world has to throw at them. Strong enough to face any threat without despair. Perhaps. It had become my only solace.

I remembered vividly a time when I mattered. When there was a woman who couldn't live without me, whose own life was so entwined with mine that our names were more often used as one, fused together rather than spoken apart. My connection to the world, my constraint and my freedom. I could have died knowing that I had left someone behind who would miss me, changed someone's life who loved me, became one with someone who deemed me worthy.

But I am no longer essential. My life brings meaning to no one. The world can continue as I disappear or fade away. If my two selves would meet, how my former self would stew in disgust over the man I am, not a husband, nor a father, unable to do anything right in the world. A truly unnecessary man. But I would remind him that he is not so just and grand, that the monster he sees in me resides solely in him, only separated by the current of time, the promise of those things that matter most.

Herb dropped his fork and leaned into Jeri. He rested his hand on my wife's shoulder, teasing out a smile that appeared as genuine as any I had seen.

I took one more sip of the flask, closed my eyes, leaned back in my chair, and urged myself to sleep so that I could stay alert through the night shift.

I can't give her what she wants. All I can hope for is that I am able to do what I need to protect her. I am no longer a husband. I was never a father.

TWENTY-ONE

Once again, I was guided through the depths of US Tech to the control room as overhead lights flickered along the way. The surrounding walls seemed even narrower than the first time, but like before, there was something very ominous about being taken into that room, a brigade of security officers walking me silently to my destination.

Robert Palmer, Agent Brody and General Day were among a dozen people inside Robert's control room. I stopped next to Robert, his gaze fixed on the large screen in front. He looked as immaculate as ever, fully suited in yet another multitude of variations of royal blue. "This wouldn't be possible without you."

His praise only led me to guilt – how different it could have been if President Walker had used the comms device when I knew it worked.

Robert stepped forward as an image of the Space Lift appeared on the screen, eight astronauts striding towards it. The floor where William had hit the ground shined with reflected light from the ceiling.

"The feed is broadcasting live, Sir." One of the comms officers stated to Agent Brody. Robert had insisted, against stern recommendations from General Day, that the people of the world deserved full disclosure and visibility of the operation.

"This is a monumental day," Robert announced to the room. "Peace can only be gained, not won. We must put past indiscretions behind us. Agreement to this operation is an impressive gesture of good faith. They are demonstrating to us that they have nothing to hide."

It took twenty agonising minutes for the eight astronauts to travel through the Space Lift to the US Pad Space Station. When I first read about the Earth-to-Orbit Shuttle, I never imagined that this would be its first mission. Except for the hum of equipment and the rare word between staff, the room was silent for the duration. I considered what peace could be like between us, how President Walker hoped we could benefit from such an advanced civilisation. Until at last, the lead pilot of the Mars Shuttle spoke.

"We are on approach to the craft. We expect to reach the destination in just eight minutes. We have a visual."

"Roger, transmitting visual." A massive oval craft appeared on the screen. It was a dull metal with small ovals protruding from it. As soon as I saw it, I knew that was where I was taken. I felt their oily, moist skin like it was sliding against me right now.

Eight minutes passed without another word from the shuttle.

"We are awaiting communication to allow us to board the craft," the shuttle confirmed, and the control room waited for the alien craft to open up a hatch or something. "We have successfully communicated our position to the craft. We are awaiting a response."

I held my breath as each second stretched out for an eternity. Everything was riding on that one moment. They're not here to kill us. If we can help them, this could all be over.

Without warning a ball of flames filled every corner of the screen then snapped away to leave nothing behind except the alien craft and no evidence that the shuttle had ever existed. Everyone in the room was reeling from the impact. The communications officer kept trying to reach the shuttle, but it was futile. Anarchy prevailed as military personnel tried to find out how the shuttle was destroyed, and if any craft were heading towards Earth.

There was nothing left, and we didn't even see them fire.

Amid the chaos Robert stood, not uttering a single word, not showing a single emotion. He held his resolve and then lifted his voice above the panic:

"They will see it as they wake. As they eat their breakfast and take their children to school. The hopes of an entire world, dashed by the actions of those who wish us harm. The death of any person is tragic. But when it is only the first of many, possibly the first of us all; that is when we must not surrender. We will not hold back." Robert's eyes bore into the screen and the empty space that was left behind. "Whatever it takes, Ryan. Whatever you need to blow the bastards back to whichever hole they crawled out of."

Our skies were clear and for the moment we were safe. But today will not be forgotten.

* * *

"Men and women have died today." Robert's speech started with the same amount of dramatic impact as I had come to expect from him. The Briefing room at the White House was brimming with press, despite the extremely short notice of invitation. There was a sombre tone, and everything seemed quieter, as though people were too afraid to speak. "A Russian man, a British woman, a Chinese man, a Japanese man, a French woman, an American woman, and two American men. Many nations of our world came together in an attempt to create peace. The lives of those astronauts, our ambassadors were taken by beings that are not of this Earth. We must now show the determination of our people, and the humanity in our hearts to defend our world." Robert held his right hand firmly in the air, "Our world!" The crowd erupted into applause followed by a standing ovation.

Darkness seemed inevitable from the moment an Earth shuttle was destroyed but felt no less welcome because of it. Neighbourhood watch evolved into local patrol parties and the city shut down after dark. Police forces became riot control while military forces policed the streets. We didn't know what was happening anywhere else because the only thing that seemed to matter was Washington DC. Robert embraced fully his place as world leader against the alien threat.

'What to do if you believe you have been abducted' posters seemed to be multiply on walls, often crowded by avid studiers. Stories spread of abductees being hauled in for questioning by military camps where people would undergo brutally old techniques like drugging and starvation to encourage them to talk. One abductee in particular was so bold to go on television stating that he was in league with our alien visitors, facilitating their migration to our planet. Amidst the plethora of pro and anti-alien and abductee propaganda, the world was ready for a reckoning.

TWENTY-TWO

I hadn't been home in days. The stench of spirits and bad hygiene that emanated from me had become unnoticeable by my own senses and the weight of the bags dragged my eyes down over my cheeks. Two weeks spent pouring over the reports Robert granted me access to, and reading Heinrich Galli's A Guide to Life cover to cover three times. I had exhausted every scenario I could dream up to arm the comms device. Still without a word to, or face to face contact with Jeri since she left me.

I had spent the last three hours in my office with Jess and Peter drawing up ideas but I felt no closer to solving it than day one. Alex Little swung the door open and paraded inside. "You never showed for our ten o'clock." My hands shook as soon as his voice started to rise. I didn't need another scathing and lacked the energy to endure it. "I don't know what the hell's going on here. I haven't seen any progress in a week."

"We're... we're working on ideas." I stumbled over my words. My head was too hazy to establish any reasoning with him.

"I don't want ideas; I want a working prototype. I'm not sure your head's even in the game. Are you listening to me?"

"Ryan's putting everything into this," Jess jumped in. "We wouldn't have a prototype to test if it wasn't for him."

He stared down at her like she was a piece of shit "I didn't ask for your opinion. You two, out. Now."

Jess and Peter froze at first, and then shuffled towards the door. A fire rumbled in my gut, ready to erupt. I raised my hand to stop them dead. My voice stayed low and almost monotone. "You don't speak to them like that. You don't speak to them at all."

Little's eyes widened before quickly developing a scowl.

"Ryan," Jess said softly, but her words were trodden on by Little's booming voice.

"You listen to me, you little upstart. I've been chewing up and spitting out shit like you my entire life. I was making seven figures when you were studying for your high school diploma. You got that?"

My face couldn't have been more underwhelmed. "You shouldn't have treated my friends like that." I selected Agent Brody from my contact list and lifted my phone to my ear. "I can't work under these circumstances. The management… Yes… Yes, intolerable." By the time I dropped my phone onto the desk, Little's cell was buzzing in his pocket.

"Hello?" he said, confused. "Yes. I'm off what?" His voice rose to a pitch that was uncomfortable for my ears. "But it's my project… I don't understand. Ok… ok." The cell phone slid down Little's pasty white face.

I kept my expression devoid of emotion, entirely calm and at ease. "Now get the fuck out of my office."

Little tensed his body and straightened his back, puffing his chest out at me. I let him hold the pose until he finally deflated and scuttled out of my office. An insignificant particle.

"Now, where were we?" I asked.

Jess wouldn't look at me, clearly unimpressed. Peter jumped to his feet and started scribbling designs on the screen pretending nothing had happened. "We can't know the success of each component of the trial because we can't truly measure our successes or failures with a great enough level of certainty to manage the variables."

"We need a live one," I said.

"You know that we can't." Jess piped up with eyes of contempt. "If we hit one, we hit them all. You know that."

"Doesn't sound like such a bad idea." I looked to Peter for support, but he backed away, not wanting to get between us.

"Are you serious?" Jess asked. "You tell me this is to defend ourselves, and that it's a last resort, but I'm not sure you see it that way."

"You know how powerful they are."

"I saw first-hand. After we held it captive then you killed it."

"What was I supposed to do? You saw what it did to those people."

"In self-defence."

"Exactly. They started taking us long before we took them."

"And that makes this right? Shouldn't we be trying to understand what they want? Trying to help them so we can resolve it peacefully?"

I shook my head in disbelief. "While they keep abducting people. What happens when they stop bringing them back? I have to stop them. Whatever it takes."

"At what cost? This isn't all on your shoulders, you know."

The office sank into darkness. My cell phone vibrated on my desk, lighting up Jess and Peter's faces. I answered and a voice spoke straight away, "Sir, we have a security breach at the lab."

* * *

The head of security for my wing was waiting to greet me outside the lab, standing to attention with his hands behind

200

his back like he was still in the military. "We lost CCTV at the same time as we lost power on this floor."

"They're on the same power grid?"

"No, sir. Each floor is on a separate grid, and security is separate again. Cameras came back online a few minutes ago, but we had static the rest of the time. Power on this floor has gone completely. ETA to get it back up is thirty minutes."

"I need to see that footage."

"Yes, sir," he said without hesitation.

"What's the damage?" I tried to mentally prepare myself for the worst.

"Critical, Sir. The comms prototype has been hit. It's completely destroyed."

Peter gasped behind me. I turned to him, "Check the plans. I want a full review of all material on central and backup drives. I want to know if anything was erased, changed, or accessed."

Peter darted towards the stairs. I headed straight to the comms device and kneeled beside it. The casing that surrounded it was melted and the device was still smouldering, along with the kit that it was connected to. Totally unrecognisable. "Were there any sightings?"

"No, Sir. No assailants were visibly identified."

"How long did it take to get your team here?"

"Two were already stationed at the entrance, and another two within the lab as per protocol, Sir."

I nodded at the acceptable response "Ok, I want this floor shut down and secured. No one in or out without my authorisation. No one."

My head of security nodded as Peter came running toward me in a fluster with a tablet in hand. "No files have been accessed within the past thirty minutes on the central or backup drives. We're doing a full audit to see if anything's been deleted but there's nothing obvious, still a shit-tonne of them there."

I stood up and looked around the room at dozens of

technicians, scientists, project managers and other personnel hurrying about the lab, staring into space in complete shock or trying to cobble together some level of recovery.

"They're watching every move we make."

Jess stood at my side, staring down at the damage. "What do we do now?" she asked.

"We react accordingly. Because now we know one thing: we must be getting close."

* * *

The comms device being hit was the first planet-based offensive we had suffered. Peace negotiations had been on hold since the shuttle attack, and Robert told me that he expected things to escalate quickly. Brody assured me that every weapon we had would be utilised to maximise security against any further attacks, but I wasn't convinced we had anything that could stop them. A quiver in his usually arrogant voice told me maybe he wasn't either.

I was desperate to see Jeri again, to hold her, or just look upon her face up close and hear her speak. I was in agony without her.

Progress rebuilding a prototype weaponised comms device was slow, so I took Sunday afternoon to stop by my dad's house and muster the courage to tell him that Jeri had left me. Just as I expected, he comforted and listened to me, which only served to poke at the wound.

"She acted like it was only temporary. I'm sure... I'm sure it is."

My dad tilted his head at me and narrowed his eyes with pity and it became harder to tell myself she was coming back. "It's difficult losing someone you love. I miss your mother every day. But she's gone and I know that I can't get her back in this life. When they're just within you're reach… Sometimes that's even harder." A tear emerged from my dad's right eye. There was only one, but it was strong, pushing its way down his face. I couldn't bare it.

"You should go and see him," I said but my dad shook his head. "Things are different now. Everything is different."

"He hates me."

"I'm sure he does. But only because he loves you." I took a long, slow breath. "He wants to see you. He told me… that he wants to see you. With what's happening… it changes everything. Maybe he's ready, you know?"

Dad had the eyes of a Labrador, never before had I seen such a mix of sadness and hope in a man's eyes. I turned away and expelled his sad eyes out of my mind.

It was a long, quiet drive to Herb's house. When my dad asked for details about what Herb said when he told me he wanted to see Dad I reiterated what I had already said and moved on. Dad was too excited to push. When Herb answered the door, my dad spoke quickly before he had time to react. "Thank you for seeing us." I could hear the anticipation in my dad's voice, he had been planning this moment the entire journey here, maybe longer. He waited for some semblance of a welcome, but Herb screwed up his face and showed no sign of inviting us in.

"We need to talk," I insisted. "It's important."

Herb turned his back and made his way into the dark corridor, like he was entering the depths of a cave. Dad hesitated so I stepped inside and prompted him to follow. I poked my head into each doorway we passed and followed Herb into the kitchen. He didn't sit down or offer either one of us a seat. He didn't speak either, a stare down permanently featured on his face, supported by folded arms. Dad braved the frosty reception, "It's been so long."

"Not long enough," Herb retorted.

"I-"

"What?" he interrupted.

"Ryan said…"

"Ryan said what?"

Dad turned to me, and his face crumpled. He bowed his

head and offered it up to Herb. I wanted the ground to swallow me whole. "Maybe I should go," Dad said. "I think there's been a misunderstanding."

Herb's voice grew louder. "Ryan said what?"

"I'll leave."

Herb turned to me. "Did you tell him to come here? Then you should both leave." Dad walked through the corridor towards the front door, still in earshot. Herb jabbed his finger towards Dad. "What the hell are you doing bringing him here?"

Eddie appeared in the doorway gazing up at my dad. Dad kneeled beside him. "Hello there, Son. It's... It's Eddie, isn't it? Uncle Ryan showed me pictures of you."

"What are you doing?" Herb squeezed between them, a centimetre away from pushing my dad over. "Don't you speak to him."

"Don't be ridiculous." Dad rose to his feet.

"Get upstairs, Eddie. Pretend he isn't here. I'm about to make it a reality." Eddie didn't move, as obedient as ever. Dad looked at his son and saw the futility over trying to overcome his stubbornness and skulked down the hallway and out the house.

This wasn't what I wanted. I hadn't thought whether Herb would welcome or at least be civil to Dad, I hadn't thought about them at all. All that was left was to do what I came here for.

"Where's Jeri?"

"She's out."

"When will-"

"She's out," Herb said forcefully. All I had wanted was to see my wife.

"I'll wait."

"Don't think we haven't seen you out there in your cheap rental every night, perving in at us."

The room became fuzzy, the light blinding me. I could hear myself panting. "I... I don't know what you're talking about."

Herb paced away then came bounding back, his arms raised over us, exaggerating his already large stature. "Next time I see you sat outside my house I'll come and bang on your window. Or I'll call the police." Herb's face was red with fury. "Now get the hell out of my house."

"I'm not leaving until I see her."

"I told you how many times, she's not here. And she doesn't want to see you. Now, I want you gone, you can go the same way he did, you're no good... Bringing him here! Get the hell outta my house." Herb didn't see me to the door.

I climbed back in the car next to my dad and drove slowly to the next block and stopped the car. "What are you doing?" Dad asked. I pulled on the handbrake and turned the engine off.

"Just wait here." I opened the door and jumped out. I heard my dad shout again as I hiked back towards Herb's house and stopped twenty or so feet away and saw her there.

Jeri lifted her hand to her mouth as Herb flailed his arms in the air. She dragged the back of her hands across each eye and then padded them with the sleeves of her maroon hooded sweater.

I should be there for her; I should be able to take care of her and help her through this. She must be terrified. But she knew I was there, and she stayed clear. So, we're terrified alone.

No one else understands what we've been through. I need you. I will love you until the end.

* * *

The sun blazed red through my eyelids. I peeled them open and cowered behind my arm. I dragged my leg off the back seat of the car and let it bang down on the floor under its own weight. It felt like my throat was eroding, the lining of my stomach carefully torn off with pliers, strip by strip, by way of alcohol or guilt. I couldn't have been filled with any

205

more hate. Bitterness crept back up my throat and snatched my attention, erupting onto the car floor. The stench was there but the embarrassment was notably absent. I missed the feeling of pride I once had. Maybe tomorrow. At least I took the rental back.

I got my things together with no care for my appearance but reserved a permanent place for my bottle, vodka being the order of the day. I couldn't bear to look at Herb's house, to see Jeri in there without me. Being here was enough to know she was safe. I turned on the engine and headed to work.

With each day that passed there were fewer familiar faces at US Tech. Some looked at me like my being there was absurd. They stared when I walked into the meeting room, but no one responded to my mumbled apology for being late. They were even more uneasy than the previous day. Jess gave a slight smile as I sat down next to her and subtly slid a packet of mints my way. There was a man at the far end of the table that wouldn't take his beady eyes off me. They talked and talked but I didn't even know what they were saying. I hoped for meeting notes. I was so tired. If it wasn't for Robert, I wouldn't be there. So tired.

I opened my eyes to a tiny bald man banging his hand on my desk. Apparently, they were waiting for me to speak. "I bet he's getting a bonus this month to piss all over," he said shaking his head.

"Sorry."

"I'm sorry. That you just daydreamed your way off this programme, White Giant boy." The bald man looked around the room for agreement from blank faces. Most of them kept their eyes to the desk. He accepted the silent response and sunk into his seat.

I flummoxed my papers and stood. I'd had enough of their incessant babble. They knew nothing about the alien race they were so desperately trying to protect themselves from. No one said a word, not until I left the room at least. I stopped in an empty corridor and took a quick drink. It burned. I couldn't bear to spend another second without Jeri. If I could only see her again, face to face.

Fool. If she saw me like this, she would surely breathe a breath of relief for leaving just soon enough.

I reached for another drink. When I heard someone coming, I threw it down my neck and pocketed it quickly. Jess crept up beside me. "I tried to wake you up. I kicked Phillip Ball instead." Her eyes wandered from me and around the corridor. "I'm worried about you… I know the pressure you're under."

I shook my head. "I'm fine."

"I know how important it is. We'll rebuild it. Then it'll work. I trust you." She pursed her lips in sympathy. Followed by a smile.

"I don't need another one of your pep talks." Jess' smile disappeared in a flash.

"I'm with you, Ryan. I'm on your side."

"I'm a married man." I said it cool and calm with a tongue of venom.

Jess took a sharp intake of breath. Her face crumpled and my chest hurt looking at it. Then my eyes stung, burning in my sockets like someone was gouging them out from the inside. "Your eyes… Oh God, your eyes."

The colour was dispelled from the world around me, blanketed by a monochrome haze. Jess looked both ways down the corridor. I palmed my face and stumbled away from her, eyes gnawing at my sockets, building up to a gallop.

Jess gripped my shoulder and pushed me along the corridor. I heard a door rattle open, and she shoved me inside to face rows of sinks and open toilet cubicles. I heard the door lock behind us. I felt around the sink for a tap and threw water at my face to wash away the sting, but it wouldn't relent. I fell to my knees and scraped my fingers down my cheeks, peeling chunks of skin under my nails.

Jess pulled me to my feet, a limp, lame corpse. Buried in agony. She placed her hand on my check and tilted my head to face her dead on. I squeezed my eyes closed.

I felt Jess' face move closer to mine. She pulled at the skin, top and bottom, until my eyeball was uncovered for her to see.

My eyes were bulging their way out of my head, scratching away at the insides of my skull, tearing me apart. "What's happening to me?" I cried out.

Jess wrenched her head away from me. She couldn't bear to look at me.

She lifted her head to face me, eyes shut tight. She took a deep, uneasy breath and opened her eyes. Two black marbles stared back at me, giant black pupils, just like my own.

TWENTY-THREE

I tugged at my skin in the reflection of the seventy-inch TV. I had never been more relieved to see the whites of my eyes staring back at me. I moved closer to make sure there were no signs of a return, the blue iris and white shell still surrounded a small black hole that limited itself to the centre.

"Why are we like this?" Jess sounded from behind me. She had sat in silence behind a glossy white desk on the meeting room floor, her legs tucked into her chest. Her eyes returned to normal as quickly as they turned black.

"You don't know?" Jess shook her head. I sipped at a plastic cup of water, stalling. "Me either."

"Have you told anyone?"

"No," I said forcefully and whipped round to face her. "We can't."

"That's what I thought… but don't we need help? If there are two of us…"

I kneeled in front of her and placed my hands on her legs. "Listen to me. You can't tell anyone about this. Not about either of us."

"We don't even know what this is. The people we've been in contact with… what if we're infected? What if it's their way of controlling us? We're building a weapon that can destroy them. We're a liability."

I jumped up and paced away from her. We could end up in quarantine, locked up until this is over or we're all dead.

"Ryan, you have drinks with Robert Palmer, there's no better example of 'who you know.'"

I hesitated. "I think we just need to-"

"You know something." Jess lowered her voice. "Shit, you do. What do you know?"

"Jess."

"*What* do you know?"

"Listen to me-"

Jess rose to her feet and stalked behind me. "This is my life. Why won't you tell me?"

I took her slender hands in mine. "I love you, Jess. You and Rick, you're my best friends. I won't let anything happen to you."

Jess marched to the door and flicked the lock open. "I'm not asking you to protect me. All I wanted from you was the truth." She swung the door open and left.

* * *

I texted Jess to tell her I was sorry and asked her to trust me. After three hours she texted me back, ok. I told myself I was doing the right thing keeping her in the dark. No good could come from her knowing she had been taken – Look how Jeri reacted. I'm sure she knew, deep down inside, but not what happens when they take you, how helpless you are. Sometimes you have to be cruel to be kind.

I didn't know how long it would be until my next episode and the wrong person saw. Until they did more than destroy my comms device. I had to go back to the start, to get answers I couldn't find in a book.

Vera Galli's scowl as she pulled back the door, one brow raised, was enough, but she threw in a deadpan, "What the fuck do you want?" just to make sure I got the message.

"I need your help," I said as I stepped towards the door, but she kept her feet planted, firmly blocking the entrance.

Both brows were raised this time, her face dead serious. "I don't think so."

"Look," I was losing patience, irritation seeping into my voice. "I can't tell you how important this is." I pulled out my ID badge. "I work at US Tech-"

"I remember what you do. However unmemorable it is."

"This has nothing to do with Rick," I said exasperated.

"You thought I was wondering if you were here to rekindle or dilapidated love, or something? See why I didn't like your friend?" She snorted a laugh but kept her mouth turned down like a grouper fish. "I don't like strangers turning up at my door. Especially from government agencies."

I took a moment to breathe and calm myself. To be at ease and look at her, arms crossed, standing firm. Dyed black hair in a bun. A billowing shirt buttoned halfway up and draped over slim black pants that stopped at her calves. She gripped the door. Her weight positioned on her back foot, ready to move away quickly. She was being cautious.

"I'm sorry," I said with as amiable and composed a tone as I could. "I really do need your help. I'm trying to build something that we desperately need, a defensive weapon, should we need it. The foundation technology that it is based on is predicated entirely on your father's theory. But I'm lost. And I'm scared. And unless I have a breakthrough soon... We have nothing."

"There is no such thing as a defensive weapon. And I can't help you."

"Please. Just let me talk to you. If you still can't help me then I'll leave, and I won't come back. Without it we don't stand a chance. No one else knows I'm here. Please."

I waited while she stared into my eyes, and I gazed right back. She took a small step back, and then another, still gripping the door. She backed up again until the door was finally open.

Vera left me in the reception room while she made a pot of tea. Her father's face was notably absent from the many photographs that adorned pale walls, white shelves, and the black glossy coffee table. She perched on the edge of the sleek black leather sofa. "So, what is it you think I can do for you?"

"I've been through everything, all of his research, his extended notes and lectures. I need more."

"I don't have it." She took a sip of tea, still steaming, and let it rest on her lips before putting down the cup.

"He talked about breaking the species barrier to access brainwaves. Maybe even to merge cognitive thought. But there were no studies produced to support the theory."

"I'm not a scientist."

"He must have had some other material," I insisted. "Something he was working on before he passed, any notes or research he had done to support his published work."

"I don't have anything."

I jumped to my feet. "There must be something. He alludes to it so many times through his work. Show me what he left you, I can take it away."

"What?" She scowled at me again and gripped her delicate teacup.

"Or I can have a look around. You said it yourself, you're not a scientist. You don't know what you're looking for. Just show me anything you have that was his and I'll look at it."

"I can't help you."

"Listen to me. This is our only hope," I shouted, furious at her for getting in my way. "We are nothing compared to them. We have nothing that can stop them. Don't you understand?" I dropped down onto the armchair. "You're my last hope."

"I'm afraid you don't understand," Vera stated firmly. She pursed her lips and clenched her jaw. "I'm as scared as you are. But if I'm your last hope that you are even more of a desperate little man than I thought. There is nothing left. He burned everything."

I sat back, confused at Vera's response. I had nowhere else to turn. She had to have something I could use. "Why would he do that?"

Vera eyes fell away from me, hollow, and glaring into space. "I was a child. He left me alone for days at a time. A child. I grew up…" Her voice quivered. Tiny clangs rung out as her shaking hands knocked the cup against the saucer. "Thinking that our society was on the brink of collapse. That some imminent destruction loomed over us."

"Your father talked of this?" I said gently.

"He was obsessed. He had me convinced, for years he had me convinced. Until I was old enough to know better… To make my own life… And then here we are." She set the tea down and rubbed her fingers into her eyes. "One day, he came home, and he wasn't the same. He wouldn't tell me what happened… I questioned him, so many times. He wouldn't tell me. He was never the same."

I saw the broken woman that Heinrich had left behind. A daughter whose father had been snatched away from her. "I'm sorry," Vera continued. "I don't know what he wrote… but it's gone. Papers, hard drives… he burnt the lot. He set it alight… and then he stepped into the flames… and took it all with him." She stopped for a moment, perfectly still. She rose to her feet, and I followed her lead. "People said he was a prophet. But he was just a man. Before anything else, he was my father."

Vera led me down the hallway and I opened the door to leave. "Wait," she said. I stopped and turned to face her. "My father. You share the same look that he had. You won't stop until you find what you're looking for. Even after dedicating his life to the study of it, my father never understood the truth about life. What it means, why we are here, the soul. He believed that to be his reason for being on this earth, never more so than at the end. His failure tortured him until the day he died."

Heinrich Galli had called death the next stage, but my worst fear was that it was final, the end of what we have here, followed only by nothingness. Death as merely the absence of life. And I felt its sinister presence once more creep closer, day by day.

"Paradoxical end. Unveil. Transcend. Do those words mean anything to you?"

She shook her head. "I'm sorry."

I nodded to Vera as I left her raw from the emotion that she had exhumed. Despite my gratitude for her eventual openness towards me, I couldn't hide my disappointment as I left.

* * *

The early evening gloom filtered in through the small grimy windows and fell on third-Tuesday-of-the-month regulars at the Bruiser bar who still hung on from a day's drinking. I emptied my glass and waved the barman for another. He didn't hesitate to fill it back up again. The next one failed like every other before it, Jeri's face callously imprinted on my mind like a burn shadow. How many times would she be violated and vulnerable? How many times until they brought her back hacked to pieces like Rebecca Jones?

I had to tell Brody. If there was anywhere that was still safe, then it would be with the other abductees. I only hoped that I could convince them that I wasn't abducted long enough for me to weaponise the comms device. I hoped she would forgive me.

As soon as Herb swung open the door, he saw me. He stopped before strolling to take the barstool next to me. I had waited all day to see his face. "You found someone else to chauffer you around then?" The words came out slurred. Herb waved the barman and kept his eyes on the deer antlers the other side of the bar. The barman set Herb's beer down in front of him. I nodded to my glass.

"I'm surprised you could tear yourself away, what with who you've got waiting for you at home. What does Carol say? Does she share your bed yet?"

The barman came back and held the bottle over my glass. Herb covered it with his hand and gave a subtle shake of his head.

I laughed. "What, you're the protective big brother, now? *Dad?* You can't speak to yours, so you have to be mine?"

Herb sipped at his beer. His silence was killing me.

"What? I'm not good enough for you?" I stumbled at him, and my stool hit the floor with a clatter. I slumped on the bar and jabbed my finger in his face. "Look at me when I'm talking to you. No one is safe. Do you understand? There's nothing we can do to stop them. We should bomb the lot of them." I turned to the boozers and shouted, "Do you hear me?"

I felt Herb's lumbering hand on my back. "Pipe down."

I pushed my face so close to Herb's I could have spat right in his eye. "I've already done one," I slurred, quiet enough for only Herb to hear. "Put metal in it. See how they like it. You don't believe me? Come and see the body."

Herb let go of his beer and towered over me. "Come on, I'm taking you home." I went quietly and without commotion in a cab back to my house. We didn't say another word to each other until Herb was taking off my left shoe while I lay sprawled on the sofa.

"You're going to help me now, are you?" Herb took his attention away from my laces and looked up my slouching body. "My big brother, the betrayer. The family man. The proud father."

"I'm getting you into bed."

"Either way she's dead."

Herb gave a ridiculously exaggerated sigh of exasperation. I felt like kicking him in the face. "What are you talking about?"

"Don't pretend she hasn't told you. Don't pretend you haven't been… sitting… laughing at me."

"I'm not gonna argue with you." Herb walked away but I wasn't finished.

"You can't just walk away from me like that." I leapt to my feet like a lion showing its teeth before an attack, but I struggled to keep my chin off my chest and my eyes from rolling in my head of their own free will. "You stole my wife. You betrayed me."

Herb stopped halfway to the door. "Don't do it Ry, don't dig into this. I just helped her out. Carol as much as me."

"Helped her out?" I slurred every word. "You're hiding her away from me! She was there the whole fucking time."

"I just gave her a place to stay. She hid herself." Herb looked at the floor. He was trying to dodge the argument, but I wasn't going to let that happen. "You pushed her out, man. I'm sorry, but… you pushed her away. I know how hard it's been-"

I charged at him, one shoe on, one off but he stepped aside effortlessly. My body expected to collide with his and my alcohol-impaired brain didn't work fast enough so my legs tripped underneath me, and I sprawled onto the table.

"I'm not going to fight you." Herb said towering over me. I stumbled upright and swung my fist at his head. Even drunk I knew I had missed by a long shot. As my whole body swung around, he grabbed me from behind and held my arms so I couldn't move. I tried to wriggle free, but it was useless. I was outmatched. "Just calm down."

Herb held my arms long enough for me to stop thrashing and then let go, gently moving me away from him. "Dad's right," I said with a sneer, "I bet Mom's so disappointed in you." As soon as the words left my mouth, Herb's fist crashed into my cheek and sent me spiralling into a shelving unit. I slid down until my face hit the wooden floor, too drunk and stunned to break my own fall. Blood trickled down my brow into my eye. I had never sunk so low.

I watched Herb's feet walk away and heard the door slam behind him. I didn't move, my mind absent. My body still, except for the blood and drool that oozed out of it. As my eyes finally closed the curtains over my view of the world, the last thing I saw was a small black object broken on the floor before me. It was so tiny I wouldn't have noticed except I recognised it. In my early days at US Tech, I helped make it.

TWENTY-FOUR

"Hello." I said as soon as Jeri opened the door. Her sequin dress shimmered purple and gold, paired with shiny gold heels. I tried so very hard to not keep staring down at her long, slender legs.

Michelle popped her head around the door. "Hello," she purred, eyeing me up and down before doing the same with Rick.

We carried wine, flowers and chocolates through the long beige hallway, shiny wooden floors leading us into the living room. "We thought we would keep it pretty casual," Jeri said.

"Your house is beautiful." The room was larger than any room in Mom and Dad's house but not big enough to stop it feeling homely. Comfortable sofas and thick rugs surrounded a short table that looked like carved walnut, untreated and laid with a platter of nibbles. Jeri slipped off her shoes and snuggled down on the rug, legs tucked underneath her.

"Thanks. My parents bought it when they married." I sat opposite her as we picked at olives, crackers and tapenade and inhaled the wood burning on the open fire. Every time I looked at Michelle, she smiled at me. It was going well.

I asked Jeri about her family, and her childhood, what it was like being an only child, and I found myself staring into her eyes and watching her lips as she released reams of beautiful words on my ears. Every time she looked diagonally into empty air when she talked, or bit down on her tongue gently, I was in a daze. I spoke less and less and became more engrossed in what revelation or captivating mannerism would come next. I watched her unfold in front of me, draped in soft light from the flicker of the fire until something got into my brain that I could never love another woman.

"What do you do for fun?" Rick said, frowning at me. He and Michelle had barely spoken.

"Jeri can hit a matchstick at one hundred feet," Michelle jumped in.

I threw Jeri a look of intrigue. "Not every time... But most times," she said, a proud smile breaking through her humility.

"Wow. Michelle tells me you're joining the academy with her?" Rick popped an olive in his mouth.

"That's right. Twenty-eight weeks."

"It's pretty tough getting into the MPD," Michelle said, refilling our glasses with wine. She smiled at Rick.

"Oh, I bet." Rick replied to Michelle, and then turned to Jeri. "There's no way I have the fitness to cut it."

"There's a lot of theory too," Jeri replied.

"And a lot of firearms training," Michelle added. "Are the starters ready, do you think, Jeri?"

Jeri looked at the clock and hesitated, but Michelle was already standing and on her way to the kitchen. I waited for them to leave and leaned in to Rick. "What are you doing?"

"What are you doing?"

"You've barely said a word."

"Because you won't stop flirting with my date." Rick said, even more aggrieved than me.

I pulled a face. "Michelle? I wasn't flirting with Michelle."

"Michelle? Michelle's your date."

"Wait, what? Who are you on a date with?"

Before Rick could answer, Jeri and Michelle wandered back in carrying miniature smoked salmon terrine, prawn cocktail and lobster tails. They took their time setting down the food and when they finished, awkward half smiles were exchanged along with averted eyes. No one touched the starters. No one said a word.

"Uhm," Rick finally braved. "Could you both just clarify something? Could you confirm uhm, who you are on a date with?"

Michelle raised an eyebrow. "What?"

"Your date," Rick reiterated. "Who is it?"

"What do you mean?" Jeri asked, perplexed.

Rick looked to me for help. "Err…" I started. "We both kind of think… we're on a date…" I looked Jeri in the eyes. "With you."

Jeri leaned back against the sofa, flummoxed. Michelle was stern rather than taken aback. "What? What?" She looked to Jeri. "How did this happen?" Then looked back to Rick and me. "So, neither of you think you're on a date with me?"

We both kept quiet.

Jeri shifted back away from us. "This isn't going to end well." We each averted our eyes from the food and each other. "I think we should call it a night," Jeri said.

"Or we could carry on?" I jumped in. "The food looks amazing. We could carry on? See how the date goes. Then tell us who you want to date?"

"What about me?" Michelle asked.

Rick and I didn't respond.

"I'm not something to fawn over," Jeri said.

"I'm not fawning," Rick said looking at me out of the corner of his eye.

"He doesn't even know how to fawn," I added. "It's just having a good night with new friends."

"Or you could just tell them who you thought you were

on a date with," Michelle said.

Jeri held her hands up. "I'm not getting between two friends."

I patted Rick on the shoulder. "We've been friends since the first day of college."

"Best friends," Rick said.

"We can handle it." I smiled at Jeri, unwilling to give up on her so easily. "We carry on, and at the end of the date, you tell us who you want to see again. If you want to see either of us."

Jeri looked back and forth between us. We had made our argument, and now we had to wait for Jeri to make her decision. I crossed my fingers under the table.

"You both accept the outcome. No grudges. Or we end this now."

"I promise." I said, hoping we had won her over.

"I don't believe I have anything to be concerned about," Rick said in a tone as pompous as his words. "But sure. No grudges."

We embraced the warmth, and the only sound was the conversation that flowed organically between us.

After the starters, we devoured Jeri's delicious chicken Thai curry with rice, eggplant, mushrooms and bok choi, and then migrated to the sofa. Jeri pulled her hair back and tucked herself up under a beige woollen blanket with long tassels dangling over her body. She lifted a steaming mug of rooibos, and I did the same, the warm aroma inhabiting my senses. A collection of wooden picture frames was hung together on the wall opposite, mostly of Jeri with what looked like her parents. On one of them Jeri was holding a baby. "Who's that you're with?"

Jeri looked over at the picture. "My cousin. She's twelve months now, just starting to walk." She took a long sip of tea. "You like kids Rick?"

"In small doses. And one at a time."

"I love kids," Jeri said turning back to me.

"Oh yeah, me too." Rick jumped in. "I love them."

221

"You want kids, Ryan?" Jeri asked.

"I do."

"A boy or a girl?"

"I don't mind."

"Boy then, huh? Every guy wants a son."

"Really, I don't mind."

"Come on, gun to your head."

"Not literally, I hope. My heads a little bigger than a match." Jeri smiled and raised her eyebrows at me, waiting for an answer. "Gun to my head? A girl."

I could feel Jeri looking at me closely, but her expression was blank. "Huh."

"You've been offered a job, haven't you, Rick?" Michelle smiled at him.

"Yeah, at US Tech. An apprentice Mechanical Engineer."

"Wow, that sounds fascinating," Jeri said, nodding to Michelle. "Do you know what you'll be working on?"

"Not yet. Not exactly. But there's some leading tech they're developing in pretty much every industry there is. A lot of experimental stuff. They showed me around the place after my interview."

"That sounds great." Michelle said. "What about you, Ryan? Do you have a job lined up?"

I shuffled in my seat, unable to compete. "No. Not yet." My grades were good, but not to Rick's standard, and I was struggling with what to do next.

"I'm sure something will turn up," Michelle said.

"I could try to get you an interview at US Tech?" Rick suggested.

"I don't know," I replied.

"Just let me know." Jeri smiled at Rick. "Listen, that food was exquisite. Now Ryan and I are going to do the clean-up."

"No way," Jeri said, jumping to her feet.

"I insist. You made it such a superb night, so please let us repay you some." Rick wasn't taking no for an answer.

"Isn't that right, Ryan?"

I nodded along and accompanied Rick. When we returned to the living room, Jeri and Michelle stopped talking mid-conversation. "We're done," Rick said, smacking his hands together.

Jeri thanked us and Rick parked himself next to her. Rick was in constant competition with every person he knew, always keeping score, always with his eyes set firmly on the prize. Time after time I sat back while he swooped in on any woman that I took an interest in. Watching him talk to Jeri and put on his best show to win her attention. I squirmed at every word he said. I didn't want the competition; I just wanted to be near her.

I sat opposite on the only empty seat. "Why do you want to be a cop?" Rick asked cosying up to Jeri.

"The usual, really…to make a difference," Jeri tilted her head awkwardly. She was biting her tongue.

"Tell me," Rick said.

"I just think it's our responsibility to do what we can. To do the right thing."

"That's admirable," Rick replied.

"I think most people see things the same way."

"Not everyone makes it their career. And plenty that do, don't do it for the right reasons. What makes you think you can make a difference?"

"Anyone can. If they commit themselves to it." Jeri and Rick exchanged bashful glances while Michelle looked on.

"Did you see the robbery by your campus last week?" Michelle asked and Jeri shook her head.

"It was rough," Rick said. "Held the guy up at gun point."

"They say he'll get six years. Out in five," Michelle said.

"He should rot." Rick shuffled uncomfortably. Michelle offered him an extra cushion that he shoved behind his back.

"He had a daughter. He'd been out of work for months. There were no bullets in the gun," I threw in.

"That doesn't matter, Ryan," Michelle frowned at me. "He still had a gun."

"He needs Jail," Jeri said. "A deterrent."

"He needs help," I countered.

"I agree with the two people present who will soon be upholding the law," Rick raised his hand and looked from Michelle to Jeri. "He needs to be punished."

"You have to admit, Ryan, he's too dangerous to be on the streets," Michelle added.

I didn't want an argument about the criminal justice system to overtake the evening, but I couldn't let it go. "I'm not saying he should be allowed to run free. I'm just saying, you throw him in jail, then what? He makes a few good contacts? Leaves thinking that society is against him? And finds it even harder to feed his daughter than the first time around. Some people, not everything goes their way. Sometimes they need help, that's all I'm saying."

"It was Rick," Michelle declared. "I was talking to Rick. He was Jeri's date." I slumped into my chair. My heart sunk into my stomach and slithered out of my body onto the cold wooden floor. Rick's smug grin expanded across his face. Michelle turned to me. "You were supposed to be my date. I only agreed to it to set Jeri and Rick up."

"I'm sorry. I should probably go." I walked into the hallway and slipped my jacket on. I heard their muffled voices and then footsteps. Jeri walked towards me, a sympathetic look on her face.

"I'm sorry. You're a nice guy and all. But…"

"I understand."

"No hard feelings?"

"To you? Never. I just wish… things were different."

Jeri swooped in and pressed her tender lips against my mouth. She grabbed hold of my shoulders with her hands and put one leg either side of me, scraping my back against the wall. She tasted like the first summers day.

"What about Rick?"

"I told him the same. He didn't take it too well."

"Oh."

"I think he's going now. Michelle too." Jeri looked at the floor. She placed one bare foot on top of the other and then switched them. "Do you like Cherry Pops?" Little did I know that they were her first love and soon I would be her last.

* * *

On the night of Herb's prom, I sat in goblin pyjamas that didn't reach passed my forearms or calves, but I had refused to give up on, watching him fix his curls back and forth across his head. With one stroke they covered the areas where hair was already starting to recede, and with another he would leave parts of his head visible for all to see. Herb had finally plucked up the courage to ask a young beauty named Carol to accompany him on that night. Carol was born the only child of a well to do family, her grandfather once a Senator of Oregon. Asked by many fine young men that year to be their date, she turned them down one by one until an 18-year-old Herbert Ellis asked her that same question. Herb played with his bowtie so many times it started to crease.

"Let your mother do it," Dad said from the sofa. Mom moved over quickly and arranged it perfectly for him. "Many a time your mom has saved my neck with the right kind of a tie. Windsor, cravat, bow, she does the lot." Dad lifted one leg and tucked it firmly onto the other to give Herb his words of wisdom. "Now the one thing that is most important is that you look after her and keep her safe."

"I know, Dad."

"There may be alcohol, but a good man like you doesn't need alcohol to get by or to have a good time. Next, you need to make sure that you're a gentleman. There's no need trying to kiss her, you've done well getting this far, no point in blowing it on the first date."

Herb slumped a little. "Thanks, Dad."

"I'm just saying, you really like this girl, I can tell, so play it safe. You want a second date, right?" Herb gave a pleading look to Mom, which was passed on to Dad, manifesting itself with firmness and a little raise of the eyebrows, softened by a smile. "Alright, alright," Dad said before getting up and leaving the room. Mom shuffled closer to Herb and took hold of his hand.

"He wants the best for you. He just struggles to know you sometimes. I don't know why, you're so alike." Herb gave a look of disbelief and Mom quickly moved on. "You just be yourself son. If the girl is as nice as you say she is, and if she's the one, then that will be more than good enough for her. Be yourself and treat her nice. You've got a lot to offer, young man." She put her arm around him, only half his size and holding on tightly. "And you, young man should be thinking about bed." Mom turned to me and gave me 'the look'. "You're another fine young man that I love."

"I want to wave goodbye to Herb," I said.

"Ok. Then to sleep." Every time I looked at my mom, she made me feel warm inside. She listened to me talk about anything for hours, always with a smile and an understanding that made me feel like the most important person in the world. She was incapable of making a decision that wasn't morally right and to the benefit of others, always above her own needs. I couldn't bear to see it taken for granted.

I didn't see Carol, only Herb's face as he opened the door to her. I had never seen him act like that before, so shy and bashful. The taunting brother seemed so far away that night. Carol's Dad drove them away – his condition to letting Carol go to the prom being that he drop them off and pick them up – while my mom and Dad watched them leave through the window. Dad put his arm around Mom, and they moved closer together.

TWENTY-FIVE

Opening my eyes, I had no recollection of how I got home from the Bruiser bar, but a hammering ache in my chin sought to remedy that. The cold wooden floor pressed against my face. I craned my stiff neck looking for clues as to what happened. A fist from nowhere. The ground rushing towards me. It felt like I was hit square on the jaw with a baseball bat. And my words. Those damned words that I couldn't take back, no matter how far they were from the truth. I let my head drop back to the floor.

Thoughts raced through my mind; of why it was so damn easy to ruin your life without even trying, how pathetic I had been to let Jeri go, why all I did was bring suffering to everyone around me. I thought about staying in my hovel and drinking myself into extinction. That was all I was worth. I didn't understand what I was supposed to do. Any minute we could all be dead, and then what? What would have been the point of me ever living on this damned planet?

I clenched my fists and squeezed my eyes closed but it was no use. There was nothing I could do lying on a cold wooden floor. I had almost resigned myself to quarantine, to be subjected to an array of tests. At least I would be of more use than lying here. Then I saw the micro surveillance camera on the floor a foot away and the final moments of last night came rushing back to me.

I clambered to my feet and picked up the tiny camera, inspecting it closely. I scoured the rest of the house, ripping apart walls and furniture. I found eight more and my home phone tapped. Each piece of technology was so carefully placed and discreet that they were invisible to anyone who didn't know exactly what they were looking for.

Maybe someone got to Jess. Or maybe they've been here all along. Either way, someone knows I was abducted.

I drew a list of suspects and tried to eliminate them: US Tech, the government, Jeremy, maybe someone I had never met. It could have been anyone.

And if they know I was abducted, then why aren't I in quarantine?

They've been watching my family, violating my home, and they went to a lot of trouble to do it.

I will not forget that.

I poured away the warm flask of whiskey, took a long shower, put on a fresh set of clothes, shaved my face, brushed my teeth, and gave myself a once over in the mirror. My head was cracking open with pain, and I felt like shit with no idea what to do next. But at least I looked like I could make it through the day. I got in my car, took out the photograph of Jeri and I at Lake Ontario and headed to US Tech, plotting my next move in my head.

* * *

Agent Brody had surrounded himself with very little inside his office at US Tech: A tablet small enough to slip easily into a jacket pocket, a glossy black plastic desk, and a tall water fountain were the only items preventing the office from being bare. "How many people have they taken?" Brody continued clicking away on his keyboard. "How many do you have?"

He sighed deeply, "That's classified information."

"I'm on a classified project and it's information I need to know."

"No, you don't."

"I want to speak to them."

Brody stopped typing and leaned forward, clearly not thrilled at the idea. "That's not going to happen."

"I need access to be able to complete my work on the comms device."

"I'll have the abductee interview transcripts sent to your office."

"That's not what I asked for."

"I hardly see the relevance of speaking to them directly."

"These people have experienced what it's like to be in direct contact with the alien race, which we know unlocks the capability to communicate using the comms device."

"And we also know, through scientific testing, that their ability does not translate to successfully utilising a weaponised comms device."

"That testing was completed outside my department."

"You have the report."

"Open your mind for a moment; maybe there's more to learn. Some way they can operate within the shared consciousness, beyond communication. Something that can help us."

"I've had teams of experts spend many hours learning everything there is to learn," Brody insisted, the corner of his mouth flaring up in irritation.

"I need to interview them to make progress. And you're obstructing my operation," I said matching his tone and insistence. "I don't want to escalate this any higher."

Brody glared at me. I gave my best attempt at looking assertive and waited in silence. Brody stood up, strolled across the office and stopped in the doorway. "Well? What are you waiting for? I'm not going to let you see them alone."

* * *

Two security officers stood guard at the facility doors. One gave a discreet nod and quiet "Sir," to Agent Brody, who was clearly a regular and paid no attention to me. Brody stopped in front of the first in a row of fibreglass boxes. I had imagined the abductees being held in sterile white rooms, empty except for a cold steel bed in the centre, perhaps with a single sheet that would be replaced and burned every week or so. But the quarantine in front of me was more like a respectable hotel room, complete with a sofa, flat screen TV, packed bookshelf, desk and four chairs, a thick pile rug and a forty something man with hair combed immaculately across his forehead reading cross-legged on the rug.

"You're prepared for this?" Brody asked.

"I have a list of questions to-"

"That's not what I mean." When I nodded, Brody swiped his card and placed his finger inside the device to extract his DNA. He scanned his retina and the fibreglass door shifted open. Brody and I entered and sat at the desk. The man carried on reading until Brody called his name. Patrick lifted his head, closed the book, shuffled over to the desk and pulled up a seat.

"This is Ryan. He's here to meet you."

"Hello, Ryan. I don't remember... the last time... I had a guest." A smile appeared and vanished just as quickly.

"I want to talk to you about what happened, Patrick." I tried to keep my voice calm, my body language relaxed and unimposing.

"What happened?" Patrick's voice was bright and child-like.

"When you were taken."

"Taken where?"

"By the-"

"The terribles," Brody chipped in. He tilted his head to me and spoke quietly: "That's what he calls them."

Patrick's face became grave. His beady eyes narrowed, almost lost in his head. "Well, they're not friendly, no."

"Why did they take you?"

"They... didn't say." He struggled to catch his breath as he talked in a faltering rhythm. His eyes rarely focussed on me and instead darted around the room. "They didn't speak. Not a word."

"How did they communicate with you?"

Patrick smacked his hand against his head, grimacing. "They get inside. They... know... what you have done. And they don't leave... without taking something. If you're not careful, they'll take everything."

Patrick scurried back to his rug and buried his face back in his book. I looked at Brody, awaiting some intervention but he gave a smug, knowing smile and stood up to leave.

In the adjoining room, I peered in through the fibreglass door at a woman in her mid-thirties, lying perfectly still. Her eyes hollow, like they were missing something and all I could see was the space where it had been. The name on the door was Louise Whittaker. "You can go in and talk to her if you want. She won't tell you anything." Brody kept his security pass firmly in his hand. "She hasn't spoken in six months. The abductee next door again has been unable to move or communicate since he was taken. He was diagnosed with locked in syndrome. There are over a thousand cases under formal investigation. Two hundred have been validated as abductions. Thirty of them are held at this facility. We believe there are many more that have not yet come forward. But this is the best place for them to be. This is the only way we can protect them. Have you seen enough?"

"Not yet." I marched down the corridor past five more rooms, each one occupied and with a name plaque fixed on the door. I stopped outside the sixth room and waited. Brody strolled up beside me, but he didn't open the door. I held my position, unflinching against the cold stare I felt upon me. As little as I knew Agent Brody, I did know that he was firm and strong-willed. And he didn't want me in that room any more than I wanted him in there with me. But I waited, and eventually I waited long enough for him to swipe his security card once more.

* * *

Brody asked me to wait outside while he spoke to Frankie Poole. After a minute or two he opened the door, and I followed him inside. When I introduced myself, Frankie smiled. Brody told me she had been reported missing three months ago, that her sister had called the police when she disappeared from her bedroom and woke up one day to find Frankie returned home. "Why did they take you?" I asked.

"I don't know."

"What did they do, when they had you?"

"I've answered all this before."

Brody gave a fixed stare, clearly questioning the point of the interview.

"I know." I smiled empathetically and kept my voice soft. "But I would like to hear it. If that's ok?"

She hesitated long enough for Brody to nod in acceptance that our meeting was over and lift himself halfway out of his seat. "I was aboard a craft," she said finally. Brody lowered his ass back into the chair and I leaned in, waiting for her to continue. "I felt the lack in gravity as soon as I woke. I was scared. So very scared."

"Did they communicate with you?"

"No..." Frankie wouldn't look at me. She turned to Brody. "Can... Can I see Laura now?"

"Soon," Brody replied firmly.

"But... I told him. Just as you said."

"When you're ready." His voice grew sterner.

"I didn't need to be scared."

Brody huffed, pushing his chair screeching backwards and standing up in one motion. "Ok, that's enough."

Frankie became more agitated, gripping the table with

both hands. "I want to see her now." Her head twisted around towards me, her voice shaky and hesitant. "Why did you come back?" She was looking straight at me. She asked me again, this time more demanding.

"I don't know what you're talking about," I finally replied but she wasn't convinced.

"You shouldn't have come back." She had a fear in her eyes like I had never seen before. "He won't let you leave."

"That's enough," Brody was almost shouting.

"What's she talking about?"

Brody was quick to respond: "She's delusional." He stayed perfectly still. Frankie's eyes bore into me without so much as a blink, calm and in total contrast with my trembling hand and racing heart. Her words rattled in my head.

"I've never been here before. This is the first time I've met you." I spoke the words but there was no conviction in my voice. It was hard to be sure of anything.

"Has she come back with you?" Frankie's voice became softer. "She's beautiful like my Laura. Is Jeri with you?" I pushed the chair screeching backwards as I jumped to my feet. I backed up slowly towards the door.

"How do you know my wife?"

"She was here. With you."

"Stop talking," Brody insisted.

The air around me felt thin, devoid of oxygen. I lost control of my arms as they began flopping and banging against my side. As my heart beat faster and faster the room started to spin, objects moving in front of my eyes. Brody didn't flinch as I hit the ground. The last thing I saw was his body towering over me as the room turned black.

* * *

Frankie sat hunched over her knees at the far side of the room. Brody's face moved into the middle of my sight where it remained for thirty seconds or so, devoid of expression or emotion. "You're awake," he said eventually. I pulled myself up, so I was leaning back onto my hands. "You blacked out. What is the last thing that you remember?"

I hesitated, the fog still lifting from my mind "I... was talking to Frankie. I introduced myself... And then everything went black. Next thing, I opened my eyes, and you were leaning over me."

Brody offered his hand and pulled me up. "I suggest we bring your visit to a close."

"Maybe that's best." I turned to Frankie and gave a smile of appreciation. She didn't speak as she watched me leave.

Brody escorted me upstairs to my floor and asked one of the assistants to get me a glass of water. He watched me drink it before checking my responsiveness to his fingers snapping in front of my face. I thought I saw genuine concern for me before he left.

I returned to my office, my head drowning in a murky ocean, struggling to piece together the hum of the lights, the desk I rested my hands on, all of the sights, sounds and smells of the world around me. I searched for Frankie Poole in the files that Robert had sent me. I found Frankie's abduction report, along with Patrick's and a dozen other abductees held at US Tech.

I had no recollection of ever being there before today but floating amongst the murky waters was a memory of Patrick, Louise and Frankie, right until the moment I blacked out and everything that had happened since. Today, I remembered everything.

TWENTY-SIX

Rick knew his way around my house and my eating habits. He returned from the   kitchen with a cappuccino, bacon, eggs, and toast and laid it down on the coffee table and sat opposite me. "You didn't feel like coming to work?"

"I'm working from home."

Rick surveyed the room, stacks of paper laid out. I spent half my time sending notes and theories into my project team to keep them busy and off my back, with barely a hope that they would be able to use it to get the weaponised comms device working. The rest of the time I spent scouring the web for something to latch onto, for some clue or lead. "And last week?"

I nibbled at the crust of a piece toast as Rick studied Jeri's photo hanging on the wall. Leaving them up after she left now seemed like a horrible idea, the changing photographs tortured me further with each new smile. "What are you going to do?"

"She's coming back," I said harsher than I intended.

"I know." Rick gave me a nod of agreement that was far from convincing. "We could do with you back at the office."

"Did Brody send you?" I eyed Rick for any micro expression to reveal the truth. He narrowed his eyes in confusion before shaking his head.

"He doesn't know I'm here. I told him you're doing research offsite. I spouted a few details, and he changed the subject quickly. But he wants you to present a summary report on progress for your division when you come in tomorrow. Apparently, you were made aware last week."

"I'm not coming back tomorrow."

"You can't stay at home any longer."

"I'm not doing the summary."

"I can help you out with it."

"I'm not doing the presentation."

Rick huffed and picked up toast with bacon on. "We've got a job to do. Everyone has to work together; you can't just sit around here dwelling and moping."

I threw my half-eaten toast at the plate, splitting the egg open until the yoke dripped out and hardened. I couldn't go back, not with Brody there.

"I know how much you wanted one…" I couldn't work out what he was saying. "At least you have someone. Someone amazing. That's more than a lot of us have. Kids. They're not everything."

"Get out."

"I know how much you love her. But..."

I jumped to my feet. "Get the fuck out!"

Rick stood slowly. I marched to the front door and swung it open as far as I could. He paused as he reached the door, giving me one final look before he turned his back and left.

"Fucking weasel." I sat back down in the living room and launched my plate against the wall, covering it in uneaten breakfast. On the table where the plate had sat was a printed draft progress update. Next to it was a flash drive that included a two-page summary and a further forty pages of supporting material, detailing information that only a few members of my team could have provided. The report had my name on it; Rick's nowhere to be seen.

* * *

A slither of light fell on Peter's face as he pushed his office door open and stepped inside. I heard a switch flick and the room lit up. "You took too long."

Peter jolted. "Damn it, Ryan, you scared the hell out of me. Why are you sitting in the dark? Where have you been? We're getting nowhere." He took another look at me. "Are you ok?"

"I need your help."

"We're still working through all the material you sent over, we're in over our heads here. Are you coming back?"

"Did you bring your tablet?" I asked. Peter pulled it out of his shoulder bag. "From work?"

"I bought a shiny new one. It's off the network."

"You were supposed to bring your work one."

"This is three times faster; nothing can be traced on this. I've already-"

"I need to get into the vault."

"The US Tech vault? I don't have access to that. Neither do you."

"That's why I need you to get me in."

"Hack security?" He laughed. "Are you serious?"

"You'll need your work tablet."

Peter kept his feet planted. "We'll be fired."

"It'll be a lot worse if we don't."

"I can't. No way." He lifted his hand to reinforce his stance, but it was shaking. Peter was more hard work than I had time for. They were on to me, and I was on to them. I needed to accelerate things, before I was taken out of the game. "There's more going on here than you know."

"On the project?"

"At US Tech."

Peter's eyes darted about the room, a million theories probably racing through his head. "A conspiracy, I knew it. There's no way a company like this shoots up so quickly without one. Especially not when they're in bed with every

237

government agency in the country. How high?"

"Maybe all the way to the CEO."

Peter snapped to attention. "He's been asking about you. Asking Bob, anyway."

"What was he asking?"

Peter shrugged. "What do you expect to find in there?"

"I can't tell you. But it could change everything. It's up to us to blow this whole thing up and find out the truth."

Peter grinned with excitement. "And what you're looking for. You think that's going to help expose them?"

"I hope so." It was the only lead I had left.

* * *

I left the crowded lift and kept my head down while I slipped a baseball cap on. I loitered in the corridor outside the vault door, casually turning away to obstruct my face from the few passers-by. I had the right level of clearance, but the vault required an additional code that was restricted to very few individuals. But if anyone could crack it, it was Peter.

As long as he didn't get cold feet and run – leave me waiting outside until security picked me up and carted me off. This time I would be sacked and prosecuted for sure.

I watched the light waiting for it to illuminate. I checked my watch – nearly a minute late. The seconds ticked by. I had already been here too long. Two minutes.

I took out my phone and dialled Peter. "What's wrong?"

Silence.

"Peter, what's wrong?"

"We're... we're doing the right thing here, aren't we, Ryan?"

I grinded my teeth to keep my thoughts to myself. "Open the door."

"Tell me we're doing the right thing."

I growled into the phone, "Open the fucking door Peter or-" I took a moment, slowed down. If he hung up, I was done. "It's the right thing. I promise you."

The green light flashed. I tapped my security card against the pad and heard the click-clunk of the lock. I grabbed the door handle and swung it open just enough to slip through.

Once inside, I marched through rows of shelves, but not too fast to draw attention from anyone else who might be inside. Racking held items ordered alphabetically, but I didn't know exactly how the system worked. I checked D for Dawson, Jeremy, J for Jeremy Dawson, and did a scan of a few rows to get a feel for how they had arranged storage, but I didn't recognise most of the names. I doubled back to L and found two columns of eight drawers labelled Libera. To the right-hand side of every drawer was a nine-digit keypad.

I checked around me and listened for anyone near and gave the drawer a hard pull. The lock was more like a bolt than the usual flimsy desk-drawers. I pulled it as hard as I could, but it wouldn't budge.

I couldn't risk leaving the storage room for equipment to break the lock and not being able to get back inside, and I knew there would be CCTV all over the place, with a hive of security watching. It was my one chance. It had to be now.

I pulled out my phone and scrolled through old messages to stall for time. I knew I had minutes before security realised I wasn't accessing anything in the vault and descended upon me. Mind blank, I kept scrolling, hoping something would come to me. Inspiration. But I had nothing.

The clunk-click of the vault door sounded, followed by footsteps at the far end of the room. A figure marched towards me in white shirt, navy blue tie, and blazer. I strolled away from the drawers and out of sight. I picked up the pace and heard the security guard's footsteps do the same. The door clunked again and a second set of footsteps joined, then a third. I darted down a corridor, knowing this was my only chance to get it and get out before they grabbed me. But they came from every side of the room; they had me surrounded. I sped down the next corridor to lead them away and doubled back to the Project Libera drawers. I screeched to a halt a few feet away from the drawers and Agent Brody stood right in front of them.

Brody tapped his finger against the keypad and a drawer slid open. The only item inside was a slim black laptop complete with a half-moon half-sun sticker. He looked down the corridor at where the nearest footsteps could be heard, then back at me. "Take it."

I froze. My gut told me to get out; it had to be a set-up. As soon as I touched that laptop, I would be arrested for stealing either US Tech or government property. I didn't even know if I would remember what happened after today.

"Go on," Brody insisted. "That's why you're here. Take it." I took a step forward and stopped to listen for the security guards. "I'll deal with them."

I stepped forward, reached inside the drawer, and tucked the laptop under my arm. Brody pushed the drawer until it beeped closed.

"That way." Brody pointed to my left. "Three rows then head straight for the exit. Now, go." I spun around and followed Brody's instructions. Halfway to the door, I heard their mumbled exchange. I slipped out of the room, kept my head down and left US Tech as quickly as I could. All I could do for Peter was hope that security hadn't traced anything back to him.

* * *

I ran to my car and sped to the nearest coffee shop with wi-fi, reluctant to go home in case the police showed up again. I flipped open Jeremy's laptop and scoured it. The hard drive was empty, there were no favourites or history saved, no email profile and no sign that it had ever been in use. Whatever files Jeremy had left for me had been erased.

I checked and checked again, searching for any trace of

something that could help me. I had risked everything for nothing.

I opened every programme installed and found nothing of interest until I got about three-quarters of the way through, and a tracer programme flashed on the screen. It was basic and outdated, with no map or any reference to where the signal was being transmitted from, except that it was three hundred and ninety miles away, and the general direction. I compared it with maps online and determined that whatever I was looking at was somewhere in Massachusetts.

* * *

I checked the signal every few miles to ensure I was still on track. The traffic was almost unbearable. As I got closer to my target, the screen automatically zoomed in, and I noticed the tracer itself was moving. What the hell is it?

Finally, I arrived at a small Boston diner. The bell startled me as I opened the door, but I kept my head down as I powered towards a table and slid into the seat. It had all the usual's – white veneer covered chipboard tables, a long counter in front of the kitchen and nothing out of the ordinary about it. I looked over each shoulder twice and opened Jeremy's laptop.

The tracer danced around in front of me like it was following a pattern, until it headed straight for me. I looked up to see a waitress stopped at my table holding a pot of coffee in the air, waiting impatiently. The programme was so outdated, and some of the features it did have weren't activated so I didn't even recognise it was based on my own design: it was a DNA tracker.

"You want some?"

I slid my cup closer to her. "Thanks."

"You look like you're having a bad day."

"Maybe it just got better. I think I need to talk to you."

"Aren't we already talking?"

241

"I think you're the reason I'm here."

She left my cup half full and hurried towards the bar. I didn't take my eyes off her. She stepped towards the kitchen door and stopped. She swung her head round and stared back at me, panic in her eyes.

I stood up slowly, and stalked my way closer, careful not to spook her. Her hand rested on the kitchen door, ready to push her way through and make a run for it. "Jeremy is dead."

She barely moved; her eyes fixed on me. But I saw them flicker in recognition. Her breathing became more rapid. I got ready to chase.

"Ryan?" Her voice quivered.

"Yes. Ryan-"

"I don't want to know," she interrupted. "How do I know you are who you say you are?"

"Jeremy left his address book for me with your name in it." I pulled out my driver's licence and held it out. "They took my wife, just like Rebecca. I dreamt about it for so long... If they take her again... I don't know if they'll bring her back."

She walked around to my side of the counter, pulled up a chair and we sat. She checked behind her, but the diner was empty except for the two of us and two customers near the window.

"Lilia Perez."

"Not anymore."

"Antonio?"

Sadness flickered on her face, but it was quickly replaced by the stern face of someone who had weathered more than any person should. "He was my husband. Antonio helped Jeremy to penetrate US Tech. You took longer than I thought."

"Are you... were you abducted?"

"We both had fragments of memories leftover. And no matter how much they tried to scare Jeremy off, he wouldn't give up." She leaned into me, her face resolute. "We couldn't let him do it alone."

"When Jeremy passed, he left me a note. He wanted me to find the truth. But the abductions went public not long after he died."

"Darling, he knew we were being taken, and he knew who was taking us. He had enough proof of that a long time ago, maybe not to convince the world, but enough to know for himself. That's not the truth he wanted you to find."

"Then what?"

"He wanted the one behind the scenes, the one who's been manipulating everything."

"Apex Guard?" She nodded. "How much of everything?"

"US Tech, NASA, the CIA, FBI, the Government. Everything." She rubbed her fingers across her forehead.

"I know... how horrific it is to be taken. I'm doing everything I can to stop them ever taking anyone again."

She gave me a smile that was somewhere between sympathy and condescension. "All I know is that they brought me back. And my husband."

"If only everyone could say that." I replied with a twang of animosity. "Jeremy's wife wasn't so lucky."

Lilia narrowed her eyes at me, confused. "Rebecca was held in quarantine at US Tech for over a year after her abduction. Jeremy found reports of the experiments they performed on her. She died on the operating table, not in some alien ship. The same people who took Rebecca took my husband. They took my life; they drove me to this." She threw her hands up at her surroundings and looked confused. "Jeremy left documents for you," she bent the top of his laptop to look closer at the half-moon half-sun sticker. "That is his, isn't it?"

"US Tech stole it from his house. They wiped everything. The only thing left was a DNA tracker I used to find you."

Lilia's eyes widened, her mouth dropped open. "You have to go." She pulled off her apron and threw it onto the floor. "You have to leave now. They can't see you with me." She eyed up the two men who each sat alone by the window, one wearing a hunting waistcoat and cap, feasting on pancakes and syrup, the other slimmer man, dressed in a suit with his head buried into a broadsheet. She searched past them, outside the diner as cars drove and people walked past us, going about their day. She raced behind the counter of the diner and kicked hard at the base of it. She bent down and came back up with a flash drive in her hand and a small but packed tight backpack. "It's not safe here anymore."

"I can help you."

Lilia jumped at the sound of a phone ringing behind me. I turned as the hunting man answered it. She shook her head. "They know you're here." She ran to the front door and grabbed a jacket. "Listen to me. There are people who can do things, impossible things. They are part of a research group, the Cognitive Enhancement Group. They can get inside your head, move things just by willing it to happen. The man who killed my husband-"

"Paradox, unveil." The hunting man stood up, knocking his plate to the floor with a crash, Lilia spun round to look at him. His eyes rolled back in his head and his arms shook violently at his sides and he shouted, "Paradox, unveil."

With a great bang, the man exploded, bursting into pieces of flesh that flew in every direction. The force of the explosion threw me against the wall. My shoulder took most of the impact as the large glass window shattered into pieces. I stumbled to my feet, ears ringing. The diner was covered in every remaining bit of the human bomb. The second customer was spread out on the table behind him, his face near flattened. I scurried to Lilia, laying on her front, dress soaked in blood. I turned her over a dent as big as a baseball in her head, the coat stand impaled into her chest. Only seconds before she had been alive and well. She still would be if it wasn't for me. I reached for her hand and opened her palm, the data stick still tucked up inside.

TWENTY-SEVEN

My heart was pounding out of my ribcage like a battering ram gradually working its way through a fort door. I raced to my car, turned on the engine and pulled out quickly. I slammed my foot on the gas to get out of there before the police arrived, or worse.

Every car behind seemed to be following me, every person I passed on the streets staring at me. A million thoughts raced through my head about what to do next, where to go. All I wanted was to find Jeri, but I couldn't protect anyone. Lilia was safe until I showed up.

I kept my eyes on the rear-view mirror more than the road in front, but the streets were so busy that I couldn't tell if I had one tail or twenty. Every time I was sure a car was getting too close, or making too many of the same turns, it turned off and I grew just as suspicious of the next one. I patted my pocket every few minutes for the data stick, carrying with it my hope that Jeremy would continue guiding me from beyond the grave.

I turned down one side-street after another until I reached a deserted back alley that I deemed as safe as any place I could find. I pulled over and watched a black Mercedes slow down as it passed the alley and then speed out of sight.

I plugged the data stick into Jeremy's laptop, which held two files and a video. I clicked the video first and Jeremy's face appeared on the screen. I held my breath and waited for him to speak while he flicked his hair out of his eyes:

"Hello, Ryan. I am sorry to leave you alone in this, but I think about your own wife, and I know you will understand why I must go. There is nothing that we won't do for the one's we love. That's why I knew it was you, I knew as soon as you knocked on my door with that crazy look in your eye; my Rebecca had that same look. I went to US Tech to find the truth. I think it was fate that I found you there."

My stomach turned at the sight of his face. An empty rope dangled behind him. Jeremy spoke each word carefully and with pause, as though he had all the time in the world. "If you've followed my leads then you know Rebecca didn't die during some alien abduction. She died by human hands at US Tech, that I am sure of." His lip twitched into a grimace, trying desperately not to break down. "I failed to find the identity of Apex Guard, but I have left you everything I have. Who knows how long Apex Guard has known about the abductions? But all this time they have been preparing for it. Preparing for war."

"The Government captured live ones. They performed tests on them, studied and dissected them. Pulled them apart, dozens of them. They are so powerful. And Apex tried to harness that power in human test subjects."

"We are bound, you and I. Bound by our beliefs, by our experiences. But I believe that you have the potential to do what I couldn't. I'm sorry I can't carry on with you, but Rebecca is waiting for me. I hope that she is. Beware Ryan; Trust no one."

Jeremy turned to face the door, and then the security camera. He looked at the rope and then back to me once more. "It's up to you now, Ryan. Farewell my friend. Find

Apex and you'll find your answers."

I couldn't comprehend why Jeremy placed so much trust in me.

I quickly opened the first file, the titled 'Apex Guard'. The only contents were five names: Elliot Brandon, CEO of US Tech, Anthony Gellar, head of the CIA, Jonathan Barnes, leader of the Republican Party, General Day and Tyler Brody, Cognitive Expansion Agent. They were among the most powerful people in the world.

I closed it and opened the last file, titled White Giant. I scrolled through twenty pages of plans for research and innovation labs, specialising in human cognitive enhancement and a fully operational miniature hospital. It was the base of operations for the CEG, Cognitive Expansion Group.

I started the car and drove back to DC, heading straight for the White Giant.

* * *

The White Giant was so huge it needed its own gravity inducers after section E, and I still felt the tug in my stomach from when they kicked in. The elevator stopped abruptly at section G; floor seven. I kept tapping the button for the top floor, but the doors kept opening. I walked out of the elevator and towards the stairs. Outside the lowbrow art exhibition at the other end of the corridor, a man stood with his phone pressed against his ear, like there was still no such thing as aliens. On the stairway door there was a large 'No Entry' sign with a small keypad next to it. I tried the door anyway, but it was a dead end.

My head suddenly felt hazed and throbbed ferociously, like a shroud had been laid over my senses. It took all my energy to stay on my feet. At the far end of the corridor stood Agent Brody. He had appeared as if out of nowhere. "Hello, Ryan."

"How long have you been following me?"

"Since you left for Boston."

"You wanted me to lead you to her."

"Lilia's been on the watch list since I popped her husband's head." A sly grin crept up on one side of Brody's mouth. "But it was already too late for her to be a problem. I just had to keep you busy. It's all about timing, you see. These things shouldn't be rushed. Well... time's up."

"So, who wants me dead?"

"You? No, no. That's not what this is."

"Then what?" I glanced at the elevator display, moving from section F to section G.

"It's time to unlock that hidden potential." Brody took out a pair of thin, mesh gloves from his jacket and carefully slid one on each hand. "I'm here to turn the key."

I shuffled slowly towards the elevator, hoping to dive in and close the doors quicker than he could pull his gun. "I know who you are."

His brow raised above his left eye. "Nice try but that's far enough. And I don't need a gun."

The elevator door opened with a ding, and I dived in. I punched the button to close it, hit the ground floor button and held my breath. I was out of his sights. The light flickered and something pulled at my chest. I flew out of the elevator and was sent crashing into the wall opposite. I fell to the ground and almost every part of my body ached. I lifted my head, blood dripping from my nose and saw Brody standing over me, his hand raised above me like an anvil about to drop. He pounded his fist into my stomach causing vomit to rise and nearly erupt from my mouth. Brody raised his hand, lifted my body into the air and pinned me to the wall without touch. He stared at me, exerting no visible effort.

I could barely move. "The comms device test on the live subject. You knew it worked."

Brody scoffed. "Every abductee within ten miles felt that thing."

"If you knew I was an abductee, why didn't you keep me

in quarantine?"

"We're going to stop them, Ryan. Remember that. They'll never hurt you again." He pressed me harder to the wall until my ribs were about to collapse under the sheer force. "Hold onto your pain. Grip it so tightly that your fingers bleed." His grin stretched too far wide and thin to be anything but a curved slit across his face, disgusting to look at, with nothing but torment and sadism behind it. All I wanted to do was to wipe that fucking grin off his face.

I heard the rattle of a door at the other end of the corridor. Two women, barely in their twenties walked towards us, four men close behind, then a family, more of them, pouring out. The art exhibit had finished. There must have been a hundred people inside.

I shouted for them to run, but it was already too late. Brody's face lit up with glee. "Get ready for it."

The two women were hurled towards me, hitting the wall with a sickening crack as their spines bent ninety degrees backwards and then they dropped to the floor like lifeless husks. It took a few seconds for the people who had been standing behind them to react. But they were too petrified to run.

Screams echoed from the other end of the corridor, as dozens of people that were backed up fled in all directions. Some took their chances running closer to get to the stairs, others dived into the first room they found, but most headed back into the exhibit, cowering in terror. Brody rolled his shoulders like he was warming up at the gym.

I heard a crack first, and then the wall split down the middle, chunks smashing on the floor. Brody sent two twelve-foot slabs of wall tumbling into the crowd in the corridor like bowling balls, exposing those hiding in the exhibition room. I wrestled as hard as I could to free myself from Brody's grip while he was distracted, but it was futile.

"Stop, they're innocent people. They've done nothing to you."

"Innocent, you say?" Brody gave a knowing smirk like I

was barely a teenager fumbling through adult life and he had all the answers. "Look closer... Any one of them could rob you, beat you and leave you for dead. Cut your throat in your sleep just to pay for their next high. Life is cruel, Ryan, you know that better than most. There's only one way to protect yourself... You have to get them before they get you."

Brody's grip disappeared and I crashed to the ground in a heap. I jumped to my feet and ran at him. I collided with Brody's abdomen and charged him into the wall. I unleashed blow after blow into his body as he laughed and groaned. I stepped back and swung my fist at his head, connecting hard. I followed it with a second, my left arm careening through the air, until it stopped far from Brody's face. Blood dripped from his nose, and he smeared it across his mouth with the back of his hand. He clenched his fist, eyes piercing, and my throat slowly closed over.

"You're just like me. We're strong, we're both so strong," his voice curdled the air, a wail of desperation. "Look," Brody dragged two men across the floor, blood smearing all the way from their two friends behind them. "They can't hurt us anymore." He loomed over the two men, their mouths gaping open, and with a flick of each wrist, he ripped their jaws clean from their heads.

I wanted to keep my eyes down, on the floor where I could have imagined that everything was ok, where there were no bodies, no blood. I couldn't look away. "You're scared. That's why you're doing this, you're terrified of them. That they'll take you again. Does it make you feel strong? Like you're not a victim?"

Brody paced in a semi-circle around me, my words bounced off him or passed straight through. He only heard what he wanted to hear. "They took your wife." He stooped down to face me, his eyes wide with excitement, taking his attention away from the crowd for the first time. "I know. And they'll take her again. And again, until they have what they want from her. And then they'll leave her a fragment of the woman you know, or they'll bring back nothing at all. President Walker wanted to make peace. To leave us vulnerable. To accept how they have violated us and say 'Welcome to our home. Come on in.' Well, do you know what I say?" He sneered in disgust, "No more pain."

Brody brought his face close enough for me to smell the stain of whisky on his breath. He pressed his lips against my ear and whispered, "Break the shackles. No one is watching. I know what you've been through. Don't pretend you don't want to take these fuckers and peel back their skin."

Everywhere went dark and my consciousness was slipping away. Maybe it's better this way. I have nothing left, no reason to go on. I can let it end, right now. I'm so close to the end, all I need is to wait. It will come to me.

Mutilated bodies covered the ground in front of me. Blood was smeared across every wall and body parts surrounded me. Brody flung innocent people through every window to fall to their deaths, dropped more onto the broken glass to slice them in half or just leave them dangling in agony. The walls were crumbling around me.

Anything I haven't already lost, I'm about to lose. Hate is all I know. Death is all there is.

A man's feet dangled, his necked gripped by Brody's bare hand. Forty feet away a woman wailed in agony, reaching out to the man and recoiling in terror before she could take a step closer. The sight should have crumbled me at the very core. It barely made a mark. Still holding the man, Brody looked down at me, the light caste from behind him, silhouetting him into something resembling a monument of a great hunter, his beaten prey in his grasp. "I know about your baby. How do you know it wasn't them? How do you know they didn't take it from you?"

Paradoxical end. Unveil. Transcend.

Brody's face fell as my head rose. I dropped to the floor and strode towards him. "No more pain."

Brody waved his hand at me. I felt the waves hit me, but I wasn't thrown across the room like he intended. My feet didn't leave the floor. I merely flinched.

I felt the power surging through me. Desperate to break out of this fleshy shell. I lifted my hand, looked Brody in the eye and smiled.

* * *

The presence of hundreds of people beamed, their very life emanating towards me. Wails of panic continued from those to scared or too slow to escape. I reached out towards Brody, a few feet away and threw everything I had at him. He fell to the ground hard. I pushed again, this time at the fire alarm. The glass cracked, the alarm wailed, and sprinklers rained down on everything in sight. It would clear out the rest of the floors and I hoped it would be enough to encourage the panicked herd that had spread through the seventh floor of section G to make a run for it.

I wanted the people from the exhibition out of the building – I wanted them safe – but more importantly, I wanted Brody. And I didn't want any distractions.

"They call it death response. Congratulations on surviving it. Not everyone is as strong as we are." Brody eyed me from head to toe curiously before he made his move. Every second he faced off against me was a second the crowd got further away from him. "Your scans were... high, yes, maybe the highest." Brody waved his hand to dismiss the fact as trivial. "But that's not all there is... Ok," he said with acceptance. "Ok, let's see if you live up to the hype."

The first wave slammed me into the concrete wall and knocked me off my feet so hard I realised Brody was no longer holding back.

He reached out and toppled the wall at the end of the corridor, crushing a mass of people under its weight, his eyes not on them but on me, waiting for me to squirm.

I lifted a fire extinguisher six feet in the air and sent it hurtling at Brody's chest. He gasped and choked onto all fours. He half stumbled to his feet trying to stay upright to convey strength.

Brody pulled a football sized chunk of concrete into the air. I saw it hurtling towards me, but I was too slow to dodge it. I came to a few minutes later to see Brody holding a fifty-year-old man above his head. He looked down on me and sneered. "You're not trying hard enough." He made a fist with his left hand and twisted it around. With the subtle movement, he ripped the man's arms from his body. The man threw his head back and screamed in agony. Blood leaked from each shoulder, his severed arms on the glossy tiles below. Brody towered over me, closing his eyes to bask in the power.

The armless man dropped to the floor with a crack of his head. I should have been able to save him.

Brody held a young woman in his hands, her arm held out in front of her, terror in her eyes. I charged at him, but I was careless. Brody sent me flying back.

He curled his hand, one finger at a time, bringing with it thick layers of skin from each of the woman's fingers, peeling up her body, curling towards her face. Brody gave a final pull and let the heap of skin flop to the floor. She shook ferociously, eyes rolling in the back of her head in shock, blood soaking her white linen clothes. Then he started on her face.

I charged at Brody. He dropped the woman, and I slammed him against the wall. He let out a cough with the impact. "That's it," he screeched "Think of what we can do. No one can hurt us."

I growled at him, seething, and smacked him across the jaw. He laughed again, with a sneering cackle. I hit him again, and again, as hard as I could swing, my knuckles numb, blood smearing across his face from the cut above his left eye. I let out an inhuman wail in fury and frustration at the animal that had butchered innocent people, wiping them out of existence. I took a breath and felt the power inside of me, working its way around my body, tingling through my limbs. I grabbed Brody's wrist with my bare hand and with strength augmented, I tore his arm from its socket.

"No!" He dropped to the floor and rolled side to side in agony. Blood poured through the hole in his white shirt, soaking his ribs and then his stomach. "No, think of what we can do to them."

"Tell me, who is Apex Guard?"

Brody's smile grew wide. "He thought he had me on a leash."

"Who is he?" I shouted, but Brody closed his eyes and crowed at me. I grabbed the other wrist and pulled again.

"Aagh! No... not like this. No, please. Please don't hurt me." His head jerked back, banging against the wall as his body went into shock. "You're just like me."

I grabbed his head and smacked it against the wall. "I'm nothing like you. They're innocent people. You're a monster. Did you take Jeri? If you hurt her, I'll rip your fucking head off."

Brody's mouth curled up through the pain into a smile from ear to ear. "Do you feel them?" His voice cracked and continued with a heavy dose of sarcasm, "They're coming, on their way to our great capital." In the recesses of my mind, buried beneath the anger and the devastation, I did. "Don't make it too quick, eh? Things like that deserve to suffer." He studied me, from my hands to my face like a proud parent. "I almost pity them."

Before he could say another word, I took his jaw in my grasp, and without laying a finger on him I ripped it from his head.

Brody rattled like he was choking on his tongue. His jaw hung loose, rocking back and forth. I grabbed his head with both hands. I could feel the death in him: every life that he had taken flickering inside, leaving a residue like tree sap on a leaf. Brody's life flowed through my hands, lighting up the room.

Dozens of abductees are sliced open as surgeons analyse every organ, every shred of humanity they can find. They were brought back alive. Brody erases every memory they had. Many don't survive the process. Many more die on the operating table.

I watch through Brody's eyes, as they suffer every cut, the removal of a body part, the inspection of their minds. I feel his delight, like it was my own, both in the pain being inflicted so liberally, and that he isn't the one lying on a metal slab.

Tyler Brody remembers the first time he was taken. And every time since. Every invasion into his mind and body. The searing pain. Being pinned down, unable to make a sound. Cowering at home, paralysed by the fear of not knowing when they will return.

Brody finally comes face to face with one on his terms, on his turf and flanked by a dozen others just like him. He cuts it off being from the central consciousness long enough to sedate it. He wants nothing more than to pick it apart from the inside while every monster feels its pain and knows that he is coming for them too. But he waits. He can be patient. Because he is the one with the power now. And no one can hurt him anymore.

* * *

President Walker sits behind his pretentious desk like it protects him from the truth of the world. I'm the only one standing, not deserving of a seat. I could rip every one of them, limb from limb.

"Our society has a great history of building peace with cultures different to our own," Walkers begins, "but often only after both sides have suffered the horrors of war. We must ascend beyond the hostility and violence that has littered humanities previous interactions with a new culture.

To enter a new era." General Day can't look him in the eye, but Palmer is listening intently, like he's swallowing every word the President says. "It is our duty to strive to be better than those who have come before us. To put aside our differences, and find a common ground, a mutually beneficial relationship that will continue. And learn to live together in peace."

"No one here wants war." Palmer stood. Even through so few words, passion radiated from him. He's playing it smart. He holds more influence over the President than anyone. Walker has to listen to him. "But we can't risk leaving ourselves vulnerable to an attack. We have limited intelligence on what they are capable of other than how exceptionally advanced their civilisation is compared to our own. And our intelligence capabilities in this situation are even more limited."

"Even more reason why we can't enter into conflict with them. Our primary efforts must be on building peaceful ground and avoiding provocation." He's weak, feeble, but Walker matches Palmer's passion, holding his hand out firmly to emphasise key words like it was a carefully rehearsed speech to the nation. Doesn't he understand what they have done to us? Those wretched few. I'll never let them hurt me again.

"William," Palmer said. His calm tone served to slow down the conversation, to appeal to Walker's friendship and respect for him. "They have already flaunted our free rights, the rights that we, and everyone in this office before us has fought so hard to protect. The first thing they did when they arrived was to take our people – innocent people – and we still don't know entirely what they did to them when they were gone. They didn't contact us to make peace. They didn't seek to understand our differences or appreciate our way of life. That tells us everything we need to know about their intentions, and what they are prepared to do to achieve their goals. It is our duty to protect the people of our world. To ensure not only their safety, but their way of life. We have to test their defences."

Walker doesn't move, doesn't even blink. I can't tell if he's seriously considering Palmer's argument, or if this man of peace is raging inside. When he finally speaks, his words echo in our ears.

"We will not justify to ourselves dishonourable actions, merely because others have chosen that path. And I will not authorise any form of attack, or any movement that shows hostility."

* * *

Red lights flash on the low hanging ceiling of the war room, in the sinking depths of US Tech. Ryan Ellis saunters in after Vice President Palmer. I can't believe he brought him here. He's not special at all.

I reposition my tie in angst of what is happening. The Tactical Interceptor pilots communicate their attempted attack on the two alien craft. One of the pilots makes a futile missile launch but the two alien craft evade it with ease, merging into one.

President Walker barges into the room. He curls forward slightly and leans against the wall with one arm. He's weak. "What the hell is going on here?" The mad bastard must be stopped. "Abort this mission! I did not authorise this." He shouldn't be here. We should have taken him out like I said.

"The missile just disintegrated! A beam of light came from the ship and the missile disintegrated!"

"Damn it we're the aggressors, stop this now!" Walker knows exactly what we're doing. His ignorance, his willingness to leave us unprotected. So weak.

I look at Palmer. He hesitates. I can see the regret in his eyes, but I'll do it either way. The mad bastard can't be left to run loose. Inviting them into our planet, into our home. I'm not weak. I won't be the victim.

Palmer finally gives the nod. Within a second, I knock Walker to the ground. With the right amount of pressure, I close over his throat. General Day looks from me to Palmer and almost chokes on her breath. She opens her mouth to cry but as she turns to Palmer his attention is already back on the skies displayed in front of him. General Day straightened her shoulders and locked her gaze dead ahead.

I let Walker get just enough air to keep him alive. It would be so easy to end it right now, to watch his pathetic life wither away. If it weren't for Palmer, I would finish the job. At least he can't make us look weak anymore.

He won't wake up again.

* * *

As I pulled out of Brody's mind a jolt sent me choking all the way to the floor. On my hands and knees, thick vomit erupted from the depths of my stomach. Froth poured out of my mouth. My brain felt like it was swelling in my head. My arms and legs trembled and every hair on my body stood on end. I fought for every breath.

Brody's eyes were open wide, glossy, and vacant but still they glared at me, his body nothing more than an empty shell. He won't wake up again.

I heard a whisper, *I'm strong. I'm strong. Please, let me be strong.*

Paradoxical end. Unveil. Transcend.

No more pain.

TWENTY-EIGHT

The screams had lessened under the continuing wail of the fire alarm as the mass of people braved the stairs. I left Brody's broken shell lying cold on the floor of section G, floor 7 of the White Giant, his consciousness stripped away. I know what he was, power hungry, afraid, full of bitterness and hatred. That's what made him the bad guy. But does that make me the hero?

I pinched the skin of my forearm and held it up for inspection, like an unknown object. The shell that held me and everything I am inside it. My thoughts, feelings, my whole being. The shell that contained this power I knew nothing about. I felt more alive, stronger. But there was something inside my head scratching to get out.

I took deep breaths to quiet my mind, but it was no use.

Apex Guard. The one person who stood to gain the most from President Walker being out of the way, the one person who may have held control over Agent Brody. The man in office, with one of the most powerful nations in the world at his whim. My friend, Robert Palmer.

I didn't want it to be true, I told myself that it couldn't be, maybe Brody was trying to throw me off or to fuck with me, but I had seen it through Brody's own mind. Robert gave the ok to put President Walker in a coma. And it seemed he had done so much more.

And he's relying on me to stop them. Because I understand their technology, and maybe I'm the only one who can turn it against them with enough destructive capability to give our world a remote chance of surviving. Or because I have looked into their eyes and saw nothingness, because I have been subjected to their decree of fear and been helpless at their mercy, perhaps that was exactly the reason why he wanted me at his side.

Now it's too late. The comms device isn't weaponised. Robert's last hope of stopping them is lost. I prayed that every other means of defence that he had produced was enough to make our planet too much of a problem to continue with. Or that Robert had something else up his sleeve.

I had tried again to reach the eighth floor, but the doors remained closed, and I was running out of time.

I paced out of the White Giant as police tires screeched and sirens polluted the air. Hundreds of people crowded the streets, reeling from the terror. I flailed against a wooden bench, panting for breath. I tried to rub the stress from my face until my cheeks throbbed.

The clouds floated in the sky like they had been painted by a divine hand. An evanescent glow. They'll be here soon. I don't know how many. Heaven help us when they get here.

On the side of the space-scraper, a huge TV screen hung on the wall that Jeri and I had often lay curled up outside for hours watching movies or live concerts. We took picnics, or sometimes an eighteen-inch pizza from across the street.

Robert occupied the screen, sat in the oval office of the White House, stern and imposing. "People of America. There are an unidentified number of invading craft that are expected to enter our planet's atmosphere in the coming hours. The majority are believed to be on a trajectory to our great country. I implore you to remain calm and strong at this time of crisis. We have a secure defence system to protect our nation against this threat. A fleet of Earth-to-Orbit Shuttles are moving to intercept the alien craft as we speak. Seven hundred Tactical Interceptors fighter planes are ready to engage any that manage to slip through our first line of defence. Specially trained ground forces will be utilised in the unlikely event that beings manage to reach the surface. We have their DNA. They cannot hide from us."

Pictures of dozens of abductees of all ages flashed onto the screen, every one of them smiling including Rebecca Jones. "All of these abductees were murdered," Robert re-appeared on the screen. "We set up video surveillance technology in the homes of many willing participants who had previously been abducted. You are about to witness footage from the home of one of hundreds of people who were taken against their will." Three alien beings entered a living room, visible only by the moonlight that seeped through the curtains and reflected against fluid metallic suits that covered their whole bodies. A bright light shone through the window and a man bolted upright from a sofa before he was lifted into the air and floated out of the room beside them. Even with poor visibility I recognised the cream leather sofa. The plain beige walls. It was my abduction. The surveillance changed to a different camera as one of the beings glided in front of it. Through the transparent metallic suit, its huge black empty eyes that dominated its mouthless head. It was no coincidence. However, many times I was taken, this was the one I remembered.

Robert was reaching out to me, he wanted it front and centre of my mind. His face returned. "They are testing our defences, measuring our weaknesses. We believe that they may be performing tests on live humans to discover a way to exterminate our race. But our world will not fall. We know their weakness. They do not breathe like you or me. Instead, they absorb oxygen through their skin. From the footage we just played for you, you can see that they are wearing high pressure suits that generate steam when they are in Earth's atmosphere. If the protective suit is removed, the lifeform inside will die within minutes."

The images being projected had become distorted, no longer a cinema screen to entertain, it was a tool of war propaganda. Robert's news report continued but I walked away, his voice fading in the background. I hurried to my car at the opposite side of the road. Robert had known I had been abducted since the surveillance cameras were planted in my house. I had betrayed myself.

I dialled Jeri's cell as I started up my engine and fled the scene, slow enough to avoid any unwanted attention. After I reached Jeri's voicemail four times, I left a message insisting that she call me back right away. Herb answered his phone after two rings with a gruff, "Yeah?"

"I need to speak to her."

"She's not here," he said, his voice growing more hostile.

"Don't fucking lie to me." The phone went dead. I hit redial right away.

"You've got a lot of nerve calling here," Herb said as soon as he answered.

"Have you seen what's happening?" Silence. "The TV, the radio?" Silence. "Turn it on and stay where you are. Don't let Jeri leave."

"I already said, she's-"

"Just do as I say." I hung up. I couldn't face any more of Herb's bullshit to keep me away from Jeri and I couldn't trust myself not to say something that might stop him from co-operating.

I called my dad, who had seen the report and was calling me while I was connected to Herb. I asked Dad to stay where he was, but he was already sealing the house with boards and furniture and had a survival kit prepared since President Walkers announcement. I called Jess, Rick, Bob and Peter but none of them answered. I left voicemails telling them to get out of DC, as far away as possible. I hoped that there would be somewhere left on the planet that was safe.

The streetlamps flickered and seemed to go out as I drove past each one, even though it had been light for hours. An army of people had congregated outside the shopping mall, blocking the road. I couldn't understand how this was the way they wanted to spend the final moments of their lives. And then I realised that they hadn't been so unfortunate as to lose all hope, they saw another day ahead, possibly one of promise. 'The soul is the energy behind all life on Earth, an entity of desire, reason and creation,' Heinrich Galli had written. Their souls beamed towards me, an eclectic of differing emotion: arrogance, ignorance, kindness, fear, hope, anguish. Something I had forgotten through the trials of life was how they are all beautiful. The most hideous of our human emotions, still human, and are all that truly distinguishes us from dog or jagged rock. I grabbed at my leg, squeezing my fingers at the underneath of my thigh. My nails dug deep, pinching at the skin through my trousers. I didn't want to stop.

Soon, they could all be dead. And I was the one that Robert expected to defend us, it is on my pathetic head that their lives rest. On my conscience they lay before they are even buried. Maybe the best I can hope for is to be at Jeri's side when we die.

You're going to cut and run? You're supposed to care about them.
You might as well be killing them by your own hand.
But I can show you the way.

I am no longer alone in my own head.

* * *

My dad had barely spoken since I told him that we were on our way to Herb's. He was horrified when he saw my bloodied state. I told him that nowhere in D.C. was safe and how I knew: that I had been developing a weapon and that we didn't stand a chance. That one of the Agents in charge had lost it and attacked me. He asked whether I should be

263

out there, helping to prepare for the attack. I didn't answer. He said his goodbyes with a few words to Mom and we left his fortified house because he said he trusted me.

My dad brought cans, bottled water, sleeping bags, matches and a camping stove with enough gasoline for a week or two, but I had no idea how long we would need to survive for, when it would be safe to return to any city or town, or if we would live long enough to use two weeks supplies.

I had barely stopped the car outside Herb's house when I jumped out of it, engine still running. I banged on Herb's door as my dad ambled up the path behind me.

The door swung open. "What do you want?" Herb said with as much hostility as he could muster. "She's not here."

"Where is she?" I barged my way past him, into the living room, then to the kitchen and dining room, screaming Jeri's name. I headed for the stairs when Herb grabbed my shoulder and pulled me back.

"What the hell are you doing? Get out of my house."

I shook his hands off me and ran upstairs. I searched every room, each one occupied by one or two of Herb's kids, but with no sign of Jeri. I ran back down to Herb.

"Please. I know you don't want me here, but it's important. Just tell me where my wife is."

"I don't know. I haven't seen her."

"How could you let her leave?" I couldn't believe what I was hearing. The light in the room seemed brighter. It hurt my eyes; too harsh. I lay my hands on the table and leaned against it. I wanted to stand but my legs trembled beneath me.

"I'm not her keeper." Herb was angry as hell. But I knew, underneath the anger was hurt. He didn't need me tarnishing his relationship with Mom in any way. She would never have said a bad word about him. Any argument or scuffle of our youth was nowhere near the brutality of that night. And with a clearer head I knew Herb hadn't wronged me, all he did was take care of my wife.

"I'm sorry. For what I said, for how I acted. There is nothing I can say to make it up to you. But I need your help."

"You were a fucking asshole." Herb said waving his fist at me.

"I was a fucking asshole. So, if you need to take one good swing at me then go ahead, I know I deserve it."

"Looks like someone beat me to it."

I kept my voice quiet and calm. "She couldn't have been prouder of you. I think you were her favourite."

"Damn right, I was." Herb leaned against the door frame and folded his arms.

"Now, we haven't got much time. Jeri's not answering my calls, she disabled her DNA tracker. How long has Jeri been gone?"

"A few hours. Six maybe?"

"Do you have any idea where she is?" Herb shook his head. "Fuck." I banged my hand against the living room door.

I saw Herb's temper flare again and then fade away. He rested his hand on my shoulder. "We'll find her."

"You don't understand. They're targeting DC, we have to get out. This place is going to be a warzone. I need you to pack as much as you can fit in your car, get in and head to Mason Neck State Park."

Herb's face changed as he saw my dad shuffling awkwardly through the hallway. Herb poked his finger at him, "I've got no business with that man."

"That man?" My dad was outraged. "I'm your dad. It's about time you spoke to me like it."

"You might be my father, but you are not my dad."

"You wouldn't be here if it wasn't for me."

Herb threw his hands up in despair. "I bet you'd like that wouldn't you."

"Listen," I said in as calm a voice as I could muster.

"Shut up, Ryan," Herb's tone devolved into a growl, his temper about to erupt if I didn't stay out of his feud. "I don't know why you brought him here."

"He's trying to save our lives," Dad countered. "Or are you too ignorant to see that as well?"

"What, so I'm ignorant now?"

"Yes, you're ignorant. You're so goddamn ignorant," Dad said, waving his finger. "All I've ever done is tried to help you, to do what's right by you. But you won't accept it. Too damn stubborn."

Herb turned his back on him. "Ryan," he said calm and slowly. "You better get his finger out of my face before I snap it off."

Dad's cheeks flared red. I thought they would put their disdain aside for a few hours at least, but their bad blood poisoned everything around them. "Enough," I shouted. They both stopped but I knew I didn't have long before they got right back to it. I had lost count of the years spent watching an offhand comment escalate to a passive aggressive remark, which provoked a blatant insult, culminating in a full-blown argument. Week's they spent apart, only to bust up again in a few minutes spent in a room together. And then they tried to make me the go between, the conduit of their attacks on each other, which I either rephrased or ignored. Never more from either of them than a tinge of regret. Until there was hatred, built on hurt, built on the worst foundation for a feud of all: love.

"You're my family," I from Herb to my dad. "Both of you. And we need to get out of here. We need to find Jeri and get to Mason Neck. What you do when you get there is up to you."

"I'm not going anywhere with him," Herb insisted.

My dad turned to me, and his eyes darted towards the door. "He's never going to put this nonsense behind us. I know that now."

"He doesn't have to. I just need you both to be safe. When this is over you can go your separate ways."

My phone started ringing in my pocket. I pulled it out; it was Rick.

"Ryan, where are you?"

"I'm at Herb's. Jeri's not answering her phone."

"I just saw her. They took her somewhere; I don't know where. But she's here, Ryan. Jeri's at US Tech."

TWENTY-NINE

"What's she doing at US Tech?" The silence before Rick replied lasted an eternity.

"They wouldn't let me speak to her. You need to get down here now."

"I'm on my way."

"I'll do what I can."

I hung up and turned to my dad. "Jeri's in US Tech, I have to get to her. You need to get on the road. I'll find Jeri and follow you."

"I told you I'm not going anywhere with him," Herb said.

"I don't have time for this shit." I grabbed hold of Herb and Dad's head, one in each hand.

"What the hell are you doing?" Herb said dazed, his mouth open so wide I could have shoved an orange down his throat. "Oh... oh fuck."

I closed my eyes and saw my dad stroking Herb's cheek, only a few hours old. His first day at school when my dad dropped him off and told him that everything would be ok. Herb's first bike, swimming, every good memory they shared that I could find. And then that devastating time, when Herb and my dad held it together. Despite their feelings of resentment and hate for the world. Amid the horror that such a beautiful person had been stolen from them and the growing agony that builds inside you, making it hard to think, hard to breathe, hard to go on living without the feeling that it is all for nothing, that one day everything you love will be stripped away. Through all of that, they stayed strong, they remained civil, and my mom saw that. When she left us, she saw a family before her that loved each other, no matter their differences, a family that was together. Even if it marked the beginning of how our family fell apart.

When I let go, they both stumbled backwards. It felt like electricity inside me, pulsing through my arms.

"What the fuck was that?" Herb asked. "I didn't know he could do that. Did you know he could do that?"

"No one knew," Dad replied.

"That's all I can do. Now, I need to get to Jeri." They both stood awkwardly, barely looking at each other.

"Herb," Dad finally said, "I'm sorry." Herb tried to reply but stumbled over his words. "Your mother loved you. Very, very much. I should have apologised to you a long time ago."

Eddie crept up beside Herb and wrapped his arm around Herb's leg, his face all but hidden. "He doesn't know who you are."

"Who am I?" Dad asked.

Herb's eyes narrowed in anger and clenched his fist. He glanced down at Eddie and relaxed his hand. "What you said. What you did. I can't forgive that." Herb paused. He flattened Eddie's hair, but it poked back up again. "This is your grandfather. We're going to go on a little trip. I think he would like to sit next to you. In the back. Then maybe... maybe your mom can... take you to see him. Not me." Herb gave a stern emphasis to the last two words and glared at my dad to ensure he understood fully. Dad's smile couldn't hide the disappointment in his eyes. He kneeled next to

Eddie.

"I would like that very much."

Herb couldn't look at them. He dashed into the kitchen to gather supplies for the car.

"I'll call you when I'm with Jeri," I said to my dad.

"Good luck, son. And thank you."

"I'm sorry. I really thought-"

"It's ok, Ryan. I know you tried. I guess I thought one day... But it's ok. I've missed so much of the lives of my Grandchildren. I think that's going to change." His eyes drooped like the sad Labrador again, but his smile beamed. "That's because of you." Dad took hold of my hands and stooped to meet my falling eye line. "Everyone makes mistakes, sometimes you make another and another, they compound, building on each other until there's too much to undo. Too much to forgive, even to forgive yourself for. Go. Get Jeri. Come quickly. And be careful, Son. Don't let your mistakes last a lifetime."

I looked through the hallway to Herb, hunched over the kitchen counter with his wrists buckling under the weight of his head. There was nothing more I could do for him. I left them packing and drove off with my dad's supplies in my car.

I felt sick at the thought of Jeri being taken to US Tech. But a part of me couldn't wait to see her again, without being a peeping Tom at the life she lived without me.

The drive to US Tech felt longer than it was. I never expected it to come to this. I had no choice with Brody. It was him or me. He was a murderer. He had to be stopped. But you don't take everything from a man but their breath and their heartbeat and expect to walk away the same.

I felt the swarms of alien craft, moving closer with each passing moment. The shroud they cast was becoming unbearable. I felt myself getting lost in the noise of their singular mind.

I need to get Jeri out before they start their attack.

You can't escape them. But you know how to save her.

* * *

The night crept closer to shade the coming events, concealing them in darkness. The US Tech building peered out between the clouds, lights in every office as high as I could see. The towering building had never looked more formidable. I took the mango wood box out from the glove compartment and opened it carefully. Jeri looked back at me, on the bench in Lake Ontario, tucked into my body. I felt content seeing her face again. I placed the photograph and the scan inside my pocket and tucked the box away.

Inside US Tech, the entrance hall was overwhelming. Nanotube girders arched overhead; each one metre thick. Security officers studied me carefully as I passed them. There were more military officers and secret service than staff. One of them was different. I didn't trust him. He glared at me, his eyes telling a story of judgement. He deemed me inadequate.

I called Rick's cell, then his desk phone but he didn't answer either.

Why doesn't anyone answer their damn phone?

I rushed to the security gate to connect to a control panel and see if I could find anything in the system about Jeri being brought in. As soon as I scanned my pass, four security guards manoeuvred towards me from every side, pistol holsters unclipped and at the ready. "Mr Ellis, Sir," the nearest one planted his feet firmly in front of me, like an immovable object.

I looked between the corridor ahead and the exit, judging whether my best option was to get past them or make a run for it and find Jeri another way. I lifted my hand, ready to clear them out of the way.

"If you're ready," the guard continued. "We've been asked to accompany you to your lab, Sir,"

I eyed him and his backup; I didn't recognise any of them. Didn't trust them. I nodded and he led the way, one

271

either side of me and another at the rear.

As the lab doors opened, the barrels of two big guns were pointed inches away from our faces by military officers. "Ryan Ellis, Sir," the lead guard said, and they lowered their weapons. The military officer insisted on taking my cell and added it to a locked drawer, then stepped aside.

Bob, Peter, and Jessica were in the lab with most of the team we had been working with, and a suited man I didn't recognise stood at the far side of the room. Jess hurried over to me "What's going on?" I asked.

"We think we're close to completing it."

"The work you sent us," Peter added as he typed away at his laptop. "You were onto something. A secondary power source means we can amplify the signal to the frontal cortex and breach the distance barrier. We can hit them anywhere on this planet, from wherever the device is."

"Have you tested it?"

"Not yet," Peter replied. "We're kind of up against it, I'm sure you'll know. We only have one prototype. And they want it ready to go like, yesterday."

"They're going to use it?"

"If we need to." Bob said.

"What if it doesn't work? If we even attempt an attack, it directly accesses their shared consciousness. They'll know we're trying to wipe them out. They'll kill us all."

"That's for the big girls and boys to decide," Bob said.

Jessica took hold of my forearm. Her fingers were cold against my skin. "It's a last resort."

Even more reason to be clear of D.C. "Where's Rick?"

"I saw him up by the production offices a few hours ago."

I hate them. For everything they have done to my family. But there's nothing I can do about that now. Using the weapon without a full testing programme was too big a risk. Surviving would no longer be finding a way to reproduce; it would be eliminating any threat that we posed. There's nothing I can do but protect my family. "Ok, let's get this done."

I fired up a laptop and while everyone was busy doing their part, I pulled up security records, meeting notes, personnel files, everything I had access to, but there was no trace of Jeri.

I hooked my laptop up to the comms device, passed through security gates and disabled the secondary power source, leaving it strong enough to communicate, but not strong enough to harm them.

I set the device to the right frequency and initiated the comms programme. The noise was deafening, pounding like a pneumatic drill in my skull. I grabbed the desk to steady myself. The lab around me disappeared, overlaid by hundreds of thousands of images of metallic control panels, clouds floating above the Earth, the sea stretched out into the horizon, large vats filled with monstrosities that burned their way into my consciousness. When I first used the comms device, I only saw fragments, but now every image merged together to create a tapestry of one unified reality. There was more than I could process, beyond my reach, casting a shadow over my perception, a light glimmering at the edges of the blunt, black object that obstructed it.

I hated everything about them. Their eyes all pupil and never turning so you never know when they're looking at you. Their slimy skin. Everything I felt was sucked inside them, dispersed amongst every being in their collective. They didn't care what happened to us, they didn't care about anything at all. I was in their world. They felt nothing and oh how I envied them. Hundreds of thousands of minds operating as one, hearing my plea, my offer of peace, a desperate attempt to deter their attack. But my desperation slipped away with my fear, and every other emotion that had raged through me moments before.

The lab ripped its way back into my senses, a jagged piece of glass forcing fighting its way into a brick wall. My mind staggered, unable to merge every sense from the hive mind with the physical world that surrounded me. I fell so hard to my knees that I almost didn't get back up.

"The secondary power source has been deactivated. It's disabled the device. I... I don't know what happened." Peter moved furiously between his laptop and the hardware, tinkering and assessing. I slumped against the desk, still reeling; my mind like it had lost a dozen limbs. Images tried to take over what my eyes could see. I lifted my heavy head to assess my exit, and the two military officers blocking it. "A comms channel has been opened up. It's running on a loop."

The man in the suit stumbled forward, one hand gripping his head, the other stretched out and feeling its way around like he couldn't see the room before him. "Turn it off."

Peter turned to me, his face a sickly pale. "Ryan, what have you done?"

* * *

The images of clouds and the sea, control panels and liquid filled vats were sucked away from me, severed from my mind in less than an instant. Peter had shut down the comms device. The connection was gone.

My head still rang, and my eyes blurred. The man in the suit marched over to me and grabbed me by the shoulders. "Fix it." I didn't answer, my head flopping groggily from side to side. "Fix it now or you will regret it."

"Now... Hang on a second," Bob was in no way physically imposing and had never done a thing in his life that wasn't by the book, protocol, following the rules. But he stepped forward and glared at the man who held me in his grip. "Let him go. Peter, what makes you think Ryan did something? Why would you say that?"

Panic left Peter speechless.

The man in the suit nodded to one of the military officers, who pointed his gun at Bob's head. He put his face inches from mine and snarled at me, "Fix it now." My eyes rolled in my head, I tried to regain control but the world around me was more like a reflection, the real world fighting for dominance.

"Listen to me," Bob said waving his finger. "That's enough. That is a good man, and a friend of mine and I'm not going to let you threaten him like that. Now you listen to me-"

The man in the suit nodded again to the officer. The officer squeezed the trigger and Bob dropped to the floor.

Jessica dived at Bob's motionless body. All the fight that he possessed was gone. She pressed her fingers against his wrist, and then his neck. He didn't move. Jess's head sank.

I saw pictures of Bob's wife and children all over his desk, every day. Now he's dead. He'll never look at them again.

He won't be the last. Their blood will be on your hands.

"Step away, Miss and be seated." The second officer barked at Jessica. Jess was in too much shock to react. Everyone else was too scared to move. The officer pointed his gun at her head. That was enough to break my static obedience. I couldn't face another death, especially not Jess. I pushed the man's arms off me. "Come on Jess, come on." I said, trying to pick her up off the floor.

The man in the suit leaned casually against the wall, grinning at me. "Come on, Ellis. Let's see what you can do." He knew exactly who I was. He wanted me to make a move. I didn't take my eyes off him.

Peter looked terrified, as though he was about to throw himself out of the window, his few words setting off the chain of events.

The man in the suit spoke quietly, barely loud enough to hear. "Fix it, Ellis." He nodded and the officer's finger stroked the trigger. "Fix it." Another nod.

The officer squeezed his finger and pulled the trigger. From over two feet away I pushed the barrel into the air. I couldn't stop it firing but the bullet shot straight into the ceiling. The other officer directed his gun at me and the first lowered his gun back down level with my head. I stretched my arm and extended my mind to rip the weapons out of the officers' hands. As I did, something hit me square in the stomach and knocked me to the ground. When I looked to see what hit me, there was nothing there. The man in the suit stood over me with a smile on his face: Cognitive Expansion Group.

* * *

The onslaught was fierce as the CEG Agent unleashed a fury of blows. He sent items from around the room hurtling at me before I could get up off the ground.

Come on, Ryan. Paradoxical end. Unveil. Transcend.

Know what is real. They're just objects.

I pulled a table across the lab until it stopped abruptly in front of me, and I spun it on its side to absorb the CEG Agents' attacks. It gave me enough time to knock the two military officer's unconscious with a tall aluminum stool for each of them. Everyone else in the lab dived for cover.

I lifted chairs and tables, glasses, and laptops around me into the air and sent them hurtling across the room. But the CEG Agent was prepared using a single chair at the mercy of his mind to deflect every attack. So, I had to take a more direct approach.

Power flowed through me, travelling through the air, invisible to the eye, to throw the CEG Agent back with enough force to create an indent in the drywall. He fell to the floor so I lifted him to his feet and did it again. He was bruised, battered, and beaten. I picked him up again and sent him crashing into the other side of the room.

"Ryan, he's unconscious," Jess shouted. I dropped the CEG Agent to the floor with a bang.

"Find something to tie them up." I reached out and dragged the two military officers across the floor to the feet of Peter and Jess.

Execution style. I didn't know you had it in you, Ellis.

I stood over the CEG Agent, grabbed hold of his crumpled blazer with my hands, his tie hanging loosely around his neck, propped him up against the wall and waited for him to regain consciousness. When he came to, he looked up at me and cracked out a laugh. "Apex was right, it's all happening as he said it would. You're going to do it aren't you?"

"Do what? Do what?" I smacked his head against the wall with my bare hands until he bled. He tensed his body and faced forward, fighting not to let my blows shift his position.

"Stop it, Ryan, you're going to kill him," Jess said. I didn't want to stop.

I stepped back. Most people would have collapsed to the floor, but he refused to go down, as rigid as a dead man. His voice croaked, "I was supposed to take you to him. After you completed the weapon."

I knelt down beside the agent and spoke in a quieter tone than before, "Where is he? Where's Palmer?"

"He's waiting for you."

"Where?"

"Here."

"What does he want with me? Where's my wife?"

I reached for his head, determined to glean whatever he knew. His eyes widened. I felt something rise into the air behind me. I whipped around to see an automatic weapon hanging above the heads of my team. It let out a rattle of gunfire. The screams filled the room as lab assistants covered their ears and engineers ducked for cover. The gun dropped to the floor with a clank. Jess stared at me in horror. The CEG Agent had slumped to the ground, a raft of bullet holes in his body and a smear of blood down the wall behind him.

I turned to face the people in the room. They were crying, screaming, fallen to the floor, or doing nothing, in utter shock. "You all need to leave," I shouted. "Get out of

Washington, it's the primary target, and there's a good chance this building is high on their list. There isn't much time. Go to your families and leave." No one dared move. "Now!"

Like a shock to the system they charged, bouncing off each other as they gradually made their way towards the door. Some went back for coats and laptops and others just ran.

"What about you?" Jess asked.

"I need to find Jeri. She's here; I think Robert Palmer has her."

"Jeri, why?"

"I don't know… She was abducted. So was I."

"Your eyes…" Jess sighed with acceptance. "So, then I…" She took a deep breath, her expression more one of acceptance than recognition. "I'll come with you; I'll help you find her."

"No. You have to leave. Please. As soon as I find her, I'll be right behind you."

Jess took hold of my hand for a moment. The crowd had turned to panic, pushing each other aside to squeeze through the door a few seconds earlier. Peter was the only one not moving. He stood over Bob's body, staring down at him. "I'm sorry, Ryan. I didn't know."

"Know what?" I spat, marching towards him. "That you were going to betray me? That I can snap your neck without even touching it?"

"I helped you," Peter hesitated. "I… I didn't know they were going to shoot him."

I got in his face and shoved him. He stumbled and just about remained standing. "They didn't shoot him, they killed him. You killed him."

"I'm sorry." Peter said, his voice shaky.

"Why should you get to live?" A burning sensation in my head wanted nothing but to make him pay. Make him suffer. I felt a pull at my arm.

"Ryan, stop it." Jess tried to pull me off Peter, but I was

too angry, growling in his face.

"You're a murderer. How many more people are going to die because of you?"

"Please, stop it. Look at him! Peter didn't put the bullet in him it was those bastards."

Peter's lip trembled like blubber and his eyes filled with tears of remorse. "I didn't mean to," he moaned. "I didn't know. I thought you were trying to sabotage us. I didn't… I didn't know…" He dove into me, burying his head into my neck, sobbing. "I'm sorry. I'm so sorry. I didn't know."

Bob lay as dead as he would ever be. Nothing was going to change that. I took a breath, trying to control the rage that churned inside me, desperate to escape. I knew the soft touch on my back was Jess's hand. She pulled the huddled mess of Peter and me closer and rested her head on top of Peter's. The fury gradually subsided. I slipped out from them and stepped back. "You need to leave. Both of you."

I detached the comms device and carefully packed it into the portable carrier that was marginally larger than a briefcase and marched out of the room, Jess dragging Peter along beside her.

The corridor outside was empty. Brody scratched at the inside of my skull, thrilled that I had annihilated another CEG Agent who had years of training. Brody's happy where he is. He thinks he's in control.

The three hundred-story building shook to its foundations. I ran to the window to see a single craft break through the clouds. The whole building vibrated.

"We've been hit." Jess said and backed away from the window. I looked out and saw an alien craft plummeting to the ground. The building vibrated again, and a huge object flew through the sky and hit a second alien craft that was breaking through the field of cloud. "We've been hit again."

"No. It's coming from this building. It's surface to air missiles."

The clouds above Washington parted for a swarm of alien craft. A flurry of missiles flew across the sky from the

279

US Tech building earning a direct hit to the first craft. Missiles erupted from half a dozen other space scrapers that were in sight, the White Giant standing tallest among them. With each wave of craft that fell to the ground, another hundred entered the night sky. Earth's fighter planes roared through the clouds to meet them. The alien craft merged together and split apart to confuse their enemies. They released an onslaught of glowing white flashes that sent hundreds of planes plummeting to the ground. Others were completely disintegrated until there was barely a fighter plane left in the sky. The crashes and flames from the ground were only just visible to us as the fire snapped up before pulling itself back down below. And when there were no more fighter planes in the skies above Washington D.C. the glowing craft turned their attention towards the bold towers that were still amassing an assault.

THIRTY

With every missile fired the building trembled, drowning out Jess's voice. I stared out at the glow of the craft that flew around the sky like fireflies, elegantly dropping their devastation over the city. They chipped away at the White Giant, the greatest achievement in my career and one of the greatest physical representations of what humankind could achieve, until it crumbled to the ground like a set of children's building blocks. Its soul had already been warped from humanity's goal to better ourselves and our lives, into a weapon of death, just like everything that Robert Palmer touched. Now its body lay broken on the ground. It wouldn't be long before US Tech was crumbling at their feet.

I did my best to shake off the enormity of what was happening outside to get to the one place in US Tech that Robert Palmer was most likely to be: the war room. I chanced the elevator not being shut down and told Jess and Peter to get out on level one and leave DC. Jess gazed into my eyes as she walked away. She didn't say a word, trying a half smile that never quite appeared. It felt like the last time I would ever see her.

I continued to the basement. With a ding, the doors

opened. Seven men stood, fully suited, thin mesh gloves covering their hands, arms at their sides as though they had holstered guns tucked into their belts, ready to be drawn. The nearest, blonde hair gelled back into a solid crisp shell on his head, touched his earpiece. "Copy that. He's here." He held a pair of cuffs with a small console attached to them. "Slow down, Sir. You're coming with me." He held the cuffs out in front of him. They think they can subdue me. They know I'm dangerous. They don't know how dangerous.

I carefully set the comms device down on the floor. "Get out of my way," I demanded. They didn't move. The one to my right was trying to stay calm but his hands shook violently. They don't want to face me. "Get out of my way."

I pulled the cuffs out of his grasp, and he held his hands in the air about to strike. Before he could, I flung them back at him and snapped them onto his wrists. He cried out, powerless. A massive force hit me in the face and knocked me to the ground. Before I could get up, one of them dragged me to him. I gripped the corrugated metal floor to slow me down and jumped to my feet.

I clenched my fists as though I was going to start throwing punches and unleashed everything that was inside me, sending all of them to the ground in one almighty blow. They got up one by one, giving me enough time to knock the first one unconscious with a crash into the wall. I did that to two more while the other four kept coming.

They sent every item they could find smashing into my body, but they couldn't stop me. The three who were unconscious didn't stay unconscious for long.

They're trying to kill us.

I told myself that I had to do anything it took to stop them. He told me it was true.

I stopped looking at what was in front of me, my vision only sought to contain what is real; only one speck of grey dirt in a spectrum of colour.

With so few objects in the corridor, I had to get creative.

I pulled bricks out of the walls, tore the doors from the elevator and picked up everything they had thrown at me, until every item was hanging in the air around me.

"I told you to get out of my way," I almost hoped they didn't. The seven men who stood in front of me watched and waited with bitterness. Their years of training had been nothing more than a fleeting moment compared with the power I had gained. All they thought about was fear. That I would get past them to the President inside, that they would have failed. That I would kill them all. Or worse. That no matter what happened down here in the dark recesses of US Tech, the alien attack would prove too much for even the barrage of defences that the now President had been amassing for so many years. "Let me past."

They didn't move.

In one brutal assault I sent everything at the seven men that stood between me and the war room. Some of them bluntly smacked into the Agents and some pierced their skin. One was killed in the onslaught. The remaining six understood that they didn't stand a chance.

I'm every bit as dangerous as they might have heard. I'll fucking kill them all.

I sent the elevator forty floors up to clear the area beneath. I reached out my arm and took hold of each one, ripping their legs from under them. I dragged them across the floor, all the way until they fell a few feet below ground level into the elevator shaft. I heard their groans and pleas to stop. But they wouldn't stop until I was neutralised. No one stopped before they took my wife.

The elevator screeched as I loosened my grip to the sound of more cries. I snapped the cables, let go, and sent the elevator whooshing down under the pull of gravity. It moved through each floor in milliseconds until it hit the bottom, silencing their screams. Their fear was louder than anything I had felt before.

THIRTY-ONE

I ventured through the narrow steel corridor in the depths of US Tech, comms device in hand, until I reached the war room entrance. Access was still beyond my clearance level alone. I pulled at the reinforced steel doors, prising them open with every trace of energy I could muster. The locks cracked under the pressure, resisting, entwined inside the opposing door. I pulled until the locks snapped one at a time and the doors flew apart.

A wave of heat hit me as soon as I stepped inside the illuminated red walls of the war room. I could barely breathe. Five automatic guns were pointed at me by five soldiers who did their best to disguise fear with a stoic face and an aggressive stance. Robert Palmer stepped out of the shadows, standing tall and seemingly un-phased by the immense heat. Mr President.

The sight of him curled my upper lip into a sneer. "You son of a bitch."

"Lower them," Palmer said. "Everything is under control. Lower them."

General Day looked incredulously at Palmer. Half a dozen people stood behind her in the middle of the floor, all staring at me, with another dozen people at their stations, trying their best not to. General Day confirmed Palmer's request and all five soldiers followed his order.

Digital projectors from the anti-stealth tech showed hundreds of alien craft above DC laying waste to the great towers that boldly stood amidst a cityscape barely as high as their knees. "Where is she?" I asked, my patience already paper thin.

"He won't let her leave." I recognised the voice instantly. I searched the faces standing with General Day. They were all familiar, but one more than the rest, the face of my best friend. "It's all about timing."

Sweat poured from Rick's head, his breathing uncoordinated. His tie hung loosely around his neck. If it had been any tighter, he would have passed out. He looked at me so desperately, almost pleading with me.

"She's safe," Palmer jumped in. He leaned forward, doing his best to make eye contact with me and adding with his most sincere voice, "I know what she means to you."

"Tell me where she is."

Palmer focused all his attention on me, like we were the only people in the room. "You can see her. I promise. But we need to talk. There is a great deal you need to know, and we don't have much time."

"I don't care what you have to say. I know who you are." I raised my hand into the air and the soldier's whipped their guns back up at me. "Tell me where she is, and we're gone."

"The Earth-to-Orbit shuttles were wiped out in minutes," Rick's tone was venomous. "The US Pad, the Space Lift, all of it, gone. Everything we've done in US Tech was to prepare for this. But we weren't ready. Your weapon isn't ready. And now you want to cut and run." He scoffed at me in disgust.

"That's enough." Palmer dismissed Rick.

"Don't speak to me. "Don't even look at me." Rick clenched his teeth and swallowed hard. "What you have asked of me. The things that I've done. You damned my soul to hell." Rick shook, taking deep, uneasy breaths.

Palmer prodded his finger at Rick. "I said that's enough!"

"No," Rick interrupted. "People should hear what I have to say for a change." He pulled a handgun from a holster under his jacket and pointed it at Palmer.

The five soldiers swung around to fix their sights on Rick, each of them resting their index fingers on the trigger. All they were waiting for was the kill signal, or to see his finger stroke the trigger. Rick wouldn't stand a chance.

"Put your weapons on the ground," I said. "He gets hurt, you're all dead." No one moved. "Do you understand me?" One of the soldier's eyes darted back and forth between Rick and General Day but the guns remained firmly trained on Rick.

I wrenched the weapons from the soldier's hands before they could get a reactionary shot off and threw them far out of reach of any itchy trigger fingers.

"Rick," I hoped that getting him out of the firing line would be enough for me to reason with him, even in the state he was in. Except for the five soldiers, everyone in the room not at a terminal had turned statue as soon as Rick pulled the gun. "Please, put it down. He knows where Jeri is."

Rick laughed to himself. "Who do you think brought her here?"

"What? Why? Where is she?"

Rick shook his head. "If only you had shown such concern for her before."

"Tell me where she is." Without thinking, I raised my hand in the air, palm directed at Rick.

"Are you threatening me? Point your magic hands away from me, you freak." Rick swung the gun from Palmer to me. I didn't understand what was happening. He was my best man, on first name basis with my mom, the reason I got my job at US Tech. He got me through college, studying, exams, booze and parties. "What, so you can treat her like shit? Sneak off with Jess again? You make me sick."

A fire set light in my belly. How dare he say that? He knows what me and Jeri have been through. "Rick, put the gun down."

"Stop telling me what to do. He has to pay."

He took your wife. Who knows what he did to her.

"I've kept Jeri safe." Palmer said. "I'm the only one who knows where she is."

Rick ignored Palmer, his attention on me. "He has to pay."

Kill him. Palmer knows where she is.

I have to save her. "Rick, put the gun down."

"Stop telling me what to do."

Kill him. He's weak; he's too scared to drop it. If he kills Palmer, you won't find her until it's too late.

The dark-haired soldier had gradually been edging her way closer to the pile of guns, thinking I hadn't noticed. Only a few feet away, she darted for them. My eyes still on Rick, I dragged the pile of guns from one corner of the room to the other. Rick fired off a shot, carving a five-cent sized dent in the concrete wall, inches above her head.

"All my life I've stood in your shadow. I have given everything for this cause. And it's all for nothing, we're already dead." Rick shook his gun at Palmer. "You have damned me to hell! Damned me to hell!" He swung the gun back at me. "And what have you done? Where would you be if you weren't abducted? There would be no White Giant, no DNA tracker for you. Nothing. And yet you get all the glory. Just because they took you. There is nothing special about you at all. He thinks you're our great hope. The one who's going to save us. We don't stand a chance."

Do it. He won't see it coming.

"How long have you known?"

He looked at me like I was insane. "Long enough. What happened to you? Was it your skin? Or the eyes?" He smiled a worthless grin. "Yeah, you got the eyes. I knew long enough to be on the Earth-to-Orbit shuttle, before its first mission-"

"Stop," Palmer cut him off. "That's enough."

"They thought they were making peace. It was all for you. That's how important you are to him. To the plan. To Project Sobek. Because you are Project Sobek." His eyes were wide with terror. "But I'm important too. That's why I was on the shuttle project. I do what needs to be done. Do you know what it's like yet? To kill a man? A Woman? To watch dozens of people react in horror at what you've done, until there's nothing left but debris and dust."

I dragged my hand across my face. "The shuttle... Oh no... Rick, no"

"Don't pity me. Don't you dare. I've been here from the start. Why do you think he brought me in? You're only here because of me. I'm only here because of you."

"How could you do it? They were innocent people. They didn't wrong you. My best friend... You lied to me. They were trying to make peace. How could you betray them? How could you betray me?"

Rick squeezed the gun tightly, his finger pressing against the trigger. "You're as bad as he is. You stole her from me. You don't even love her. How many times has she left you? And you keep dragging her back."

"How can you talk like that? You know what we've been through."

"It was two years ago. Get over it." His face crumpled, his eyes welling up with tears. "I have loved her since the moment I saw her. She danced like an angel."

Kill him.

"Tough shit." Rick stepped back, his face aghast. "She picked me. Not you. Me. And we sure as shit have had our tough times, but who the fuck are you to say what I feel about her? You sad, pathetic, murdering piece of shit."

Rick glared at me. His lip shook, tears welled. He pointed the gun back at Palmer but kept his eyes fixed on me. Everyone in the room reacted – they froze, backed away, held a hand to their mouth – except Palmer. He didn't flinch. Rick swung the gun and squeezed the trigger like a cold-blooded murderer without a flicker in his eye. The hammer hit the bullet and put a hole in Rick's skull and the concrete wall behind him. It was the most sickening noise that killed instantly.

He was dead. And I did nothing to stop him.

THIRTY-TWO

Rick lay sprawled on the floor, eyes open wider than usual, as though in shock of what he had done. I thought there would have been more blood. What he kept from me, the things he did, I could never have forgiven him. But what about now that he's dead?

He got what he deserved.

Palmer stared down at Rick, as composed and in control as ever. "He did what needed to be done. He was unstable. But he made his contribution."

"Why did you bring him into this?"

Palmer bowed his head and furrowed his brow. "You don't have a lot of friends, Ryan. I saw what you did the first day I met you, when you answered the difficult question Rick Stenson couldn't. You've certainly got guts. But it wasn't the White Giant you were fighting for, and it wasn't US Tech. You were fighting for your friend."

"So, what, you used him to get to me?"

He tilted his head back and peered down at me like a disappointed father. "I think we both let him down."

All the anger I felt towards Rick was now directed at the man responsible for his demise. It raged inside me, like a fury about to take over. "Don't dare. Don't you fucking dare. You have ten seconds to tell me where my wife is."

Palmer paused for no more than a second before he gave a subtle nod to the half dozen people who had barely moved from the middle of the war room since I entered the fray. A brunette woman in a tailored navy-blue suit emerged and hurried to the control panel. She pressed a few keys and entered her fingerprint and retinal scan, which triggered a thick section of the far wall to slide to one side and reveal a doorway. The woman rushed inside and reappeared with Jeri behind her, inhibitor cuffs wrapped around her hands.

I ran to her, I studied her eyes, her face, her bare arms, looking for any sign of harm or ill treatment. "Get them off her." The suited woman freed my wife's hands and stepped away from me. I took Jeri's cheek in the palm of my hand. "Are you ok?"

Jeri nodded and wrapped one arm around my neck, pulling our heads together. Her oval blue eyes were as bright as the day I met her. She explored the room in a daze, stopping at Rick's lifeless body collapsed on the floor with a gasp of horror. She turned back to me, aching to know what had happened.

"We're leaving," I said and marched towards the open exit, doors in a heap against the wall.

"We need to talk," Palmer shouted after me. "You can't run away from this." I kept going towards the door, doing my best to block out his voice. All that mattered was that I finally had Jeri back with me. That we could go to somewhere safe, out to Mason Neck, away from the terror that had befell our city. "I'm sorry, Ryan." There was a break in his voice that made him sound regretful. I could barely hear him. "Out of everything in your life, she was the one thing, the one person that more than anyone else… you would kill for."

I stopped dead; Jeri came to a halt a few steps behind me. I saw my car ahead of me, a clear road, a way through, a hope to escape the attack until it was over, until they got what they came for and left us to rebuild. But we would still be alive. That would be enough. But Palmer's words echoed in my mind, his slow, calming tone harrowing to my ear. "What? What have you done?"

"The reason they are attacking with such force, it's not because we attacked them first, though we did. They want to make sure they achieve their goal, because it is finally within their grasp. They are here to get what they need, and because of this facility, they don't know where it is, or rather, where she is, so they are tearing this city apart until they find her. It's Jeri. They're coming for your wife."

I couldn't comprehend his words, the implications of what he was suggesting. Why Jeri? What has he done?!

"I know this is difficult for you to understand. But I want to be honest with you. We have thousands of years' worth of experience with reproduction to draw on. We made progress targeting their abductees, but we were unsuccessful with any of the live alien subjects that we were able to cut-off from the central consciousness. Until we went back to the role of both genders in reproduction. Until we found you. We immediately recognised your potential and adjusted your abilities to enable DNA replication, carrying with it the ability to reproduce, crossing genders, and ultimately species. I'm sorry to say this, but one of the benefits of the state of your relationship, was that we could allow you to walk around free and still control the timing of the impregnation. Or so we thought...until well, unexpectedly... you forced our hand to accelerate events."

Jeri froze, her body faltered a held breath away from fainting to the floor. My torso tingled, sending sensations through my body until my hands shook uncontrollably. The last remnants of my grasp on consciousness nearly slipped through my fingers. I held on tight, trying to stay present, to keep my mind contained inside my head. I watched Jeri again, hoping that seeing her face would ground me. Watching her fight so hard to keep the wave of emotion from erupting out of her nearly killed me. She tamed her quivering lip, took a breath, and let the words out.

"I'm pregnant."

It rushed over me, almost unbearable to my senses, the air around me tingling at my skin, my neck getting tenser and tenser like it was gradually turning to stone. I wanted to hold her, to pull her into me and squeeze until my arms turned numb. To cry together. To never stop crying. But the unwelcome sound that came out of Palmer's mouth took me back, deep underground, a return to death and the smear of blood that Rick left behind, subtly fading into the bright red light that illuminated the war room in the depths of US Tech.

"She's the key. The answer to how they reproduce. We made her fertile. You made her fertile. They won't bring her back this time."

I reached out across the room and threw Palmer into the wall as hard as I could. I felt the blood flowing through his body, pumping oxygen through into his brain. Felt the air being pulled in by his lungs.

Kill him.

I charged towards him, pinned to the wall. I got into his face, snarling like a depraved predator and he was the last piece of meat. "Why? Why did you do it?"

"What would you have me do? Try to make peace? While they control our minds? How long until we ceased to be useful to them? Until they decide to use their infinitely superior technology to launch an attack on their terms? We could never allow creatures so powerful to survive to destroy us. They can manipulate our minds; make themselves invisible to our eyes. We don't know how they think. How far they're prepared to go to get what they want. We invited the ultimate stranger into our home. Look," Palmer motioned towards the anti-stealth display. There was anarchy in the skies, an armada of alien ships dropping an onslaught on the ground below. "I have dedicated my life to being ready for this fight."

"You're not the one they're coming for."

Palmer pushed his chest out, bitterly offended and

standing proud. "I would gladly die to save our planet. Every scenario we ran, we lost. Not a few million lives, total annihilation of the human race. Our whole society, decimated. Everything we have worked for, everything that our ancestors have died for, over thousands of years. Gone." Palmer paused and let the passion in his voice subside. "I'm sorry you were brought into this. I wish it was different, I truly do. But you progressed far faster than any of our own subjects. There is no one else that can do this. I had to give them what they want."

"What right do you have to decide who's bait? Who lives and who dies?"

"I'm afraid there is no price too high for the preservation of the human race. I never wanted to be President. These are not decisions that we want to make. They are decisions that we must make."

Palmer rested his hand on my shoulder. "It doesn't have to be this way, Ryan. Right now, they want us, they want Jeri so they can reproduce and continue their species. But what next? Do you really think they will stop there? That they will travel off into the galaxy and decide there is nothing else they want from us? You think they won't need a planet to colonise? To terraform, so it can sustain their newly formed species that can reproduce for a thousand years to come? There's barely enough space for the life that's here now."

"We don't stand a chance. I've seen it happen, over and over. Night after night."

"I'm sure Noah felt the same before he saved all of the lives he did. I can imagine how he felt watching the rain pour down from the skies. When I found out about them, about what they can do, about what they're here to do… I felt as terrified as I imagine Noah did. Only without the boat. And then you dropped into my lap. And I knew the human race was meant to survive this. We were going to make it through... Because you're our miracle."

I strangled his disgusting neck. I didn't want to hear another word.

I could close it completely. I could close his throat right now. I could stop his heart from beating, pull his manipulative brain out of his fucking head. He deserves it. He started this. He'll pay for what he's done.

Murderer.

Lights flickered and flashed and one by one, every item in the room blew up around him. A phone smashed into his face, cutting his cheek, a cabinet crashed into his chest and pressed him tightly against the wall. But I kept him alive. I wanted him to suffer. I was in complete control, and I wanted Robert Palmer dead.

I want to rip out his soul.

Murderer.

He stopped breathing. I felt his life slipping away. Just like President Walker, like Bob and Jeremy. Like Rick.

But this isn't going to save her.

You know how to save her.

I let Palmer drop to the floor in a heap, fighting for every breath.

Jeri hadn't moved from the doorway. She stared at me like she no longer recognised me, a familiar stranger more than her husband. It was only a matter of time before they find us here. There was only one way to save her.

"Come on," I said to Jeri and started towards the door. She watched the alien craft in the anti-stealth display, low in the sky, focusing their attack on the ground forces that had been assembled to respond to them, land to air missiles shooting into the air like they were being fired from pea shooters. She ran to the pile of guns in the corner, picked up the two-handed weapon, weighed it in her hands, slung another onto her back and followed me to the exit. Barely larger than a suitcase, I held in my hand what I hoped would be the only weapon we needed.

THIRTY-THREE

Three severed fingers lay outside the elevator where one of the CEG agents had reached for their escape. Jeri recoiled but she didn't suspect it was me who put them there. She doesn't know what I'm capable of, what I would do to protect her. I prised apart the doors and followed Jeri inside. The doors didn't close, and the mechanics were broken, but I lifted the elevator until we reached the ground floor, far away enough from the war room, away from Robert Palmer. I let the elevator back down gently to the basement. I felt Jeri watching me, but she maintained her usual appearance of calm, showing no sign that she was phased by the struggle that lay ahead of us. I was sure I looked like a wreck, about to crumble at any moment. But I no longer faced the struggle alone.

Vibrations shook the building, but this time was different. They were more violent and lasted longer. The impact of one was so severe it nearly knocked us to the ground. The alien craft occupying our skies had turned their attention to US Tech.

The chaos outside echoed through the reception area, gunfire and explosions reverberating through the room. I looked down at Jeri's stomach, but I couldn't comprehend what was inside, what I never thought possible.

I crouched down and laid the comms device on the floor. Jeri gave me a questioning look, and then looked to the exit of US Tech, only forty feet away. Another tremor.

"We can't leave, not yet," I said, loading the programme.

"We have to get out of here… You said we have to leave DC."

I sighed, the words like razor blades crawling out of my throat. "He's right. Whatever he's done, he's right. We don't have a choice now." I felt a great sadness of what had become of my life. For the life that could have been. "Listen to what's happening out there. We can't slip away… Not when they're coming for you."

Jeri stepped closer to me. "I saw what you can do." She pulled the long automatic weapon tightly into her shoulder. "We can make it… We can go where they won't find us."

I shook my head from side to side. "Wherever we go they'll find us." Whatever it takes. That meant accepting the decisions I had to make. Being at peace with them. As peaceful as still waters. "Brody was right. You have to get them before they get you."

"Get them how?" Jeri asked slowly, but she didn't want to hear the answer. The second time she asked wasn't so hesitant.

"A hit to their shared consciousness. Like a psychological payload. It will end their brain waves simultaneously. Every one of them"

"You can't. There has to be another way."

"I tried. They are… singularly focused on their goal. I've been inside their heads; I've seen what they want. They'll do whatever it takes to survive. And all I did was get Bob killed."

Jeri smothered her face with her hand. When she re-emerged, her skin was bright red, but her eyes had all the determination that I felt inside, but knew my weary appearance was far from. "I know what they've done to you. I know, Ryan, I do. But please, don't do this."

"I wish it wasn't painless. I wish they could agonise as I have." I stood up to face Jeri.

"You have to forget about what they've done," Jeri was desperate, she dodged the words, but she was telling me to get over it. Her pleas didn't scratch my resolve. "We have to go, now."

"We don't know when they first took you. What if they took her away from us? What if they took our baby?"

I leaned down to enter the access codes. Jeri grabbed my arm and wrenched me back up to face her. I could almost see the crack forming, about to split her open. But like everything else she plastered over it and stood tall, like she could weather any storm. "You can't do this. A whole race, you can't just kill them all. Do you understand what that makes you? I know people who have taken a life... A single life. I've seen what it does to them. There has to be another way."

"It won't be my first." I pulled my arm free, pumped in the activation code.

No more pain.

"No more pain."

Within seconds the clarity of their hive-mind let out a wail, immediately aware of the pulse that I released into their consciousness. I saw what every alien being saw across Washington, in the skies, above Earth. I felt their singlemindedness to retrieve Jeri. They were fighting for their own survival, and she was everything to them. But they had given me no other choice.

The US Tech reception area became one of thousands of scenes that I saw, all fighting for dominance over the one right in front me. Emotionless minds merged together. We were almost as one.

The vibrations within US Tech stopped. The noise outside subsided. It won't be long until it's over, until their ships fall to their ground, their bodies drop to the floor.

We waited and I wondered if Jeri held any of the hope that I did for it to succeed.

Boom. The whole building shook like a nine on the Richter scale, rumbling through the ears of anyone within miles of US Tech. And again, just as loud. I heard pieces of the building crash to the ground outside, felt the lives, human and alien slipping away in the streets and on the floors above. My hands trembled and my heart beat out of my chest. I rose to my feet.

It can't be. After everything. My one hope. The only way.

"It didn't work. The weapon failed. They know what I tried to do." The blood drained out of Jeri's face before me, her eyes grew wide. "They're not going to stop. Not until every human on the planet is dead."

THIRTY-FOUR

I stared into space in a trance, unable to break out of it long enough to process my surroundings. They won't leave anyone alive to create a weapon that does work. I've doomed the whole planet.

I felt a hard slap hit my cheek. I blinked repeatedly, came to, and saw Jeri standing in front of me with her hand raised, about to deliver another. I jerked my head to look in her eyes and she let her hand drop to her side. "We have to get out of here," she said. I didn't answer. Another tremor. "This building is about to come down."

"Not with you in it. They're trying to flush you out."

Jeri paused. "Do they know for sure I'm in here?"

I nodded.

"We leave, or we wait for them to come for me," she said. "Out there, at least we'll have a chance to escape." Jeri charged forward, two hands gripping her weapon, the sight positioned just in front of her eyes, poised and ready. But we were far removed from chasing down thugs. Jeri had only fired her gun at a living thing once, hitting an armed robber in the shoulder before he fell to the ground and dropped his weapon. Michelle tried to take the kill shot. Jeri stopped her, moved in, and arrested him. She saved his life.

I ran to catch up, copied Jeri sliding over the top of the waist-level security gates in the deserted reception. Another rumble as US Tech was hit and dust from the ceiling crumbled down onto our heads. The sounds of gunfire from outside grew louder with each footstep closer to the exit.

Two bodies were huddled in the doorway, out of sight of anyone outside. Jeri and I slowed our run to a jog, and then a stroll, but our footsteps alerted the nearest person, quickly followed by the second. Jess jumped to her feet. Peter rose slowly, his eyes hollowed out, gazing into nothingness. He barely lifted his head from his chin.

"It's horrible," Jess said. "It's… people are dead everywhere…" Jess looked at Jeri, eyes wide with anticipation of how Jeri would react seeing her here.

"We have to go. It's more dangerous here than it is out there." Jeri eyed Jess and then Peter to reinforce her command. Jeri had no time for animosity during a crisis like this, her only concern was getting us out alive. "We get as far as we need to until the roads are clear. Then we find a car. Motorbikes are even better. Get on them right away and dodge anything blocking the way. Double up and we'll meet at the corner of Fairfax Drive and North Meade Street and move on from there until we get to Camp Springs Air Force base."

"Dad, Herb, Carol and the kids have gone to Mason Neck State Park."

"Even better. Most importantly, stay alive. Stay away from fire, stay low and don't be seen. And keep moving." Jeri looked back over her shoulder, at me on her left side, and then at Peter and Jess on her right. "Let's go."

The doors of US Tech automatically swung open to expose a mass of anarchy and destruction before us. The scream of an air raid siren raged through the streets, ordering people to get inside where it's safe. But nowhere was safe. Not in your house, not in your bed. Not behind the hundreds of heavily armed soldiers that lined the streets, or inside the tank that had been flipped, sixty feet away. A white glow shone from the left, an alien craft slowly lowering itself to the ground, unaffected by the land to air missiles that scored direct hits against it. Behind it, a second craft had already landed and a third was quickly descending from the sky, each blocking one of the three routes of escape from US Tech.

Jeri stayed low and ducked behind the nearest car. The three of us followed, heads down until we reached her. We watched carefully as the glow of the three craft darkened until it was unlit, leaving a metallic liquid that fluctuated like a ripple but retained its oval structure. Three holes grew out of the centre and each side of the one-hundred-foot-wide craft. They poured out of it, spreading in a perfect line, bodies hanging low to the floor, backs arched and long, thin arms curled underneath them. In perfect unison, they delivered a massive blow that knocked the first hundred soldiers soaring until they hit something – a building, a streetlight, a tank, every one ending in blood. One hit the car that we hid behind with a terrible crack. She didn't get up.

The only light was that of artificial buildings and lamps that gave a dim caste to midnight. One by one, the human made lights went out. I feared what it would be like when we reached morning and whether there would be anyone left to see it. Alien beings swarmed towards an army of humans while gunfire filled the streets. They ran faster and hit harder than they should, enhancing everything with their abilities. If they could feel anger, they would be enraged. CEG Agents ripped the protective suits off aliens who decomposed before my eyes, dried out in seconds. Military officers unloaded hundreds of bullets a second; most of them shooting randomly until shots got too close and they were pounced on, their throats sliced open, and their eyes gouged out. A perfectly formed row of alien beings threw humans around like soft toys, breaking bones and shattering skulls. And we four stayed perfectly still, the horrors that we

302

witnessed rendered us unable to move, terrified of how long it would play out and what would happen to us when it was over.

Humanity was losing. We were always going to lose.

Within minutes, the battle was over. There were less than a dozen humans left alive and the crumbling bodies of less than fifty alien beings dead, thousands more still alive inside just three alien craft. The beings who invaded our planet may not have asked for a war, but they were more than prepared to win one. In the thoughts that we still shared, they knew their first battle was won, that there was little opposition left. They had bested Earth's greatest defence, and this was merely their preliminary assault. In perfect alignment, they crawled forward. After finishing off the last dozen soldiers and a pair of CEG Agents, they finally turned their attention to the last four humans left alive.

THIRTY-FIVE

A screaming wave of bullets silenced my thoughts and nearly pierced my eardrum as Jeri gunned down the nearest of ten creatures that approached. I followed her lead, quickly ripping the head from the torso of the second.

The remaining eight charged at us, lifting themselves into the air to strike from above. One pulled Jeri's gun from her hand and charged at her. Jeri whipped her second gun around swiftly to meet it. Eye trained, she sprayed bullets until it hit the ground like a husk.

I ripped the protective suits from two simultaneously then smashed the heads of four more into the front and back passenger side windows. Before they could move, I pulled their bodies down and held their heads in place until they ripped away from their necks entirely. Another three had slipped past, edging towards us from the rear. I sent one flying backwards into the crowd, and Jeri reeled off another dozen bullets into the head of the second. The third got too close, inches from Peter and Jess. There was a scream and the alien lunged at Jess, its hand smacked her face when the side of its body was hit with a round of bullets. Jess fell back onto the car, wheezing.

The alien body lay dead at Jess's feet, multiple bullet

holes in its thin metallic suit, its black eyes reflecting the light above. Its thin arms lay sprawled out across the floor, fingers extended fully like some twisted version of the Vitruvian man.

Peter lay next to it, barely conscious, his chest ripped open so badly that dark thick blood poured out of him, dripping from his exposed ribs and clotting on the edge of the wound.

I leaned down and closed his eyes. I couldn't save him. No more.

A line of them charged at us. I threw them back a hundred feet until they crashed through the glass of an apartment building. I lifted one above our heads and pulled hard at its arms until they tore from its slight body. I ripped the protective suits from the rest of the next line of attack and watched each of them slump to the ground, suffocating from the lack of oxygen.

Another four approached. I bent their bodies one hundred and eighty degrees backwards, but they didn't snap. I kept going until their heads smashed into the floor. I did it over and over until there was nothing left but a set of bashed in helmets full of mush.

They kept coming, edging closer. They pulled away the car, our only cover away, forcing the three of us back against the walls of US Tech. I did my best to thin their numbers and Jeri barely missed a shot. They always moved forward, more cautiously, but replacing their losses with what seemed like an endless supply.

Something jumped on me from the side and climbed onto my back. It crawled over my head and lowered itself in front of my face. Its black eyes met my own through the semi-transparent metallic visor covering its face. I grabbed its arms and tried to pull the thing off me, but it wouldn't let go. I gripped its head with both of my hands, about to throw it. Before I could, I saw my body drop to the floor in front of me. I looked down, standing over it. I felt a tingling sensation through my body that stopped at my head.

Everything felt new, the hate, the love. It was like seeing beauty in the world for the first time: hope, a future. More than new life, a new way of life.

I looked down at my hands, missing a few fingers. They were grey and slightly translucent covered by a metallic suit that flexed around my body, moistening my skin. My emotions were so great that they almost overpowered the body I inhabited. But it yearned for more. Every mind that my emotions seeped into wanted more.

Jeri pointed her gun at my head, devoid of emotion. I closed my eyes as a stream of bullets raced towards me until Jeri clicked away at an empty clip. When I opened my eyes again, I was lying on the floor. The alien dead next to me. Jeri crouched over me, tightly squeezing my hand. I grabbed hold of her arms, and she pulled me to my feet.

I looked up from the ground and my heart started to beat faster until I found it hard to breathe. My arms trembled at the sight of that monster Robert Palmer holding a gun to Jessica's head.

THIRTY-SIX

"Which is it, Ryan? The wife or the lover?" Palmer positioned Jessica between us, covering enough of his body to shield him.

"I didn't tell anyone. About our eyes. I promise. It's ok, Ryan. It's ok." Jess smiled to me and closed her eyes.

"Stop." I only hesitated for a moment, but it was enough. Palmer pulled the trigger and Jessica fell to the floor. The only name in my head was Jeri's. Jessica's dead eyes stared up at me. My true friend.

I couldn't look away.

Palmer dived at Jeri and wrapped his arm around her neck, pulling her inside of the US Tech building. He pressed the same gun so hard against her head that I didn't know if I could stop a bullet before it hit her. I trailed inside, praying for an opening. "Your weapon failed. Let her go."

"It was a failsafe. And a way of gaining your commitment. Your peace attempt failed. They can handle everything we threw at them. Except you... You are the only one who can stop them. You're the weapon, Ryan. You are project Sobek."

"You bastard." All I wanted to do was to smash in his skull.

"Listen to me. It's why you were the only one able to initiate that first communication. Why you can understand their technology like no one else. You can get inside their consciousness. There is no one else that can do what you can do."

Jeri wrestled to loosen Palmer's grip to speak but he tightened his choke hold and drilled the gun harder into her head.

"What right do you have to decide who lives or dies? Look around. There's no one left to follow your orders. You're fucking dead."

"You and I, Ryan, we're not important. What's important is that you know I speak the truth. You can shut down their consciousness. In one hit. And you don't need the device to do it. Here," Palmer reached inside his suit jacket and pulled out a pair of thin, mesh gloves. His stern expression quickly changed to a welcoming smile that extended to his eyes and reminded me of my father. "I had them made, just for you."

A wail of frustration burst out of me. "All this time... Getting me into the war room, faking the shuttle bombing, making me weaponise the comms device. You've been feeding me, building me up to kill them."

"I didn't make you do anything. You came back to me to weaponise the comms device. You knew what it could do."

"As a last resort. You've been planning to kill them the entire time."

"Whatever it takes. That's what you said to me."

"This isn't what I meant. What you did to President Walker. To the abductees. You made Jeri their target."

"I'm sorry, Ryan. I wish I had known you under different circumstances. What I have asked of you, of your family… it is a regret I will hold to my last breath. I've failed you. But we must accept the consequences of our decisions, every one of them. We have a responsibility, to make those decisions based not on ourselves, or our loved ones. But for the good of the billions of people that are too scared to leave their homes, who are unable to do anything to stop what is to come, the people who might not live to see tomorrow."

"Don't try to justify what you've done."

"I won't. I know what I am asking of you. But I'm asking, one more time. For your country. For our entire civilisation. Don't let this be the last of humanity."

Palmer nodded to himself, with the satisfaction that comes with great realisations. "I'm afraid it all comes down to one thing: power."

"Look around you. All your power is gone."

"Not me. You. You have more power than I ever did. You can end this. Then you can go home. All three of you."

It surged inside me – what he called my power. I saw the alien conscious in front of me, with only a thin veil of my own crude vision draped over it. Felt them moving closer, surrounding the building, ready to wage another assault against us.

"Do it, Ryan. After everything they've done. They're not like us, they're not even human. Do it, or God help me I'll kill her. I can't let them win."

I couldn't comprehend what was happening, how I had been caught so deep. "You don't have to do this. I thought we were friends."

Palmer's face was filled with disappointment. "We are, Ryan. But we each need to do what is right." The weight in Palmer's sigh could have dragged a weaker man into the ground he stood on. "It is not for me, that I do this. Please, forgive me. When the paradox ends, unveiling of the human mind is the path to transcendence."

Something clicked inside my head. I straightened up. A great clarity washed away every thought I had. My body hummed with electricity. I held out my hands, felt the tingle that extended from each fingertip back to the centre of my body and up to my brain. I barely managed to regain enough control to speak. "What... have you done to me?"

Palmer mustered a sympathetic smile. "Don't try to fight

it."

My body turned to face the entrance. I was immersed amongst them, even louder and in deeper than ever before, my own mind one amongst them. The little control I had was being suppressed by my own subconscious. I couldn't beat it. I was about to do exactly what Palmer wanted.

"Do it, Ryan. We did not invite them to our planet. We don't know where they came from, how many others are out there. Wipe the bastards out. They are insects. Are you going to let them take your wife and rape her until she reproduces their spawn?" Palmer gripped the pistol harder and pressed his finger against the trigger. "If you don't kill them, I swear, I'll-"

Before he could finish the sentence, I dragged the slug out of Jess's head and sent it tearing into Palmer's skull. His body cracked as it hit the ground. His jacket was crumpled, his tie hung loosely over his shoulder.

Jeri dropped to the ground and grabbed Palmer's gun. Within a few seconds she had it gripped in both hands and stood pointing it at him, assessing the assailant. When she saw his body was still and his forehead pierced, she lifted the weapon to eye-level, reloaded and had it aimed the doors in seconds.

I still felt the pull of Palmer's words bubbling beneath the surface. "Are you ok?" I would sacrifice everyone before I would watch her die.

Jeri's eyes darted around the room like a bird's head watching for a predator. "I don't know how he got the drop on me. I... I couldn't get him off me."

The foundations of the building shook. Plaster and concrete fell from the walls. Nanotube girders separated as the entire building was snatched from above our heads and cast aside, crashing to the ground. They crept through the entrance of US Tech and floated over the broken walls that remained, their pores pulsating as their shiny metal suits kept them alive. A horde edged their way towards her, their bodies and suits still intact. I ripped them apart, limb from limb before they could get near her, every one of them. Jeri watched their bodies dissolve into nothingness, only ruins and rubble to protect us.

In a second they can all be dead, their shrivelled carcases leaking small amounts of fluid as they fade away. I can become Brody or Robert Palmer, save everyone on the planet. Commit genocide. Make an entire race extinct in one moment to save all of humanity. I can be the man who justifies his means with the end result. Palmer called them insects; I can crush them like insects.

I can save her. I can do whatever it takes.

Hundreds of them surrounded us, waiting for my next move. I had only one thought in my head… what if they took my daughter away from me?

THIRTY-SEVEN

Jeri grabbed my arm and pulled me into her body. Her solid posture was gone, her eyes weary. She rubbed at her neck, still red. She knew it was the end. "I know what she meant to you." Jeri took a deep breath to compose herself before she restarted. "Our daughter. I know what our daughter means to you." It had been so long since I had heard her say the word and when she did it was slow and purposeful, like it took all of her concentration to say it and not fall apart. "I'm sorry. For not understanding… I know… I know what you've been through. What we've lost… Our daughter will always be with us."

I cried out in agony, a wave of emotion boiling over, too much for me to take. I tried to speak. The pain in my chest was excruciating, taking over my body, pulling me under. "I know you carried her, that it was you she was inside. But it… It's so hard… to carry on… Knowing. That she was with us. That I was hers. I miss her so much. I never even got to hold her. Oh…" I fell apart, broken. On my knees, my arms limp, barely able to move. I couldn't utter another word.

"It's ok." Jeri placed a hand on each of my cheeks and lifted my face to look at hers. "I know that now."

Guilt burned through me, that this is what it took for us to understand each other and now we may never live beyond it. The guilt took me to Robert's lifeless corpse that we ignored like it was just another chunk of rubble. "Look what I've done."

"You had no choice."

"I wanted him dead." Protective suits were littered around me and through the streets of DC. I wanted to blame Brody but he had been gone since the war room and I knew it. I still wanted them dead. Hundreds of thousands of them, an entire civilisation. Dead.

I shook my head at the ruins around us. "I won't let them take you."

"Whatever happens now, whatever they've done," Jeri let her gun drop to her side. She placed her hand gently on her stomach. "There is a life inside of me. Do you know what that means?"

Jeri took my hand to rest alongside hers. I felt the precious life, finding its way through existence. The life that we were never meant to have. The life we created together.

THIRTY-EIGHT

Jeri lay before me, her clothes thrown to the floor only. I followed her lead and then leaned towards her, my eyes closed. The softness of her lips made me surrender myself; there was nothing I could do but love her. She fell back onto the bed, and I smothered her body gently, hearts racing, struggling to breathe, our lips never apart. Unconscious desire controlled our every move while we held hands in the perfect moment. I believe time stopped and the universe changed, the creation of life.

Only a few months later our world changed. It was the end of hope, the end of the way things were.

I could never go back to that time that I missed so desperately. But the life that we created never truly left us, something created from so much love could never end. That life is a part of us as much as we are a part of life. Watching over us from above.

A true creation: the most beautiful thing in the world.

A perfect soul.

THIRTY-NINE

I knew I was speaking the last words I would ever say to her. "I'm sorry... for everything." I expected Jeri to nod or agree, but she jolted in surprise instead. "You're the only thing that kept me… If not for you…" I leaned towards her and whispered in her ear, "I love you."

Jeri's eyes darted from my eyes to my mouth, like she was trying to catch the lie. I thought she knew how I felt about her, how much I cared. She kissed me with as much love as anyone could show. Side by side, we stood. I shrouded Jeri's hand in mine; embraced. I held it out as though I was about to twirl her away and then back in close to me for one last dance.

We gazed into each other's eyes, like we were the only people that existed, like we would stay in that moment forever.

I was so lost in Jeri's emotions that poured out of her and clung to me – great warmth and a sharp fear that gradually became subdued – that I could have forgotten about the soulless creatures of the unknown. They felt nothing, loved no one. They didn't ask permission for the horrors they wreaked, and they would never ask forgiveness.

"They didn't kill Jess. Or Rick, Bob, the shuttle crew,

President Walker." I looked down at my hands, the most ordinary looking hands I could imagine. "Or Robert. They're just trying to protect what's important to them. I can protect you. I can kill them all. But what if there's another way? I don't know if it would work. I don't know if it would stop them from taking you."

"You have to try," Jeri said without hesitation.

"I've been inside their mind. They can't reproduce because they have no soul. They're empty inside. You can't create life without a soul. The things Palmer did to me… when I reached out to them, I felt like my entire consciousness was almost lost to theirs. All the light, all the emotion drained out of me, seeping into them. If I hadn't stopped, I don't know if there would have been any of me left. When I look at you, at our baby inside you, I can see that light burning in you. That's what they want from you. But I think I can give it to them."

Jeri held her hand to her stomach. "Ryan, you can't."

There was one thing I was sure of. "Whatever happens, our daughter is gone. I'm not going to lose you too."

Jeri's hand stiffened. Her whole body had become a statue, unable to move. They swarmed, long fingers spread towards her, grabbing at her body. Her rigid hand slipped away from mine as they dragged her away. I reached out to protect her, but I was too late, and her head bounced off the granite floor. A scream wretched from Jeri's throat, more from fear than pain.

Almost instinctually, as though waving goodbye, I reached out and ripped them apart, limb from limb, every one of them. Jeri stopped, spread across the ground, her arms still stretched out beyond her head. Her hopeful eyes were as big as the moon. She was burying her pain, showing me her brave face. The fury raged inside me, crying out to be free to rein terror on every creature that surrounded us. I knew I had to be brave too.

I trembled, summoning every ounce of power inside me, invading their singular consciousness. A deafening drone sucked all sound from my ears. Searing pain overwhelmed me while I looked upon Jeri one last time. I closed my eyes and with every drop of hope I had left, I whispered, "Whatever it takes."

I slowed my breathing, each breath deeper than the last, straightened out my arched back and lifted myself high into the air above them. Every hair on my body stood on end. As I dripped with oil and the blood drained from my face, I remembered the words Palmer spoke to me: 'When the paradox ends, unveiling of the human mind is the path to transcendence.' Somewhere, the wind blew a fury and buildings stopped falling. Every alien being on this planet and beyond came to a standstill to see what I would do next.

Their emptiness reached all the way from their eyes into the depths of their shared consciousness, a hollow existence. One being in multiple bodies. One thought and no feeling, not a single emotion among them. Millions of beings with no soul. It is the gift that I was prepared to give.

A bright light soaked the dull grey sky in colour and seeped down onto all life below. I soared higher until the buildings and trees, the dogs and people were blended together like some amorphic chunk of living matter rather than the billions of separate pieces I had always seen them as. The air sizzled around me as my body burned white hot and I smiled as the photograph and the scan inside my pocket melted into my skin until they were as much a part of me as my own skin. In the blackness of the night sky, I could smell a whole meadow of white lilacs.

I choked, trying to breathe until the realisation that I no longer needed to. My deepest emotions radiated around me and penetrated their empty shells all at once. It seemed like the cold night had disappeared before my eyes. Time would soon be gone. And I was no longer afraid.

They left humanity behind with the devastation they brought to our world. But it wasn't my world anymore. I am them and they are me. Their consciousness fused with my mind and soul.

I watched a thousand places through thousands of alien eyes. Earth's invaders had withdrawn to their craft and were leaving the planet's skies. My lifeless body slipped through Jeri's fingers as she tried to catch me. She squeezed my hands as though to squeeze the life back into me. Stroked my cheek and pressed my head tightly against her chest as she called out to me to come back. I said her name and hoped that she could hear me. In a moment, I would be gone.

It was the moment of creation. A new cycle of life. An imperfect soul.

The first black-eyed child was born.

For a time, my human body lay crumpled on the floor, a lifeless shell. If I could have done anything with my body, it would be to tell my family how much I love them. I would shake my father's hand and hug him. I would thank him for all of the many things that I have to thank him for. I would tell him that Herb loves him, that one day, in the next life, he will find Herb's forgiveness, when there is no more reason to hate, when Mom is at their side.

I would hold Jeri's hand. Take her delicate fingers and fold them in between my own. I would stroke her cheek and run my fingers through her soft hair. I would close my eyes, kiss her lips, and love her.

I would hold my son. I would be there for his birth and watch him grow. And I would be the father that he deserved. I would tell him that one day, he would be united with his sweet sister who was out there waiting for him to join her after he has lived his long life.

But 'I' was now only an illusion, the suggestion of a separate entity from a skewed view through fractured glass. Their race would live on, and I could finally let go of this world.

Form gradually disappears and I'm on a bench in front of the glistening Lake Ontario at Scarborough Bluffs. The gleaming pink sky creates a rose cast on the white rocks and lush greenery, brighter than any summer's day. A fresh, sweet smell of a meadow of white lilacs surrounds us. We have the whole place, just for the two of us. Her bright smile and the glint in her eyes appear as she sees my face. I lift her up above my head and she laughs with glee, shaking her golden hair from side to side. She gazes into my eyes with more love than I have ever felt. I am finally there for her. My beautiful little girl. I bring her in close to me, feel the softness of her cheek against mine, and we smile together. Our eyes filled with tears and never letting go.

It is beautiful.

And I am home.

If you enjoyed *We Come In Peace*

Then read the new novella from Mark Turnbull

Doomsday

As the sky turns pink and the end of the world looms, young Timmy enlists the help of a stranger to protect him from the dangerous streets and find his way home.

But everyone has their secrets, and the stranger who has spent a lifetime drifting, might finally have to face his past.

Sign up to the mailing list at markturnbull.net to read free & exclusively

ABOUT THE AUTHOR

Mark Turnbull was born in the UK in 1984. After studying acting for a number of years, Mark pursued a successful career in business, whilst spending ten years dreaming of life as an author and harnessing his craft. We Come In Peace is his debut novel.

Reviews are important to Indie authors. We really appreciate it when you leave one.

Sign up for a free novella, exclusive news, and updates:

www.markturnbull.net
Instagram: @markturnbull23

Printed in Great Britain
by Amazon

20209345R00192